Praise for Nicky Pellegrino

'A novel about the joy of learning to live again. It also made me very hungry!' Jojo Moyes

'Warm, engaging and truly delicious' Rosanna Ley

'A delicious and sensual adventure . . . as evocative and captivating as Venice itself' Fiona Gibson

'A wonderfully evocative setting and mouth-watering descriptions of Venetian food' Pamela Hartshorne

'Full-bodied as a rich Italian red, it's a page-turner combining the missed chances of *Captain Corelli's Mandolin* with the foodie pleasures of *Chocolat*' *Eve*

'Three generations of Italian women talk romance and cooking . . . an evocative foodfest of a novel' *Prima*

'A slice of pure sunshine' *Good Housekeeping*

'A lovely read . . . with a genuine heart and true observation' Elizabeth Buchan

'A touching story about one woman's search for love' *Sunday Express*

'Set against a backdrop of love, friendship and food . . . The descriptions of Italian food will make your mouth water' *Cosmopolitan*

'Sink back on the sofa with this delightful read' *Now Magazine*

Nicky Pellegrino was born in Liverpool but spent childhood holidays staying with her family in Italy. It is her memories of those summers that flavour her stories: the passions, the feuds but most of all the food. Nicky now lives in Auckland, New Zealand with her husband, two dogs and two horses.

Find out more at www.nickypellegrino.com

Also by Nicky Pellegrino

Delicious
Summer at the Villa Rosa
(*originally published as* The Gypsy Tearoom)
The Italian Wedding
Recipe for Life
The Villa Girls
When in Rome
The Food of Love Cookery School
One Summer in Venice
Under Italian Skies
A Year at Hotel Gondola
A Dream of Italy

Tiny Pieces of Us

Nicky Pellegrino

ORION

An Orion paperback

First published in Great Britain in 2020 by Orion Fiction
This paperback edition published in 2021 by Orion Fiction,
an imprint of The Orion Publishing Group Ltd,
Carmelite House, 50 Victoria Embankment
London EC4Y 0DZ

An Hachette UK company

1 3 5 7 9 10 8 6 4 2

A CIP catalogue record for this book
is available from the British Library.

ISBN 978 1 4091 7901 6

Typeset by Deltatype Ltd, Birkenhead, Merseyside

Printed in Great Britain by Clays Ltd, Elcograf S.p.A.

www.orionbooks.co.uk

For Stacy Gregg, with heartfelt thanks

How it begins …

Jamie can't wait to get home. Normally after school he likes to hang out with his friends – kick a ball around, share a carton of fries, have a laugh – until the very last minute when he pedals as fast as he can to be back home in time for dinner.

Today a good thing happened and Jamie is excited about seeing the look on his mum's face when he tells her. She doesn't even know he applied for the scholarship. It seemed better not to mention it as there was so much competition and he assumed he didn't stand a chance. Jamie worked really hard on the application. He explained all the reasons he wanted to do the summer school in robotics, describing the dreams he had for his future. Some day he hoped to design super-cool bionic arms and legs, so cool that kids who weren't amputees would be sorry they couldn't have one. Jamie had filled a notebook with drawings of his ideas but there was so much he needed to learn and he couldn't wait to get started.

His mum is going to be really pleased. She is always telling him he can do anything he sets his mind to. He is sure she would have found the money to pay for the summer school if he had asked. But Jamie didn't want that. Not that they are poor exactly but his mum spends very little on herself, saving to buy things for him instead – the mountain bike for his last birthday, the trip to London to visit the science museum, his new iPhone. It seems important that he shouldn't always be asking for more. He is sixteen now and wants her to know that she doesn't have to worry about him all the time. So when he heard about the scholarship he put in an application and hoped for the best. He didn't believe it when the computer science teacher told him he had been chosen. Like, he really didn't believe it. But it is official; he has a letter now to prove it. It is tucked inside the school bag he wears slung around his shoulders as he cycles home along Cowley Road in a hurry to show it to his mother.

It has been raining and the tarmac is glossy but Jamie has all the proper safety gear; a helmet, a high-vis vest and really good lights for his bike. His mum insisted on it. She seems to worry more than other mothers do, probably because there's only the two of them. Jamie used to wish his dad hadn't walked out when he was a kid, and that he had a brother or sister maybe, but now he kind of likes the way things are. His friends seem to have endless whinges about their families. Little sisters are annoying, big brothers are bullies and parents are always spoiling things. Jamie gets on with his mum mostly. In the evenings they watch television together and on weekends she always has time to drive him wherever he wants to go. She isn't one of those mothers who is always getting upset, going on and on about things, or even worse, shouting. Jamie can't remember the last time they argued.

He wonders what she has planned for their dinner. Maybe when she hears his good news she will decide to take him out for a celebration instead. Just McDonald's; it is his favourite place, and always where he asks to go when she wants to treat him.

Jamie pumps the pedals of his bike, flying along the busy road towards home. It isn't a particularly long ride and it is pretty flat. On the weekend he might get his mum to drive him out to a mountain biking trail so he can have a proper blast. He wants to get fitter and stronger, perhaps even do some races. He loves the feeling of his heart and muscles working to power the bike forwards, faster and faster. It would be great to have a go at a few jumps too; he has heard there are some in the Shotover Woods. Maybe she will drive him there then they can go to Pizza Express afterwards because his mum really likes the American Hot with the spicy pepperoni and jalapeño peppers.

She is going to be so proud of him; Jamie can't wait. He plans to give her the envelope and not tell her what is inside. She will probably think it is another boring school letter; details of new gear he needs or a parent/teacher appointment. She will tell him to leave it on the kitchen bench for her to look at later and wonder why he is so insistent that she read it right away. He imagines her surprise when she sees that her son has won a scholarship; out of all the kids who applied he was the one who was chosen. This is his lucky day, thinks Jamie.

The road is slick and wet, and a car is making a clumsy right turn through the heavy traffic. Jamie realises the driver hasn't noticed him and he brakes hard but too late. His last thought is that this is going to hurt, then the impact, then nothing. He doesn't see the shocked bystanders, one of them crying softly as she kneels down and takes his hand, waiting for the ambulance somebody has called. The lights, the sirens, the paramedics checking vital signs, the race to the hospital, Jamie isn't aware of any of it. His heart is still beating but his life has ended.

Later on his mother will find the letter tucked carefully into the school bag that has been returned to her. It will be a long time before she opens it though. Not until well after the days and nights in hospital when the miracle everyone is praying for never happens. Not until after the hardest decision of all, the one that still wakes her up in the middle of the night filling her with an awful mix of regret and panic.

Jamie is breathing with the help of a ventilator when she says goodbye to him. They tell her not to feel rushed, she can stay as long as she likes. But no time will ever be enough, how could it be? She sits very close as Jamie breathes in and out. She can't quite let go of the last of her hope, but he is gone, this is what they keep saying. Her boy with all his energy and brightness and life. It seems impossible; it is too huge a thing and she can't take it in. She doesn't want to.

For years the school bag stays on the desk in his room. She dusts around it from time to time, but touches nothing, assuming she knows exactly what is inside. The iPhone Jamie was so proud of, the notebook he was always scribbling in, his dented old laptop, schoolbooks, a few pens, coins. The bag sits there until its fabric starts to fade slightly from the sunlight that pours through the window. She isn't sure what makes her pick it up one day, sit down on his bed and empty out its contents.

These are all the familiar things that Jamie touched everyday. She leafs through a notebook full of complicated diagrams, glances at the dark screen of his phone, opens the laptop and rests her fingers on the worn keys. Finding a slim envelope deep in one of the bag's pockets, she tears into it and starts to read.

Grace hadn't thought it was possible to feel any worse than she already did. But now she reads the letter and sees it all; the life Jamie should have had, the future he was cheated out of, everything that has been lost, all those beautiful dreams.

Her son is gone and she is broken. Mostly what she wants is to be gone now too. Grace longs to curl into herself, disappear, be nothing at all; it would be such a relief.

The only thing that has ever made her feel slightly better is knowing that out there somewhere Jamie's heart is still beating, that his death meant other people had a future. She thinks about the ones that have tiny pieces of him inside them, about the stranger who sees the world through his eyes, and most of all, the one who was gifted his brave heart. She wonders about them, what their dreams were and if they are making the most of their chance to live them. At times it makes her angry – they got so much, Jamie lost everything – but often it helps just a little. Right now it seems to make no difference at all.

Grace wants all of this to be over.

16 November 2010

Tragic teen saves lives

But more donors are desperately needed.
By Daily Post reporter Mary Moore

All Jamie McGraw wanted for his sixteenth birthday was a new mountain bike. Tragically, only weeks after being thrilled to receive the dream gift, his young life was cut short after he was knocked off his bike by a motorist while pedalling home one wet, dark evening.

Thanks to a brave decision by his heartbroken mother Grace, the Oxford teen's death has meant the gift of life for five other people. His undamaged kidney, heart, liver, lungs and pancreas have all been donated to patients who were running out of time, and his corneas have saved someone's eyesight.

'Jamie had a heart of gold,' said Grace, 45. 'He was such a lovely boy. I still can't believe he's gone but I'm trying to find some comfort in the fact he has helped so many others.'

'There are thousands more sick people that are desperate for a transplant, and the need for organs is urgent and growing,' says Lynda Fyfe, coordinator of Harefield Hospital.

'Across the UK people are dying while they are waiting for an organ. Every day in my job I see the amazing difference a transplant can make. There are currently 165 sick children alone on the waiting lists and meanwhile healthy organs are going to waste. Signing up to become a donor really is giving the gift of life.'

Vivi

London, spring 2017

My heart is less than one per cent of my body, it weighs hardly anything; it is only a tiny piece of me yet it is the part that everyone finds most interesting, even me. Whenever I wake in the middle of the night, with one of those 3 a.m. spikes of anxiety, it is my heart I reach for first. Is it beating properly? Is one thud following another, slow and steady, or is it skittering a little, out of rhythm, is it about to fail me? I press my hand against my chest and feel each soft resting beat and it always takes a while before I am reassured enough to think of sleeping again. For now, everything is as it should be. For now, there is nothing I need to worry about.

I was born with a heart that couldn't be trusted to pump my blood properly. In and out of hospital, fainting at school, always exhausted; I was the child who couldn't go places or do things, the sick kid, the special one, the girl who was going to die young.

Growing up with a body that keeps letting you down isn't much fun. People feel sorry for you but they must resent you too. My sister put up with years of me getting the best of everything – all the attention, the biggest bedroom, the nicest presents – while the doctors bought me time. First drugs, then a pacemaker and finally they put in a mechanical pump to keep my failing heart going while I was on the waiting list for a transplant. No one expected to keep me for long; it was an unspoken thing but somehow I knew it. So for years I got everything I wanted, until at last I got someone else's heart.

I have tried not to think of him, the kid who died so I could live. I didn't want to imagine a screeching of brakes or the crash of a car accident, sirens, shocked bystanders, a still, bleeding body. I never wanted to know his name, or where he came from or how sad his family was. All of that was too much. Once I knew I had a future, it seemed better not to look back.

My mother called it a miracle; that was how we all thought of it. In the beginning everyone was focused on me recovering from the transplant surgery. There was a scare when my body started rejecting the new heart, so they had to fill me with steroids and that fixed things, although I still have to take drugs and be really careful. I was in hospital for ages and when I finally got home we had this big party with all the family and neighbours coming through and everyone telling me the same thing, 'You've got your whole life ahead of you now.'

Not a single person mentioned him, the boy whose heart I had taken. I suppose they thought it wasn't appropriate over cups of tea and chocolate cake in a room hung with bunting, not very nice to mention death when I was celebrating being alive.

The transplant nurse encouraged me to write a thank you letter to the donor's family; she even suggested what to put in it. Keep everything anonymous, mention how grateful you are, describe what it was like before and say how things have changed for the better, offer words of comfort such as, 'I hope this letter will help you through your loss, because you have helped to save my life.'

I wrote it fast and sealed the envelope, not really considering who would open it and read those words. I was nineteen when I sent that letter. Now seven years have passed and there is nothing wrong with my heart. It just isn't the one I was born with.

There are scars, of course, but the smaller ones on my

neck are fading and the dramatic long one down my chest I keep well covered most of the time. Hardly anyone at work knows, only Dan because we were sleeping together and I had to tell him.

Dan is my boss, an editor on the tabloid newspaper I've been working at for the past four years; the one who is always making me interview reality TV stars even though he knows I would rather be working on newsier, investigative pieces. I can't say no to him, not with the tricky state the print industry is in right now. Probably the only reason I still have a job is that I can turn my hand to pretty much anything – royal rumours, disgraced politicians, soap star weddings. If Dan asks then I write the story. One evening, following after-work drinks at the Prince of Wales pub, he asked for something more and I found myself saying yes to that too, then going back to his place.

Dan was fascinated by my scar, kept touching it with his fingers, putting his hand flat on my chest and feeling my heart beating. And he asked the question anyone else might have shied away from. 'Whose is it? Who did it belong to?'

'I don't know,' I told him, pushing his hand away and pulling the duvet up to my chin.

'Seriously?' He propped himself on one elbow and stared down at me. 'You've got no idea?'

'It's all confidential,' I explained. 'They don't tell you anything.'

For a while Dan and I had been having one of those secretive workplace flirtations. We would buy each other coffees and send messages back and forth; it was a way to break up the day, and Dan was a laugh, I liked him. And then there I was lying naked in his bed.

'Don't say anything, OK?' I pleaded, as his fingers strayed back beneath the duvet and traced the long ridge of scar tissue scoring my chest. 'There's no need for people to know.'

'Sure,' Dan said, too casually.

'I've had all those years of being a sick kid, I just want to be normal now.'

'Aren't you curious to find out though? I'd have to know.'

'You mean who my heart belonged to?'

'Yeah, it must be possible to get more details. You could start by looking back through the news archives for accidents on dates that match up with your surgery. That would give you some clues.'

Dan was an expert at chasing people down and uncovering stories. It had been his job for years and, when I arrived on the scene as an intern, he devoted a lot of time to showing me how. But this wasn't just another story, it was my life and I didn't necessarily want to solve all its mysteries.

'I could try and find out more about my donor but what good would it do?' I asked. 'There's no point really.'

'Maybe you'd feel a connection with the family, an emotional link. It might make a really good feature for the weekend paper.'

'No,' I said hesitantly, almost testing the word, because it wasn't one I had used with him before. Then with more certainty, 'No, I can't.'

Dan must have assumed he would be able to talk me round. He mentioned it again several times when we were in bed together, or at the pub, or out for dinner and I always gave him the same answer. No way. I was not going to be clickbait for the *Daily Post* website. There would be no bittersweet video of my first meeting with the donor's family, no moving first-person piece.

'Think of all the good it would do. It might encourage readers to register as donors and help other sick kids,' Dan pointed out.

It was the sort of line he had taught me to use when trying to coax a story from a reluctant interviewee, and I couldn't believe he was trying it now.

'I already wrote a big feature for organ donor awareness week,' I reminded him.

'Yeah, somebody does one exactly like that every year. Dull, isn't it? Not likely to stir any feelings or touch a reader's heart. Your own story could be really powerful.'

'No,' I repeated, shaking my head, because even though he was my boss I didn't think he could make me do this. Briefly, his expression seemed to darken.

By then Dan and me were in a routine where I would spend a few nights a week sleeping over at his place, but still we weren't officially 'together' and at work we were keeping things discreet. I hadn't pushed for more because I didn't think I wanted it. Guys like Dan are my unhealthy addiction – like cigarettes or alcohol are for other people: not good for me, a temporary pleasure I ought to give up at some point, just not quite yet.

'OK Vivi.' He treated me to a smile that widened into his most mischievous grin. 'You can't blame me for trying though.'

One of the things our newspaper is always doing in a bid to boost its readership is launching these big campaigns. In recent months there had been one to tackle loneliness and another to raise funds to pay for a dying woman's dream wedding. Readers love that sort of thing and Dan was constantly on the hunt for another good cause to back.

It was him who came up with 'Donate for Life'. Hearing about my transplant must have put the idea in his head and then me reminding him about that article I had written, filled with statistics about the numbers of people needing organs, had got him thinking. Thousands with faulty hearts, kidneys, lungs, livers ... some of them dying while they were waiting for new ones. Surely something could be done to help them.

'I've had a brilliant idea,' he announced. 'This has to be our next big crusade.'

Newsrooms are quiet places these days. There is no pounding on typewriters or yelling down phones any more, just a lot of people jammed into a large room, all staring at their screens and not saying much. So when Dan spoke up everyone heard and half the office got in on the discussion, with even the editor-in-chief coming over and leaning on the edge of his desk as they brainstormed.

'In lots of other countries all adults are potential donors unless they opt out,' Dan explained, 'but not in England. Here you have to be proactive and sign up to a donor register. Lots of people never get round to doing that. We need to push for a change in the law to bring us in line.'

'Great, great, this could be huge,' enthused the editor-in-chief. 'Find me a good face for the campaign though. A cute-looking kid on the waiting list or someone young and attractive who would have died if they hadn't got their transplant in time.'

'Yeah, I'll get onto it right away,' promised Dan.

I was hunched behind my computer, trying to look busy. It was often me that was assigned articles like these. I had written the lead piece about the loneliness epidemic and followed the dream wedding story through to its inevitable unhappy ending. Mostly I liked working on those campaigns – it felt as if we were helping make a real difference – but I didn't want to touch this one.

'Vivi?' Dan called.

Looking over the top of my computer screen, I shook my head. 'Not me, sorry; I've got too much other stuff on.'

'Park what you're doing, this is more important.'

I couldn't say no to him in front of everyone. Even if we hadn't been sleeping together, which added a whole extra layer of complication, a journalist on the *Daily Post* didn't refuse to chase up a story. There had been times I had put things on my list then quietly forgotten to get on with them, but that wasn't going to work this time.

'OK then, I'll start hunting out a case study,' I said, reluctantly.

'Come on Vivi, forget boring case studies, write me a first-person piece, how a heart transplant changed your life. Knock it out this afternoon and we'll get a quick shot of you, then we can have it up online tonight and in tomorrow's paper.'

Everyone was looking my way curiously: the editor-in-chief, the other people at the desks around mine, a couple of sub-editors heading back from the kitchen with their cups of tea.

'Put loads of emotion into it,' Dan urged. 'We need to hear how close you were to death and how thankful you are to the family of the donor. I want our readers smiling through their tears.'

He was talking fast, full of his own brilliance. He may have been good-looking with his shock of fair floppy hair and boyish smile, but right at that moment his charm was missing entirely.

'This is your opportunity to raise awareness and save lives, Vivi,' he was saying. 'Give other sick people the second chance you've had.'

The trouble was there was no denying he was right. If a stranger hadn't given me a healthy heart I wouldn't have been sitting there at all; my own would have stopped beating years ago. Didn't other people deserve the same gift of life? Shouldn't I be helping them if I could?

'This is a way for you to give something back,' Dan pushed on, 'to repay a debt. How can you say no to that?'

'I suppose I can't,' I admitted.

'Then why are you staring at me like that? Get on with it.'

And so I did. It came out more fluently than I expected, as if the words had always been there in my head ready to flood out onto the page and be a story. Afterwards, feeling slightly stunned, I put on some make-up, swapped my black shirt for another woman's brighter top, and managed to smile down a photographer's lens. They even shot some video of me talking about changing the law and saving lives. And when it was all over I went to the Prince of Wales and ordered a large glass of wine.

'Should you be doing that?' wondered one of the senior reporters. 'Don't you have to take care of your health?'

'I don't have a moral obligation not to drink Chardonnay just because I've got someone else's heart,' I snapped.

'That's not what I meant at all,' she protested, but of course it was.

Dan must have expected me to go home with him that night. He was there at the pub, drinking pints of beer, and he looked surprised when I grabbed my bag and headed off alone. I went to my own place, a tiny rented room in a Victorian bay-fronted villa in Highbury. There was barely enough space for a large single bed and a clothes rack, but mostly I used it as a place to crash so I didn't particularly care.

That night I slept badly and woke with a headache. Normally I would never ring in sick. I've had enough days of resting in bed to last me a lifetime and would rather be at work. But with the thought of my face spread across the pages of the *Daily Post*, I texted Dan a feeble lie about having a stomach bug, rolled over and tried to go back to sleep. My phone kept ringing and I ignored it for a while but eventually needed to climb out of bed and open a window because the stuffiness of the room was making my headache even worse. I checked the calls I had missed: a couple from Dan, one from my parents, and several from my sister Imogen. Clearly she wasn't going to give up. The phone rang again and her picture flashed up.

'So, you're a celebrity now,' she said when I answered.

'It's only one article.'

'Vivi's Law – help our brave reporter Vivi Palmer save the lives of thousands.'

Grabbing my laptop, I checked the *Daily Post* website. There I was on the home page, forcing a smile and wearing clothes that didn't suit me. I could hardly bear to read the story. Dan had been late to the pub the evening before and now I saw why. He'd had a good go at rewriting it. In this new version I was a little battler, literally days from death and saying goodbye to the world when miraculously I was saved by the anonymous donor whose family I dreamed of thanking in person some day. My life was devoted to making Vivi's Law a reality and helping other sick kids have a future.

'I didn't write most of this,' I told Imogen. 'Shit, it's terrible.'

'Well, Mum and Dad love it; they couldn't be prouder, their little girl helping others.'

'That's good ... I guess.'

The *Daily Post* is the third most read online newspaper in the world, everybody looks at it. My dad has the app on his phone and checks for my stories now and then. I hated the thought of him reading this one.

'They forced me into being the face of the campaign,' I told Imogen. 'I'd much rather not have done it.'

'That's ridiculous. How could they force you?'

Imogen is married to a lawyer. Since having kids she hasn't gone back to work because they don't need the money.

'I can't afford to lose my job,' I pointed out. 'There's always talk of redundancies these days. And besides, the campaign might work; it may help save lives.'

'Mmm,' she sounded distracted. 'Farah, Darya, stop that now, you know the cat doesn't like it. No, she'll scratch you. What did I say? ... oh God, sorry, hope stardom goes well for you, talk soon.'

And my sister was gone.

*

I had spent the past few years talking other people into sharing their stories. Heartbreak, love, dreams; I had a talent for finding out the most interesting details and crafting them into a feature article or news piece, I prided myself on being good at it. Now I realised how exposed all those interviewees must have felt, and I felt a bit queasy.

A spike alert pinged on my phone to say my story was getting a high number of views. It was quickly followed by a message from Dan telling me to get in sharpish because *London Live* were sending a crew over to shoot an item about Vivi's Law for the evening news.

There was no avoiding this so I took a paracetamol, bought a can of Coca-Cola and a Snickers bar on the way to the tube station, and made my way to work more slowly than I should have.

Like I said, the newsroom is never noisy but an extra hush seemed to fall over the place as I walked in.

'Really great piece, amazing,' a couple of people murmured as I walked past their desks. 'I had no idea. You never said.'

There was a grin on Dan's face when he saw me. He seemed even more pleased with himself than usual, as he called me over to his desk.

'Hey Vivi, I've got some really amazing news for you. I reckon I've found him. Come and see this.'

'Found him?' I faltered.

'Yeah, here he is – look.' Dan swivelled his screen so I could see a picture of a smiling kid with a mop of dark hair and dancing brown eyes. 'Jamie McGraw, the boy who gave you his heart.'

Back on my very first day at the *Daily Post*, when I was still feeling overawed to have landed a job on a national newspaper, Dan gave me one important piece of advice – never, ever cry in the newsroom. Up till now I had managed it, although there had been a few private tearful moments in toilet cubicles, but now, looking at the face of the dead boy on his computer screen, the tears came from nowhere. They rushed from my eyes, and Jamie with his tangle of curly black hair, big smile and ears that stuck out, almost blurred from view.

Dan stood and put an arm around my shoulder. 'Hey, it's OK,' he said. 'It's a big moment for you; this kid probably saved your life.'

'How did you find him?' I wanted to know, once I could trust myself to speak.

'The story was in our archives, so it was easy enough to find. He saved four other lives actually – one got his undamaged kidney, another got his liver, one his lungs, one his pancreas. And his corneas saved someone's eyesight. Imagine that, five people out there linked to you, almost like a family. Wouldn't it be great if …'

'No.'

'Ah, come on, think of the campaign; there's the potential for some great pieces here.'

I didn't want to hear about the Vivi's Law campaign. I even stopped worrying about hanging on to my job. If it meant going home and living with my parents, giving up on journalism and training for some other career, I didn't care any more. My sister had been right after all. No one could force me to do anything.

'You're not meant to try and contact each other,' I told Dan. 'There are rules.'

'Right, and what are they going to do if you break those rules, take the heart off you?'

Someone had pushed a wad of tissues into my hand and I blotted my tear-soaked eyes, hating Dan, thinking I should turn round and walk away, but held there by the image now clearing on his screen, the boy who had died but whose heart was still beating.

'We need to keep up some momentum on this,' said Dan.

'At least track down the mother, Grace McGraw. She might be pleased to know that you're happy, healthy and successful. It may help bring her comfort.'

'She wanted those things for her son, not me.'

'This is an opportunity to do some good, to help other people,' repeated Dan. 'How can you say no?'

'I wrote the first piece and that's it.' The words burst out of me. 'Why don't you do the TV interviews, the radio or whatever else? It's your campaign.'

For a few moments people's fingers stilled on their keyboards and a phone was left to ring as everyone waited to see how this would go.

'I'll find the woman myself then.' Dan was flinty-faced. 'It's not likely to be too hard.'

Sympathetic glances were darted my way as I headed back to my own desk but no one spoke to me. Sitting there pretending to work, failing to concentrate because my stomach really was churning now, I couldn't get that photograph out of my mind: Jamie McGraw. Who had he been? What had he liked doing? Where was life set to take him?

My desk was tucked away in a corner of the newsroom, which I always liked because no one could see my screen unless they came and stood right beside me. It meant a lot of time wasted on Facebook when I ought to have been writing. I logged onto it now and searched for Grace McGraw. Just as Dan had thought, it wasn't too difficult to find her. In her Facebook profile shot there she was with her son, a pleasant-looking woman with a smile a lot like his. Obviously she didn't know much about privacy settings. There were sad little posts about grief, more photographs of Jamie, even a short video clip that was difficult for me to watch. I really wanted to contact her but not for any story or campaign, only to say thank you and that he looked lovely, her son.

I shut down my computer, picked up my bag and left without bothering to look back. Dan would be furious but

I wasn't about to waste time worrying about it. Walking up to Kensington Gardens, I sat on a bench beside the Round Pond and watched the swans and geese for a while. It was sunny and the park was busy. Mums wheeled their toddlers past in buggies, people walked dogs, couples smooched. They were normal people and for them it was an ordinary sort of day. I felt envious of them all.

There was always a chance Dan might be wrong about Jamie but I didn't think so. The dates of his death and my new heart transplant matched and so did the few details I had been given. Besides seeing his cheeky, smiling face I just had a feeling. This boy was dead and I had his heart.

12 April 2017

Donate For Life: Support our campaign for Vivi's Law

Your chance to help make a difference.
By Daily Post senior editor Dan Parker

Today Vivi Palmer is one of our talented reporters but as a child every day was a struggle to survive because her heart was failing.

Vivi was 19 and running out of time, when the miracle of a heart transplant changed everything. We believe it was this boy, Jamie McGraw, who gave her the precious gift of life. After Jamie's tragic death in a road accident, his heartbroken mother agreed to donate his organs. He also helped four other people survive and his corneas saved someone's eyesight.

Forever grateful for her second chance, Vivi is now battling to help other sick people get that same opportunity. She needs your help to change the law and make sure no more healthy organs go to waste. Sign up to our life-saving campaign and hear more from Vivi about why it's so important at donateforlife.co.uk.

This is your chance to make a difference.

Vivi

I had spent all afternoon composing a message to Grace McGraw, deleting and rewriting it several times. This time I did picture the woman who would read my words. I imagined her surprised to hear from me but hopefully pleased to know her son was being remembered. Perhaps she had a husband she would show my message to, or Jamie might have had brothers and sisters. From her Facebook page I could tell she lived in Oxford but Grace had been sparing with other personal details.

Each day it was my job to sit in front of an empty screen and fill it with words. Even though this was only a few lines, getting them exactly right was the hardest thing. Several times I came close to pressing send, then changed my mind, ran my eyes over the message and tinkered with it again, altering a word here and there.

Dear Grace, I hope you don't mind me contacting you. I saw a photograph of your son Jamie and I'm convinced it is his heart that is keeping me alive. Seeing his face has made me think about him so much. He looks like such a gorgeous boy. I'm very sorry you lost him and extremely grateful you agreed to donate. All the other recipients must feel the same way. You saved our lives and I wish I could do something as huge and meaningful for you, but it seems I can only say thank you again even if it's not enough. Please know, I will always be thinking of Jamie and you – Vivi Palmer.

It took hours for me to get that far. I started out typing on my phone while sitting on a bench in Kensington Gardens. After a while I moved to a nearby café where I sipped tea and frowned out at a view of the Italian fountains. Finally, I went home, lay on my bed, switched to my laptop, and tried again. Nothing I said seemed to be enough. Disheartened, I considered deleting the whole thing.

Taking a break, I went to the fridge, looking for something I could call supper. There wasn't much to be found, which is par for the course, unless my mother has recently sent a healthy food parcel, so I opened a can of chilli beans and microwaved a potato.

Sitting down to eat, I flipped open my laptop again to check the *Daily Post* headlines and make sure I hadn't missed anything big. That was when I found it, Dan's follow up story for the Vivi's Law campaign. I wasn't surprised to see he had gone ahead and written one without checking in with me first; if anything, I had expected that. It was the photograph at the head of the page that shocked me – Jamie with his curly hair and happy smile, the same shot that had been used on the original piece Dan had shown me that morning. He had even gone ahead and used his name. I couldn't believe it.

I was too agitated to sit still, never mind eat, but pacing back and forth across the short stretch of worn carpet in my bedsit wasn't especially calming. I was furious at Dan and almost as cross with myself for not predicting he would do this. All he cared about were headlines and the number of views on a story. I knew that and it had always kind of bothered me, but now I was the headline, and Jamie was the story, I felt hot and angry.

All that time spent crafting a warm and friendly message to Grace, trying to get the tone exactly right, and there was no point in sending it now. Instead I would have to find some way to apologise.

My head was starting to ache again. Scraping my dinner

into the bin, I dropped the dirty plate into the sink, lay down on my bed, and wondered if there were any words I could come up with to fix this. I fell asleep still thinking about it.

In the morning I tried telling myself it had been a short news piece and there was every chance Jamie's mother hadn't seen it. She might be a *Guardian* reader who wouldn't dream of looking at the *Daily Post* website. And even if someone had drawn her attention to the story, perhaps she supported the campaign for Vivi's Law, maybe she wouldn't mind too much. By the time I got to work, I had almost convinced myself that naming Jamie hadn't been such a big deal after all. I wanted to believe it. The last thing I needed was a showdown with Dan about it in front of everyone, so I decided to stay quiet for the time being.

Dan too was playing it cool. He didn't mention his Vivi's Law piece or the fact I had stormed out of the office the previous day. Instead he assigned me a couple more stories – an internet romance gone wrong and a guide to having a better night's sleep – and left me to get on with them. It was run-of-the-mill stuff and not especially taxing. Still it was a struggle to concentrate on anything. I had always loved seeing my name in print, attached to the pieces I wrote, and I liked the idea of people reading my words. But I had never spared much thought for the impact those words might have; now it was all I could think of.

By mid-afternoon, I wasn't getting very far. The pace of work is fast at the *Daily Post* and I couldn't afford to slack off for long but, if I coasted through a few more hours without anyone noticing, hopefully I could go home and then be back on form in the morning.

The phone on my desk rang and I picked it up with the usual, 'Hello, Vivi speaking'. All I could hear at the other end was the sound of someone breathing. Assuming it was a nuisance call, I hung up. It happened twice more and the second time a woman's voice said a faint 'hello' then I heard a click as she disconnected.

By then it was getting late. Dan had left for the pub and I was giving it a few last minutes before I escaped too, when my phone rang again. This time I picked it up and didn't say anything at all.

'Hello?' It was the same voice as before. 'Is that Vivi Palmer?'

'It is,' I said, levelly.

'Your trashy newspaper used my son's picture without my permission.'

'What?' My hand tightened around the phone as I realised who I was talking to. 'Is this Grace McGraw?'

'I want to make an official complaint.' Her voice was shrill. 'Surely you're not allowed to do that. It isn't ethical.'

'I'm so sorry,' I began, but she wasn't interested in an apology.

'And now this Dan Parker keeps sending me messages,' she continued, angrily. 'He wants to interview me, make me join the campaign you're running. Well I'm not interested. There's no way I want to be a part of anything like that. I'm a very private person.'

'I'm so sorry,' I repeated, doing my best to sound calming when my own voice was shaky. 'I'll tell him that, and hopefully he'll stop chasing you.'

'I don't even support Vivi's Law. Actually, I think it's a bad idea. It's not all about the people crying out for organs, you know. What about us, the ones who have lost somebody we love.'

'I sent you a letter, after the transplant,' I told her, when she gave me a chance to speak.

'Yes, I got that letter. You hoped the fact I had saved your life was helping me through my loss. Just so you know, it wasn't.'

She sounded bitter and sad, and I understood why she

must be, but it made me feel guilty, like I had stolen her son's life from her, taken everything and left Grace with nothing at all. I took a deep breath, touched my hand to my chest, and searched my mind for the best words.

'I was so young,' I told her. 'I didn't know what to write, how to explain how I felt. But when I said sorry … and when I said thank you … those weren't just words. They came from my heart, from Jamie's heart.'

There was a moment of silence then Grace said in a softer, quieter voice. 'It's inside you beating right now, as we're talking.'

'Yes, it is.'

'A little piece of my little boy.'

'It's keeping me alive, every single day, it's given me seven years I wouldn't have had otherwise.'

'Have you done good things with those years, Vivi? Because Jamie would have, I'm sure of that.'

'I've tried,' I told her, although I couldn't come up with anything I had achieved that seemed impressive enough to share with her.

'Have you had any children?' Grace wanted to know.

'No, but I have two lovely nieces who I adore. Farah is four and Darya is almost three.'

'Are you married?'

'Still single … just dating.'

'I suppose you're still young. You've got plenty of time ahead of you. Years and years.'

'Hopefully,' I said, because I struggle to think that way, having grown up knowing my life could be cut short at any moment.

Grace must have heard the doubt in my voice. 'More time though, enough to achieve whatever you want, to have all the things you've dreamed of.'

'More time,' I agreed. 'Thanks to you and Jamie.'

She breathed a soft sigh. 'I'm sorry if I was rude earlier. I got such a shock when I saw that article with Jamie in it. It was the last thing I expected.'

'Grace, I'm the one who needs to say sorry. I had no idea my boss was going to use his name and picture, otherwise I'd have tried to stop him if I could.'

'Ah well, it's happened and no harm done, I suppose. And at least it was a nice photo, the one they used.'

Now she was calmer, Grace's voice was low-pitched and pleasant. I put the timbre of it together with the photographs I had seen of her on Facebook and tried to imagine what sort of woman the mother of my donor was.

'Jamie looks like such a lovely boy,' I told her.

'Oh, he was. They all used to say so, his teachers, the parents of his friends, everybody we met; they'd tell me how lucky I was to have such a great kid. And then my luck ran out, didn't it?'

'Oh Grace ...'

'What I'd like is to be close to him again.' Grace said it very softly. 'Close to his heart.'

I wasn't sure what she meant, not at first, then it dawned on me. 'You're saying that you want us to meet?'

'Yes ... I could come up to London any time that works for you.'

The thought was unnerving. 'When were you thinking?'

'The sooner the better; do you get a lunch break?'

'Most days.'

'Tomorrow then?' Grace sounded eager now. 'Or are you too busy? Would another day be more convenient?'

How could I be too busy to meet the woman who had saved my life? As if anything else I had planned to do with my time was more important than that.

'Tomorrow should be fine,' I agreed, apprehensively.

Where would we do this? It needed to be somewhere informal, not too intimate, an easy spot to come and go from, full of other people who wouldn't pay us any attention. My mind went blank until suddenly it was obvious.

'What about McDonald's on Kensington High Street, say at 1 p.m?' I suggested

'Yes, McDonald's; good idea,' she agreed. 'I'm sure I'll recognise you from your photo in the newspaper.'

'Right, well, I'll see you then,' I told her, and my stomach churned at the thought of it.

Once it was arranged I started to feel better about our meeting, excited and curious too. I called my sister Imogen as I was walking back to the office and heard the usual soundtrack of her family in the background – a child yelling, Peppa Pig playing, the clinking as a dishwasher was emptied and plates were stacked.

'I need to talk,' I told her.

'What? Sorry? Hold on a minute.' On the other end of the line everything went quiet. 'I've shut myself in the bathroom; it's the only place I get any peace. Now what did you say?'

'I'm meeting her, the mother of the kid who was my heart donor.'

'Bloody hell.'

'I know.'

I described what had happened and Imogen wasn't distracted once, not even by the unmistakable sound of a small child screeching from somewhere beyond the closed door.

'How do you feel about this? Is it going to be weird?' she asked.

'Yes, probably.'

'Do you need me to come with you? I'll find a babysitter.'

'Thanks, but I think that might be weirder.'

'Call me straight afterwards then, OK?'

'Shouldn't you go and see what's going on out there?' The screaming was definitely louder.

Imogen sighed. 'Most likely it's only someone hitting their sister over the head with Lego bricks ... but yeah, I'd better check. Hope it goes OK. I'll be thinking of you.'

*

Back at work I had another distracted afternoon. Every time I thought about my donor's mother, adrenalin surged through my body and my heart seemed to beat faster. In my head I kept running through the questions I wanted to ask her, the things it would be appropriate for me to say. I don't remember ever being so nervous about meeting somebody.

That evening instead of going home I walked to Selfridges and spent too much money on a new outfit. It looked exactly the same as everything else I own – fitted black top, slim-leg trousers. I have variations of that outfit for summer, winter, daywear and evenings. But it would make me feel good to dress in something new and I wanted to give myself every chance to make the right impression.

Grace McGraw had to like the girl who had got her son's heart.

Vivi

When I was a kid my mother wouldn't allow me near junk food. I was fed low-fat everything. And after the heart transplant I was still meant to be super careful about what I ate, but I developed a crazy passion for McDonald's. Whenever I'm desperate for a treat I go there and always have the same thing – two Big Macs. I love everything about those burgers: the crunch of iceberg lettuce, the melting orange processed cheese, the sour bite of dill pickle, the sauciness and greasiness, all sandwiched up in a sesame bun. And I take a stroll from my office to the branch on Kensington High Street far more often than I ought to.

Today I walked there briskly, dressed in my new outfit having spent a lot of time tidying my hair, which is thin and wispy these days, whilst focusing on my reflection in the mirror and telling myself it was absolutely normal to feel so jittery.

Even so I arrived at McDonald's fifteen minutes early. Settling at a table by the door, my eyes were trained on the faces of the women coming through it, and there was no denying my nervousness now.

Grace's hair was shorter and greyer than in her Facebook profile picture but still, there was no mistaking her. She was taller than most women, more slender too.

I stood up and smiled in her direction. 'Hi, I'm Vivi.'

She paused a couple of arm-lengths away. 'Your editor keeps sending me messages,' she said, accusingly.

Silently, I cursed Dan. 'Sorry, just ignore him. Please sit down. Can I get you a coffee or something to eat?'

'Maybe.' Grace moved closer, resting her hands on the back of a chair. There were no rings on her fingers, no jewellery at all, and she was wearing faded jeans and a long-sleeved navy-striped T-shirt. 'I'm not sure how long I'll be staying.'

Grace seemed ready to take flight and I didn't want that. Now she was here, I needed to know everything; all the details I had tried for years never to let myself consider.

'Please sit down,' I repeated. 'Tell me all about Jamie.'

'Are you sure?' She took a step closer. 'I'm not going to pretend that everything's fine now, because it isn't. I regret it, you see; I wish he hadn't been a donor. That's not what you want to hear though, is it, that it haunts me?'

'It would haunt me too,' I told her.

With a low sigh, Grace pulled a pack of tissues from her bag, dropped them on the table and took a seat opposite me. 'I cry,' she explained. 'And I get angry because he was taken too soon and it isn't fair. Whenever I speak about him ... often even just thinking ...'

'What was he like?' I asked, gently.

'My lovely Jamie ...' Grace leaned forward, resting her elbows on the table, and as she did so her sleeves rode up and that was when I noticed the scars; there was no way of missing them. I know all about scars, the way they silver as they age, and the curved lines scoring both her wrists looked raised and red, not old at all. They made me feel afraid for her.

'My Jamie was funny, smart, a good writer like you, so talented. And he was kind too, such an affectionate boy, a hugger. Not that I'm saying he was perfect; he got up to mischief like most kids do but never anything too bad. I know he would have grown up into a lovely man ...'

Some people want to tell you their stories; it helps for them to be heard. But this woman Grace was so on edge and I was wary of asking more questions, of pushing too hard, in case I made things worse. So I waited, while she took a deep breath and steadied herself.

'The terrible thing is, it was me who bought that bike for him. Everyone says not to blame myself but if I hadn't then he would have been safe on the bus with the other kids. It was his sixteenth birthday present and I surprised him with it. Jamie always loved my surprises and this one was meant to be the best yet.'

Following my gaze, she pulled the sleeves over her thin, scarred wrists and, leaning back, dropped her hands beneath the table, out of sight. 'I suppose you want to know what happened?'

'Only if it's OK for you to talk about it.'

Grace gave me a bleak look, making it quite clear nothing would ever be OK again, then began talking in a low, flat voice. I could tell she had told this story in the same way before.

'It was such an ordinary evening. Jamie had lots of friends and after school he would usually hang out with them so I didn't start worrying until after it got dark. I was heading out to look for him when I saw the police car pulling in right by my front gate. Two of them got out of it, a man and a woman. They told me he'd been knocked unconscious when he came off his bike.'

'Was there never any hope?'

'I hoped. Of course I did. In the hospital he looked almost perfect and I sat by his bed, held his hand and talked to him. I begged and begged him not to leave me. There were machines keeping him alive and I thought if we just waited for long enough his body would heal and it would all be fine. He was always so healthy and strong, you see. And he was only sixteen.'

Grace's voice faltered. For a few moments we sat staring at each other across the plastic table until I reached over it to grasp her hand, holding it tightly like she once held Jamie's.

'They told me to stop hoping,' said Grace, the tears falling now in such a steady flow I wasn't sure her single pack of tissues would be enough to stem it. 'I must have gone into shock because it was almost as if I was detached from the whole thing, like it wasn't really happening and I would wake up any moment and find everything was OK again. Does that make any sense?'

I nodded. 'Yes, of course.'

'The more I thought about it, the more it seemed a waste of this lovely, healthy boy. Jamie would have wanted to help others; that's the kind of kid he was. So it was me who brought it up, I offered his organs for transplant and they were happy to accept them.'

'You regretted it afterwards?'

'Not straight away, only after I saw an article about an American boy who was declared brain dead and then came back to life. His parents had been about to sign the donation papers. I screamed and screamed when I read about that. Do you people ever think properly when you write these articles? Do you realise what they do to mothers like me?'

'Probably not,' I admitted, helplessly. 'I'm so sorry. If there's anything I can do ... any way at all to help you ...'

'There is something, that's why I'm here.' Grace looked me in the eyes. 'I'd like to listen to it, to Jamie's heart. I've dreamed of hearing it beating. Would that be OK, do you think? Would you mind?'

I held my hand over my chest and felt my heart's dull, regular thud. 'Now?'

'I've brought a stethoscope. My brother is a GP. He lent it to me.'

How could I say no? The heart beating away inside me, so strong and steady, suddenly felt more hers than it did mine. Once it had been inside her body, a tiny piece of the son she gave birth to.

So I nodded my agreement and Grace picked up her bag

then stood. 'I suppose it would be best if we went to the bathroom?'

That was how I found myself standing in a disabled cubicle in a fast food restaurant while a tall woman with a neat figure and dark eyes pressed a stethoscope to my heart and listened intently.

It was far more awkward than it was moving. For a few seconds both of us held our breaths. I was aware of my heart's steady rhythm and imagined how it must sound to her, a soft drumbeat. We stayed there as she listened and the lunchtime crowd came and went, as doors slammed, toilets flushed and taps ran. At last she gave a faint sigh, removed the stethoscope from my chest and, for first time since we had met, Grace managed a smile.

'Thank you ... it's like Jamie's not gone from the world completely, you see, not while you're still alive.'

There was another tricky moment when we exited the bathroom together and neither of us was quite sure what we should do next – chat a while longer, say goodbye and walk away?

'Can I buy you some lunch?' I offered.

'Yes, why not,' Grace agreed. 'I haven't had McDonald's in ages.'

Standing and waiting in the queue, she asked about my life. I was describing my job as we reached the counter and automatically put in my usual order.

'Two Big Macs please.'

Turning towards Grace, I saw she was staring at me, a curious expression on her face.

'One is never enough,' I told her and, assuming she thought I was being too greedy, added. 'They're not actually that big.'

She made a gasping sound. 'That's what my Jamie used to say as well. Two Big Macs, it was always what he wanted.

And if I commented, it's just what he'd tell me. They're not really that big, Mum.'

Not for one moment did I believe there was anything significant about this. I have read those articles about people who suddenly develop a taste for their donor's favourite food or take up the sport they loved – I had even written a couple – but I don't believe having Jamie's heart has changed me in any way. I'm still entirely me. Most likely I would have always loved junk food if I had been given a chance to taste it. Grace, though, was staring in wonder. To her this must have seemed far more than a coincidence.

'I'll have the same thing,' she declared. 'Two Big Macs.'

We sat together at another of the plastic tables. I wasn't especially hungry but the warm, savoury smell of burger as I opened the box was enough to make me want to eat. Picking it up in both hands, I took a decent bite, then realised Grace was still watching me.

'That was how Jamie ate his too. Exactly like that, with his hands wrapped round it.'

I put down the burger and wiped my fingers on a paper serviette. This was starting to freak me out. 'It's probably how everyone eats a Big Mac,' I said, as lightly as I could.

'Perhaps there are other connections between the two of you.' Grace sounded hopeful. 'You never know. It's a heart, isn't it, so it must have changed you.'

I could sense her watching and waiting for something else that linked me to her dead son. When I picked up the burger again it was with one hand. I only nibbled at it and didn't bother unwrapping the second.

Afterwards we said goodbye on the pavement, with a clumsy hug and a promise to stay in touch. I gave her my mobile number, but still, as I turned and walked away I was pretty certain I would never see her again.

I didn't know Grace, not then. And I had no idea that she hadn't told me what she really wanted.

Grace

She doesn't like to say goodbye to Vivi Palmer. As they stand on the pavement, crowds eddying around them, she tries to prolong the conversation and keep her there a little while longer.

It took such a long time to accept her son was gone. Grace would think she had caught a glimpse him on the sofa, call for him to turn the television down, wonder what he might like for his dinner, see or hear some random thing she couldn't wait to tell him about. A hundred times a day she would remember with a jolt that everything had changed. Then one day all that stopped and now the dark shape on the sofa is only ever a cushion, there is no need to worry about cooking dinner, she hardly ever turns on the television, and she is used to the silence and loneliness.

To Grace, grief seems like an ocean; at times rough, at others calmer, but there is always a current she has to fight against, and often she doesn't feel strong enough.

If only she had worn a different top, one with longer sleeves, because she is ashamed of the scars and certainly didn't want this girl to see them. It had been her brother who found her that day. As a doctor he knew the signs so he had taken to popping in, coming over from Didcot without calling first, and he had his own key so when she didn't answer the door he could let himself in.

Grace felt bad about him finding her like that. She felt bad about wishing that something else had come up and he hadn't found time for the twenty-minute drive. But now watching the slight, dark-haired girl turn and walk away down Kensington High Street she has the glimmer of a feeling she hasn't known in a long time. Not hope exactly, certainly not excitement, but an interest in finding out what will happen next.

As she walks to the bus stop to catch the number twenty-seven back to Paddington, every step she takes has the steady rhythm of the beating heart she has just listened to.

The heart is love isn't it? That means this young woman has a piece of her love inside her. And just when it had seemed to Grace that there was none of it left.

Vivi

My sister lives very close to me geographically, but a world apart in every other way. She has an elegant Islington terraced house in one of those squares with a little garden at its centre. Imogen has filled her home with too much of everything – books, paintings, shabby leather chairs, pot plants and Persian rugs – and since she had kids it is always cluttered with half-finished craft projects and tiny discarded socks. Wine time starts earlier these days too. There was a bottle open on the kitchen table when I arrived.

'Where are the girls?' I wondered. My nieces are adorable but noisy and the house seemed strangely silent.

'They're upstairs in our bed watching TV with a large pack of Milkybar Buttons. I decided my 1200 thread count Egyptian cotton sheets were worth the sacrifice for a few moments' peace. And besides how much damage can white chocolate do?'

'Isn't feeding them sugar practically considered child abuse nowadays?'

Imogen wasn't interested. 'They're going to grow another set of teeth at some point, aren't they?' she argued.

What my sister really wanted to hear about was the meeting with Grace.

'Chocolate will only stave them off so long; you'd better start talking,' she warned, pouring more wine for herself and a glass of Coke for me.

When I told her about the whole business with the stethoscope, she shuddered. 'God, was that creepy?'

'No … it was odd I suppose but she's so terribly sad and it felt good to be able to do something nice for her.'

'Really?' Imogen sounded dubious.

'It wasn't such a big deal.'

'Will you be writing another article then? Interviewing her for the newspaper?'

'No, she's too fragile, I'd never try to make her do it.'

'Won't that boyfriend of yours expect it? The handsome, untrustworthy one?'

I had taken Dan to her place one Friday evening for impromptu drinks and Imogen seemed charmed but had later declared him completely unsuitable.

'He's not my boyfriend, not even my friend at this point,' I told her. 'Just another of my mistakes.'

Imogen raised her eyebrows. 'Hmm, I might have told you …'

'I know, I know.'

'So I assume it's over?'

'Oh yes, very, very over.'

There was a noise above our heads, like a stampede of small but solid animals. They thudded across the bedroom floor, down two flights of stairs and drummed along the parquet hallway, so heavily it seemed improbable that all we were about to encounter was two sweet little girls.

'Here they come,' warned Imogen.

Attaching themselves to me, squealing my name, covering me with wet chocolate-coated kisses: Farah and Darya, my two favourite little people in the world. They were only a year apart in age and seemed so alike with their dark hair, dark eyes and cuddly little bodies.

'Aunt Vivi is staying for supper,' Imogen told them. 'What do you want to eat?'

'Not hungry.' Farah was wriggling into my lap.

'More Milkybar Buttons,' demanded Darya, pushing in next to her.

Imogen shrugged. Most likely she didn't have any food in the fridge anyway. Last time I was over she served up boiled pasta shapes squirted with ketchup and called it bolognese.

'White chocolate is calcium-rich; I'm sure it says so on the packet,' she told me now.

Whenever I am there I get to do bath time and stories. Imogen doesn't care how much water gets splashed about, and there is no limit to the number of picture books I am allowed to read from in silly voices. Who knows where she got her parenting style from, but it certainly wasn't our mother.

'OK, so we'll do Deliveroo,' she announced, grabbing her phone and starting to scroll. 'What about Ottolenghi? Let's have the roasted aubergine with spiced tomato, lots of the little pea and mint croquettes, tempura sweet potato. Oh, and Hamid will want something meaty – venison kofta?'

'Sure,' I agreed, grateful that she never expected me to cover the bill.

By the time I had the girls tucked up in bed, Hamid was home and the food had arrived. Imogen was pushing all the clutter to one end of the kitchen table and crowding takeaway containers, forks and paper towels into the space she had cleared.

'No need to dirty plates,' she declared and Hamid beamed at her as if she was some sort of unrivalled domestic goddess.

Mostly I find Imogen's husband intimidating. He is older than us and it can be difficult to understand what she sees in him. My sister is all about fun but Hamid doesn't seem to know the meaning of the word. He is a leading light in the legal world, an expert in immigration and human rights, and he has this rather stern patrician air. Still he adores Imogen. She – and now the girls – are at the centre of his world, and when he is around them Hamid almost takes himself less seriously.

'Sit, eat, drink, enjoy,' Imogen instructed, pouring wine from a fresh bottle.

I know that Hamid thinks of me as the rackety sister, always overspending then having to borrow cash to cover her rent and showing no sign of growing up and settling down. But he tries to hide his feelings behind impeccable good manners.

'So Vivi,' he said, spearing a venison kofta with his fork. 'I see you are lobbying the government to change the law around organ donor registration.'

'Um, not me really, the newspaper.'

'I think it's a worthwhile cause. It may be time to look at the Human Tissue Act.'

Imogen was dipping the hot croquettes into a pot of green tahini sauce and dripping all over the table. 'Tell Hamid what happened today,' she said to me through a mouthful, 'with that creepy woman and the stethoscope.'

'She's not creepy,' I argued. 'Really, she isn't.'

Hamid looked solemn when I described my meeting with Grace, dabbing at his lips with a strip of paper towel and suggesting I should be careful.

'There are good reasons for the guidelines around contact. People can have unrealistic expectations.'

'I don't think Grace expects anything else from me.'

'You can't know that,' Hamid said, his tone reasonable. 'I'm quite sure you have a sense that you owe her something, even feel a little guilty because you're alive and her son isn't, am I right?'

Reluctantly, I nodded. 'Yeah, I do feel a bit like that.'

'So you see, you're vulnerable.'

'Do you really think so?' Imogen sounded concerned. 'Surely there are not likely to be any problems?'

'Hopefully not, but nevertheless I wouldn't advise her to see this woman again.'

At that my sister smiled. 'When did Vivi ever take any of our advice?'

*

After dinner Hamid had some sort of conference call so he disappeared to his study to prepare for it while I helped clear up. Since this only involved stashing the leftover takeaway in the fridge and rinsing forks, it was hardly onerous, but still my sister seemed tense.

'You're worrying about what Hamid said,' I guessed.

'A little bit,' she admitted.

'Why? You know I wouldn't do anything really stupid.'

'This woman Grace, she's sort of connected to us now isn't she, to our family? Have you spoken to Mum and Dad, asked what they think of you meeting her?'

'Not yet.' I had been avoiding it.

'I think you should.'

'Mmm,' I said non-committally because my parents are worriers, at least where I'm concerned, so it has become a habit for me to edit what I tell them.

'Are you going to show us a picture then ... of this boy ... the donor?' asked Imogen.

'Jamie.' I retrieved my phone from the clutter on the table and logged onto Grace's Facebook page, choosing that same first photograph I had seen, the one of him tousled and grinning.

'He looks very sweet, doesn't he?'

My sister stared at the screen. 'Poor kid. How old was he when ...?'

'Sixteen.'

'God ... what if it was Darya or Farah?'

'Don't.'

'But really, what if?' Imogen couldn't let go of the thought. 'It would be like my own heart had been ripped out; the grief would never go away, how could it? That poor, poor woman,'

I hugged my beautiful sister, chest to chest, heart to heart, wrapping my arms round her shoulders.

'I'm glad I let her have a listen with her stethoscope,' I

murmured into her glossy dark hair. 'Even if it was a bit weird.'

'I'm glad you did too.'

Later on, walking back to my place because it wasn't very late and Upper Street is always busy, I felt my phone buzz in my bag and assumed it must be Imogen checking in to see if I had made it home yet. But it turned out to be a text message from Grace. Later still, in my cramped little room I stared at it, wondering what she wanted now.

Vivi please can I see you again? There's something I need and you're the only person I can think of who might be able to help me …

Vivi

Saturday morning and Paddington Station smelt of warm cookies and coffee. People were rushing to buy tickets and catch trains, everyone on a mission, trailing umbrellas and dripping coats as it was raining outside. Drifting among them, I wasn't sure if I should be there at all. What had made me agree to a day return to Oxford to visit Grace in her semi-detached house on Cowley Road?

Boarding my train, I found a seat and pulled out the magazine and newspapers I had picked up on the way. The *Daily Post* was fat with weekend colour supplements. Flicking through I found another headline about the campaign for Vivi's Law. It was an interview with a mother who had lost her son from an asthma attack and given his liver, kidneys, corneas and skin to grateful recipients. Lives and eyesight were saved so that was a great consolation and had given her strength, she said. This woman was passionate about organ donation and much more on message than Grace with all her unsettling regrets.

It was still raining when the train arrived in Oxford. Catching a taxi to Grace's place, I tried to shrug off the sense that this might be a mistake. All I was planning to do was listen and find out what she needed, because I couldn't begin to guess and was much too curious not to have come at all.

Grace's house was neat and filled with photographs of Jamie. They were framed on the walls and arranged on furniture – there he was as a baby and a toddler, in his school portrait, hanging out with friends, posing on his bicycle, a whole gallery showing every stage of his short life.

'Come and sit down.' Grace ushered me into the lounge. 'Would you like some tea?'

'Thanks, but I'm fine. I had one at the station.'

More pictures of Jamie decorated this room. As I perched on the sofa there was nowhere to rest my eyes without finding another image of his face.

'I was a single mum,' said Grace. 'It was the two of us, now it's only me. Do you want to see his room?'

'Maybe later.'

Grace accepted this with a small frown. Picking up the nearest photo frame, she dusted its glass front with her sleeve and stared at the print inside.

'This one of him was taken when he was playing at a Saturday morning football club. Every week I was there on the sidelines cheering him on, no matter how cold it was, I never let him down. Afterwards we'd go for lunch, usually to McDonald's if Jamie had his way ... two Big Macs, just like you.'

I nodded, not sure what to say.

'I let him down at the end though, didn't I?' she continued, still looking at the picture, 'that day in the hospital. When I said they could carve him up and give away pieces of him to strangers. What sort of mother does that to her only child?'

'But if you hadn't done it ...'

'Then you wouldn't be here and your parents would be the ones grieving now.' Looking up, she met my eyes. 'Yes, I know all that.'

'Not only my Mum and Dad; it must be the same for all the other recipients. If you hadn't made that decision things would have turned out differently for every one of us.'

Grace put down the photograph and looked around the room at all the other versions of Jamie smiling back at us. 'Instead it's only me grieving.'

'You said there was something I could do to help ...'

Turning her back on me completely, Grace stared out of

the window at the busy, rain-swept main road.

'There is one thing,' she told me, tentatively. 'Jamie helped five other people. Someone is looking at the world through his eyes, someone is breathing through his lungs. I want to meet them all.'

'Why now?' I wondered. 'Why seven years later?'

Wordlessly, Grace left the room. When she returned it was with a letter that she handed over to me.

'Not very long ago I found this. He'd won a scholarship that I didn't even know he had applied for. He was going to do something amazing with his life; and then he was gone. So now I have to know it was worth it. That Jamie's life wasn't completely wasted. I want to be sure you people are making the most of the second chance you got thanks to him.'

'What if you manage to track them down and you're disappointed?'

Grace shrugged. 'I listened to Jamie's heart and felt better for a while. Now I'd like to look into his eyes and hear his breath and see how the person with his liver is, and the one who got his kidney and his pancreas.'

She came and sat beside me on the sofa. Her cheeks were flushed and suddenly the room felt stifling. Remembering Hamid's words of warning, I felt I ought to reason with her.

'My sister's husband, he's a lawyer, and I don't think he'd recommend you trying to look for the other recipients.'

'Oh, I'm not going to,' she interrupted. 'I wouldn't know where to start. But you're a journalist so you must be good at finding people. It's what you do every day isn't it?'

'Not exactly.'

'You'll help me though, won't you?

'I'm not sure … sorry Grace …'

That was when she insisted I went and looked at Jamie's room. It was small and unremarkable, a few posters on the walls, a desk that had been dusted, clothes still hanging in the wardrobe, an empty school bag on a single bed.

'People keep telling me it's time to start getting rid of his things,' said Grace, standing shoulder-to-shoulder with me in the cramped space. 'But no one else needs this room.'

There were no photographs of Jamie on these walls, but still I felt closer to him here, in the place where he had slept each night.

'What would he want, do you think? What would he say to you now?' I asked Grace.

She bent to smooth the cover on the bed. 'Jamie hated to see me sad, so I think he'd be hoping you'd help me.'

I wasn't sure if I knew how or even where to start. Some of the old-timers on the *Daily Post* used to talk about how much tougher it was to chase up leads before the arrival of the internet and social media. They thought we younger ones were soft because back in their day it was all about networking, getting to know cops, court clerks, lawyers, debt collectors. You were only as good as your contacts and, if all else failed, you would be sent to scour the electoral register at the local library. All those older guys had retired now or died or gone to work in corporate communications. An unwelcome thought occurred to me – I was going to need Dan's help with this.

'I'll think about it, is that OK?' I was desperate to escape this room, this house, Oxford.

'Yes, I suppose so. But before you go I should give you all the letters.' Grace must have noticed my blank stare. 'The thank you letters, from you and the other recipients who bothered to write.'

She was keeping them in an old shoebox stowed in Jamie's wardrobe. Mine was on top, although I barely recognised the careful handwriting as my own.

'Are you sure you want me to take these?'

'You'll need them. They're the only clues I have. Oh, and this one sent a photograph, not a very good one though, it could be anybody really.'

She gave me the picture. A man, blue eyes, short hair, quite good-looking but, Grace was right, not especially distinctive.

'Did you ever write back to anyone?'

Grace shook her head. 'For a long time I was just so sad, then it seemed too late and I thought you wouldn't want to hear from me, you'd all be busy with your lives.'

'If you contact the Donor Records Department they should still be able to pass on letters.'

'I can try that but everything will be anonymous, won't it? And I want to meet these people, see them with my own eyes, talk to them properly, so I'm going to need your help no matter what. Please think about it and let me know.'

I took the letters from her hand, tucking them inside the pages of the magazine in my bag so they wouldn't crease too much.

'I'll be in touch,' I promised.

Over the rest of the weekend I did the usual things. Went for a long walk beside the Thames, lazed in a café, took my nieces to the park and ate another meal conjured up by my sister via Deliveroo. I chatted to my parents on the phone and had a long discussion about media ethics with Hamid. I didn't mention my visit to Oxford, avoided bringing up anything at all about Grace, knowing they would be tempted to tell me what I should do.

I also knew what they were likely to say. Be careful, be careful; it was the mantra I had heard my whole life and it was starting to drive me crazy. Being careful took up so much of my time but my heart depended on it, so I did everything the doctors told me, I was as careful as anyone could be.

This, though, was entirely different; there was no risk of hurting my heart. And I wanted to help Grace, repay my debt to her, do whatever I could to ease her sadness.

Late on Sunday evening, I looked up news stories about recipients who had met their donor families. Mostly it happened in America and it seemed like a good thing, a happier ending. Watching YouTube footage of an emotional meeting, I reached a decision.

I was curious now too about these strangers who were linked to me by tiny pieces of our bodies. Who were they and what had they done with their second chances at life? I might not be sure how to go about it yet, but I was going to give this a try.

First thing Monday morning I was at my desk seeking out organ donor support groups online and making a list of options worth exploring. Admittedly it was a short list. I had Grace's letters and the one photograph in my bag but all they told me was that two of the other recipients were as grateful as I had been.

Dan appeared half an hour later clutching a takeaway coffee and something greasy in a paper bag. He made a few pointed remarks about how little I had achieved the week before and rolled his eyes when I claimed that the stomach bug I had invented must have really knocked me about.

'I've worked a lot over the weekend to make up for it.'

'Doing what?' he wanted to know.

I didn't really want to tell Dan about Grace, but I needed his help because I wasn't confident of finding any of Jamie's recipients without it.

'I've made contact with the mother of my donor.'

'You've talked to her?' Now he sounded interested.

'Actually, I went to meet her.'

'Seriously? Good work, Vivi.' Putting down his coffee, Dan took a bite from the bacon and egg bap he produced from the grease-stained bag. 'What did she say? Will she do a story with us?'

'I don't think so.' I said. 'All those messages you've been sending, she's feeling pressured.'

'Right, so you've got nothing so far then?' Dan asked through a mouthful of food.

'Only a couple of letters she received years ago from the other recipients, and a picture of one of them.'

'Really?' His eyes lit. 'Gold dust!'

'I'm not sure how useful they are really.'

'Let's see them.' Dan sounded impatient.

Reaching into my bag, I pulled out the sheets of paper and the passport-sized photo. 'One is from the man who got Jamie's kidney and the other from a woman who has his lungs,' I told Dan.

'So the corneas, pancreas and liver didn't get in touch at all? How rude.'

'I guess for some people it's too difficult, too emotional, and they don't know what to say.'

'Hmm.' Dan had started skimming the letters and was nodding his head, muttering under his breath, 'OK, that's interesting.'

'What is?'

'This one, from Fiona the lung woman, there's a lot of praying and giving thanks mentioned here, so she's a God-botherer, right?'

That term makes me flinch. My parents are churchgoers and even though I'm not religious myself I don't love it when those who are get disparaged.

'As for the kidney guy, Tommy, he's big into triathlons.' Dan continued. 'He says he's hoping to get back to competing now he's off dialysis. I wonder if he ever managed it.'

'Lots of people are religious or sporty,' I pointed out. 'It's not much help really.'

'What you need is to go online and start making connections; it might not be as hard as you think.' Dan stuffed the last of his breakfast into his mouth and took a swig of coffee. 'Hey, do you want to have a drink later? Come back to mine tonight maybe?'

I glanced up at him. 'No, I don't think so.'

'Suit yourself.'

It wouldn't be too long before he moved on, surely. There was a new editorial assistant; a posh girl with lots of swishy, glossy hair, or he might revive his on/off fling with the lifestyle editor of the weekend magazine. I told myself that I didn't care.

'Put in a bit of legwork, hey? And Vivi,' he called, reaching his own desk. 'Check to see if there are any special events for athletes who have had organ transplants. That's where I'd start.'

'Thanks, yeah I will.'

As usual Dan was on the money. It didn't take me long online to find the Gift of Life Games, an annual sporting contest for recipients who wanted to celebrate living to the full.

Quietly excited, I checked through their website. The last event had taken place in Manchester and yes, it had been a triathlon. Some guy called Tommy Moran had taken the gold medal. A speedy search of his name led me to a headline in the *Liverpool Echo*.

23 August 2016

Kidney Patient Triumphs

Race triumph for local miracle man. By Ron Deakins.

A Merseyside man has swum, cycled and run his way to victory in this year's Gift of Life Games. Six years ago he was on dialysis and his health was failing. Today after a successful kidney transplant Tommy Moran, 34, of Wallasey, is again competing as an elite triathlete.

'I do this because I can and it's all because of my donor,' says Tommy who ran a personal best at the event and vows he will continue to take part in the sport he loves. 'After a kidney transplant you never know how long you've got, so I'm trying to make every moment count.'

In the photograph accompanying the article Tommy Moran was running down a city street. His body looked muscled and he was wearing sports gear in tight, bright Lycra. It felt unreal, the idea of me sharing anything with this stranger.

I looked more closely at his face in the picture. It could easily be the same one that was staring out at me from the passport photo on my desk. The hair colour was the same, the square angle of the jaw.

The first thing I decided was not to say a word to Grace yet. Knowing how fragile she was, it seemed wise to meet up with this guy first, explain the situation, see what he was like and how possible it was that he had got Jamie's kidney. Not that I had actually found Tommy Moran yet. He didn't seem to have a Facebook account or even be on Instagram. Trying all the other obvious routes, I hit more dead ends.

'Anything?' Dan was back from the Monday morning meeting.

'Not really, but I'll keep looking.'

I could have done with more help, but was wary of asking him a second time. Instead I started searching for sporting events in the area Tommy was from. There was a half-marathon coming up in Liverpool and if he were super-keen perhaps he might be competing in that. Still so would thousands of others and picking one man out from the crowd wasn't going to be easy.

Dan caught me not quite managing to stifle a sigh. 'This story is bigger than us now, you know, Vivi,' he said, serious-faced. '*London Live* is all over it. If you don't find these people, someone else will and they might not treat them so well.'

That's the sort of thing editors say all the time, but what if it was true? I hated to think of reporters on Grace's doorstep, making the most of her grief. Of them finding Tommy Moran, and intruding on his life. At least if I did it, then I could make sure it was with kindness.

All around me other reporters were pounding on their keyboards, producing content to feed the fire that was the *Daily Post* website, all those articles every day, constant news updates, more was never enough. If I didn't write this, then one of them almost certainly would.

'Actually, I may have found a lead,' I admitted. 'His name is Tommy Moran and I've got a hunch he'll be at the Liverpool half-marathon. Do I just head up there and see if I can find him?'

'Get media accreditation,' suggested Dan. 'Ask for a list of the competitors, request interviews after the event, tell them you want someone who has overcome all the odds to race.'

I ought to have come up with that idea myself. Perhaps the old-timers had been right and younger journalists like me relied too much on social media.

'Hey, and good work.' Dan grinned at me. 'Are you going to let me buy you that drink now. Prince of Wales in half an hour?'

'Sure,' I agreed, even though I knew there was one place a drink with Dan was going to lead.

At the pub I was reminded of how much fun Dan could be. He drank bottled beer, I had a glass of wine and he made me laugh. In the softening light all I noticed was the good things about him, the golden-fair hair curling over his collar and falling over his forehead, the soft hazel of his eyes, the charm of his smile.

My sister was right; Dan was entirely unsuitable. He was never going to provide me with a lovely home and a stable future, or father our adorable children. But what did that matter since most likely I couldn't have any of those things anyway?

If you start looking up life expectancy after a heart transplant the numbers make unhappy reading. This is not a cure; I'm not completely fixed, I'm in recovery. Most heart transplant recipients are lucky to get about fifteen years of borrowed time; and there isn't a moment of it when you are allowed to stop working to stay alive.

All I ever wanted was to be normal and the reality is I never can be. There is always the risk my body will reject this foreign heart, which is why I have to be so careful. My system is weak because of the immune suppressant drugs I need to take twice a day, which means I reek of hand sanitiser all the time and need to steer clear of sick people. I'm not even meant to eat sushi in case of food poisoning. Then there are the pills to combat the side effects of the other pills and all the regular medical check-ups to look for signs of rejection, which can happen any time, for no apparent reason, and without any symptoms at all. It means always living on edge; waiting and wondering, fear never far away. And it means endless fussing too from the people who love me, even my sister.

Mostly Imogen was great when we were growing up. On days when my mother insisted on keeping me inside – because it was too hot, too cold, too wet, too windy or just because she didn't like my colour – Imogen, with her perfectly reliable heart, would stay home too. We painted each other's portraits, watched daytime cartoons, read the same books together.

It is why we are so close now. Ours is the sort of closeness that means we like to talk to each other several times a day even though there is nothing important to say. It has been harder lately with her little girls demanding her attention but she sends constant messages and emojis. And I'm sure she worries even though to my face she is breezy and unconcerned.

Not telling my sister about the whole deal with Grace, not mentioning I may have found a kidney to match my heart, it felt wrong. I kept picking up my phone then changing my mind.

It isn't that Imogen can't keep a secret, more that she genuinely doesn't see any reason why Hamid and our parents shouldn't know everything. Personal privacy is not her forte. What she fails to understand is that often people are happier not knowing. It saves them a lot of unnecessary worry, when they have enough to be concerned about.

A heart transplant is only a temporary miracle; there is still a lot that can go wrong, and it affects the way I live my life, the things I choose to do, and those I don't. After mine they did say it should be possible to have a baby – so long as I was careful, always careful, obviously – but how could I be a mother when I had so much hanging over me, when I knew my life would still be cut short? Besides, I might pass on the heart condition I had inherited from my mother's side of the family – dilated cardiomyopathy – and how guilty would that make me feel? So Imogen was living that life for both of us. She had the lovely children and a husband to rely on. I slept with unsuitable men.

Dan was only the latest in a long line of my unwise choices. I never let things get serious with any of them; never even chose the kind of guy who wanted to get serious. But when fear wakes and stalks you in the night, when you touch your chest and feel where they cracked it open to pull out your old sick heart, when you count up the borrowed time and wonder how much more of it lies ahead, when your new heart thumps harder at the thought of it … it helps to have someone lying there beside you, a warm body to curl against, the sound of their breathing, another heart beating alongside yours. That is all.

It is why I agreed to a drink with Dan and why, when he suggested a curry at the Indian place around the corner from his flat, I said yes to that too. Over dishes of spicy chicken madras and tamarind-laced okra, he gave me a pep talk.

'You're good at this Vivi, you've got a bright future ahead of you. Just look at the response to this story. It might actually happen, a change of law, and that would be huge for you; it'd really get you noticed. So track down these people, your donor brothers and sisters, and we can get a whole series of brilliant attention-grabbing pieces out of it.'

'Maybe,' I said, because I did like being good at my job, although increasingly I wasn't sure if I liked myself for it.

'I've been thinking about the God-botherer with the bad lungs; there has to be a way to find her. The others are going to be harder. It's a bummer they didn't send letters. Could this woman Grace write to them or is it too late?'

'She can try; the Donor Records Department will have all the details, although I'm not sure if they will pass her letters on. And I need to go softly because she's still in such a bad way.'

'Would it help if I had a chat with her?'

'Definitely not.' I didn't want Dan anywhere near Grace.

He smiled at me over the rim of his beer glass. 'Are you sure? I can be very persuasive.'

'Yeah, I know all about that.'

As we walked back to his place, he slung an arm round my shoulders. As soon as we were through the front door he pushed me against the wall, leaned his weight into me, and moved us towards his bedroom.

Nowhere was Dan's self-confidence more evident than when we were in bed together. He liked to take charge of things, strip me naked fast and set an urgent pace. It was almost a relief to let him shape my body to his and have my mind empty of everything but the pleasure of it, at least for a few moments. All I had ever wanted was to be normal and these sorts of moments were the closest I could get.

Afterwards Dan's body spooned mine and I felt him nuzzling into my neck.

'So we're fine now, you and me,' he said. 'You're not shitty with me any more.'

My response was a murmur, and non-committal.

'That's good … because I really like you Vivi …'

Dan

He likes it when she falls asleep first, her wispy hair spread across his pillow, her eyes shut tight. He listens as her breathing softens and slows, and keeps an arm curved around her.

Vivi Palmer isn't Dan's usual type, at least not to look at: pretty enough but unremarkable. He might struggle to pick her out of a line up of other small, dark young women if not for the scar, the long ridge engraved on her chest that normally stays concealed behind high-necked tops and buttoned-up shirts. Dan was fascinated the first time he saw it. He thought she looked broken and badly mended. He still likes to touch it and think about what they must have done to her body, all those surgeons.

Dan likes having her here. He sees himself more clearly through other people's eyes and he is sure that Vivi admires him. From the moment she arrived at the *Daily Post*, a nervous intern, he has worked at fostering her talent, because she could be good, very good, with a decent push.

Helping Vivi succeed is a bit of a buzz actually. He can see how she struggles at times to take a story as far as it needs to go and give the readers what they want. Tabloid journalism is tough, and not everyone understands the thrill of it, but he thinks Vivi does. She is good at getting close to people, asking them the right questions, really listening to the replies, and best of all she can string together a sentence, which is where a lot of them fall down.

Dan has made sure she has a chance to shine, thrown her some good stories and lots of the big campaigns, but he thinks this latest is the best. The personal angle is the winner. And the chance of it influencing a law change: well, that would be good for both their careers, as well as for the newspaper. Vivi's Law, it was a stroke of genius: what woman wouldn't love a law named after her?

She feels warm and small next to him, vulnerable. He had known she wouldn't stay angry for too long. It was obvious to everyone that she should write that first-person piece and she did a decent job with it too. Once Dan had fixed it up, injected more emotion, deleted some of the medical facts, it had been a great read that really gave a sense of how it must feel to have a dead boy's heart inside you. Dan is pretty proud of it.

Vivi isn't really his type but he likes the way she makes him feel. The more he gets to know her, the more sense it makes.

Before he drifts off to sleep he moves his arm and rolls away, sure that by morning she will have moved closer again, her head on his pillow, her scarred chest against his smooth back. Dan has decided to like her; he thinks it was one of his smarter decisions.

Vivi

Flags were flying, music was playing over a tannoy and people of all shapes and sizes were wearing numbered bibs and stretching out their quads and hamstrings. On a brisk spring day at Liverpool's Pier Head, this was how a half-marathon started. Beyond the queues for the Portaloos and the runners sucking on energy gels there was a wide ribbon of river and a row of grand old buildings lining its banks, but the thousands gathered here were more interested in the challenge ahead and there was a mounting sense of excitement.

I flashed my media pass at a man in a high-vis vest and he let me through a barrier. The organisers had been pleased to get my request for accreditation. Now I had access to all areas and a list of potential interviewees, people running in costume or to raise funds for charity, a blind athlete and, yes, a kidney transplant recipient called Tommy Moran. That had been the lucky break I wasn't expecting and, while I wasn't planning to interview them all, I was equipped with my digital recorder and a notebook.

It was still early and I was hoping to find a decent coffee somewhere once the race began. The course covered more than thirteen miles, which wasn't going to take the front-runners long, so there wasn't much time before I needed to be back on the finish line.

Apparently, Tommy Moran would be happy to chat after the race. A bid to extract his contact details hadn't got me anywhere and I hadn't quite decided how to approach things when we met face-to-face. Dan had been all in favour of me getting an interview done before I broke the news about why

I was really there; possibly he thought the quotes would be stronger that way. But to me seemed better to be completely honest from the outset and hope that Tommy wasn't so surprised that he turned around and walked away.

You don't become a journalist unless you're the curious type. The ones that are good at this job really care about the details of other people's lives whatever they do and whoever they are. I would have wanted to hear about Tommy even if there weren't a chance we were both alive due to the death of the same teenage boy. Why he ran, what drove him, how it made him feel – I would have had a whole list of questions. But now, because of the person I suspected he was, I wanted to know everything.

With the loud hooting of a horn, the runners were off. I searched for Tommy's face amid the front pack but couldn't pick out anyone who looked like the photographs I had seen. As the last of them trailed off I headed to a coffee cart then moved away from the crowds and walked a short length of the river, a stretch of choppy grey with a ferry ploughing through. The more I considered it, the more I wondered if Dan was right after all. Going in gently with Tommy might be the smartest tactic.

The first competitors started threading their way back, the winner throwing his arms in the air as he ran beneath the finisher's banner. Fair-haired and lanky, he definitely wasn't Tommy Moran. Neither were the next fifteen or so. Then I thought I saw him, running strongly over the smooth cobbles, well-muscled body, short-cropped dark hair, smiling as he crossed the finish.

'And just in, Tommy Moran in a very competitive time of one hour, thirty minutes and thirteen seconds,' announced a voice over the loudspeaker.

As the crowd cheered, I watched him follow the other runners down the finish chute to surrender his bib number, collect his medal and refuel on Powerade and bananas. I pushed my way through the spectators and eventually managed to find him at the other side, sitting alone on the ground, busy massaging his calf muscles and munching on a granola bar.

My first impression was of someone very masculine: a square jaw, a close-trimmed beard, bright blue eyes and, down one muscled arm, some sort of intricate tattoo of flowers, birds and leaves. He was in great shape

'Hi, I'm Vivi Palmer from the *Daily Post*. Congratulations, it looked like you ran a good race.'

'Not too bad,' His voice was low with a strong hint of a Liverpool accent. 'But it was an easy enough course.'

'Doesn't look easy to me.'

Tommy smiled 'It's all relative I suppose.'

'I'd love to sit down and chat to you about it. I'm working on a piece about marathons.'

'Oh yeah they said a reporter might want to interview me.' With a last stretch of his calf muscles, he got to his feet. 'What is it you want to know exactly?'

'I'd just like to hear your story. But do you think we could get out of here? Find somewhere quieter.'

'Sure, I'd prefer that too.'

Leaving the crowds behind, we walked a little way past the museum towards the Albert Dock and sat on a bench overlooking the river.

'What sort of article are you writing exactly?' Tommy wanted to know. 'Is it about marathon running in general?'

'I'm looking at more of a human interest angle about the people who run them,' I told him.

'And you want to include me because of the kidney transplant?' he guessed.

'That's right.'

'Others are out there competing at sports after a transplant. I'm not exceptional.'

'Maybe, but I don't think it's something that is generally well known. Our readers will be interested.'

'OK, fine,' he agreed. 'Ask whatever you like.'

I started off with questions about his life before the transplant, when his own kidneys were still functioning properly. Like lots of interviewees, once he warmed up, Tommy seemed to enjoy talking about himself.

'I was fit and healthy, really strong. That's why it was such a shock when I got sick, because I thought I was bulletproof. It started with a headache that wouldn't go away. Everyone was nagging me to get it checked out and when I finally went to the doctor it turned out my blood pressure was sky-high. It didn't take them long to diagnose me with kidney disease, glomerulonephritis, such a stupid name.'

'Your kidneys were failing?'

'I was basically dying and fast. So, then I'm on dialysis and I can hardly get out of the house, never mind run a marathon. I was exhausted, nauseous, my feet swelled up, my brain felt muzzy. I felt like shit and it was tough on everyone around me. People offered me kidneys – friends, family, even a guy from work I hardly knew – but no one was a good enough match so then I had to wait for somebody to die.'

'And finally they did.'

'He was a kid, starting out in life, terrible really. He died in a road accident, that's what they told me.' Tommy had been looking out at the river; now he dropped his gaze to the ground. 'It's why I do this. There's no sitting round feeling depressed because of all the shit that's happened. I push myself, train hard, try to win, because I can and that boy can't any more.'

'Yeah, I understand,' I told him. 'Plus, it's got to be good for you, right? Stay healthy and your kidney should last longer.'

'I want every minute I can have. The thought of going back on dialysis ... God ...' Tommy half closed his eyes and shook his head. 'But doing the Ironmans and marathons is about more than staying healthy. These races, they're kind of my only way of showing I'm grateful, of saying a thankyou to that boy and his family.'

'What if there was the possibility of saying thank you in another way? Would you want to?'

'How do you mean?' He glanced at me.

'If you could meet the donor family?'

'It would be weird after all this time but yes, I'd want to. It won't happen though. I wrote a letter at the time, even sent a picture when they said it was allowed, but I heard nothing back.'

'Things might have changed.'

His expression was wary, so quickly I added, 'Look, I've got some explaining to do.'

When I told him about the *Daily Post* and the Vivi's Law campaign the wariness cleared from his face.

'Ah, that's where I know you from. I kept thinking you seemed a bit familiar. I read that article about your heart transplant the other week, thought it was great. Hopefully it'll help make a difference.'

'We've had loads of feedback,' I told him. 'And it's had an unexpected consequence. I've connected with the family of my donor for the first time.'

'Wow, and how was that?'

'Oh you know, strange and sad.'

'So, who was your donor?'

'Well, that's it … the reason I'm here. I'm wondering if it was the same boy who gave you his kidney.'

His eyes widened. 'You're kidding?'

'I'm not entirely sure, obviously, but it seems very possible.'

'Bloody hell.'

I gave Tommy a few moments to let it sink in and then we compared notes, what he had been told about his donor, what I knew about mine. More convinced now that I was right, I pulled out the letter and photograph he had sent to Grace all those years ago. 'This is you, isn't it?'

'Where did you get that?' Tommy sounded wary.

'Our donor's name was Jamie McGraw. I have a picture of him too, on my phone. Do you want to see it?'

Staring at the screen, Tommy looked stunned. 'What is it you want from me, exactly? You're not writing an article about marathons, are you?'

'No,' I admitted. 'But it's not me that wants something, it's Jamie's mum. She has this idea she needs to meet all the recipients. You're the first one I've tried to look for.'

'She wants to meet everyone who got a part of her son?' His tone was subdued and I couldn't tell how he felt about it.

'Yeah, I know it seems kind of freaky ...'

'It doesn't really,' said Tommy, thoughtfully. 'I've got a couple of young kids myself so I can understand. We're all that's left of her boy, aren't we?'

'In a way, yes.'

Tommy looked at me then, really looked, as if seeing me properly for the first time. 'Is there a word for what we might be? Co-recipients? Donor siblings? We have some of the same DNA now right.'

'I guess so ... Is that important though? We're still just us.'

'Maybe ...' Tommy stared out at the river again. 'I lost a lot of people when I was sick. It was my own fault; I was a complete arse so I don't blame them for not being able to put up with me.'

'How were you an arse?' I wondered.

He gave an embarrassed shrug. 'When you think you're dying you don't care about a lot of things. I didn't care about people. I was a crap husband, crap father, crap friend. All that mattered was being near the phone in case a call came through to say I had a kidney. Then I got my transplant and was healthy again, which seemed like a miracle. But life didn't go back to the way it was before. Things had changed ... My marriage broke up for a start ...'

'That must have been hard.'

'Yep.' Tommy nodded. 'So I get it, why that mother would want to know us: that's what I'm trying to say.'

'Would you like to meet them too, all the people with organs from your donor?'

'I think so, yes.'

I told him a little more about Grace, how grief seemed to have roughened her edges and worn away at her. I described her house, the gallery of photographic memories, and tried to prepare him for her unsettling honesty.

'When would we meet?' Tommy wanted to know.

'I'll need to tell her about you ... but soon, I'd think.'

'OK.'

'If you go down to Oxford, then maybe see her somewhere other than the house. It's pretty overwhelming.'

'You'll be there too?' There was an edge of anxiety to his voice.

'If you want.'

'Please.'

'Take lots of photos to show her,' I suggested. 'Of you competing in triathlons, pictures of your family, tell her about your life.'

'What about the rest of them, the other co-recipients, are you going to keep searching?'

'It looks like it.'

'If there's anything I can do to help ...'

We walked back towards the finish line, me only just managing to match Tommy's long, fast stride. Runners were still straggling in and most looked in worse shape than he had been in: falling to the ground, heads plunged into hands, bodies broken with exhaustion.

'It's difficult to see why people do this,' I told him.

'Nothing else makes you feel as alive. And it starts to take over: eating right, training, getting enough sleep, it gives you structure.'

In my job you meet a lot of different people and get used to sizing them up quickly. I wondered if Tommy was one of those intense types. Certainly that was the sense I was getting. His eyes were such a startling blue and there was something about the way they fixed on my face as I talked, as if he was paying careful attention so he could mull over every word later on.

'Hey, do you want to get some food?' he asked. 'I'd offer to take you to a café but I need to get changed. Perhaps we might go back to my place though. I make a pretty decent omelette.'

'Thanks, that would be great.' I was intrigued to get a look at where he lived. Most people like to reflect their personalities in the way they decorate their homes and I wanted to see what Tommy's place would tell me about him.

We caught a taxi that took us through a tunnel running beneath the river and out the other side to a suburban sprawl. It was leafier and greener than the city we had left behind, but nothing about the area suggested wealth. We passed a row of terraced houses and some boarded up shops and then the taxi pulled in beside a pebble-dashed bungalow with a neatly mown lawn and a worn welcome mat beside the front door. Inside the house everything was the same, shabby but tidy. Tommy didn't seem to own much furniture. He showed me into the front room, which was dominated by a gold velour sofa, a low coffee table and a glass-fronted cabinet.

'Do you mind if I take a quick shower?' asked Tommy. 'Make yourself at home. If you want a cup of tea I'll put the kettle on.'

'I'm fine, thanks.'

I was glad for the chance to look around. As soon as I heard the shower running I crept through for a glimpse at the other rooms. A small kitchen with a few dishes in the drying rack, a spare room with two single beds and a box of toys, Tommy's room with a king-sized bed neatly made, a dining room that didn't look like it was ever used. Back in the lounge I checked out the contents of the glass-fronted cabinet. It was filled with medals and trophies from races he had taken part in.

'This place is a rental,' said Tommy, still towel drying his hair as he came back into the room. He had changed into jeans and a white T-shirt. 'I moved here when my marriage ended and haven't bothered doing anything to the place because I keep thinking I won't be here for much longer. It's handy though, you know. Close to my kids, not far from work.'

'What job do you do?' I had forgotten to ask.

'I'm a joiner, fancy kitchens mostly. I used to have my own business down south but that went under when I got sick so now I'm back here and working for a mate.'

Tommy must have enjoyed years of being a healthy person, built his business, fallen in love, had a family, with no suspicion that his kidneys were going to fail. Would that have been harder or better than the way things happened for me? I wasn't sure.

He did make a spectacularly good omelette. Lots of eggs laced with pepper and beaten with a whisk, sautéed spinach and finely chopped parsley, all folded in with a quick flick of his wrist and slid onto a plate he had warmed in the oven.

We ate sitting on stools at the kitchen counter and this time it was Tommy who asked all the questions. That happens surprisingly rarely to me. Even in social situations I tend to be the one listening to other people's stories and staying quiet about my own. Still I owed this guy a few details, so I walked him through my life – sick kid, heart transplant miracle, brand new future etc.

'Sometimes it feels odd knowing you have a part of a stranger inside you,' Tommy admitted, when I had finished. 'Don't you think?'

'Yes ... but not as weird as it would feel being dead.'

Tommy laughed at that.

'And Jamie had gone, hadn't he?' I continued. 'There was nothing more anyone could do to change that. So me having his heart made no difference.'

'It makes a difference to her though, to his mother,' said Tommy, a frown deepening on his face. 'Otherwise she wouldn't want to meet us.'

'Grace needs to know what has happened to everyone, to see we're doing well and prove to herself it was worth it. Her son lost out on his dreams so I think she wants to know what we made of ours.'

'Fair enough, she gave us our lives back.'

'It's a bit of risk for her though, isn't it?' This was something I had kept thinking about on the train up from London. 'She's bound to be pleased with you – you've got kids and you're keeping yourself healthy. The lung recipient seems to be religious so hopefully that means she's nice. But the others, the ones who got his liver, his pancreas and his corneas, what if they're heavy drinkers or chain smokers, or not good people, what if Grace doesn't think they deserve a piece of her son?'

'You can't do anything about that,' said Tommy. 'You can only find them.'

'I'd like her to find some peace too. Otherwise what is the point of this?'

'At least you're helping give her the chance of finding some.'

Tommy rinsed our plates and loaded them into the dishwasher. He washed the omelette pan and wiped down surfaces.

'What's the next move?' he asked me, as he cleaned so meticulously. 'Are you actually planning to write an article about me?'

I screwed up my face. 'It's what my boss expects. I'm

definitely not going to involve Grace because she's much too fragile. I'd rather not put myself into another story either to be honest. But if you and I did something together it might help us to flush out the others.'

'I said I'd do anything to help and I meant it.' There was that intensity again – the seriousness in his expression, the bright gaze of his eyes.

Showing me out of his house, Tommy leaned across to open the front door and I caught the clean scent of his skin and a base note of muskiness. When he hugged me goodbye, and held me for a moment, it took me by surprise.

'See you then,' he said.

'Yeah, see you soon,' I replied, climbing into the waiting taxi.

On the train home, I made a few notes and thought about Tommy. My instincts are good; I have been out with enough rogues to recognise a nice guy when I meet one, and Tommy was a definite win. Finding him had given me the same buzz I got whenever I was working on a story and knew I had something really good on my hands.

Grace was going to like Tommy; that was the most important thing. I kept remembering those scars tracking up her arms. If I found enough of us, could we stand between her and anything as bad happening again? Could we be enough of a buffer against her despair? I hoped so. Surely we owed it to her and Jamie to try.

It had been surprisingly easy to track down Tommy and, flushed with my triumph, I hoped everything else was going to fall into place as easily. But after that one win I made no progress at all for ages. Days and days were spent trawling through newspaper archives and stalking strangers on social media. I put up hopeful enquiries on message boards, forums and Facebook groups, and nothing, not even a hint.

Dan had found an MP to publicly back Vivi's Law, so the story still had legs. Grace knew about Tommy and was excited to meet him. Still both of them wanted more than that, and it was up me to get it.

I hated disappointing people; no one likes that, do they? But this search was starting to feel personal now too. Having met Tommy, and liking him, I was curious to see the others who had this strange connection with me. All of our lives had been changed on the exact same day; we had been slowly dying then suddenly we weren't, and it was all thanks to a boy called Jamie. It felt as if I knew so much about these strangers already.

So I stepped up my efforts, sending emails that were never answered, trying the official channels only to be told what I knew already. Recipients could send letters, their friends and family were permitted to as well, photographs were allowed so long as there were no identifying features, we could tell our donor's family what we had been through before the surgery and how our lives had been changed, we were allowed to express our gratitude as much as we liked, but we had to stay anonymous.

It was frustrating to keep hitting up against brick walls. Even Dan seemed to have run out of good ideas for me. And every time I called Grace, it was to tell her there had been no progress at all. She was nice enough about it, thanking me for trying and hoping there would be a break soon, but I could sense her disappointment.

When I came across Laura Bria, I started to feel excited again. I first found her on Instagram where she posted images of herself in sportswear and bikinis, showing off the fish-hook-shaped scar that scored her upper abdomen, and telling all her followers: '*I love my body, I love my scar, it is a battle wound, there is no shame #livertransplant*'

Then I found Laura on a YouTube video, blithely contradicting herself by sharing scar-covering make-up tips and her favourite products. I read about her in a woman's magazine where she said a lot about body positivity and healthy lifestyles, and not much at all about liver cancer or her transplant. None of this was much to go on; still, I had a sense she was the one. It felt right.

I sent messages via social media and hoped she would accept them. I told her I was a journalist and that I thought we shared a donor, expecting a quick reply because social media influencers aren't usually shy, so I was surprised by her silence.

'Find her address on the electoral register,' instructed Dan. 'Doorstep her.'

Turning up at someone's front door, out of the blue, was never my favourite part of the job. Some of the reporters loved it – one proudly boasted he had been on so many doorsteps people called him the milk bottle – but it seemed bad manners to me. If I could avoid it then I did.

'She's pretty isn't she?' Dan was looking at Laura's Instagram profile. 'All that blonde hair: you'd look great together in the pics. Maybe you could show off your scar too?'

Not bothering to respond, I logged on to the electoral register, found that Laura Bria was registered to vote and, as her accent suggested, lived in South London. Her flat was a short walk from Clapham South tube station, in a tall terrace a little off the main road. I went there at the very end of the day, a part of me hoping she wouldn't be home and I could find some other, less intrusive way of making contact.

Laura didn't look quite as pretty in real-life, with her hair scraped back, and her make-up worn away, and a frown on her face rather than a dazzling Instagram-ready smile.

'What do you want?' she demanded. 'Are you trying to sell me something? Not interested, sorry.'

She tried to close the door and I put my hand flat against it, leaning in to stop her. 'No wait, I'm a journalist; I've been trying to get hold of you.'

'Oh yeah?' She sounded more interested. 'Where are you from?'

'My name is Vivi Palmer, I'm from the *Daily Post*.' I was trying to pass her my card when she started to laugh.

'That's right, I saw something really weird from you. Have you been sending me messages?'

'Yes, because I had a heart transplant and think we might share a donor . . .'

'You're barking up the wrong tree,' she said, shortly. 'My donor was my mother, and she's still alive.'

I took a step backwards. 'Oh I see, I'm so sorry, I've got it wrong . . .'

'If you want to do an interview get back to me in a few months. I'm planning a range of scar-healing oils, all natural and organic.' She took the business card out of my hand. 'Actually, why don't I call you when I'm ready to do some publicity?'

'Sure,' I agreed, not bothering to stop her this time as she closed the door in my face.

Laura Bria was my most humiliating failure, but not the only one. Over the next few days there were more hopeful leads that all finished in dead ends. I knew that out there somewhere were four other people who were linked to me, strangers who might be anyone at all, and I couldn't seem to find them.

At least there was Tommy. We had stayed in touch and he was definitely up for helping me. By now our only hope of managing to conjure up anyone else at all was to do an article and put out a plea. The plan was for him to come south so we could have a photo shoot together and then he could meet up with Grace at the same time. But it seemed difficult for him, escaping his family, getting time off work, and committing to a date. I was beginning to worry that I had got Tommy wrong, and actually he was a bit flaky, when late one evening I had another message from him.

Hey Vivi, You said the lung recipient is religious. I've been doing some research. There's a thanksgiving service for the families of donors and recipients at Westminster Abbey in a couple of weeks. She may well be there.

There was a link at the bottom of his message and I clicked through to a page filled with details of special services at Westminster Abbey. Most were to celebrate the lives of priests, missionaries and politicians, or mark an anniversary, but I spotted the one that Tommy was referring to. There weren't many more details, only a date and a note that tickets were free by application.

I messaged him back straight away.

Great, thanks! I think you're onto something. I'll definitely go.

I was the journalist and ought to have been on to that thanksgiving service. It wasn't as if I hadn't been trying, yet somehow, I had missed it completely. Imagining what Dan would say if he knew, a low-level sick feeling of failure set in and I curled up on my bed, feeling useless. When Tommy FaceTimed me, I almost didn't respond.

'Hi Vivi.' He was sitting on his sofa, in a chambray shirt that brought out the indigo of his eyes, holding a cup of tea and smiling. 'Nice to see you.'

'Good to see you too.' It did feel nice to have his face right there, looking back out at mine. 'That was a stroke of genius, coming up with the thanksgiving service. How did you find it?'

'I knew they had them occasionally because I was invited to one here; but I didn't bother to go because I'm not big on religion, not since my Mum and Dad stopped forcing me to go to Sunday school.'

I smiled at him; it seemed like another thing we had in common. 'Same here.'

'Still, this is one church service I will gladly attend,' he told me.

'You're planning to come?' I was surprised and pleased.

'Yeah, I was going to apply for three tickets actually, in case Grace wants to join us. I thought that could be a good place to meet her.'

It didn't seem the best idea to me. A thanksgiving service was bound to be emotional and Grace, with her fresh scars and raw grief, might not be comforted. But Tommy talked me round, pointing out that this service was meant for people like her, designed as a healing experience, and with us there, two of the people that her son had saved, it would be extra special, even if we didn't find any of Jamie's other recipients.

Tommy didn't know Grace. They had spoken on the phone, and sent messages back and forth, but he had never looked her in the eyes and seen all that pain for himself. I should have considered that but I didn't. Nor did I think about Hamid's lawyerly words of warning, about the guidelines and how we were about to break them. It felt good to have Tommy on my side; it was such a relief, that I put everything else out of my mind.

'See you in church then,' I told him.

Vivi

What do you wear to a service at Westminster Abbey? I went for basic black, the uniform that takes me everywhere. Grace had made more of an effort. She was dressed in a cream blazer, her hair sleeker and properly blow-dried, her face powdered and lips glossed.

She was wide-eyed and jittery when we met beside the lawn in Parliament Square, with the gothic Abbey looming beside us, and Tommy due to appear at any minute.

He had brought her a gift. From its shape it looked like a book and as Grace put it, still unwrapped, into her bag I could see her hands were trembling.

'I can hardly believe I'm here with you both,' she admitted. 'I keep wishing I could tell Jamie.'

Already she was shivery and on the edge of tears. Tommy pulled her into an easy hug and they stood together still and quiet, as other people walked past us and into the Abbey.

I was beginning to question whether we should really be here, but it was too late now because Tommy was suggesting we head inside and Grace was linking an arm through his and walking at his brisk pace, as I fell a little behind.

There was organ music playing, filling the whole of the grand space, echoing from the stone pillars and soaring ceilings. The three of us paused, overawed for a moment, and then continued on over the marble floors looking for a place to sit together, Tommy and I flanking Grace.

The choir raised their voices as we sat down. It was some sort of sung psalm and it seemed as if everything we felt was being expressed in those pure, perfect voices: sadness, hope, gratitude. When Grace pulled a packet of tissues from her bag, I accepted one just in case.

She whispered something to me that I couldn't quite hear so I moved my head closer.

'Sorry?'

'Do you think she's really here, the woman who got Jamie's lungs? I'm not sure how we'll know.'

'Me neither. I'm sorry. I guess we should just wait and see, and try to enjoy the service in the meantime.'

There was no way to tell whether the people surrounding us were donor families or recipients. They were such a mix of ages and ethnicities, most listening to the choir, a few shifting uneasily in their seats. Searching their faces, I wondered if any of them were Jamie's recipients, and noticed Tommy doing the same.

We sat through a lot of speeches. A minister talked of sacrifice and faith, then some of the congregation shared their stories, echoing each other as they expressed deep sadness or great thanks. One woman told us how her heart had started failing when she was pregnant with her second child and now, with her new heart, every day was a good day. A man thanked the nameless angel who had given him a kidney. A mother shared the story of her sick little boy's liver transplant and how full of energy and joy he was. I glanced at Grace and saw tears streaming down her cheeks.

It was a relief when the choir began singing again. I wasn't sure if I could bear to hear more about the loved ones who had died, the lives that had been saved, and feel the mix of grief and joy rippling from all these strangers.

As a child, the church was one place my mother would reliably allow me to go. There is something about being in one; light filtering through stained glass windows, dust motes in the air, old stone and varnished wood, music and prayers; the smell of hymn books; it is a language I understand. Normally I find it quite soothing, but now it all seemed too much.

There was a lesson to be read, of course; there always is. The woman who gave it was extremely slender and beyond middle-aged. She had grey hair swept up from her face and was dressed in a simple black shift dress worn with a string of creamy white pearls.

Her voice was shaking with nerves as she introduced herself. 'I'm Fiona and seven years ago I received new lungs from a young man who died in a road accident. I'm grateful for every moment of life it has given me.'

Grace grabbed my hand. 'Do you think it's her?' she asked, excitedly.

'I'm not sure,' I replied, cautious about raising her hopes.

'Seven years ago, and it was a young man, a road accident.' Grace squeezed my hand hard. 'It's her; I know it.'

The woman began to read, cheeks flushing, voice still shaky; all those eyes on her face. I recognised the verse she opened with:

> *There is a time for everything, and a season for every activity under the heavens: a time to be born and a time to die, a time to plant and a time to uproot, a time to kill and a time to heal, a time to tear down and a time to build, a time to weep and a time to laugh, a time to mourn and a time to dance …*

'We have to talk to her,' said Grace, in a loud whisper.

'After the service, no rush,' I replied.

She nodded her agreement but continued holding onto me, her hand radiating warmth and the pressure from her fingers revealing her level of tension.

Next the minister invited all the recipients present to come forward and light candles. Tommy glanced my way but I shook my head. I wasn't going to stand up in front of everyone.

Staying in my seat, I watched him walk the aisle with that

long, panther-like stride of his, fidgeting in the queue waiting his turn, standing out from the others. Soon rows of candles were flickering and solemn-faced people stood in the soft light saying quiet prayers of thanks; I noticed Fiona among them.

Now the families of those who had donated organs were invited up. They moved more slowly along the aisle, some needing encouragement before rising from their seats, one man holding his wife as she struggled with her tears. Grace surprised me by standing too. She followed the other families as each was given a gift, a small camellia plant wrapped in white tissue paper and tied with ribbon.

As they returned to their seats, the glossy, green leaves marked them out: the ones who were grieving a lost life.

The minister ended the service with a blessing: 'Go forth with a passion for living and loving; with the humility to learn; with the tenderness to understand; with the strength to endure; with the trust to believe.'

Grace was clutching her plant; eyes fixed on Fiona who was sitting opposite us now, playing with her pearls with nervous fingers, apparently quite alone; no husband, child or friend beside her.

'She looks elegant,' Grace commented.

Fiona's shift dress was beautifully cut, the pearls lustrous. 'Yes, she does,' I agreed.

'Every breath she is taking is thanks to my Jamie.' Grace said it with wonder. 'The air in here is filling his lungs.'

Fiona was picking up her handbag now, standing, getting ready to leave. I felt Grace stiffen beside me.

'This is our chance, we should go and speak to her,' said Tommy.

'Are you sure?' I wondered. 'Is now the right time?'

'Of course it is. I'll go and have a word first if you like.' Before I could say anything else, Tommy was springing up and moving forward, all animal grace, each step a surge of energy.

I was watching Fiona as he approached her and saw the feelings in her face. First there was polite surprise, then confusion as Tommy began to speak, a widening of her eyes and falling of her jaw, one hand pressing to her chest and the other flying upwards to half cover her face. I hoped he was being gentle; surely he would be.

When she stared towards us, I sent Fiona an encouraging smile. She looked like every friend my mother had ever introduced me too. Well-dressed, well-spoken women whose lives revolved round church and charity work, shopping trips to town, long lunches and literary festivals. That was what I pegged Fiona as; she appeared to slot neatly into type.

She was saying something to Tommy and whatever it was seemed to concern him. He touched her arm and, although she didn't pull away, I noticed she held herself more stiffly. He started talking again and Fiona's eyes were on his face, drawn to the blue dazzle of his eyes. Was he persuading her into something? It seemed so.

Fiona was nodding now. She brushed a few specks from her dress, adjusted her pearls, smoothed her hair then nodded again. Following Tommy's lead, she began to move towards us.

'You go,' I said to Grace. 'You talk to her.'

'Don't you want to meet her?'

'There's no rush. I can wait. And we don't want to overwhelm her.'

Grace nodded, biting at a thumbnail nervously, as if uncertain herself now. 'OK, if you think it's best.'

As she arrived at his side, Tommy put an arm around Grace. I watched as he introduced her to Fiona and there was an odd moment, a sort of silent stand-off, before the two women began talking. I was too far away to listen in but could see Fiona was smiling and, while Grace had her back to me, there was nothing about her stance that seemed especially tense.

I noticed Tommy stepping back to give the two women some space. He waited for a moment or two then moved away altogether, coming to stand beside me.

'Shit, that was quite difficult,' he said, in a low voice.

'What happened?'

'She was fine at first but when I told her Grace was actually here, she freaked out a bit. Then she seemed to pull herself together. And look at them now, chatting like old friends.'

That wasn't quite how I would have put it. Grace had a tissue in her hand and was dabbing at her face as she listened to Fiona talking. Then I noticed her shoulders beginning to heave and could tell she was properly sobbing. The noise reached me; primal and awful, Grace crying out and gasping. Fiona was concerned, her hand went to her mouth again and she looked around as if desperately hoping for help to come.

Two women swooped in. There was something brisk and efficient about both of them. After a quick exchange one took Grace's arm and eased her back towards us. The other herded Fiona away.

It turned out they were nurses, they worked in a transplant unit and were fully aware of all the rules about contact. They didn't tell us off exactly but made it clear we had done the wrong thing. By then Fiona had disappeared entirely and Grace was still distressed.

'I only wanted to talk to her,' she said. 'I think she has my son's lungs.'

'Meetings are meant to be initiated by the recipient,' the nurse was speaking briskly to Tommy as though, as the man, he must be the one in charge. 'They happen very rarely and before a visit is arranged there are letters, maybe a phone call, people have time to prepare and take things very slowly.'

'She's alive because Jamie died.' said Grace, her face clouded with sadness.

'We'll find her, again,' I promised.

One of the nurse's gave me a sharp look. 'The rules are in place to protect people.'

'Perhaps you don't understand, but I miss him so much,' said Grace. 'I miss hearing his voice when he comes home from school and walks through the door wanting to know what's for dinner. I miss the smell of his hair when he hugs me. I miss him and his mates watching football, lying all over my living room floor; and him playing his music too loud, and the sound of him laughing. Why is it so wrong for me to want to get to know the people he helped? Why do we need protecting?'

Tommy moved to put an arm around her and I saw how Grace leaned into him and hoped his strength felt reassuring.

It was time for us to get out of there. Smiling at the nurses, I murmured polite words of thanks. 'Such a wonderful service. Lovely of you to help us, we really appreciate it but now I think we should be off.'

Tommy and I kept Grace between us as we walked past the few people left who must have witnessed the scene, and out of the Abbey. A couple of them stared but no one stopped us or tried to say anything.

'Well, that went badly,' said Tommy. 'I'm sorry, I should have listened to you; it wasn't the right time.'

'What did she say that made you so upset?' I asked Grace.

'Nothing awful, it wasn't her fault, it's me, thinking about Jamie and being surrounded by all of you, knowing that in a way he's here with us ... but not really here at all.'

'God, I'm so sorry, we should never have brought you, it was insensitive.' Tommy paused in the doorway of the Abbey and stared into Grace's face. 'It was my fault, I didn't realise how it would be for you.'

'I wanted to come,' insisted Grace. 'Really I did. It was a beautiful service and I enjoyed hearing all those people speaking. It was just ... almost breathing the same air as him again ...'

Tommy tightened his arm round her shoulders. As the three of us emerged from the Abbey, we caught sight of Fiona. She was standing in Parliament Square, a little way down the path, beside the statue of the suffragette Millicent Garrett Fawcett.

'Stay there,' I told the others. 'Don't go anywhere.'

Fiona watched as I approached. She looked older in the bright afternoon light, a small woman in a black dress with a grey pashmina wrapped round her shoulders. Smiling, as I drew nearer, I held out my hand to shake hers.

'I'm Vivi Palmer.'

'Fiona Lambert.' She even sounded like my mother, plummy and posh.

'We handled that so badly, Fiona. My apologies.'

'It was my fault entirely. I wasn't prepared and said all the wrong things and upset her. How can I make it right?' She looked over to where Tommy and Grace were standing in the shadow of the Abbey, staring back at us.

'Perhaps it would be better to take things slowly,' I suggested. 'That's what everyone advises. Start with an email or a letter.'

'I don't want to distress her again, that's the thing.'

'Grace is ... well, she ... Look, can you and I meet another time? If her son really was your donor then there's stuff you need to know.'

I gave Fiona my business card and saw the distrust flash across her face. 'You're a reporter. Oh, the *Daily Post* ... I'm afraid I never read it.'

'I've got a personal involvement with this. I'm not here to write any articles,' I promised.

'You're a friend of hers?'

'Kind of, yes I am.'

'I was trying to thank her.' She glanced towards Grace again. 'I wanted her to know how blessed I feel, but when I told her that I talk to my donor every day and said how much I treasure the gift he's given to me, she started to cry and ... she seemed inconsolable.'

Fiona pulled the pashmina more tightly round her. She glanced up at the statue of the suffragette who was holding a banner emblazoned with the words 'Courage calls to courage everywhere'. Her expression looked more strained and anxious than ever.

'Oh dear,' she said. 'Yes, I'll send a card, that would be best, don't you think? I'm so sorry.'

'A card would be perfect.'

Stepping back, Fiona repeated how sorry she was. 'I would appreciate the chance to thank her properly but I need a little time. Please let her know I'll be in touch. I do hope she understands.'

I watched her walk away, a slight figure taking short, slow steps, until she mixed with a crowd of tourists and I lost sight of her. She had pushed my business card into her bag and I wondered how long it would stay there with the lipsticks, keys, phone and whatever else she toted around.

'You let her go,' Grace sounded disappointed.

'Yes, sorry.' I was disappointed too. 'But she says she'll be in touch. I'm sure you'll hear from her when she's ready.'

Grace was still staring in the direction Fiona had gone. 'She seemed nice, didn't she? Quite old though ... I'd always imagined since Jamie was young they would give his organs to other young people. I hope she does get in touch.'

I hope so too,' said Tommy. 'But hey, you've still got us.'

He was booked onto a late evening train back to Liverpool and the idea had always been for him and Grace to have some time together after the service. Any hopes I'd had of spending the rest of the day with my nieces ebbed away, as looking at me, blue eyes catching mine and widening, Tommy made it clear he wanted me to stay.

'Shall we have a quick bite to eat together?' he suggested.

'Yes, good idea,' Grace agreed, cheering.

'Where do you both fancy going?'

'McDonald's?' she suggested.

'You're kidding, right? You don't actually eat that junk?' Tommy sounded shocked.

'I do, every now and then,' I admitted, slightly shamefaced.

'It's Vivi's favourite,' Grace put in. 'Like it was Jamie's too.'

I felt drained after all the emotions of the church service, not to mention the awkward scene afterwards, and I couldn't stomach eating another Big Mac in front of Grace, as her eyes drilled into me, and she searched for signs of her lost son in the way I tackled a burger.

'What about Pizza Express instead?' I suggested.

Grace drew in a breath. 'That was Jamie's other favourite. We always used to share the American Hot.'

'Well, let's go and have one now, shall we?' Tommy linked an arm through hers. 'I'd love to hear more about him.'

'He was such a great kid.' Grace didn't need more encouragement. 'Sporty too; he'd have been into doing races and triathlons like you.'

Again it felt good to have Tommy on my side, someone else to care about Grace, to help make things better. It wasn't all my responsibility; there were two of us now. Hopefully, once Fiona had taken the time to reconsider, soon there would be three.

Fiona

She has no one to tell. Fiona is accustomed to that because it is the way things have been for a while. There was a time when her mother or older brother would have been the ones to listen but sadly both of them are gone. And in all those years of nursing other people and being ill herself, so many friends drifted away. It wasn't their fault; they had families, jobs, busy lives and problems of their own. Fiona hadn't liked to bother them. She managed on her own.

Shivering a little, as she unlocks the front door of the tall mansion block where she has her little flat, Fiona is glad of her pashmina. She takes the stairs slowly, holding the handrail, pausing to rest more than once.

It is good to be through the door and inside her home. The kettle goes on, the tea is made. Removing her pashmina, she folds it onto the back of a chair. Lifting off her pearls, she pools them on the table next to the phone that hardly ever rings these days. Fiona does have people: old colleagues, friends she shares a chat with at the places where she volunteers, but no one who ever calls now for a proper talk.

Life is full, and Fiona is perfectly happy. There are books to read and concerts to go to and documentaries she wants to see. She wakes every morning with a plan and is never bored. But sitting down, sipping tea, catching her breath after the unexpected events of the day, she is a little shaky. It would be nice if there were someone she could talk to.

Every year she goes to the service at Westminster Abbey, looks forward to it as a chance to give a heartfelt thanks to the unknown boy who saved her life. This is the first time she has agreed to read the lesson. Standing up in front of all those pews lined with strangers had been daunting but Fiona did her best and, once her voice stopped wobbling, it hadn't gone too badly at all.

Then there was the man, his eyes boring into hers and a strong northern accent. As she was trying to get to grips with what he was saying, there was the woman, formidably tall and unnervingly sad, and an upsetting scene right there in the middle of everything.

Fiona struggles to her feet, draws the curtains, turns on lamps, makes herself a slice of toast and spreads it with honey. These are the things she does every evening. Tonight, though, Fiona is more fatigued than usual and anxious. She misses the people she used to tell things to.

She eats her toast, wipes up crumbs, puts the dirty plate and teacup into the dishwasher. Then she stands in her kitchen, leans against the bench, drops her head into her hands and breathes as deeply as she can. There is one person she still talks to. Although he can't hear her, she tells him almost everything.

'I met your mother today,' Fiona begins, her voice echoing in the empty room. 'I now know your name is Jamie ...'

Vivi

It wasn't an especially warm day but Imogen wasn't going to let that spoil her plans. She'd had me help carry containers of water over to the nearby park and now we were sitting together on a wooden bench while the girls filled cups and watering cans, splashing and soaking themselves, shrieking and giggling, loving every moment, trampling the grass into mud.

'Won't they catch a chill?' I worried.

'You know who you're sounding like now,' Imogen warned.

There were never any water games when we were kids, not even in the height of summer. My mother wasn't going to risk it. Fortunately, I quite liked staying indoors and reading, as we certainly did a lot of it.

'I'm a fun mum,' said Imogen, watching her daughters play. 'We're having adventures together. I'm not constantly saying no to them.'

A familiar sense of guilt crept over me; I was the one who had spoiled everything with my endless, boring need to be careful. 'It wasn't so bad for us all the time was it?'

'No, but it wasn't a very carefree childhood. That's what I want for Farah and Darya. Lots of great memories.'

Imogen is a high achiever when she sets her mind to it. She did brilliantly at school, was successful in her career and now it seemed she was going to excel at having happy children.

'Their Aunt Vivi needs to be a big part of those memories,' she told me. 'So you will come away with us this year, won't you?'

She and Hamid had rented a house somewhere in southern Italy. They were taking the place for the whole summer even though Hamid would only get away from work for a couple of weeks at best. Imogen's plan was that I should stay the entire time, hang out with her and the girls, while she drank a lot of the local wine and got a suntan. She didn't seem to have factored in my job, or at least didn't see it as important.

'You know I can't take that much time off work.'

'Stop making excuses. It's a horrible job. You don't even like it that much.'

'It pays the rent; mostly.' There were times I needed to turn to Imogen for top-ups although I hated asking.

'I don't understand why you won't accept help from Mum and Dad. You know they'd love to buy you a place to live and if you need cash they'll give you whatever you ask for. It's not like they can't afford it.'

This was a familiar refrain. Imogen was exasperated at me spending so much time stuck at a desk when all that lovely family money could have made everything easier. I was always explaining my reluctance to take it, but she refused to understand.

'If I let them pay for my life then I have to allow them into it – can you imagine? Mum would be here every second day filling the fridge with superfoods and taking my temperature. They'd interfere; they wouldn't be able to help it. And I need to be independent, it's important to me. Anyway, I don't hate my job. I like telling stories.'

'Just one summer, Vivi, in a beautiful villa, seeing your nieces everyday, getting closer to them,' Imogen wheedled. 'You could resign from your job and look for another one when we get back. And if you're short of money in the meantime I'll sort it out.'

'I'll think about it, OK?' I said to fob her off.

'It's a huge villa, amazing, so many bedrooms, you should invite friends over, whoever you like ... we'll have fun.'

'The timing may not be great, that's all.'

Imogen tossed her head impatiently, dark hair flicking over her shoulders. I looked at it tumbling down her back in thick, shiny tendrils. Once mine was just like that; now it was thinning, barely covering my scalp.

Whenever I look in the mirror I have to remind myself that other transplant patients suffer far worse side effects from the anti-rejection drugs we all have to take. They have tremors, get diarrhoea or feel nauseous, their arms and legs swell, skins bruise easily, they can't sleep. Losing my hair is a smaller price to pay but even so I'm vain about it. I spend a fortune on products to hold the strands in place; I'm always splurging on some new wax or miracle hair putty. And when I look at Imogen, with so much beautiful hair, it is hard not to feel a pang.

'You'll come, I know you will.' She was still gazing at her daughters. 'You can't miss out on all that deliciousness.'

'The thing is there's something happening; it may be quite big.'

'A story?'

'More than that.'

Imogen looked away from the girls, tilted her head and waited.

'Well?' she prompted, when I didn't offer any more.

'You have to promise not to say anything, not even to Hamid. They'll know eventually but not just yet.'

Now I really had her attention. 'What's going on, Vivi? It's something to do with that woman, isn't it? The mother of the donor boy.'

Imogen is smart and she knows me well enough to be able tell what's on my mind more often than I might like.

'I'll tell you about it but I think we should get the girls inside and dry them off. I'm worried it's getting cold.'

'Fine, but I want to know everything.'

Imogen listened like the lawyer she once was, her

expression mostly unreadable, taking in every detail, committing it to memory. Once or twice she nodded but didn't interrupt. I kept talking as we bathed the girls, towel-drying their smooth-skinned bodies, wrapping them in fleecy robes and heating up tomato soup from tins. Imogen opened wine, of course, and we sat on a window seat in the late afternoon sunshine as I explained about Grace, Tommy and Fiona.

'Well, shit,' she said when I had finished.

'I know.'

'So what's the plan here, what are you trying to achieve exactly?'

'I'm helping Grace.'

'It's more than that though, isn't it?'

'Yes, probably,' I admitted. 'There's something about meeting other people who have been through so much of the same stuff. Even though they're strangers, we're connected. And the fact we all share the same donor ...'

'Are you sure, though? Have you had official confirmation?'

'Not yet ... Grace is writing to the Donor Records Department but they may not agree to release any information. There are all these rules about contact and we seem to be breaking pretty much all of them.' I laughed as I said that, but Imogen didn't respond with a smile.

'There'll be good reasons for those guidelines, you know.' She was brisk. 'They've been put in place to protect people and by not respecting them you may be opening yourself up to all sorts of issues. Perhaps you're prepared to take that risk but what about the others? Are they prepared emotionally ... psychologically? It doesn't sound like it.'

'I really don't need a lecture.'

She screwed up her face. 'I'd really prefer not to lecture you. But I'm worried about what you're getting yourself into. I'm not going to pretend everything seems fine if it doesn't.'

We've never been sisters who argue all the time. Even as

kids there was none of the hair pulling and pinching that can go on with little girls. We're on the same team, Imogen and I; we look out for one another.

'This woman Grace, she may be manipulating you,' she said, now.

'You're just looking at this from a lawyer's perspective ...' I began.

'More from a sister's point of view actually,' she interrupted. 'You don't need another family, Vivi, you've got us.'

The girls had finished their soup. They were sitting beneath the kitchen table playing a game with the empty bowls and giggling a lot. Distracted by the noise they were making, Imogen only smiled.

'I'm not trying to replace you,' I told her. 'What makes you think that?'

'You're busy searching for your donor twins,' she murmured, 'the ones who really understand you; so busy you're prepared to miss out on a summer in Italy with us. These people are the reason the timing is wrong, not your job, admit it. And they are actually strangers, whatever you might think you have in common.'

She wasn't entirely wrong, but I wasn't going to admit it.

'It's not like that,' I insisted.

'Prove it then by coming to Italy.'

'I'll be there with you for some of the time.'

'At least a month,' insisted Imogen. 'And you'll back off this search for the other donor recipients, won't you? I'm worried it will lead to problems. Don't put any more of your energy into it.'

There was no way for me to make that promise. I was committed now, and I couldn't let Grace down. Besides I wanted to know these people too, find out who they were and what they had done with their lives.

'I'd really like you to meet Tommy. He's lovely,' I said, because it was easier to distract Imogen than lie to her.

'Oh yeah, lovely in what way?'

'He's a nice guy, that's all.'

'Not lovely as in hot, then?'

In my mind I conjured up an image of Tommy; that compact, muscled body, that animal grace. 'I hadn't been thinking about him that way but you know what … maybe …'

Imogen smiled at me. 'Well, that sounds a bit more promising.'

Sometimes my heartbeat is so strong it keeps me awake. Lying in Dan's bed later that night, my chest pressed to his back, I thought that surely he must feel it too, although judging by the soft snoring it wasn't stopping him from sleeping.

I'd had no intention of seeing him after leaving Imogen's place. But then reluctant to return to my bedsit, and wanting more than my own company, I had called him impulsively. Dan answered straight away and it was easy enough to talk him into our typical Sunday night. A lamb rogan josh and then back to his place for fast, sweaty, mind-emptying sex before drifting off to sleep together.

Only I didn't fall asleep. The room was airy, the bed completely comfortable, there was no loudly ticking clock and only a hum of traffic noise. So it must have been my heart pounding and the thoughts that each beat brought with it: Jamie and Grace, Tommy and Fiona.

Shifting over, I lay on my stomach with my face pressed into the pillow, then wriggled over to my other side, then tried lying on my back, and finally returned to spooning Dan again.

'Jeez Vivi,' he complained drowsily. 'Can't you lie still for a minute?'

'Sorry, I can't sleep. Perhaps I'd better go back to my own place.'

'Wait … what is it?' He rolled towards me, face next to

mine on the pillow, breath warm on my cheek. 'Are you worrying about something?'

'Kind of,' I admitted. 'It's this whole thing of tracking down the other people who got organs from my donor. I'm stuck.'

'You got the triathlete though? You're in touch with him?'

'Yes.'

'Get on and write a piece with him then, as part of the Vivi's Law campaign.'

I wasn't especially keen on the idea but it didn't seem like I had any other option.

'We're losing momentum,' Dan continued. 'Let's get something in this week.'

'OK then ... I'll talk to Tommy about it.'

'Great. You could really make your name with these stories. If you don't want to do them someone else will. Suzy Ambridge is desperate for a chance and she's a good little operator. But Vivi's Law needs some more of Vivi.'

His words were meant to fire me up and I knew he was right; there were always younger reporters who would sell their grandmothers to get a good story. What he didn't realise was these people meant more to me than that: Jamie and Grace, Tommy, and Fiona, they weren't just great quotes and a killer angle.

Faking a yawn, I nuzzled my face into the pillow and managed to lie still. It took a while for sleep to come. And in those empty minutes I kept listening for the beat of the heart echoing in my chest, soothing myself with its soft steady boom.

Vivi

The advantage of always dressing in basic black is I get away with morning-after outfits. No one could tell I had come straight from Dan's flat and, just to be sure, I stopped for coffee on the way to the tube station, which meant I arrived at work ten minutes later than him. People might have guessed there was something going on but if there was any gossip it hadn't reached my ears. To be fair ours was hardly the only office affair – people were always falling into bed with one another – but Dan seemed to want to keep it quiet, so I was careful too.

Mondays on a newspaper are hectic. Everyone is looking at the stories that broke over the weekend, the news reporters getting a hard time about stuff they missed, the features team trying to decide what they should be following up on. That meant Dan was preoccupied for most of the morning, leaving me free to waste my time online.

Free-ranging round the internet I came across another forum for transplant recipients and lost myself in the chat room. There were other women struggling with hair loss, people bickering about the safest diets to be on and discussing their health regimes. It was a window into worlds just like my own. Then I started reading a long thread dealing with people's feelings about their deceased donors and, tears pricking at my eyes, hastily stopped reading.

I had started seeing Jamie by then. He was everywhere I went. A barista who made my takeaway coffee had a smile like his, a young guy beside me at a pedestrian crossing the same shock of gypsy dark hair; a face glimpsed through a window might have been him, but several years older. It took my breath away, every time it happened.

Around mid-morning Dan reappeared at his desk so I made a show of getting on with my work. I was meant to be writing a story about the pros and cons of all the latest fad diets and had several lengthy interviews with experts that I had been putting off transcribing. When I had my headphones on and was typing furiously, Dan was less likely to interrupt me.

Transcribing is dull and I am always happy to be distracted, so every time an email pinged I paused to read it. Fiona Lambert's message arrived around lunchtime. In the subject line all she had written was the word 'transplant'. I opened it straight away:

Dear Vivi,

As you may have guessed, I had no intention of contacting you. I was very shaken the other day in Westminster Abbey and when I learned you're a tabloid journalist naturally I was wary. But I must have been intrigued as well because last night I checked the Daily Post website and saw that you are a transplant recipient too.

I'm not sure if I feel ready to meet Grace again but if you wanted to talk to me, privately and off the record, then I'm willing. It's always good to meet people who have been through the same things. And also, perhaps you might be able to tell me something about my donor. I talk to him you see, almost everyday, I tell him what I'm doing and thank him for the gift he's given me. I have a name now, Jamie. I feel as if I ought to know a little more about him.

Please don't mention this to Grace. It might distress

her again, and that's the last thing I want. But if you would like to chat then email me or call on the number below whenever it's convenient.

Thanks,
Fiona Lambert.

I didn't waste any time. Grabbing my mobile phone, I punched in her number and headed over to the far end of the office, hoping she wouldn't answer until I was safely out of Dan's earshot.

'Hello, Fiona speaking,' came that mannered, genteel voice.

'Hi, this is Vivi Palmer, I just got your email.'

'Oh!' She didn't hide her surprise. 'You're extremely quick off the mark.'

'I'm keen for us to talk,' I told her. 'There are things I need to explain. But could we get together rather than do it over the phone?'

'I suppose so.'

'Where are you based? Would you have time today?'

'Not really, I was about to head out. I'm a volunteer at the Chelsea Physic Garden, you see. I'm due to lead a guided tour at 2 p.m.'

'Perhaps I'll come on the tour with you and we can chat afterwards?'

'Well,' she said, dubiously. 'Yes, you could do that.'

'Great, I'll see you in a little while.'

I had never heard of the Chelsea Physic Garden. Looking it up on my phone as I headed back to my desk, I saw it was only a short cab ride away so put on my jacket and called out to Dan that I was heading out to get some lunch.

'Bring something back for me, will you?' he asked. 'Not some anorexic's salad though, a decent sandwich.'

Out on the street I hailed a black cab and, settling onto

its vinyl seat, thought about Fiona. It would be important to go in gently when we met. Women like her, all polish and perfect manners, don't enjoy feeling ruffled, and we had messed up that first approach in the Abbey. This time I was going to get it right.

Chelsea Physic Garden is concealed behind high brick walls. I must have passed by many times and never realised it was there, through a narrow gateway, beneath a canopy of trees. I paid my entrance fee at a small kiosk and was told to wait for the tour beside the statue at the centre of the garden. There were a few people milling around, mostly tourists with backpacks and middle-aged women, and I glanced about as I stood with them. It was a lovely spot, peaceful despite the hum of traffic and the planes overhead. Hemmed in by mansion blocks: a profusion of plants, willow sculptures and rustic greenhouses.

Then I spotted Fiona hurrying towards the group, looking a little flustered. She was wearing a battered-looking beige Burberry trench and sensible shoes. I managed to catch her eye and she acknowledged me with a tight smile.

'I'm sorry I'm a little late,' she told the small crowd. 'Please gather round. Can everybody hear me? Do let me know if you can't.'

She launched into a long speech about the history of these four acres in the middle of the city, and the medicinal plants the apothecaries had begun propagating almost four hundred years ago. As she talked, Fiona shepherded us along the brick and gravel paths that crisscrossed the garden. I drifted in and out of listening to her monologue, distracted by thoughts of the conversation to come and how I was going to handle it.

After the tour everyone had questions. One woman kept her talking for twenty minutes, chattering on mostly about her own garden while somehow Fiona resisted interrupting. I waited impatiently, thinking of Dan back at the office still expecting his sandwich.

At last everyone disappeared and it was my turn.

'Thanks, that was great,' I told Fiona. 'I can't believe I'd never heard of this place before.'

'Many people haven't; it's a hidden gem,' she said.

'Have you been a tour guide for long?'

'Oh, I've volunteered here for ages. I'm a gardener at heart but now I'm doing this instead. It's very rewarding but I do miss having my hands in the soil.'

'Have you got a garden at home?'

She shook her head. 'Sadly no, I'm in a tiny flat these days. But I have lots of plants; I'm always coming home with another one.'

'My mother has a garden, she's completely obsessed with it,' I told her.

'What sort of plants does she have?'

I wasn't going to admit that my family's garden spanned forty acres fringed by woodland or that at least four men were employed full time to care for it.

'A mix, all sorts,' I said.

'A bit like this one then,' said Fiona. 'I do love hodge-podge gardens, with lots of treasures to be found, rambling and a little untidy. Mass plantings can be so boring, don't you think? A mix is much more charming.'

My mother has a large sunken garden inspired by the Italian Renaissance and a Japanese-style area designed for contemplation. There's an English wildflower meadow and a promenade of pleached linden trees in homage to the writer Edith Wharton's landscaping.

'I suppose Mum's is a bit of a hodgepodge,' I agreed.

Fiona led me to the café, really just a small marquee and a few courtyard tables.

'It's not too chilly for you if we sit outside in the sunshine?' she asked. 'I do prefer fresh air.'

We ordered tea and lavender scones and chatted about the

garden some more, with its thousands of species of plants, small ponds and tropical hothouses.

'I'm sorry, I could talk about this forever and you didn't come here to hear about any of it, did you?' Fiona said, at last.

'No,' I agreed. 'Partly I've come to apologise for the last time we met.'

'There's no need ...' she murmured politely.

'Tommy and I shouldn't have rushed in like that ... We shouldn't have brought Grace either.'

'I kept asking myself why you were all there at all. What the link might be between the three of you.' Fiona looked at me, held my gaze for a few moments and answered her own question. 'Then I realised, it's Jamie, isn't it?'

'That's right.'

I explained everything as she crumbled up pieces of lavender scone in her fingers and let her tea go cold. Fiona bit her lip when I described how badly Grace needed to meet the people who had a part of her son, and how much it meant to her.

'She is so lost in grief that I think this search is almost like a form of therapy,' I explained. 'And meeting all of the recipients may help her accept that Jamie is gone. It's what I'm hoping for anyway, that it might be healing, because I think things have been desperate ... really desperate. I'm worried about her.'

'Oh dear.' Fiona pushed aside the plateful of deconstructed scone. 'Perhaps she might come here to the garden some time. It's such a healing spot; at least it has been for me.'

'That's a nice idea.'

'Over by the woodland garden in particular, that's my place of peace.'

I needed to extricate myself now. Get back to the office, preferably in the possession of some sort of giant sandwich to pacify Dan. I was pretty sure he had been trying to call as my phone was buzzing in my bag, and he wouldn't be impressed at me disappearing for half the afternoon without an explanation.

The trouble was Fiona didn't seem ready to be left. She was sitting very still, breathing in a way that sounded ragged.

'Are you OK?' I asked.

There was an almost imperceptible shake of her head and I noticed a slight tremor in her hands. 'Fiona?'

She started talking about her illness then, hesitantly at first, describing the pulmonary fibrosis diagnosed later in life, the shortness of breath, the coughing and exhaustion, the worry about what she was facing.

'I didn't think I was sick enough for a transplant,' she admitted. 'There are so many others waiting, younger people, mothers with families to care for, husbands who are needed. I've had a long life already, I have no one depending on me and I can't help wondering ... what if Grace thinks I didn't deserve my new lungs? What if I'm a disappointment to her? That's what is really worrying me.'

I had never had a thought like that about myself. Of course I deserved my heart, I deserved a chance to live, be fit and healthy like every normal person.

'If you hadn't been a good candidate they wouldn't have gone ahead with it,' I said to Fiona. 'And I think Grace will more disappointed if she doesn't get to see you again. But there's no need to rush. Weren't you going to write to her first, send a card?'

Women like her always have a stash of greetings cards ready to be inked with messages of thanks or condolence. They also have lovely handwriting and know the best things to say.

'That's right,' she said. 'I'll do that. Perhaps you might email her postal address to me later.'

I insisted on paying the bill and together we walked along the gravel paths towards the small ticket kiosk at the entrance. Fiona was meant to be hurrying to a meeting about some sort of schools programme she was involved in, but her good manners dictated that she should escort me to the gate.

As we paused to say goodbye I gave her another one of my business cards, to be sure she had all my contact details if she needed them. Also, I quite liked handing out those cards and seeing the words printed on them, *Vivi Palmer, features writer, Daily Post* – that was who I was, who I had worked so hard to be.

Glancing down at it, her brow furrowing slightly, Fiona said, 'You seemed a little familiar and now I realise why. You're related to Sir Lance Palmer. That's right isn't it?'

I frowned too, more deeply, because Sir Lance Palmer, wealthy industrialist and noted philanthropist, is my father, and I tend to try and keep that quiet.

'How did you know?' I asked.

'I'm a great admirer of his. I read his autobiography recently: so inspiring. The chapter about his daughter's heart problems made a particular impression on me, how humbling it was that his money couldn't help her, how transformational that turned out to be. It resonated.'

I wasn't surprised Fiona had read my father's book – everyone seemed to have. Whenever I caught a train or travelled on a bus I would spot someone with their nose in a copy. There were a few photographs of me in there; nothing recent though, I had insisted on that. So Fiona couldn't possibly have recognised me that way.

'And, of course, you were at Harefield at the same time as me. There was quite a fuss about it. I always did wonder if we shared a donor.'

It made sense that we'd had our transplants at the same time, in the same hospital. Possibly I had encountered Fiona back then, or even seen her at one of the follow-up clinics, but she was a quiet person and I wasn't interested in making friends at those places, so I had no recollection of her.

She smiled at me. 'You're that Vivienne Palmer.'

'Yes I am.'

Money always changes the way people treat you. With Fiona it wasn't glaringly obvious but I heard it in the inflection of her voice, the warmer softer tones, and saw it in her sudden smile.

'You must be very proud of your father. He's done so much good. And his philosophy of life, his faith ... well, he seems an amazing man.'

'Yes, he is,' I said, shortly.

Fiona glanced at the watch on her wrist. 'Oh dear, I'd better run or I'll be late. It was lovely to meet you Vivi.'

'We'll talk again?' I said.

'Yes, yes, absolutely, I hope so. And I'll send that card to Grace like you suggested. I'll do it this evening.'

Most people don't make the link between my family and me. What with the anonymous layers of black I wear, the chain-store shoes, the lack of bling, nothing about me screams money. And I prefer it that way.

For a long time I didn't actually realise we were rich. The manor house, the extensive gardens, the staff; it was a while before it occurred to me not everyone has those things, but when you're brought up that way, and your life is sheltered and small, it seems normal.

Not that my parents raised us to be extravagant. Lessons about the value of money were very important in our house. And it didn't pay to get attached to possessions as they were forever being boxed up and given away to the needy.

I stay quiet about my family because money complicates things; it creates expectations, changes relationships. Besides, I am not the wealthy one; they are. So I am very careful to segregate the people I know. My workmates on the newspaper have no idea at all, although there have been a couple of times I've come close to being found out. There was a particularly bad moment when my father's book came out and it seemed I might be the one assigned to write a profile of him. Luckily Dan picked an older, more senior writer for the job.

My father talked about me a lot in that article; his heart transplant daughter, I am always a part of the story because my illness changed everything. But otherwise I keep a low profile. I'm careful not to get photographed with him, stay away from all the cocktail evenings, charity galas and ceremonies, and so far I was certain no one had made the link … not until Fiona.

As my taxi crept back towards the office, slowed by heavy traffic, I knew my background would be what swung things for her. Fiona trusted me now. I would be able to talk her into almost anything. She wasn't likely to say no to Sir Lance Palmer's daughter.

Any hope that the salami and cheddar baguette I had picked up would mollify Dan was shattered by the first words that came out of his mouth.

'What the hell, Vivi, where have you been?' he said, striding towards my desk, voice raised.

'Sorry, I was chasing up a lead for a story.'

'And you couldn't answer your phone?' He was standing over me.

'It was in my bag … it must have been on silent.'

'I need that piece. You said it wasn't far away.'

'It isn't, I've transcribed most of the interviews and writing it shouldn't take long.'

'I want it by the end of the day.'

I was pretty sure the diet article wasn't scheduled to run. It was one of those any-time pieces, useful for slotting into the pages on slow days, decent clickbait for the website but hardly critical. If Dan was going to make me stay at my desk while I finished then it was to prove a point: he was still the boss.

'No problem,' I said. 'I'm onto it.'

'What were you busy chasing up anyway? Was it for the organ donor story?'

My first instinct was to lie. I had a good reason now not to appear in any future articles. The higher my profile was, the greater the chance other people would put two and two together like Fiona had. Then they would all treat me differently; I'd be the little rich girl, Sir Lance's daughter, not just me any more. And I really liked being me.

Since I couldn't conjure up a lie quickly enough, I fell back on the truth. 'It was Fiona, the woman who got Jamie's lungs, I went to meet her.'

'Brilliant.' Dan's face changed, the glower gone. 'She agreed to talk to us, right?'

'Well, not quite ... I didn't ...'

'What I reckon is, we run a big feature with the three of you, heart, lungs, kidney. Then we have a first meeting with the mother. We'll do loads of video, maybe *London Live* will want to shoot it ... we might even get you all onto *This Morning*.'

Dan was in that almost febrile state he gets into when he knows a story is set to be big. Cheeks flushed, eyes too bright, voice overloud. It was pointless trying to put the brakes on this now. In fact, there were no brakes. It was going to happen and the best I could do was fight to keep Grace out of it.

'Fiona's not over the line yet,' I warned him.

'You'll get her there, right? And the triathlete guy, he's good to go?'

I nodded.

'Good work, Vivi. Hey, and I still need that other piece, OK?'

'Sure.'

Dan loped back to his own desk. I watched him grazing on his baguette and checking his emails. Catching my eye, he treated me to a quick boyish grin then focused on his screen again. It was weird to think that we had been in bed together only a few hours earlier. Now he was my boss again, making me work late, pushing me into stories I didn't want to cover. It occurred to me that my sister might be right; this job really wasn't worth it and probably neither was he.

Who would I be without it all though? That was the question keeping me there, at my desk, working late, writing about intermittent fasting and the keto diet, as the hum of the newsroom died down, other desks emptied, people went for one quick drink or hurried home to their families. That was what always kept me there.

26 May 2017

Vivi's Law gathers pace

MPs back campaign to save more lives.
By Daily Post reporter Suzy Ambridge

A plan to change the rules on organ donation consent has now been backed by even more MPs. Spearheaded by a campaign that *Daily Post* readers have taken to their hearts, a new opt-out system will save hundreds of lives every year.

There are thousands of sick people hoping for a transplant and many are running out of time. Manchester cystic fibrosis sufferer Diana Brown is on the waiting list for new lungs and is praying that Vivi's Law will be the difference she needs.

'I want to thank *Daily Post* readers for caring about this campaign,' says Diana, 30. 'Even if the change comes too late for me, I know so many others will benefit.'

Right now in England, organs can only be used if a donor has signed the register or told a family member of their desire to donate. Around 500 people are dying each year because of a shortage of organs.

'That's not good enough,' says Labour MP Rowan Stuart. 'We can do better than this.'

Launched by *Daily Post* reporter Vivi Palmer, who is only alive today because of a heart transplant from her donor, tragic teen Jamie McGraw, our campaign is set to make a difference.

Help us change the law by signing up at www.donate-forlife.co.uk

Vivi

Tommy was so good about staying in touch with Grace. It was a rare day when they didn't exchange a few messages. Sadly, the news he brought back from her was never that great. There had been no word from the Donor Records Department. The anniversary of Jamie's death was coming up and she was feeling down. So when Tommy heard I had met with Fiona he wanted to tell Grace straight away; but I talked him into waiting.

'Fiona's sent her a card,' I explained.

'I'm pretty sure Grace hasn't had any cards; she'd have mentioned it.'

'It's probably in the post.'

'Why is Fiona sending something by mail anyway?' Tommy sounded impatient. 'Is she aware quicker forms of communication have been invented?'

'Some people just like to send cards.'

'If you say so.'

I was lying on my bed staring at the ceiling. All the windows were open because it was warm and my room felt stuffy. I could hear the sounds of the neighbourhood – someone's music, someone else's television, a child's high-pitched screaming, the heavy-footed person who lived above walking from room to room. I looked at the bare walls – I hadn't even bothered tacking up photos – and thought about Tommy in his unloved bungalow.

'I'd really like to talk to Fiona again,' he told me. 'I mucked things up when we met and I owe her an apology. And no, I'm not sending a card.'

'She'd love it if you did.'

'No way.' I could hear the smile in his voice. 'Seriously though, wouldn't it be good for the three of us to meet? We've got so much in common.'

'Only Jamie,' I said, and that picture of his smiling face flashed up in my mind.

'More than that,' said Tommy. 'We've all been sick. And we've all thought we might not make it then got the call that changed everything – mine came at 2 a.m.'

'Mine too.' I remembered my mother waking me up, calling out that I had a new heart, repeating the words over and over as she turned on the light and helped me out of bed. And then the drive to the hospital, my father at the wheel, wiping tears from his own eyes whilst telling my mum, 'Don't cry darling, don't cry.' And all the way me wide-eyed with excitement that my life was going to change, but terrified too because they were about to break open my body and what if I didn't survive it?

'You never forget that call, right,' Tommy said softly.

I had always avoided transplant friends, stayed away from the support groups and off the online forums, kept to my family, the way I always had, because it seemed safer. There is usually an empty chair at those support groups, someone is gone who, like you, started out with so much hope. If you have transplant friends there are always going to be funerals, organs are rejected, hearts stop beating, hearts are broken, and I didn't want that to happen to mine. Now I had met Tommy and Fiona; I was beginning to wonder what I had missed.

'Yeah we do have a lot in common,' I agreed.

'Let's get together then.'

I was surprised how pleased I felt at the thought of seeing him again. 'When?'

'I'll come down again as soon as I can get a couple of days off work. Things are busy for the next week or so, unfortunately. We've got a couple of big jobs to get out and I can't ask the boss to let me go right now.'

'Tommy, do you like your work?' I wondered.

'Can't say I love it but it pays the bills, looks after the family and means I get to do other stuff. Why?'

'Don't you ever think that we got this second chance at life so should be doing something more important?'

'Like curing cancer or negotiating world peace?'

'Perhaps not that important.'

'I don't know.' Tommy sounded thoughtful. 'We can't live our best lives all the time, can we? Sometimes we just have to get through the day, same as anyone else.'

'Fiona told me she's not sure if she deserved Jamie's lungs.'

'That makes me sad for her,' said Tommy. 'But you don't feel like that, do you? About your heart?'

'I didn't, but now I'm wondering. What have I done that's so special? I go to work, hang out with my family; shouldn't there be something more?'

'Train for a triathlon,' Tommy suggested. 'Or a marathon.'

'I don't think so.'

'Do whatever your version of that is,' he advised. 'The thing that makes it worth being alive.'

'I'm not sure I have a thing.'

'There must be something you've always dreamed of doing.'

'Nothing special.' Everything I ever wanted seemed ordinary yet still out of reach. It seemed easier to stop wanting it.

'So do you like your work, Vivi?' Tommy asked.

I thought about that for a moment. 'It can be fun, exciting … It's hardly ever boring, but sometimes I wonder why I'm doing it.'

'It sounds more interesting than making kitchens.'

Tommy was good at staying in touch with me as well as Grace. If he had his kids staying over then he called at night once they were asleep. Often we talked for an hour or more; me lying on my bed; him stretched out on his sofa. We laughed at similar things, discovered we had watched the same Netflix shows and that we shared a taste for Eighties music. One night he played Queen and David Bowie really loud and I listened to it down the phone. A couple of times we watched football together; him in his lounge 350 miles away, cheering every time Everton scored. On the evenings I spent with Dan, I missed talking to Tommy.

'When you come to London you can stay at mine,' I offered.

'I thought you only had one room.'

'Yes, but I could sleep over at my sister's place.'

'Let me talk to the boss then, and work out some dates.'

'Great. And I'll catch up with Fiona in the meantime, see if she got round to sending that card, maybe suggest we get together.'

On the other end of the line, Tommy yawned. 'Sorry, I should get to bed. Need to be up early for a run tomorrow.'

'OK, goodnight then.

'Night Vivi, talk to you soon ... see you soon.'

This is how I courted Fiona. First an email, with photos of my mother's garden, the most celebrated parts like the glasshouse filled with sub-tropical palms, the lake in springtime hemmed with swathes of daffodils, and the parkland dotted with sculptures. Next a suggestion she might be able to visit and see it all for herself some time soon. While the garden isn't open to the public, over spring and summer my parents allow charities to auction off limited numbers of tickets for exclusive tours. Then there are the garden parties, the outdoor operas and picnic events and usually some sort of art show – all to raise funds for causes my family supports. I avoid these occasions, so does Imogen. We've been through enough of them. But my parents are the hosts and always put in an appearance, which meant Fiona might get to meet them too.

She was so excited by my email she called straight away.

'You could really do that for me?'

'Yes, of course, it would be a pleasure.'

'I can't tell you how many times I've applied for a ticket and never been successful; Sir Lance Palmer's garden, that would be wonderful.' She was talking faster than usual. 'I'd love to go soon while the wildflower meadow is in full bloom. Would that be possible? Of course any time at all would be absolutely lovely.'

'I'll check. And I'll ask for two tickets, you might want to take a friend.'

'Just one ticket would be lovely. Oh Vivi, I don't know how to thank you.'

'There's really no need. My parents are always saying to let them know if I have any friends that want to visit. I'll ask them to sort one special guest ticket.'

'This is the nicest thing that's happened to me in ages ... it really is, the nicest.'

Fiona was so thrilled that it made me feel better about being manipulative. We talked a little more about what she was likely to see in bloom and then she told me all about the schools programme at the Chelsea Physic Garden while I feigned interest.

'I haven't forgotten about sending that card to Grace,' she told me. 'I've picked one out and now I'm just trying to decide what to say in it.'

'That's fine, no rush,' I said. 'But Tommy is going to be in town again and he'd really like to see you so I was thinking we could meet up in that little café where we had afternoon tea last time.'

'Oh ... I see ...' she stammered in surprise, then recovered. 'Yes, of course, I'll put it in my diary.'

'I'm not sure exactly when he's coming yet; I'll let you

know. Wouldn't it be great if it coincided with one of your tours?'

'Tuesdays and Thursdays at 2 p.m., rain or shine,' she said. 'Let me know and I'll organise it so you don't have to pay the entrance fee. It's only a few pounds, but still.'

I wondered about Fiona's life. There seemed to be no one important in it – no partner or children. Perhaps there was a sibling she was close to or a tight circle of friends, but she never mentioned anyone. She had been alone at that service in Westminster Abbey, was adamant she only wanted a single ticket for the garden tour. The sense I got was of a solitary person keeping busy.

Not that I have tons of friends either; Imogen and the girls are my closest circle. And my parents too, Sir Lance and Lady Deborah Palmer, who lead busy lives but are clear there will never be a day when they wouldn't drop every single thing for me. Their love is boundless, sometimes suffocating. I don't really see enough of them; it's a thing I feel guilty about but it seems easier not to. All the questions, every time the same ones, and I can sense the anxiety coming off my mother in waves. Is my temperature raised? Am I especially tired? Have I been peeing enough? She blames herself for my heart condition since it stems from her family; her sister had the same thing and died young, so my mother can't worry enough about me.

My parents have had years of worry and I feel guilty about that too, even though it isn't my fault I was sick. The story my father tells in his autobiography is of how my illness changed his life. All the wealth he had worked for, all the success and status; seemed irrelevant as he faced losing a child. He prayed a lot and says God told him there was a reason he was so good at making money. It was to be used to ease the suffering of other children; that was his real mission in life.

Our family had always donated to charity, but after that

they pledged to give away most of their fortune. They set up a foundation to fund everything from medical research to vaccinations for kids in developing nations. I have lost track of the good works they do; possibly they have too. There are people who look after that side of things, a whole team now, while my parents circle through endless functions, smiling and shaking hands.

Imogen calls it 'doing the gooding' and rolls her eyes when she says the words. As in, 'Mum and Dad hope to make it to Italy if they're not too busy doing the gooding all summer.'

The gooding has been going on for as long as I can remember and doesn't seem special any more even if people like Fiona tend to be impressed. Photographs of my parents crop up from time to time – Dad sleek in a suit, Mum bright in her trademark florals – alongside details of some dizzying sum they have recently donated. Those huge numbers seem meaningless. Besides, nothing about their life changes, no matter what is given away. They still have the Oxfordshire country house and estate, the ski chalet in Val D'Isère, the apartment in New York, the cars, the boat, even a helicopter.

Often Imogen and I wonder what they would have done with all that money if there weren't so many worthy causes needing handouts. It might have just kept piling up until eventually we inherited the lot and had to decide where to put it.

'I'm not cut out for doing the gooding,' said Imogen, shuddering whenever the subject came up. 'All that listening to speeches and being fawned over; I don't know how they stand it.'

I hated the idea too. But my parents are relatively young and very healthy. They have years ahead of them to carry on shedding their riches. Chances are they have many more years than I do.

And that is why my mother worries. It is the reason she calls my sister all the time to check in on my health. Why she sends me organic fruit and vegetable boxes, even though she knows I hardly cook, and pays for a gym membership I am mostly too lazy to use. Why she makes me promise to be careful.

All the signs of organ rejection have been drummed into us. If my mother could, she would have had them laminated and hung around my neck. I try not to get caught up in worrying as I'm also aware there can be no signs at all that your body has started rejecting a donor organ. Even so quite often I stop and tune into my heartbeat, to check it's still there doing its thing, to make sure I've been careful enough.

Did Fiona ever fill her lungs with air and hold her breath? Could Tommy somehow sense his kidney was working? No matter what we might have in common, neither of them had what I did, that faithful beat to reassure me, the drumming of Jamie's heart.

Tommy

Tommy is running. It is always easier to think when his body is moving. His regular route takes him down past the golf course and along the promenade and the windswept beaches where the River Mersey flows out into the Irish Sea. The air that fills his lungs seems fresher down here, the horizon far away, and there are miles ahead of him.

It is Vivi that Tommy thinks about as his feet hit the concrete and his muscles work. She has been on his mind a lot lately.

He liked her the first time they met, when she came and found him at the marathon. Her sharp curiosity, the way she has of listening so carefully, her face, her smile. He liked her a lot and now every time they speak, he likes her a little more.

Talking to Vivi is often the best part of his day. Tommy looks forward to the moment when he is done with work and the kids are sorted and he finally has time to relax and call her. He hopes he isn't overdoing it, coming on too strong. Sometimes he thinks about not picking up the phone at all but then she always sounds pleased to hear from him.

Tommy isn't kidding himself. He knows Vivi is out of his league. For a start she is posh and quite a bit younger than him. Why would a girl like that be interested in an older guy with two kids, no cash and an ex-wife? He wishes he had more to offer, but he can't see that he ever will.

He likes talking to Vivi, likes making her laugh. Since his marriage broke up Tommy hasn't bothered dating other women. He prefers to keep life simple. And there is always an event to train for, roads to be run, lengths to be swum, bikes to pedal, weights to lift. Tommy's fitness feels good to him. It is all he has been interested in.

Now though, as his body moves, Vivi is on his mind. He is looking forward to seeing her again. He isn't kidding himself; still it will be nice to hang out, have a laugh and get to know her better.

Tommy has reached the long stretch of promenade facing the Liverpool docks. He is feeling good and could easily go further but there are things to do. Turning off at Vale Park he runs up past the bandstand and starts to head home.

He is still thinking about Vivi, wishing things were different and that he had more to offer. Tommy isn't usually one for giving up. That is not how you finish a marathon or win a triathlon. But he can't change who he is.

His kids are with their mother this morning so the house is quiet and empty. He eats a quick breakfast – a banana, a couple of boiled eggs, wholegrain toast – and after a shower, is ready for work. The day is set to be a long one and Tommy puts Vivi out of his mind for now. He will be seeing her soon.

Vivi

Tommy was sleeping in my bed. I may have been half a mile away at Imogen's place but I couldn't help thinking of him lying beneath my duvet, my books piled on the table beside him, my clothes on the rail against the far wall, the clutter on the counter of my kitchenette.

We had spent the evening together having dinner with my sister, who made more of an effort than usual. She cooked a risotto from a recipe she had clipped from a magazine and even cleared the table and set out cloth napkins. As she hovered over the cooktop, wielding a wooden spoon and frowning over the instructions, the rest of us sat with our drinks and made polite conversation.

Whenever he is around me, Hamid has this faintly disapproving air. My sister insists I am imagining it, but I know I'm not. Tommy didn't seem to notice. He chatted away about politics and art, things I hadn't realised he knew so much about, and by the time the risotto had been served it was clear he was winning Hamid over.

Imogen was more interested in hearing about Tommy's children, Ava and Liam. He looked proud as he showed off photographs and described their achievements – how well Ava had done in the school sports day, how funny the younger one Liam could be, how much effort they put into their schoolwork, what bright futures he saw for them.

'So I assume it's not heritable, the condition you had with your kidneys?' Hamid asked, unflinchingly direct as usual.

'It can be, but thankfully not in my case. I'd hate my kids

to go through the stuff I have,' said Tommy. 'To pass all that on to them.'

Imogen was fiddling about arranging cheeses on a platter. She paused and looked over. 'I suppose that's why you and Vivi seem so easy together: you've had the same experiences, you know how it feels.'

'That makes a difference, yes,' Tommy agreed. 'There's a lot we don't have to explain to one another.'

'It will be interesting to see if you feel the same way with this other organ recipient tomorrow.'

'Fiona … yeah, I don't know about her yet. But I take people as I find them.'

Bringing the platter over to the table, Imogen sat down and smiled at Tommy. I could tell her smile was genuine. When my sister isn't sure about someone she shows it by being slightly too polite. She asks lots of questions and shares very little about herself. At first she had been that way with Tommy, but now she was relaxing; smearing cheese onto a water biscuit whilst making him laugh with a story about the time Farah found some scissors and decided to play at being a hairdresser.

'You would be amazed how fast one little girl can cut off most of her own hair and then start on her best friend's,' said Imogen.

'Oh no, I assure you I wouldn't,' he smiled back.

My sister liked him, that was clear, but even so it took me by surprise when suddenly she said, 'Did Vivi tell you we're spending the summer in southern Italy? We've leased a villa for three months. You should come over and stay with us.'

'Well, I …' began Tommy.

'Seriously, come in the school holidays and bring your kids; there's loads of space and it would be nice for my girls to have other children there, even if they are older. Also Vivi needs someone to go sightseeing with while I get a suntan.'

'Is there a pool?' I asked.

'Yes, a natural rock pool you can swim in ... and an almost private beach ... oh, and lovely gardens. The owner is a landscaper. Mum put me in touch with him.'

'Why isn't he spending the summer there then, if it's so perfect?' I wondered.

'He's working on a big project somewhere. Mum did tell me ... it might have been Palm Springs ... I wasn't really interested so didn't bother remembering. The main thing is we've taken the place and now need to fill it with fun people. So Tommy, you'll come, yes?'

'That's a really generous offer.' He still sounded surprised. 'But I'd need to talk to my ex-wife first, check whether I can get the time off work, count my pennies and see if I can afford it.'

'It'll be super cheap,' Imogen promised. 'Everyone says food and wine is so affordable there. You'll hardly spend a thing.'

I had to smile at that. As if Imogen would know the first thing about living cheaply. She spends generously and without thinking, always has, and doesn't really understand that other people need to be more careful.

'I've never been to Italy,' Tommy said, wistfully. 'And it'd be great to get away with the kids. They could do with a break.'

'Think about it, then. There's no need to commit to any dates yet but we're taking on the property in June.' Imogen picked up her phone and started tapping on the screen. 'The guy emailed me some more shots. It looks so lovely. I can't wait to be there soaking up the sunshine.'

Most of the houses Imogen has found in the past have been flashy. Once there was a small chateau in France and, last year, a villa in Greece with an infinity pool and Doric columns. This place was different, I realised, peering at the pictures on her screen. A simple farmhouse backed by mountains, its walls blush pink, its gardens terraced down to a rocky coastline.

'Villa Rosa,' said Imogen. 'An authentic taste of southern Italian life and exclusively available to us because the owner knows our mother.'

'It looks fairly small,' I said.

'Yes, but it's a part of a complex,' my sister explained. 'There's another house right next door that we get to use too. So our guests will have their own space, which is perfect.'

'Now you're really tempting me,' said Tommy, as she passed the phone to him. 'But if I did come I'd have to contribute to the rent.'

'No, no, it's all sorted, isn't it Hamid?' said Imogen, cheerfully.

'I believe so,' said my sister's husband, who wouldn't have had a clue. Each year he holidayed wherever she chose and seemed entirely happy.

'Oh yeah, this place looks special.' Tommy was gazing at the photographs. 'I love it.'

'Great, that's settled then,' smiled Imogen. 'Now who else can we ask?'

If Fiona ever got tired of delivering the same spiel then she was careful not to show it. I trailed along the paths in the Chelsea Physic Garden, listening to her enthuse about the plants and their history, staying beside Tommy, who seemed genuinely engaged. He even had a few questions at the end.

Fiona was casually smart as usual, wearing her trench coat, slim-fitting jeans and sturdy ankle boots. As soon as she was free she made a beeline for us, lightly kissing my cheeks and shaking Tommy's hand.

'Well, here we are,' she said, as if surprised but delighted by the situation.

Tommy started apologising for the whole Westminster

Abbey upset but she brushed away his words, insisting there was no need to worry, it was all forgotten now.

We walked together towards the café, with me a little way behind so they could talk, but close enough to join the conversation if I wanted.

'I've had a letter from Grace,' Fiona was saying. 'We're just going to correspond for a while I think. Get to know each other that way.'

At the café we ordered tea and scones while we went through our stories again – Tommy's kidney disease, my broken heart, Fiona's failing lungs. We told them quickly, in a sort of shorthand, and once or twice we laughed at things no one else would find funny.

'There are three more of us out there,' Tommy told Fiona. 'One had a liver transplant, one a pancreas and the other got Jamie's corneas. That's all we know about them so far but we've promised Grace we'll find out more.'

'How do you plan to go about it?' she wondered.

'The only idea we've had is to do an article for Vivi's newspaper in the hope it will strike a chord with someone. Perhaps they might have had their transplant at the same time, or been given similar details as us. It's worth a try anyway. It seems like our best chance.'

'And you want me to be part of this article?'

'Ideally, yes ... Grace would appreciate it.'

Fiona's brow creased. 'I suppose so then ... as long as Vivi is going to write it ... I'd rather not deal with a complete stranger.'

If Tommy had been paying proper attention, he might have asked himself why Fiona was no longer thinking of me as a complete stranger; after all we hardly knew each other. But he was focused on being persuasive.

'Absolutely, Vivi will write it. Won't you?' he turned to me. 'This is something Grace really wants, that's why we're doing it, to help her.'

'In that case I can't really refuse,' Fiona said, softly. 'She has given me so much.'

None of us could say no to Grace and I was beginning to see the potential for a problem. She was such an unknown quantity. Who was to say meeting us all would be enough? What if it didn't help her at all; what might she want next?

'I wonder what Grace was like before Jamie died,' I said.

'Any kind of grief leaves a mark on you.' Fiona was demolishing another scone, reducing it to crumbs with quick, nervy fingers. 'At least that's been my experience.'

When you are interviewing someone, the hardest thing of all is to leave a silence for them to fill. The temptation is always to leap in with another question. Since becoming a journalist, I have trained myself how to be quiet. It is when the secrets are spilt, in those empty spaces; it is when the important things are said.

Tommy was a good listener; he seemed to know all that stuff instinctively. Both of us watched Fiona, fiddling with her uneaten bits of scone, neither of us saying anything.

'I lost my brother to cancer and then I lost my mother,' she explained at last. 'She was frail at the end and I nursed her until I got too sick myself and couldn't any more. When she died it left such a gap. They say there are stages of grief, but I think that's nonsense myself. Grief is just grief and it changes you.'

I'm not a great one for touching people. In fact, I'm an awkward hugger, aside from with my close family. Fiona seemed so wounded I felt I ought to touch her thin shoulder or still her busy hand with my own. But I didn't; I left that to Tommy, who with an ease I envied, reached out to her, saying, 'I'm so sorry.'

Fiona tried for a smile but didn't quite manage it. 'She was very old, and we all have to die some time, but that doesn't make it any easier when you're the one left behind. What makes it worse is that she was so worried about me. I wish she'd lived for long enough to know I got my transplant.'

'It must have been such a terrible time,' said Tommy.

'It wasn't the best. Still I'm here, and I have these gardens which have been such a solace, and I'm so grateful for this time and to be healthy again because I didn't think I would. The fact it's due to someone else's loss ... that's always going to be difficult, isn't it? Especially when you know how loss feels.'

When I'm in cafés, very often I look at other people and try to guess how they fit together. Is that a mother with her daughters; a group of friends or colleagues; a business meeting? I wondered how we looked from the outside, three such very different people caught in conversation. Surely no one would have guessed what linked us.

'Do you think it's going to help Grace, knowing us all?' I wondered.

'She thinks it will, and I suppose that's all that matters,' said Tommy.

'What if we didn't bother with this article though? Grace has contact with the three of us now. Do we really need to keep trying to find the others?' I wondered.

'You don't want to do it?' Tommy asked.

'Not really.'

'Why not?'

'I became a journalist to tell other people's stories, not my own. I didn't mean any of this to happen. I'd rather keep a lower profile.'

Before our meeting, I had called Fiona and asked her not to mention my family situation to Tommy. Naturally she appreciated my need to be discreet and now she was nodding at me, with tacit understanding.

'Seeing my personal details spread all over a tabloid newspaper doesn't appeal to me much either,' agreed Fiona. 'I suppose they'll want photographs too? I hate having mine taken.'

Tommy shrugged. 'It doesn't seem such a big deal from my perspective. And it might help Grace in some way; that's the important thing. She's been through a lot and she's not through it all yet.'

'Then it seems we have to,' Fiona conceded.

'It may not get us anywhere, but at least we'll have made the effort,' said Tommy. 'And the campaign the newspaper is running, Vivi's Law, we've got to back that, haven't we?'

Fiona was of the same mind. 'Yes, absolutely, that's a good cause.'

Two days later we had a photo shoot together in the gardens. The photographer was one I had been out on a few jobs with and he knew what he was doing. He grouped us closely together, Tommy in the middle with his arms round both our waists; had us smile, look solemn, gaze at the camera and each other.

Fiona looked lovely. She had put on a narrow skirt and short boxy jacket covered in a pattern of pink peonies. It was an outfit that might have been taken from my mother's wardrobe and the photographer adored it. I had been persuaded out of my uniform of black and was wearing a borrowed dress in a shade of pink that Tommy said suited me. He was casual in jeans and a blue T-shirt that clung to the taut lines of his body and brought out the tones in his eyes.

As well as the photographs, we shot some video, all of us talking about our special bond, how grateful we were for the gift we had been given, speaking in the clichés that the *Daily Post* trades in.

I had already written most of the article. It was coming out in Sunday's paper, a big spread. It would be on the website too and shared on social media. For a day or so at least there would be no escaping us.

'OK, let's get a few shots of you walking down the path, chatting to each other,' the photographer called.

'Aren't we nearly finished?' Tommy was showing his impatience.

It was harder to know how Fiona felt as she faced the photographer with a bright smile. Having agreed to do this, she was giving it her very best, showing the kind of fortitude that years of boarding school undoubtedly had taught.

I knew a little more about her now and none of it surprised me. She came from a family with some money, but not lots. Had worked for years as a cookbook editor and loved the precision the job required. But her mother's long illness and then her own had put an end to all that and now she was retired, living on a modest income that was enough for her to manage on so long as she was careful.

It seemed a quiet, neat life, the one she had. In the photograph she showed me, of a much younger version of herself sitting with her mother, she didn't look so different. Well-dressed, properly groomed, less wrinkled and not quite so thin.

Fiona had agreed to this photo shoot and now was determined to make sure it went well. She was suggesting we move to another part of the gardens and Tommy was shaking his head at the idea, growing impatient now.

'How many pages is this article going to be anyway? Surely we have enough?'

'Just a few more to make sure we've got every angle covered,' I told him. 'We don't want to have to do this again, do we?'

'Definitely not,' he agreed.

I knew it was going to make for a good piece, one that people would talk about over their weekend eggs and bacon, but I wasn't convinced it would further our search. And it was likely to create problems for me if someone else made the connection with my family. My days of being ordinary Vivi would be numbered and then who would I be? All those other rich girls, with their expensive handbags and even costlier cocaine habits, I wasn't one of them. But neither did I belong in the world I wanted to be a part of.

'Well, that wasn't so bad really,' Fiona said, once the shoot was finally over.

Tommy had dashed to catch a train home but I wasn't in any rush to head back to the office so had agreed to her suggestion of a restorative cup of tea. She seemed tired but this time actually ate some of the scone I bought for us to share. Cutting it into tiny squares, and treating them to barely a scrape of butter, she chewed carefully.

'Too much lavender,' she said, thoughtfully. 'I should suggest they put in a little lemon to balance it out.'

Thin bordering on bony, Fiona didn't look like a woman who cared about cake.

'Do you bake?' I asked her.

'When my mother was alive, I used to make treats for us on the weekends. Now I don't bother because who would I give all those cakes and biscuits to? But I do rather miss the process, the measuring and mixing, and the alchemy of it, seeing batter or dough become a wonderful light and fluffy thing.'

To me it seemed such a user-up of time, not only the actual cooking, but all the shopping and cleaning it seemed to involve. When you can buy perfectly good ready-made things from the shops then why would you bother?

'What about you ... do you like to bake?' Fiona wondered. 'Perhaps you used to do it with your mother?'

'God no, she's too busy.'

'Even when you're busy it's nice to slow life down for the duration of a recipe. And then you have that glorious sugary smell filling the house and a tray of goodies to share. It used to be my favourite way to relax on a Sunday morning.' Fiona sounded wistful.

'I don't think my mother does much relaxing' I told her.

'She was always a whirlwind, even before all the gooding got out of control.'

'Sorry ... all the what?'

'The charity work, it dominates her life these days. That and the garden, which just keeps getting bigger and bigger.'

'She sounds like such a fascinating woman,' said Fiona, admiringly. 'Just like your father, she's achieved so much.'

The thing about my mother is, she doesn't care about being admired, it is not why she does anything. What she is proudest of is Imogen and I. She might have had lots more children, if I hadn't been such a sickly one. Instead there was the garden and the gooding to distract her.

'I need to talk to my parents before this article comes out,' I told Fiona. 'They don't know yet about me finding Grace. Or about you and Tommy.'

'How will they feel, do you think? Perhaps a little worried about what you might be getting yourself into?'

'Perhaps.' I was playing with the food now, rolling bits of scone into pellets. 'In fact, yes, definitely.'

'I do understand, because I did my share of worrying,' Fiona admitted. 'I never imagined I'd be in this position. But having had time to consider, I can see it as a good thing that I've met you and Tommy. It feels like honouring Jamie, don't you think?'

'Yes, I guess.'

'I'm not sure about the other recipients though,' she admitted. 'What if they don't turn out to be quite so nice? It won't bother me if you never manage to find them. I suppose you have to keep trying?'

'Grace is so set on it. I think she's looking for reasons to live.'

Fiona frowned at that. 'And we are those reasons?'

Wordlessly, I nodded.

'It's a lot of responsibility to put on us, don't you think?' Fiona said, carefully. 'I do want to help Grace but I can't have her relying on me. It wouldn't be good for either of us.'

From her expression I could tell how concerned she was, and I understood, or at least thought I did. Because Grace was on my mind so much these days, I owed her everything. She had given me the future her son should have had, seven years more life, time to study and get a job and meet my nieces and travel and lose my virginity. But whenever I thought of Grace and how much she had given up so I could do all those things, it felt as if I owed her something more. It was an uncomfortable feeling and I couldn't seem to shake it.

Vivi

My mother's latest project was a series of fantasy gardens with eight-metre-high topiary figures, oversized flowers, fountains and lily ponds. It was all she had talked about for ages and lately she had been emailing me photos and hoping I might come to visit to check on its progress.

Those weekends with my parents are always more fun if Imogen and the girls come too. That means getting my sister organised, helping her pack and steeling myself for her driving. She and Hamid own an old Range Rover with every panel scraped or dented, which apparently only ever happens in the supermarket car park, and has nothing to do with Imogen's erratic driving.

Still she's fun on a car journey to Oxfordshire. There is always lots of music and singing, old-fashioned sweets like pear drops to suck on and crazy 'short cuts' that take you miles in the wrong direction to the perfect pub for lunch or the loveliest little tea shop.

My parents are in a daze of love for Darya and Farah; they can't get enough of them. But my mother is enough of a multi-tasker to still manage plenty of fretting about me.

'Are you eating properly? How are you feeling in yourself? Sure you're not at all down or depressed? Are you being careful to steer clear of colds and flus? Had you thought of getting those masks you often see Asian people wearing when you're travelling on buses and the Underground?'

She said all this over the course of half an hour as we were walking through the garden, the girls on scooters exploring the pathways ahead and apparently oblivious to the spookiness of the topiary figures looming over us.

'If only you would text me every day and let me know that you're OK, Vivi. Just send a smiley face or a thumbs-up. I know you don't want me worrying.'

'I hate you worrying.'

'Well then.'

Beyond the crazy topiaries was a large stretch of lawn where an amphitheatre was in the process of being carved out. There were going to be charity performances here, small concerts and exclusive appearances by very famous names. I had read about it in my own newspaper.

'This is looking good,' I said. 'But how will you get Lady Gaga's piano all the way in here?'

'Anything is possible with the right planning.'

'She's not seriously coming?' asked Imogen.

Our mother smiled and tipped the wide brim of her hat down to cover her face. 'It's all top secret. I couldn't possibly say.'

My mother Lady Deborah Palmer is a celebrated beauty. She has the glossy dark hair we both inherited; hers is still as thick as Imogen's and she wears it quite long. She loves florals and today's outfit is typical – a floppy hat printed with sunflowers, a top covered in appliqué daisies and flared black trousers splodged with yellow roses. I think the very fact she pulls off this look says everything.

'If Lady Gaga is coming, I want tickets,' said Imogen.

'You can apply with everyone else.'

My sister actually gasped. 'You wouldn't make me.'

'Yes, I would. And they won't be cheap.'

Beyond the surreal garden was a Gothic ruin with ivy clambering over its walls. It was here we found a picnic set up, with a wicker hamper, tartan rugs on the ground and a bottle of champagne chilling in an ice bucket. Farah and Darya squeaked with delight, dropping their scooters and rushing to be the first to open up the hamper and see what was inside.

'Cupcakes,' called Farah, 'with our names iced onto them.'

'Thanks Mum.' Imogen smiled at her.

'It's such a lovely day that I thought it would be a waste not to eat outside. There's some actual food in there too. I asked for those little chicken and almond finger sandwiches that you love, Imogen; the ones with curry powder in them.'

My mother wants to keep us safe and make us happy. Her world is fine so long as she feels she is managing both.

'I love cupcakes,' I told the girls. 'I want my share.'

We settled on the rugs and Imogen poured champagne while the rest of us helped ourselves to food.

'Your father was hoping to join us but I think there's been some sort of crisis he's averting.' My mother didn't take a huge interest in the minutiae of my father's work. She trusted in his ability to deal with anything, because he always had.

'He'll definitely be joining us later though?' I checked. 'There's something I need to talk to you both about.'

As always, my mother's antenna was ready to pick up on any signs that there might be something wrong. 'Why? What's happened?'

'Nothing bad.'

'You need to tell me, I'm not waiting.' The smile had gone from her voice. 'What is it, Vivi?'

And so I took a deep breath and explained, about Jamie and Grace, about Tommy and Fiona. It was a long explanation, particularly because she kept interrupting with questions. My sister sipped champagne and stayed silent, while my nieces devoured cupcakes with little regard for whose name was iced onto them.

When I had finished, my mother still seemed concerned. 'I don't know how Lance is going to feel about this. When they did the transplant they said there were rules and it seems to me you are breaking them.' She looked over at Imogen. 'Is that such a good idea?'

As always Imogen's instinct was to side with me. 'I've only met one of these people so far – Tommy – but he seems a nice guy.'

'You'd really like Fiona too,' I said. 'She's a decent type.'

'And what about the mother of the donor; what does she want from you?'

'Only my help.'

'You're sure that's it?'

'She doesn't know who we are,' I reassured her.

My parents might have played down how wealthy we were but they were wise to all the ways it made us vulnerable. Money tends to make you distrust other people's motives; it makes you more careful.

'So you are absolutely sure?'

'The only person who knows is Fiona and I can't imagine her taking advantage of anyone. She's religious. And she does voluntary work ... in a garden.'

'Oh.' There was quite a lot in that one word. Relief. Approval. Interest. 'Is the garden in London?'

I nodded. 'Some place called the Chelsea Physic.'

'Yes, yes, I know, it's charming. So, she's a gardener.' My mother thinks anyone who digs holes in the earth and plants things can't be entirely bad.

'Used to be but now gives the tours. And actually I promised her a ticket to come and see this place. Not while Lady Gaga is on obviously ...'

'Oh yes, absolutely, she must.' said my mother. 'I'll take her round myself.'

'And Tommy, the kidney recipient, may come to Italy to stay with us this summer,' Imogen told her. 'So hopefully there'll be a chance for us to get to know him better then.'

It can be stifling at times to have your family so protective, but things have always been this way for me, and even though I chafe at times, I keep telling myself I would most likely miss it if they weren't.

'Is that why you invited Tommy?' I asked my sister. 'To be able to check him out properly?'

'Obviously yes; if he's in your life then I'd like to know him better. But as I said, he seems a nice guy ... not like that Dan person.' Imogen pulled a face.

'What Dan person?' asked my mother, looking from one of us to the other, confused.

'Didn't she tell you about him? Oh well, not to worry, he's off the scene now,' said Imogen.

I didn't set my sister straight, didn't mention that I had slept with Dan only the night before after a glass of wine to celebrate me finally delivering the story he wanted.

'It seems there have been all sorts of developments in your life that we've heard nothing about.' My mother wasn't happy.

'You've been so busy ...'

'Not too busy, Vivi, never too busy.'

There were more questions, the same ones my father was going to ask later when we met him at cocktail hour, for dinner, or for milky drinks before bed if the crisis really had taken some averting. With him we would examine the situation from every angle, searching for what could go wrong.

'I suppose this is a good thing you're doing,' my mother said, cautiously. 'And backing the change to an opt-out system for organ donation certainly seems the right idea. But Vivi?'

'Yes, I know, I'll be careful. I'm always careful,' I said, trying not to sound as impatient with all this fuss as I felt.

'Is that breeze freshening up a bit?' she asked, looking up as the topiary started to sway. 'Should we head back indoors?'

Getting up, we left the picnic behind us, the rumpled rugs still on the ground, the hamper with its lid open, glasses smeared, empty champagne bottle upended in the ice bucket, confident someone would be along soon to clear it all up.

We set off through the gardens, my mother a few strides ahead, while my sister and I lagged behind, waiting for the girls to catch up with their scooters.

'That went OK, I think,' said Imogen.

'Yeah ... hey, and thanks.'

'Thanks for what? Being nice about Tommy? Well, he does seem a good guy, so I'm not fudging it.'

'You're not trying to matchmake us, are you?' I asked, because it seemed the obvious explanation for such an impulsive invitation to join us in Italy.

'Of course, I am.' Imogen shrugged. 'Come on Vivi, someone's got to.'

My sister longs for me to have all the things she values most in her own life – a happy home, a caring husband, lovely kids. She is always trying to hook me up with someone she thinks is suitable, and there have been awkward dinners, strained lunches, drinks parties and picnics. I keep pushing away the nice guys and she keeps persisting. I don't know why Imogen refuses to understand that it's not going to work. I'm better off with the unsuitable men, the ones like Dan I don't have to care about hurting, the guys there is no need to worry about leaving behind some day when this heart stops beating.

'We're friends, me and Tommy, transplant family; that's enough,' I told her. 'No matchmaking, OK?'

Imogen tossed her head at me. 'Yes, well, we'll see about that.'

My parents live in a Georgian manor house that looks impressive from the outside. Inside nothing is especially grand. There are lots of over-stuffed sofas and fires that blaze in wintertime, mismatched floral wallpapers and battered antiques.

If we are at home they always make time for breakfast in the wood-panelled morning room that opens out onto a walled garden with a swimming pool surrounded by cypress trees. The pool is heated so even on cooler days Farah and Darya can splash about in it while we relax with pots of coffee and keep a careful eye on them. With Radio 4 in the background, his dogs at his feet and his family around him, my father is always happiest.

Sir Lance Palmer is older than his wife. He has reached that stage in life where his eyebrows straggle and craze if she doesn't remind him to get them trimmed, and his hair is snowy white. My father has always been the calm one, the strength of the family, the person we turn to for advice although he doesn't often give it, because he believes in the importance of making your own decisions.

He hadn't told me not to continue the search for my donor siblings, but asked enough questions so I could see for myself where the pitfalls might lie. Now at last he seemed to have got all that out of his system and he read my piece in the *Daily Post* without too much comment.

'Very nice outfit,' my mother remarked of Fiona's suit. 'You must ask her where she got it.'

'Probably some designer recycle shop.'

'You seem good friends already.' She was gazing at the shot where Tommy had his arms round us.

'I suppose we are; I like them both.'

'In that case I would love to meet them.'

Imogen hadn't seemed to be paying attention. She was leafing through a colour supplement, crunching toast and marmalade and watching out for the girls. Still like our mother, she is a skilled multi-tasker.

'I don't know why everyone doesn't get together at the house in Italy over summer,' she said. 'This woman Fiona too if she's as lovely as you say … it's obviously the best idea. A perfect opportunity to get to know each other.'

'I'm sure everyone has commitments,' I said, in the tone of someone who is always having to repeat herself.

'I don't have any commitments, and I'm going to be there all summer so I'd like to think my family and a few friends will make time to join me.'

'Of course we will, darling,' my mother soothed. 'We'll finalise the dates and have flights booked, won't we Lance? And Vivi will be there.'

'Imogen wants me for the whole summer though.' I was sitting on the floor, next to my father's legs, patting one of the dogs. After the transplant my parents had re-homed all their pets, concerned about the risk of infection. But my father loved his dogs and, so long as I was careful, they didn't pose a threat. A few years ago I had convinced him to get two roly-poly black Labradors.

'Wash your hands,' my mother reminded me reflexively, as I stood to fetch more coffee and I rolled my eyes, turning my face away so she wouldn't see.

Setting aside his newspaper, my father got to his feet and stretched. The dogs looked at him expectantly. 'These guys need a walk,' he said. 'Vivi, why don't you come with me?'

It sounded like a suggestion, but what he meant was there were things he wanted to say in private. I expected a caution about Grace or discussion about my finances so was surprised when it was my sister he wanted to talk about.

'How does she seem at the moment?' he asked, as the dogs trotted ahead through the sculpture gardens.

'Fine … the same as usual I think. Why?' I had been wrapped up in my own life lately and hadn't noticed much else.

'It's been difficult for her, that's all, putting aside her career to have a family. I think there must be times she struggles with that.' My father smiled as the boy dog, Boston, cocked his leg and peed on a silver reflective Anish Kapoor sculpture that had probably cost millions.

'Imogen can go back to work if she likes, surely?' I said.

'And perhaps she will once the girls are older. But for now she wants them to have what you had, a mother who is there. And we should all do what we can to support her.'

'Of course.'

My father threw a stick for the girl dog, Betty, in the vain hope she might chase and retrieve it. 'You could start by spending the summer with her in Italy. And yes, I know what you're going to say ...'

'My job ...'

'I admire your work ethic, Vivi, but don't you think you've gone as far as you can on that tabloid. Reality TV stars, fad diets, royals; you're capable of much more. You proved that with this morning's piece, which was beautifully written.'

'They do run longer stuff too, premium content.'

'A few senior journalists will get to work on that while you young ones are stuck in the daily churn.'

My father was right. The sort of journalism I cared about were the meatier investigative pieces but at the *Daily Post* we were all about chasing clicks on the website. They wanted us to do podcasts and pieces to camera not spend months following leads for a story that might never happen. If it hadn't been for the Vivi's Law campaign I would never have been given the time to spend on this one.

'What do you suggest I do instead then?' I asked him, because it wasn't as if I was fending off any other job offers.

'Take the summer to think about what you really want and how to get it. You could do some freelance work in the meantime, travel articles maybe, write a blog ...'

'Blogs are over,' I argued.

'Maybe, but it would be an opportunity to explore a different style of writing. You've shown you've got what it takes to work on a tabloid; it's time for a new challenge. Strike out, do something different instead of repeating yourself.'

That had been my father's philosophy in his own career.

He was always pushing forward, learning something new and taking risks others would find dizzying. I admired him for it, but didn't think I could ever live that way.

'It would be a chance to do something nice for your sister too,' my father finished.

Beyond the sculpture park lie acres of woodland criss-crossed by paths. We had reached my favourite part, a fairy glade of ferns, mossy boulders with a stream bubbling through; and we paused for a moment, while the dogs drank noisily from it and my father searched for more sticks they would be too lazy to chase.

'OK, I'll think about,' I told him.

'While you're in thinking mode, there is another thing I'd like you to consider. Why don't you give up that nasty little bedsit and move in with your sister for a while?'

'Hamid would hate that,' I said, quickly.

'But it was Hamid's suggestion.'

'Is he worried about Imogen?'

'He's looking after her, and caring about you.'

My father put an arm round my shoulders as we strolled on. His jacket smelt of the cigars he smokes outside, thinking my mother won't notice, and his pace was languid. He was a busy man and he had all the time in the world for me.

'I'd never try to push you into anything, Vivi; this is your life. But I also want what's best for you and Imogen. And right now, this is what I hope you'll choose to do. Spend a summer in Italy with your sister. It won't exactly be a hardship, will it?'

'I don't know about giving up the bedsit though. And I'd need some help with the rent if I was going to be away the whole summer.'

My father nodded. If he was surprised at me asking for money, when for years I had determinedly not, then he didn't show it.'

'As you say, I could try to drum up freelance work. The

Daily Post might even take a few pieces. You never know, there may be some reality TV star staying in the same village that I can spy on.'

'Yes.' My father smiled. 'Or even better, a member of the royal family.'

I looked carefully for any signs of angst in my sister as we demolished a Sunday roast and as she drove us slowly back to town in the evening traffic. With the girls safely strapped in their car seats and playing with my phone, I managed to probe a bit, asking questions about her job and whether she ever missed it. Imogen made several rude and very funny comments about the senior partners at her old firm then changed the subject. She seemed entirely herself.

If Hamid was suggesting I go and live with them then surely it was only because he thought I couldn't be trusted to look after myself. He wasn't worried about Imogen; she was fine as always.

Imogen

She slips into bed beside her husband, who is already asleep, face pushed into the pillow, creasing his forehead. He works so hard and is always half distracted. When they both had careers Imogen didn't mind so much. But now, untethered from the life she used to have, everything seems different.

Often Imogen pretends she is an actress, playing a role to the best of her ability, the same role every day, good wife and fun mother. Her house is a stage, set with its lovely clutter of family life, and she is almost word-perfect.

Imogen isn't sorry she had the girls; she could never be sorry. But sometimes, as each day runs into the next, she wonders if they might be better off with a different mother. So she does the only thing she knows: works harder, tries and tries.

When she was pregnant Imogen studied for it; read all the books. She learnt about raising happy, healthy kids, about smart mothering and creating a peaceful, joyful home. She thought she was prepared.

Imogen is almost sure no one has noticed how things really are. Hamid is caught up in work, her parents have their gooding to do, the girls are still young and Vivi is wrapped up in her own problems.

The most important lesson Imogen has learnt is how to put on a good performance. The effort is exhausting. She knows she has to change something. Maybe the long summer away will make a difference. Perhaps in Italy, with the sun on her skin, and swimming in the sea, with good food and people around her, perhaps there she might feel different. What she needs is to get away. She needs a party to distract her, colour and life, real fun rather than the kind she has invented.

Imogen lies down beside her husband and switches off the light. Next to the bed she still has the baby monitors, even though her daughters aren't babies anymore. This house is a tall narrow one and the girls have rooms on the floor above. What if Darya calls out and she doesn't hear her? What if Farah has a nightmare?

When she met Hamid she always slept naked. She was carefree then. Now Imogen can only ever sleep if she has a plan. Pyjamas she could quickly throw a jacket over, sneakers within reach, car keys by the door. Imogen is ready, although she is not sure what for.

All those years when Vivi was young and often sick, their mother must have been ready too. Lying there during the longer, lonelier hours, listening to her husband's steady breathing, Imogen remembers those times and wonders how they got through them.

Vivi is leading her own life now and these new people have arrived in it; her transplant twins, strangers with a connection. Imogen is being careful. After a lifetime of being the one who worries, looking out for problems and trying to protect, it has become a habit. Imogen needs a plan; she needs to be ready.

Vivi

Half the world seemed to have read my article over the weekend. I spent most of Monday morning dealing with reactions to it. Messages from friends and strangers and hundreds of comments on Facebook; a few emails from other recipients wanting to share their experiences, several from nutters who thought that organ transplants were unethical, even one who wanted me to know the shade of pink I was wearing in the photographs did nothing for me; but unfortunately no one who thought they might be one of Jamie's recipients.

Only a single person made a phone call: Lynda my transplant recipient co-ordinator. Seven years ago she had been the one to ring and say there was a heart for me and she has stayed with me every step of the way since then, preparing me for surgery, helping me to adjust to life afterwards. I recognised her voice immediately, a Scottish burr, bright and breezy.

'Vivienne Palmer, what have you been up to?'

'Lynda, it's so good to hear from you.' She had been my life raft for such a long time. Never dazed by worry like my family, always calm and full of the facts I needed to know. I had clung to her.

'You are the talk of the place this morning,' she told me.

'Because I'm disrespecting all the guidelines?'

'Ah well.' She dropped her voice. 'The reality is we can't do too much to stop that happening, not with all the social media these days; everyone is connected, aren't they? And the publicity you're getting is priceless. People are talking about organ donation, changing the system at last, so a little bit of disrespect is probably worth it.'

I lowered my voice too, although in the *Daily Post* office we're all elbow-to-elbow and people could overhear if they wanted. 'Lynda, can you help me track down the others?'

'You know I can't, not officially.'

'What about unofficially?'

'Vivi, I love you to bits but …'

'Could we meet at least? I haven't seen you in ages.'

'That's because you're doing so well; you'd see me quick enough if things went wrong.'

'Just a coffee, surely you have time.'

'OK then,' agreed Lynda.

'And not in the hospital, let's meet somewhere nicer.'

'There's a newish café on the high street. They do very nice buns.'

'Sounds great, let's say tomorrow morning then?'

'Tomorrow?' She sounded surprised. 'You must really want to see me.'

'Or I must really want a nice bun.'

She laughed and it was such a good sound, warm and reassuring. If Lynda was laughing then everything must be OK; that was how it had felt seven years ago and there was the exact same sense now.

'If you want a bun, darling, then that's what you shall have,' she told me.

So many people were involved in getting me through that transplant, so many doctors, nurses, social workers, an entire team, even a psychiatrist, but only ever one Lynda.

'We've got this, darling,' she would say whenever my courage was failing. 'You and me, we've got this, and it'll be fine.'

I trusted that Lynda would never say that if it weren't true. I kept watching for her smile and listening for her laughter, and they helped me feel safer.

People tend to think of an organ transplant as a happy ending. This is partly the fault of newspapers like mine; it's the way we tell the story. But when my old heart was gone and the healthy one was beating, it was the beginning of something new – we call it the recovery journey – and it wasn't always easy.

My body was weak. It had never run fast or lifted anything heavy; it hadn't climbed a mountain, barely even walked up a hill. Lynda helped me believe I would be able to do all those things. She was hope and kindness. During the long nights when the steroids were stealing my sleep, I thought about all the good she did and all the people she helped, and was so grateful to have her on my side.

Maybe Lynda knew where those other pieces of Jamie had gone – his liver, his pancreas and his corneas. Perhaps there were records she could access or administrators to check with. I had never asked her to break the rules for me before, and did feel bad about it, but the rules were in my way. All I wanted was to connect with these people. I wasn't going to force them to be my friend or make them get in touch with Grace. What harm could it do?

I felt a little lighter knowing that I was going to see Lynda. For the rest of the morning, she stayed in my mind. I thought about her holding my hand before the surgery, as I was almost breathless with terror about what was to come. Encouraging me in the days afterwards, as I lay in bed so weak and tired I wanted to close my eyes and let my broken body sink down through the mattress into oblivion rather than get up and walk round the ward like everyone wanted. Patiently she talked me through all the many drugs I needed to take, and called me every day for weeks after I had been discharged. Hearing Lynda's voice again always made those memories much more vivid.

Going up to Harefield to meet her was going to take half

a day so I had to tell Dan about it. He smiled at the news, as always thinking of the potential for another story.

'Get some shots of the two of you together and a few good quotes supporting Vivi's Law,' he reminded me. 'We'll use it on the website, or maybe as part of a longer piece.'

'I'm not sure ... It might be against the rules.'

'It's a photo and some quotes. It'll be fine; just do it, OK?'

Dan reckoned it was acceptable to break rules so long as it led to an exclusive and you didn't get caught. Sometimes in the pub people got drunk and started telling tall stories, and his were always the most outrageous. Lying, cheating, snooping, I laughed along with the others, even if I didn't always feel entirely comfortable about it.

The reason I became a journalist was that I love writing. It is my favourite part of any assignment, when the research is done and the interview transcribed and all that is left is to marshal the words. I used to write other things, poems and short stories, but they were awful no matter what my family say. My talent is taking real life and giving it a beginning, a middle and an end. That is why I am here at the *Daily Post*; it is what got me hired. I can make almost anything read well, it is all the other stuff I have had to work at: chasing the story, hunting down interview subjects, talking them round; it doesn't come as naturally.

Arguably my father was right and I was reaching a dead end in this job. It certainly felt that way today as I composed several hundred words on Kate Middleton's parenting secrets, quoting myself liberally as a 'royal watcher', in the absence of any genuine material.

'Want to have lunch?' Dan surprised me. He didn't normally take a break during the day.

'Don't you need me to finish this piece?'

'No rush on that, let's go somewhere nice, my treat.'

He took me to The Ivy Brasserie and we sat side by side on a banquette and ordered shepherd's pie and bowls of thick-cut chips. Mostly Dan talked about work, some restructure they were planning for the website; but there were always changes and this one didn't seem to affect me, so I only half listened to his fast-paced chatter.

We were almost finished with our food when Dan paused, smiled boyishly, touched my arm, and said, 'Anyway, that's not really what we're here to discuss,'

I looked at him blankly, 'It isn't?'

'White tablecloths and glasses of the house champagne ... are you kidding? Of course not.' Dan smiled again. 'I want to talk about something far more important ... us.'

'Us?'

'Yes, Vivi you and me.'

My eyes widened; this had never happened before. 'What about us exactly?'

'Well, when these website changes happen I won't be your direct boss any more and so I thought the timing was right for us to start living together.'

I was so taken aback; I didn't say anything.

'You're always staying over at my place anyway. You may as well move your stuff in.'

I stared at him, still silenced by surprise.

'I like you, Vivi.' Dan's hand fell on my thigh and his fingers stroked upwards. 'And you like me. So it makes sense doesn't it? Besides, that place you're living in is a shithole.'

His hand was curved round my inner thigh now and he didn't seem to notice that I hadn't responded. He was talking about having a good clear-out of his things to make room for mine. Saying he didn't expect much contribution to the rent, since he earned more, but we could split the power and grocery bills. Suggesting he might borrow a mate's van and help me shift at the weekend.

'This weekend?' I said, faintly.

'Why not? No point wasting time now we've made the decision.'

Perhaps it was because I was so used to doing what Dan told me at work, but it seemed difficult to say no. Besides, he was right, his place was much nicer than mine and I spent a lot of my time there as it was.

'I suppose it might be a good idea,' I said slowly, even though my sister was going to kill me and I didn't want to think about what my parents would say.

He had never kissed me in public before. But now he took hold of my face and tilted it to his. I felt a flicker of desire as his lips touched mine and his hand tightened on my leg. He must have felt it too.

'Aw Vivi,' he said, his voice a groan.

Dan kissed and touched me as the waiters cleared our plates and brought us coffee, and I let the thrill of the moment override any doubts in my mind.

Did I really want to live with him? It wouldn't be such a bad thing to have the chance to find out. Falling asleep together at night, waking with him each morning, mingling everything from our future plans to our laundry pile. Even if my sister was right and Dan was unsuitable, I'd never had that kind of intimacy with any man before. Deep down I knew it wasn't going to last for long but wouldn't it be nice to live like a normal person? To know how that felt, just for a little while?

'So will we be telling everyone, and meeting each other's friends?' I asked later, as we walked back to work.

'Yes, eventually, all of that,' he sounded amused. 'I believe it's traditional.'

Dan held my hand the whole way, letting it go only as we reached the revolving doors that sucked us back into the *Daily Post* offices. And all afternoon I caught him looking over and smiling, like he was pleased to share a secret.

It was Tommy that I messaged first with the news, probably because I thought he was the one least likely to judge me.

My boyfriend just asked me to move in with him!

The reply came back almost straight away.

I'm assuming you said yes?

Apparently I did.

He asked about my moving plans, where Dan lived, what his flat was like, but before too long we found our way back to Grace again. She seemed to always be there, standing between us, finding her way into our messages and conversations; we couldn't escape her for long.

Tommy was concerned that the article I had written about us might have stirred up more difficult emotions.

Have you spoken to her since it came out? If not one of us should give her a call.

I'm seeing my transplant co-ordinator tomorrow. I'll call after that, there may be more to say.

OK let me know how it goes.

I sent him a smiley face and a thumbs-up, then Tommy sent back a heart in reply. That was how he always ended a back and forth of our messages – with my symbol, bright and red and cheerful.

It doesn't take long to get to Harefield by taxi, it is just a quick zip up the A40, and normally I spend most of that time trying not to get anxious. Blood tests, electrocardiograms, chest X-rays, biopsies: all the checks to make sure Jamie's heart is in good shape and my body hasn't started to reject it; that is what Harefield means to me. To be going just for coffee and a catch-up felt almost indulgent.

Lynda was waiting for me at the café in the high street. She folded me into a warm, firm hug then stood back and looked at me properly.

'A little too thin,' she declared. 'Definitely in need of a bun.'

She wanted to know about everything, my health, my life, my plans; asked to see a photo of my unsuitable boyfriend Dan and hear how my job was going; made a fuss about whether I was eating the right things and getting enough exercise. The buns were finished and the coffee drunk by the time we talked about why I was really there.

'You're a big girl, Vivi, and I'm not going to lecture you but ...' she began.

'You think I shouldn't be looking for the other recipients?'

'I don't understand why you'd want to.'

'Mainly to help the donor's mum.'

Lynda raised her eyebrows.

'It's more than that,' I hastened to add. 'The people I've found so far, it's like we've got nothing in common but also everything. We've been through the same journey. Does that make sense?'

'You might feel like that way, even if you didn't share a donor,' she pointed out. 'You could join a support group and meet like-minded folk.'

'It wouldn't be the same.'

'You've set yourself a challenge then.'

'So everyone keeps telling me,' I said. 'It's so frustrating. All the information is there at the Donor Records Department and they won't share it because of the policy. Even getting them to confirm what we already know has been a mission. I understand the reasons for it, it's meant to protect everyone. But me, Tommy and Fiona don't need protecting from one another. Why shouldn't we be friends?'

Lynda sighed. 'It's drummed into us, you know, the anonymity, so we accept it. People do meet up, of course, and I've never heard of anything terrible happening as a result, but I can't tell you a thing, I'm sorry.'

'You do know something then? Or you've got contacts who might be able to help?'

She shifted in her seat. 'Sorry, my darling, but you'll have to keep trying through the official channels.'

'Just a little hint,' I pleaded. 'It might benefit the Vivi's Law campaign.'

At that Lynda smiled. 'You seem to be going perfectly well there without me. It's a great job you're doing. I'll give you any help that's in my power, obviously.'

She agreed to pose for a photo. The owner of the café took it, Lynda and I arm-in-arm and smiling. Then she promised to have a think about some quotes I could use. After that it was time to say goodbye and go our separate ways, but I prolonged the moment, keeping her chatting for another ten minutes as we stood on the pavement outside, showing her photos of my nieces and talking about our plans to spend some time in Italy.

'It's great to see you healthy and happy.' Lynda hugged me one last time. 'Keep taking good care of yourself, OK? And have the best time in Italy.'

I watched her walk away down the high street, a broad-shouldered stocky figure. She didn't turn and look back. There were other people depending on her now, transplant patients whose hands needed holding, families who were facing worry and worse. Not everything went as well as it had for me, not always.

A couple of days later, Lynda phoned me again. She had some officially approved quotes to run with our photo on the *Daily Post* website, predictable words about the desperate need for donor organs and the way lives could be changed for the better.

'Is there enough for you there?' she asked. 'Will that help?'

'Yes, definitely.'

'Great … keep up the good work then.'

'Thanks Lynda, I'll let you know when it's up on the website.'

'Please do … Oh, and Vivi, there's one more thing.'

'Yes?' I asked, hopefully.

'I was thinking about your trip to Italy this summer and there's a place I've heard about that you should visit if you get the chance.'

I wanted more from Lynda than tips for my holiday, but it seemed ungracious to say so. 'Oh right, well, we're heading south so …'

'This place is in the south, although I'm not sure how close it is to where you're staying. They make organic mozzarella and raise the water buffalo. There's an English cheese maker there who you might find interesting.'

'Mozzarella?' I said it loudly enough for people at the neighbouring desks to glance over.

'Yes, the place is called Masseria Perretti and apparently it's really worth a visit. Since you're going to be in Italy anyway I thought I should mention it. There's a tour you can take to watch the cheese makers at work.'

'Have you been yourself?'

'Me, no.'

'But you reckon I should?'

'That's right, Vivi, I do.'

'To meet this cheese maker?'

'I didn't say that exactly, did I? Just that you might find him interesting.'

Putting down the phone, I turned to Google and typed in the name 'Masseria Perretti'. The website detailed farm tours, a restaurant and tastings and said bookings were advised, but there was nothing about any specific cheese maker.

Again my first instinct was to message Tommy.

Hey do you have a moment to chat? Something just happened.

Give me ten minutes and I'll call. I need to talk to you too.

Waiting impatiently for my phone to ring, I spent the time wondering. If Lynda was hinting about cheese makers, there had to be a really good reason. Maybe this was another lead at last, and right when I had thought my search was hitting its final dead end. I felt a quick sting of excitement and couldn't wait to tell Tommy.

Vivi

We had a problem, a tricky Grace-shaped one, and now Tommy was trying to find a way to solve it. Just as he had predicted, the article and photos of the three of us together had created an upset.

'I think Grace is feeling left out,' Tommy explained. 'It must seem like you, me and Fiona are becoming friends without her.'

'But she didn't want to have any part in the article,' I objected. 'I was trying to protect her by keeping her out of it.'

'Yeah, I know. Still, if that's how Grace feels then we need to do something about it.'

I could hear wind and traffic noise, so Tommy must have been standing outside. Our conversation had probably interrupted him installing someone's kitchen.

'Such as?'

'What if we get together in Oxford this weekend?' he suggested. 'It would be an opportunity for Grace to meet Fiona properly, and we could all do something nice.'

'I'm not sure if Fiona is ready for that.'

'Talk to her, find out.'

'Also I'm meant to be moving house this weekend,' I reminded him. 'It's all organised.'

'Can't you delay it?'

'I suppose so … if I really have to.'

It was hard not to feel a hint of resentment. Whatever Grace needed, we were meant to jump. We had our lives thanks to her; we owed her everything, so even if I didn't want to go to Oxford, if it wasn't the least bit convenient, that didn't seem to matter.

'We don't have to go to her house,' Tommy reassured me. 'Not if it bothers you. Just a nice lunch somewhere, a walk by the river, it'll be good.'

'OK then,' I agreed, as what else could I say? 'I'll check with Fiona, talk her into it if necessary.'

My weekend had been holding all the nervous promise of a fresh start. Moving in with Dan was a risk, one I'd had a couple of sleepless nights over, but things were going well enough so far. Dan had gone to the trouble of borrowing a mate's van and made space for me in his flat; everything was ready and if I tried to change the plan now I worried he would be put out. It seemed a bad way for us to start off together.

What I hadn't taken into account was how keen Dan was on me pursuing this story; if I wanted to spend a weekend with my transplant friends it was fine by him. He even suggested I should take the Friday off work to pack up my stuff and he would move it for me.

'Then you can come straight to my place on the Sunday evening,' he said. 'And everything will be there waiting for you.'

'Are you sure?' I was grateful to have Dan solve the problem.

'It's no trouble. I'll get my mate to help me. Probably easier without you there getting in the way, actually.'

So that was a relief, but still I couldn't relax because there was the issue of Fiona to contend with. She and Grace had been exchanging cards and letters, a polite ritual that seemed set to be drawn out interminably, and now I was the one who had to hurry it along.

It seemed better dealt with face-to-face, so I texted Fiona and suggested we meet later that day for a cup of tea, and she agreed to see me at the usual place.

Afternoon tea would be lovely. Lots to catch up on, I'm sure.

It turned out that Fiona had been feeling like a celebrity all week. Lots of people had seen her in the *Daily Post,* other volunteers from the garden and the congregation at her church, folk she'd never have imagined would read a tabloid newspaper. All in all, the feedback on my article had been very positive. In fact, a couple of friends she hadn't heard from in years had been in touch, so now her diary was filling up with dates for coffee and lunch. It was all rather exciting.

'You did such a lovely job with it, as I knew you would.' Fiona beamed a smile at me. 'What sort of a response have you had?'

'My mum loved your suit,' I told her. 'She asked me to find out where you got it.'

'Oh.' Fiona pinked with pleasure. 'I have a dressmaker I use. I'd be happy to pass on her details if you think your mother might be interested.'

We ordered pots of tea and yet more scones because they are one of the safer things to eat from a café menu. All the bacteria that might make us sick are lurking in the sandwiches and salads, and maybe in the cheesecake. Normal people never stop to consider that, as they have whatever they fancy. Fiona and me; we choose scones.

As we nibbled and sipped, I updated her on the reaction to my article. I even told her about the strange business with Lynda and the Italian cheese maker. We discussed that for a while, neither of us completely sure whether she had been giving me an unofficial tip-off or genuinely making a holiday suggestion.

'Normally Lynda is so straight up,' I explained. 'It's not like her to drop hints about things. But I guess if this guy really is one of Jamie's recipients then she's breaking the rules, so ...'

'You're going to Italy for a holiday anyway, aren't you?' Fiona asked.

'My flights aren't booked yet but I'm meant to be, and this gives me another good reason. It would be nice to have some positive news for Grace as Tommy says she's not doing too well.'

Then I explained about his plan, our weekend in Oxford together, and Fiona's face showed signs of strain, her lips down-turned and her brow creasing, as she murmured something non-committal and her gaze moved from my face and towards the windows.

'Do you know, I think it might rain,' she said, in a weak bid to change the subject. 'Look at the colour of the sky, like bruised lilac, very pretty actually but darkening now.'

I wasn't going to let her off the hook that easily. 'Fiona please, won't you come?'

'For the whole weekend?'

'Tommy is travelling down from Liverpool so I suppose it makes sense.'

'Couldn't I join you for lunch?'

'I guess so, if that's all you can do.'

Outside rain was starting to fall. People were putting up umbrellas or hurrying for the shelter of the building. Fiona continued to frown towards the windows as they blurred with raindrops.

'My lungs have been such a gift, they were my lifeline, but …' She began coughing, and needed several breaths before she could speak again. 'I can't be Grace's friend; I'm not the right one to help her. Transplanted lungs don't last long; you probably know that, don't you? Given my age, I'm doing well. Seven years and, as I always say, I'm grateful for every moment. I try not to worry about what lies ahead, to stay positive.'

'Me too,' I told her.

Fiona rummaged in her handbag. Like everything about

her, it looked expensive and well worn. She pulled out a handkerchief, pressed into a neat square, and dabbed lightly at her face with it.

'When you can't breathe, nothing else matters,' she told me. 'I'll never forget the relief of not needing oxygen, having energy again, just being able to cook a meal or go for a walk. That's all down to Grace.'

'Yes,' I said, encouragingly.

'So I'll come along and thank her in person. But I think you should call a halt to this search after that. Don't put the other recipients in the same position. Leave them alone to get on with their lives and allow Grace to continue with hers. That's my advice, for what it's worth. I think it would be best.'

Perhaps it had been a bad idea, writing the articles, making contact with everyone, but I'd done it now and couldn't see a way back.

'Consider it from Grace's perspective,' Fiona said, and there was a steelier edge to her voice. 'It's fine while all of us are doing well but that's bound to change eventually, for one of us at least, and then there'll be more reasons for grief. I hate saying it but that's the reality.'

I swallowed hard, because there was every chance she was right, and I didn't like to think about it either. 'It's lunch, that's all'

'Yes, of course.' Fiona managed a smile. 'Lunch, this one time, that I can do.'

The rain was still sluicing down, and neither of us was in any hurry to get wet. I didn't even have a raincoat, so by the time I found a cab I would be soaked to the skin. We stayed and drank more tea. Fiona breathed through Jamie's lungs, I sensed his heart beating softly in my chest and we talked about other things; films we wanted to see, places we would like to go, like other people do.

Eventually the sky lightened and the rain softened to a drizzle.

'I'd better head off,' I told Fiona. 'Before it starts pouring again.'

'You'll be in Italy soon, all that lovely Mediterranean sunshine.'

I thought of the pretty pink house my sister had rented for the summer, how many bedrooms it had and how thrilled Fiona would be at the chance to occupy one of them. Should I invite her to join us like Imogen had suggested? For a moment I considered it then remembered Grace; guilt-inducing, spiky, sad Grace. Wherever we went together, with our tiny pieces of Jamie inside us, surely she would want to come too?

A hotel in Oxford was hastily booked, a lunch reservation made; and I spent the rest of Friday packing everything I owned into boxes so they could be moved to Dan's place while I was away, feeling ridiculously forlorn at the thought of leaving my little bedsit. It had been my first real taste of independence. As I stuffed a weekend bag with the essentials that go everywhere with me – my blood pressure monitor, the log book where I record its reading every day along with my heart rate, temperature and weight, all my various pills, and there are lots of them – I recalled the thrill of moving in to my very own space, behind my own front door, where I could live however I wanted.

I taped closed the last of the boxes and thought ahead to when I would open them up again at Dan's place in Bethnal Green and start settling in. His flat was small, but it had actual rooms and I was hoping he would be OK with me buying a few bits and pieces to make it more homely: cushions for the sofa, pot plants, artworks for the walls, things to look at other than his widescreen TV. Perhaps I might even learn to cook a couple of dishes so we could have friends over for dinner. Life seemed full of new possibilities and it made saying goodbye to my bedsit a little easier.

With all my belongings stripped away, the place looked even more dismal. I had one final night's sleep in my extra-wide single bed then the next day closed the door on it for the very last time, hoping I was ready for my future.

It was a golden morning and I was pleased to be going somewhere. As I carried my heavy duffel bag down Grosvenor Avenue, I thought about Tommy and realised I was looking forward to seeing him again, to hanging out together in Oxford. I even found myself wishing it could be just the two of us, having a nice weekend, having fun, without the complications of the others being there.

We had booked into a riverside pub for the night. It seemed a good place for Grace to meet us for lunch as there were outdoor tables with views, and the menu wasn't pricey.

I was the first to arrive and, since it was too early to check into my room, I ordered a coffee and sat in the sunshine, watching the ducks on the river. As soon as he got there, Tommy came and found me. It was good to see his smile and be hugged firmly and capably.

'Right,' he said, settling on the wooden bench seat opposite, 'before the others arrive, what do you and me need to catch up on? How's it going: work, the boyfriend, your health, everything?'

'It's all fine,' I told him. 'Still moving in with Dan this weekend like I'd planned.'

'So you're going ahead with that? You're sure it's the right move?'

'No,' I admitted, 'but I think it's worth a try.'

Tommy was looking at me searchingly, holding me in the blue dazzle of his eyes. 'You're not exactly making it sound like you're madly in love.'

I shrugged because people make such a big deal out of being in love but it never guarantees anything, as he surely knew. 'I'm going to give it a few months and if it doesn't work out then it won't be the end of the world.'

Shaking his head, Tommy seemed as if he was about to launch into an argument but then, glancing over my shoulder, he smiled a welcome instead.

'Fiona, hi,' he called, holding up an arm to attract her attention.

Moments later Fiona was standing beside us, looking stylish in indigo jeans and a light merino scarf arranged round her neck in that artful way I never seem to manage. She was a little breathless, as if she had been walking quickly.

'Has Grace not arrived yet?' she asked.

Tommy checked his watch. 'She shouldn't be long.'

Fiona was paler than usual and I noticed her hands were trembling.

'Are you feeling OK?' I asked.

'Not brilliant,' she admitted. 'I woke with a headache. Often it goes away but this isn't one of those good days.'

'Yeah, I know about those headaches,' said Tommy.

'Do you take anything?' Fiona wondered.

'Nah.' He grimaced. 'More pills, I don't think so.'

'Me neither. Sometimes I do find a peppermint tea helps; at least that's what I tell myself.'

'Sit down then while I go and order you one,' offered Tommy.

When Grace arrived she found us sharing a pot of herbal tea and reading the menu. She was also smartly put together, but even so she looked flustered. This must have been a difficult lunch for her to get ready for.

'Have you been here long?' she asked. 'I'm not late am I?'

'Not at all.' Tommy sprang from his stool and squeezed her into a hug.

I embraced her too, more stiffly and awkwardly, feeling dwarfed as she towered over me. Then it was Fiona's turn. She may not have been feeling great but this was a woman who had been properly schooled in good manners. Taking

Grace's hands in hers, she brushed cheeks, then stood back, smiled warmly and admired her cream blazer.

'It's so beautifully cut,' she said. 'Where did you find it?'

'It's only a chain store buy.' Grace brushed at the fabric with her fingers, dismissively. 'Nothing special at all.'

'My mother always said a good blazer could take you anywhere,' said Fiona, settling back onto the bench, and with an easy gesture suggesting Grace should sit beside her. 'Those classic pieces are so reliable.'

'I wear this one all the time,' said Grace. 'Actually I had it on the last time we met, in Westminster Abbey. I'm so sorry about that day, I don't know what came over me.'

'No more apologies.' Fiona held up her hands. 'I think we all had a shock, but it's best forgotten now.'

Reading over the menus, making decisions about what we wanted and ordering our food kept us occupied for a short while. After that Fiona continued to lead the conversation. She asked about Jamie, looked at photographs of him, talked about her illness and how grateful she was for those extra years of easy breaths, offered more thanks for the gift she had been given.

'When I took that first big lungful of air, it took me by surprise. I couldn't believe I didn't need my oxygen anymore. It's impossible for me to ever thank you enough. I don't even know how to begin.'

'It's Jamie who deserves the thanks,' said Grace, gruffly.

'I know that.' Fiona hesitated, as if unsure of the right thing to say for once. 'I thank him all the time, actually. I've been having conversations with Jamie ever since my transplant ... Does that seem strange?'

'Not to me; I do the same.' There were tears welling in Grace's eyes. 'I wonder does Jamie hear us?'

'I like to think so,' said Fiona. 'I hope he's up there somewhere, seeing all the good he has done.'

It felt like the air was thickening with emotion, just as it had in Westminster Abbey, and I was shy of another distressing scene right here in the pub garden with people all around us eating their lunches.

'Isn't it great that we're all together?' I interrupted, with forced cheerfulness. 'When Grace asked for my help, I never imagined a day like this. I wasn't sure if I'd find anyone at all.'

Tommy suggested some alcohol-free bubbles so we could make a toast and, when everyone agreed, he went back to the bar and fetched it. Then we raised our glasses, clinking them together awkwardly, murmuring 'cheers then' and 'here's to Jamie' and 'to us'.

At least it seemed like Grace was pulling herself together. 'What about the others?' she wondered. 'Has anyone else contacted you since the article you did?'

'Not so far,' I admitted. 'Still, it's not too late, those stories stay up online pretty much forever so there's always a chance someone might get in touch.'

'I hope so,' she said. 'I want to meet everyone.'

Fiona gave her a concerned glance. 'This seems very important to you.'

'Yes, it is.'

'Can I ask you why?'

'It was just an idea at first but then . . .' Grace's eyes passed over our faces, as she reached into her memories. 'I always wanted a big family, you see, lots of children. But my ex-husband, he was a waste of space, selfish and lazy. Even Jamie was too much responsibility for him. After he left there was just the two of us and I was happy with my little family, I didn't want any more. Then on that last night, when he was being kept alive by machines, and I made the decision to give away his organs, I felt so lost. There were other people there: my brother Tim, coordinators from the transplant team, nurses, but in a way it seemed like just Jamie and me still. I don't know if I realised I was never going to see him again.'

Tears were running down her face and she let them fall. There was no packet of tissues pulled from her bag; this sadness was too much to hold back or hide.

'That's how it often is,' Fiona said, very softly. 'I've never stopped expecting to see the people I've lost, and it's been years for me too.'

Grace turned to her, seeming grateful. 'I thought it would get better in time but it hasn't. Every year the anniversaries, his birthday, Christmas, the day Jamie died. You're supposed to move on with your life, heal, that's what they always say isn't it, but not me. I've stayed in the same place, stuck.'

'Oh dear,' Fiona said. 'I'm so sorry ...'

'My brother has this theory that everything happens for a reason. But what reason could there be for a young boy to die just when he was about to start living his life? When I read that article in the newspaper and then met Vivi, I thought maybe if I met you all, found out what you've made of your lives ...'

Right then, with Grace weeping and Fiona trying not to, was the moment the waiter chose to appear with our meals. The food looked good, but none of us wanted to eat. We pushed it around our plates as the river flowed by and the swans drifted past.

'You are the closest I can ever be to Jamie now,' said Grace, putting down her fork. 'I've heard his heart beat and I can see his lungs are breathing and I know his kidney is working.'

'I'm going to keep searching for the others,' I promised her. 'I won't give up.'

'Thank you.' Grace smiled at me. 'I need to know they deserve the miracle they got, that Jamie's life wasn't wasted. Perhaps then it will start to seem like there was some sort of reason for everything that happened.'

Grace

They are walking together alongside the river, the four of them in the sunshine and for a moment she is happy. It is such an unfamiliar sensation, this lightness and brightness, that Grace barely recognises it.

When did she last feel this way? It must have been at some point in the days before Jamie died, but they are a blank in her mind. She has tried to remember; she doesn't want to lose any of the time they had together, but they seem to have got lost in the shock, those final precious days.

Grace must have made him breakfast that morning and packed a lunch for him to take to school. Jamie's appetite had been raging as his body did the last of its growing, and she never could seem to get enough food into him. Perhaps the evening before she had helped with his homework, although it had started to get so complicated – maths, computers, art and design – and Jamie didn't seem to need her as much: he was clever. Grace couldn't even remember if they had made any plans for that coming weekend.

Mostly life had gone on being a blank; there was nothing worth remembering. She had signed the donor forms, said a hundred goodbyes, torn herself away from him, and after that, the best she could do was get through each day. She went to work, secretarial jobs mostly and nothing too demanding because she didn't have the concentration. On Sundays she went to her brother Tim's place for lunch, but only because he insisted. It didn't give her much joy to sit there eating roast chicken with his wife and three children – Jamie's younger cousins – trying to find something to chat about that wouldn't lead straight back to him. Talk of school, sports, hobbies, whatever they had been watching on TV, it all reminded Grace of her son, and it was a struggle not to say so.

Now with these people, almost strangers really, strolling along the riverside, she feels a little freer. Fiona wants to know about the boy whose lungs she breathes through. They are walking side by side and she is listening to Grace's stories of the things he used to do. That time he was playing with matches and almost burned down the garden shed. The camping holiday in Cornwall when he tried surfing and the instructor said he was a natural. The cake he baked for their last Mother's Day, carrot with cream cheese icing. She sifts through her memories and tells Fiona stuff she hasn't talked about in years.

Grace realises she is happy, a little, and only for these few moments, but it is a good feeling; she welcomes it.

Vivi

Grace was emotional during that weekend in Oxford but meeting Fiona seemed to spark some brightness in her too. We went for a long walk along the river, through meadows and past rowing teams practising out in their boats, and the pair of them chatted for ages. Then later at dinner, with Tommy and me, Grace told lots of stories about Jamie, mischief he got up to, things he did to make her proud. The tissues were there, ready beside her wine glass; still, some of the memories made her smile.

It was tough for me hearing those stories while Jamie's heart was beating in my chest. When Grace talked about how well he had done at school, told us about the scholarship he won and the plans he had for his future, it was like I had cheated him out of it; I had survived while he died.

'I'm doing all the talking,' she said, after a few glasses of wine, 'when what I really wanted was to get to know you better.'

Tommy started telling her about his kids, his hopes of getting another business up and running some day, and buying a place of his own. He spoke about events he was hoping to compete in, Ironmans and marathons, and how much training they required. Grace nodded, listening intently; and I could tell she was impressed. She thought Tommy deserved her son's kidney; there was no doubt about it.

When he had finished, they both turned my way expectantly, and I couldn't think of anything worth mentioning at all.

'Tell me about why you became a journalist; is it your passion?' Grace wanted to know.

'It was my father's idea,' I explained. 'I've always been good at writing and after I had the transplant, when I was well enough to train for something, he suggested it.'

'Why the *Daily Post* though?' Grace made a face as if the wine she was sipping had turned bitter.

'Only because they gave me an internship, after I did my journalism diploma, then they offered me a trainee job.'

'Do you love it there?'

'I'm not living my dream exactly but it's fine.'

'What is your dream then?' wondered Grace. 'What do you really want from life?'

'I don't know,' I said, my voice faltering, because it felt like my response was important, that she was going to judge me on it. 'To be healthy and happy, just like anyone else.'

'But the *Daily Post* ... a tabloid ... surely you could do better?'

'It's one of the big national newspapers, a lot of people dream of working there,' I argued, defensively.

'You just said it's not your dream,' Grace reminded me. 'You're a talented writer, you've got all this brightness and potential, why waste it?'

My father had said something similar, Imogen too, but hearing it now from the mother of my donor, felt like a gut punch.

'I mean the *Daily Post*.' Grace screwed up her face again. 'It's trashy.'

'It's my job and I'm good at it. Sure I'd love to work on more serious, investigative pieces but so would loads of other people ...'

'That's no reason not to try though, is it? You've got another chance at life; shouldn't you be making the most of it?' Grace wasn't going to let this go. 'I'm sure my Jamie never would have settled for second best.'

Again her words almost winded me.

*

Later on, after she had left, Tommy and I drank hot chocolate together in the bar. The wood fire was blazing because there was a chill in the air and we settled back together on an old Chesterfield, me a little shaky inside after Grace's words had rattled me.

'It was easier when our donor was a stranger, wasn't it?' I said to Tommy, ruefully.

'She gave you a hard time, but she means well.'

'What if she thinks I don't deserve Jamie's heart? What if I'm the one who's the disappointment?' It had been Fiona's worry, now it was mine.

'Don't be silly.' Tommy cupped his hands round the mug of hot chocolate and breathed the steam. 'She'd had a few glasses of wine, that's all.'

'Do you think it's helping her, meeting us?'

'Yeah, I do ... At the very least it's giving her something else to think about.'

'But she seems to feel as if Jamie's life is carrying on in some way through us all.'

'If that makes her feel better, is it an issue?'

'I don't know ... maybe.' Now I understood why Fiona had been so cautious; I was seeing the potential for all sorts of problems. 'What if Grace starts wanting more from us? Say she asks to spend Christmas with you, or join you on holiday or wants to talk to you every single Sunday, become a part of your family. Do you let her interfere in your life? At what point is it OK to say no?'

Tommy's expression was thoughtful. He didn't answer straight away but stared into the fire, at the flames flickering and hissing.

'I suppose it's going to be different for each of us,' he said, eventually. 'Like I wouldn't mind if Grace wanted to come for Christmas, but that may be a bigger deal for you, and that's fine.'

'Christmas I could cope with maybe but I'm not having her come away on holiday with me.'

Tommy laughed and then looked at me sideways. 'So how did you feel about your sister asking me to join you in Italy?'

'That's not the same at all,' I told him. 'I'd love to get to know your kids and hang out with you; it would be fun. But with Grace there's always so much else going on, so much grief and guilt. It's a lot to deal with.'

'Like I said, each of us is different. If all you can manage is to make time for a chat with her every now and then, that's going to be enough.'

'I'm worried that I've put you and Fiona in an awkward position,' I admitted.

At that he smiled again. 'You don't have to worry about me, Vivi, I can look after myself.'

Tommy was such an easy person to be with. Sitting beside him on the battered leather sofa, I thought how lucky we were that Jamie's one undamaged kidney had gone to someone who was so good at kindness. In the glow of the firelight his eyes looked darker and the fine lines around them were softened. I liked being here with him. It was a shame we couldn't stay longer.

'Are you thinking that you really might come to Italy?' I wondered.

'I'd love to but I wasn't sure if your sister was serious about the invitation.'

'She's not someone who says things she doesn't mean.'

'Isn't your boyfriend going?' he wondered.

'Dan? I haven't asked him. He may be there I suppose, but Imogen's not a big fan.'

'What does she think about you moving in with him then?'

'She doesn't know yet . . . I haven't mentioned it,' I admitted.

'Seriously?' Tommy's eyes widened. 'You're moving in with this bloke tomorrow and you haven't told your sister yet?'

'My family likes to interfere in my life,' I explained. 'Sometimes it's easier to do things first then tell them later, once everything is sorted. It saves everyone a lot of worry.'

'I can't imagine that approach working out well for me. Harder when you've got kids though, life is more complicated.'

We were so different, Tommy and I. Our backgrounds, our families, our day-to-day lives, there seemed to be no points where any of it touched and yet we got on so well, I never felt awkward around him; we always had things to talk about.

Both of us were reluctant to say goodnight. I ordered another hot chocolate and Tommy sat with me while I drank it. The bar staff were collecting glasses and cleaning up by the time we started yawning.

'Don't worry about Grace too much,' he told me. 'You may have her son's heart but it's still your life and you get to make your own choices.'

Saying goodnight, I grazed his cheek with a kiss and catching me with a strong arm, Tommy squeezed me into a hug.

'And I'd love to come to Italy,' he said, before heading off to bed. 'If I can make it happen, I'll be there. But don't mention it to Grace, OK? We don't want her feeling left out again.'

After he had gone, I stayed in the bar a while longer, watching the glowing embers of the fire start to settle, as the staff turned the lights off around me. I needed time to let what Grace had said to me settle.

For so long I hadn't bothered making plans for the future; I wasn't sure if I even had one. My way was to take opportunities as they came along, and it had worked out well enough so far; at least I thought so. The guys I met, the job I was offered, they were the easy options at the time and it seemed pointless worrying about where any of it was going to lead.

Now I couldn't shake the idea that I should be aiming

higher and doing better. I wondered if other people thought of me that way, if everyone did, and it wasn't a good thought.

Standing next to Grace always made me seem small, but tonight she had made me feel tiny.

I slept in the next morning and missed several of the trains I could have taken back to London. By the time I made it to Dan's flat he had started opening up the boxes that were stacked in his living room and my belongings were strewn about the place.

'Lots of books,' he said, as I walked in. 'Black clothes, of course, loads of them. Oh, and scented candles.'

'My sister gives those to me,' I told him. 'It's kind of a joke; she knows I think they're ridiculous.'

'But you've kept them.'

'I keep everything she gives me.'

'Where's your real stuff then? Your nice things?' Dan flicked a finger at one of the boxes. 'There's nothing much here.'

'What do you mean, my real stuff?' I assumed he was joking.

'This can't be everything you own. Do you have more belongings stored at your family's place or something?'

'No, this is it.'

I had never talked to Dan in any detail about my parents, only mentioned that they lived in the country. He didn't seem especially interested in hearing more. Now I searched his face, the seed of a thought blooming. He knew it all already; who I was, what my family had.

'Why would you think I own better things than this?'

'Come on Vivi, stop acting coy.' Dan sniffed at a vanilla-scented candle and wrinkled his nose, tossing it back into the box. 'I'm a journalist, my job is to find things out. I wouldn't be much good if I hadn't worked out by now who your mother and father are.'

'Does everyone at work know?'

'Probably.' He shrugged then nodded. 'Yeah, obviously ... and we've all been wondering why you're slumming it with us. Shouldn't you be too busy having fun with all that money?'

'I don't have any money, Dan.'

'Yeah right.'

'My parents are wealthy, it's true, but they're giving it to charity, not me.'

'They're hardly going to give it all away, are they?'

'I assume so, but I don't really know.'

This is exactly why I don't talk about my family. People make assumptions, and it changes the way they feel about you. Some are envious, some like you less for it, others like you more. I wasn't entirely sure yet which category Dan was falling into.

'So sorry but no secret riches,' I said, lightly. 'What you see is what you get, just a lot of books and candles.'

I began closing up the boxes nearest to me. There seemed no rush to start unpacking.

'Damn, and I was going to suggest somewhere really flash for an early dinner.' Dan treated me to his boyish smile; the one that is pretty much irresistible. 'If there's no platinum card then I suppose we're just having the usual curry.'

'Curry would be fine,' I told him. 'I'll pay if you like.'

At the local Indian place we ordered our favourite dishes – butter chicken, lamb biryani and lots of naan bread – and talked about the usual stuff. A big story one of our competitors had broken over the weekend, how there were going to be questions in the morning over who had missed it, and someone was bound to get a roasting but hopefully not him. For a while it was like nothing had altered.

Then he started on what people were saying about me. How the business writer reckoned people as rich as my parents found that their money grew far faster than they could ever give it away. How the editor wondered why I wasn't making a lot more use of my contacts. And how no one could understand why I didn't have a cooler apartment, a nice car, a better handbag, fancier clothes.

I listened and didn't say much at the time but all night long, lying in bed, I replayed those conversations in my head. How was I going to face the people at work who thought of me as some rich kid playing at being a journalist? And more importantly, was this the reason for Dan asking me to live with him? I turned my head on the pillow. The street lights shining through his thin curtains were bright enough for me to make out his face, eyes closed, lips pursed in a gentle snore, fair hair messy. I knew him well enough to be pretty certain. The money had changed everything, like it always did. That was what Dan liked; not me.

I lay there, wide awake, listening to my heartbeat, but its steady rhythm didn't soothe me. As daylight broke and before Dan's alarm went off, I rolled out of bed, shoved everything back in my duffle bag and slipped out of the flat without waking him. I would have to come back later for my boxes, or better still, send someone. For now there was only one place I wanted to be.

Imogen was still in her dressing gown, the furry Bugs Bunny one with ears. I smelt coffee as she opened the front door and heard Peppa Pig playing loudly.

'Vivi, why are you here ... what's wrong?' She stepped aside so I could haul my bag inside.

'I seem to be homeless,' I told her.

'What? You moved out of the bedsit?'

'Yeah ... although actually there's more to it than that.'

'Come and get some coffee, tell me what's going on. Are you OK?' She stared into my face. 'You're not really, are you?'

'No,' I admitted. 'I need a place to stay.'

'Vivi, you can stay here as long as you like. The girls will be thrilled ... So am I.'

My sister took my bag and put it down on the hallway floor. She pulled me into a hug. 'But what's the story, how are you homeless?'

'I gave notice on my flat and moved in with Dan.'

'Shit, you didn't.'

'Yeah, and you won't be surprised to hear it was a huge mistake.'

She didn't ask for all the details. Nor did she bother mentioning that she had told me so. Instead Imogen gave me coffee made by her fancy machine, and slices of toasted sourdough bread pasted with honey.

'One more thing,' I said, filling my mouth with crunch and sweetness. 'I may need to borrow some cash because it looks like I'm quitting my job too.'

'Truly, you've resigned?'

'Not yet but I'm going to. I can't go back to that place.'

Imogen cheered. She jumped up and down on the spot so energetically the bunny ears on her dressing gown flapped around. 'Farah, Darya, come here,' she yelled. 'Your Auntie Vivi is moving in with us!'

She was still dancing around the kitchen as the girls came running in to find out what all the fuss was about. 'Good news, Aunt Vivi's left her awful job and her unsuitable boyfriend,' she told them, 'and now we're all going to Italy together!'

Biting into the only slightly burnt toast, I shook my head at her.

For once I decided to let the money be useful. I asked my father to send one of his assistants to pick up my stuff from Dan's place. I let him top up my bank account and have his lawyer draft a resignation letter, making it clear I was owed so much annual leave that I wouldn't be returning to the

Daily Post to work out my month's notice. The money made escaping easier, and I tried not to mind about taking it.

Over the next few days there were several messages from workmates wondering why I had disappeared and I replied telling them the same thing; that I was taking time out to spend with my family. With Dan it was trickier. At first he tried to charm me, then he became angry. His final text, most likely composed after a long night at the pub, said I was a heartless bitch and he wasn't going to miss me.

Imogen laughed wryly when she read that one. 'Pun intended I assume?'

'Let's hope so.'

I didn't admit to her that I missed my job, or that without it I wasn't sure who I was any more. I didn't say I missed Dan too, that I felt small and crushed with disappointment. At night, sleepless in bed, I listened to the clock ticking loudly in the hallway as more time passed that I wasn't doing anything great with, and fought down the panic.

But I didn't tell any of that to Imogen. Every morning she and the girls stampeded into my room and woke me by bouncing on my bed, as happy to find me there as they had been the morning before. They pulled me into the play of their days: finger-painting and duck feeding, fort building and cake baking; games where we hid from each other, hunted for treasure, followed the leader. There seemed no end to the fun my sister dreamed up for us all.

She told me every day how pleased she was to have me there. 'As much as I love the little terrors, it's a relief to get some grown-up conversation,' she said as we watched them on swings at the park, or eating ice cream covered in sprinkles, or cooing over the lambs at a petting zoo.

The trouble was, this was Imogen's life, not mine. As welcome as she and her family had made me, everything about it felt borrowed.

It was Tommy I talked to about that, on Skype and

FaceTime calls, made quietly from my room with the door shut later in the evening once everyone's kids were in bed. I was starting to depend on it, Tommy's soft Liverpool accent coming from my phone or laptop, his smile ending my day, his words making it all seem a little better.

'It's like I've failed at everything,' I told him.

He laughed, dryly. 'Ah yeah, I know that feeling. It's crappy.'

'What should I do now? Find a new job ... look for another boyfriend?'

'You're going on holiday soon, aren't you?' he said. 'Why do you have to do anything? Just take it easy while you can. You must be looking forward to it. Lazing in the sunshine, swimming in the sea, eating delicious food.'

Lately I had been mostly looking backwards. All I could see were the missteps taken.

'It will be good to get away,' I told Tommy, because that at least was true.

'Enjoy the summer, Vivi. Eat well, get lots of exercise, be healthy.' He ended the call with the words he often said. 'Look after your heart, OK?'

20 June 2017

Find Vivi's transplant twins

The search is on, can you help?
By Daily Post senior editor Dan Parker

As MPs continue to back Vivi's Law, bringing hope to thousands of sick people on the transplant waiting lists, the woman who gave her name to the campaign is searching for the others whose lives were saved by her donor, tragic teen Jamie McGraw.

Vivi was given the gift of life when she received Jamie's heart. Meeting the recipients of his lungs and kidney has been a dream come true. Now Vivi longs to track down the strangers who have her donor's liver, pancreas and corneas, so they too can form a special bond.

Sign up to support Vivi's Law, read her story and contact us if you think you can help with any information that might lead to her finding her transplant twins.

Vivi

I left it all behind: the newspaper that was still publishing headlines about me even though I didn't work there any more, the man who only wanted me for my family's money, the woman who made me feel I wasn't good enough. I got on a plane and ran away to a house in Italy.

Villa Rosa was so beautiful, just being there made me smile. It was far more than I had ever imagined. What the photographs hadn't shown was how its pink walls glowed in the early evening light. It was decorated mostly in soft whites and sea blues, but the hallway was painted with a bright fresco and the garden was insane. This wasn't the sort of landscaping my mother favoured, with its careful palette of texture and colour. Whoever owned these terraces stepping down towards the rocky coastline preferred allowing plants to be themselves. Bougainvillea rioted over a pergola, wisteria festooned the terrace, caper bushes spread over the rock walls. There was a grove of citrus and an orchard of pomegranates, and a pathway twisting down steeply to a saltwater pool that nature had carved from the rocks.

'This is the best place to spend a summer,' declared Imogen, who had insisted on dumping our bags and going exploring immediately.

She was all for swimming straight away but then we dipped our toes into the sea and found it was much too cold.

'Let's choose our bedrooms and unpack instead,' I suggested.

'OK, and we'll eat dinner out tonight.' Imogen stretched up her arms and tilted her face to the sun. 'I'm so happy to be here. It's such a relief to be away from London.'

My sister must have caught me looking at her questioningly, because she shrugged and smiled. 'So many people, so much noise, Hamid working too hard, everybody stressed. It's nice to escape that, isn't it?'

As we headed back up the steep path we glimpsed pine martens scurrying along the branches of the trees, and the song of the cicadas was almost deafening. The hill was hard work for me, a reminder that I really did need to work on my fitness, to look after my heart as Tommy kept saying. Reaching the top, the villa came into view again, pretty with its soft pink walls and weathered terracotta roof, all the life of the garden springing up around it. At times I have these moments when gratitude sort of breaks over me like a wave and I feel swamped by it. I had one right then, walking with my sister and her girls, looking at all that beauty and realising I was only there to see it because a kid called Jamie never could be.

'Imagine if I'd missed all this,' I said, standing still to catch my breath for a few seconds.

Imogen misunderstood me. 'Yes, I'm so glad you dumped Dan and walked out of your job.'

'I didn't walk, I ran as fast as possible. I feel bad about that now; I should have handled things better.'

'Dan was wrong for you; so was the job,' said my sister, dismissively. 'How many people out there are trapped in the wrong situations and wishing they could escape? You actually did it. And you're such a good writer, Vivi. It was a waste of your talent being there. You're better than the *Daily Post*.'

'Maybe.' I wasn't sure if that was true. 'It was a good job, I learnt a lot there.'

'Yeah, sure, but it was definitely time to leave.'

'I could have made a more graceful exit.'

'You're here with me now, that's all I care about,' said

Imogen. 'Remember when we were kids and I wanted to give you my heart. I didn't realise I'd have to be dead for that to happen, I thought we could share.'

Of course, I remembered. My sister had cried when it had been explained to her why her plan wouldn't work

'I still want to share stuff with you Vivi.' She turned and smiled at me. 'I'm really glad you've run away with me.'

My room was small but had its own terrace and once I had settled in I stood out there to watch the sky blush as the sun set. Behind us were mountains, above so much sky, and the air smelt of wood smoke. If there was anywhere better to be I couldn't think of it.

'Aunt Vivi, hurry up, we're hungry,' Farah called from the courtyard below.

I peered down to see her waiting with Darya, both clutching little beaded bags, spruced up and ready for their evening out, and I actually felt my heart swell with love for them.

'I'm coming now, you little tyrants,' I called back

We drove down to the marina and ate at a restaurant right at the water's edge with a view of the sleek yachts and old fishing boats. At the height of the holiday season this place was going to be jammed but now, with summer so new, we had the place nearly to ourselves. The girls played at being grown-ups, sipping mineral water from wine glasses, while Imogen chose too many dishes from the menu.

'Ordering food might be my superpower,' she said, as a dazed waiter retreated to the kitchen.

'Do you think they have Deliveroo around here,' I teased.

'They most definitely don't have a McDonald's,' she shot back. 'But don't worry, I've thought of everything. I have the phone number of a local woman who will come and cook for us. Not every night, because I'm sure even we can boil up a bit of pasta, but definitely once our house guests start arriving.'

'Who exactly have you invited?' I asked. 'The usual crowd?'

Like me, Imogen doesn't have a lot of friends, only a few she was at school with and has never let go, a handful she made at work. Our childhood was so intense, and particularly when I wasn't well, which was quite a lot of the time, it was all about each other.

'My lot have been crap,' Imogen told me, sounding disappointed. 'They've all got their own stuff going on this summer so I don't think any of them will come. What about you?'

'Just Tommy, hopefully he'll come.'

'It was me that invited him,' she pointed out. 'So you need to choose someone else. Why don't we get the whole transplant family together – Tommy, Grace and Fiona?'

'I've been wondering about Fiona. She'd go crazy for the garden here, but I've got a feeling she doesn't have the budget for foreign holidays.'

'Ask her,' my sister encouraged. 'What about Grace?'

'Not her,' I said, quickly.

'Are you sure? I'd like to meet her,' said Imogen.

'I expect you will at some point, but not now.'

There was guilt at the thought of Grace being left out, but there was always some guilt now where she was concerned. And after that night in Oxford, when she had said words that were still stinging, I was wary of letting her too far into my life. She certainly wasn't coming to this place.

Imogen didn't try to argue. 'Whatever you want is fine by me.'

Waiters appeared bringing dishes filled with the kind of food we would never cook ourselves. Plates of gnocchi cloaked in sharp pecorino cheese and crisply fried sweet peppers, a piping hot dish of baked aubergines and melting mozzarella, spiced sausage on a velvety sauce of peas, a salad of nutty roasted fennel tossed with fronds of wild rocket, lots of grassy olive oil and lemon. For dessert the girls shared a sugary tart of goat's cheese topped with berries, and my sister had a final glass of wine. It was such a feast, and sitting there, grazing on it and staring out at the bay, it felt like my spine was softening and my shoulders were lowering. Running away had been a good thing.

'What shall we do tomorrow?' I asked my sister.

'Absolutely nothing.'

I thought about the mozzarella place. We had driven past a turn-off for it on our way down earlier but uncharacteristically Imogen hadn't been keen on a detour. It was tempting to forget about it now, stop searching and just relax. But I was much too curious for that. I wanted to find out if this guy Lynda had suggested that I look up really was connected to us; if he had a tiny piece of Jamie.

'You're not planning to go chasing round the country after more transplant twins are you?' asked Imogen, guessing at my thoughts.

'Not tomorrow, but I'll need to sooner or later. It's my only lead and probably it won't come to anything.'

'Can't you leave it then? Just hang out here with us?'

'I'm going to do that too,' I promised. 'There'll be plenty of hanging out, loads and loads.'

I managed a couple of very quiet weeks. Each day I woke early and took some exercise, thinking of how pleased Tommy would be with me, as I walked the hills, my heart pounding aerobically in my chest. By the time I got back to the villa the sun was taking the edge off the early morning chill and we could sit outside to drink our coffee and eat buttery slices of toasted crusty bread.

Imogen didn't want to explore much further afield than the nearest town. Fortunately, Triento appeared to have most of the things we needed. Places selling cheese and olive oil hidden in the twists and turns of its lanes, a bustling market in the piazza, a bar for more coffee and, of course, *gelato* for the girls. We went there most days to browse through shops selling leather goods, linen and over-priced scarves, or people-watch the locals.

On the hill above us was a statue, a huge white one of Christ the Redeemer with his arms outstretched, and there were churches everywhere you turned, graceful old buildings made of honey-coloured stone.

'It's adorable,' Imogen decided, and I waited for her to get tired of losing herself in its narrow, steep streets or dawdling in its piazza, but it didn't happen.

While I wasn't bored exactly, it was a struggle to power down. In the afternoons when Imogen pulled out a lounger and dozed in the sunshine, I played with the girls and tried to shake off the sense that there was something more important I ought to be doing. Darya and Farah were obsessed with the green lizards that darted over the rock walls, and their favourite game was trying to catch one, although neither of them was quick enough. They also loved helping me pick wildflowers and arrange them in jars. And lots of time was spent looking at the brightly painted tiles on the terrace, with me making up stories about the scenes they showed – happy peasants dancing with garlands of flowers. There wasn't a lot else for little kids to do and Imogen seemed to have forgotten she was meant to be the maker of fun. This was a version of my sister I had never seen before – a quieter, sleepier, slower Imogen.

When the cook appeared to make us Sunday lunch I was pleased to find she spoke decent English. She was an older woman who drove through the open gates of Villa Rosa in a dented old Fiat, announcing her arrival by hooting loudly on the horn.

'I am Raffaella,' she said, loading us with the baskets of food she had brought and leading the way to the kitchen, where she moved around with the ease of someone who had cooked there before.

Soon she had us all involved, the girls rolling out pasta dough, me chopping vegetables, Imogen in charge of stirring the sauces as they began simmering on the stove.

If she hadn't been wearing such a shapeless black dress, if her hair wasn't grey and caught in the messiest of top-knots, and her olive skin so lined, then Raffaella might have been beautiful. Actually she was almost beautiful still. There was something in the way she held herself, she moved like a younger woman.

Catching my eye, she smiled. 'I worked here in this house, when I was about your age, cleaning and cooking.'

I imagined what she must have been like then, with her skin taut over those high cheekbones, her lips fuller, her hair loose, glossy and dark. Getting old was cruel, but it was better than the alternative, and if I ever got to see myself like that, with grey hair and deep wrinkles, then I'd be very happy.

'Didn't you used to be a chef in a restaurant?' Imogen asked her. 'That's what I was told.'

'Yes, I was that too and now I am retired. But if someone asks and I am in the mood then I cook.'

'I hope you'll be in the mood a lot this summer,' said Imogen. 'My sister and I are terrible cooks.'

'You are doing fine I think.' Raffaella smiled, and I realised she hadn't so much as touched a knife or a wooden spoon so far. Her version of cooking seemed to be purely supervisory.

Actually, it was fun to be involved. With the girls, I made pasta parcels stuffed with piquant blue cheese and walnuts. The results were misshapen and variously sized but Raffaella only shrugged and said they would taste as good. She kept Imogen busy cooking a deep red soup of fish, spiced sausage and tomatoes, laughing as she splattered the sauce up the walls with a clumsy flick of her spoon. A quick salad and a basket of bread, Parmesan was grated, and lunch was almost ready.

Raffaella found the pasta bowls and pulled out four ready to serve the ravioli.

'We'll need another,' said my sister. 'You're going to join us, aren't you?'

'No, no, I don't want to intrude on your lunch,' said Raffaella. 'I will clean up and then leave you to enjoy it.'

Imogen wouldn't hear of it. 'But we'd really love the company. And you can tell us all about the area. The best places to visit, where to shop, the nicest beaches.'

Shrugging, Raffaella took out another bowl. '*Va bene*, there is plenty of food, so why not. And I can always eat.'

In fact, she talked as much as ate. Raffaella told us some of the history of Villa Rosa and the people who had lived there. The artist who painted the fresco on the walls; the rich family who let it go to ruin and the landscape designer who restored the place but was too busy creating gardens in Australia right now to enjoy it.

'We're lucky being able to lease the place for so long,' said Imogen.

'You won't get bored? Nothing much happens in Triento.'

'God no, we just want to relax, don't we Vivi?'

I nodded my agreement although I already felt restless. Beautiful as it was, I couldn't imagine what we would do with an entire summer here. Imogen's vision of filling Villa Rosa with lots of friends didn't seem like it was going to happen. My parents had so much gooding to do they were only planning to come for a short time. Who knew when Hamid would get away from work to join us? That only left Tommy if he managed to make it, and Fiona if I decided to ask her.

'I have lived here my whole life,' said Raffaella. 'I am used to the pace of life. If I visit a city I come home exhausted and sleep for a week.'

I glanced towards the sheltered corner of the terrace that my sister had now colonised. Her sun lounger was surrounded by the rubble of her belongings: hat, book, espadrilles, empty water jug, towel, pile of magazines, tube of sun cream, nail file, hair clip. It seemed like she had been dozing there on and off for days.

'You will get a chance to relax here,' continued Raffaella. 'And swim a lot, take walks, play on the beach, eat good food ...'

'You'll come and cook for us again?' asked Imogen, hopefully.

'I am sure I can be persuaded.'

Perhaps it was because we were eating outside in the sunshine with all that colour around us – the blue of sea and sky, the pinks of the house and bougainvillea, the lilac wisteria flowers – but every mouthful of that food tasted ridiculously good. I thought about the things I ate at home, the greasy meat sandwiches from McDonald's, the endless stodgy scones, and I tasted the ravioli we had made together and looked at the people I loved, heads bent to their own plates; and the gratitude lapped over me again, as warm as the sun on my skin.

I had all this, I was lucky, and the knowledge made me remember Grace, who seemed to have nothing at all. Hadn't I made her a promise? And now mustn't she be thinking I was letting her down?

'I may go to that mozzarella place in the morning,' I told Imogen, seeing her instantly frown.

'Really? I thought you'd decided to leave it.'

Raffaella glanced from my sister's face to mine. 'Which mozzarella place?' she asked.

'It's called Masseria Perretti,' I told her.

'Ah yes, it is famous. The produce is organic, extremely high quality.' Raffaella began telling us about some big cheese scandal. Local gangsters illegally dumping toxic waste in the Campania countryside, contaminated mozzarella, farms where the buffalo were mistreated, so many problems, such a disaster. 'But at Masseria Perretti the mozzarella is pure and the animals are cared for. It is a nice place to go.'

Imogen was still frowning but at her own thoughts apparently, not Raffaella's words. 'Does this mean you're going to take the car and strand us here for the whole day on our own?'

'You could come too. Apparently there's a tour. It might be fun.'

'This is fun, being here together, eating and hanging out.'

'It's just a day, Imogen.'

'I know but …'

'I will take you in my car,' offered Raffaella. 'I would like to eat good mozzarella.'

The thought of all those dents in her old Fiat made me dubious about that.

'What if we all went together? A road trip with cheese,' I suggested.

'There is *gelato* there too, a leather shop, a restaurant for lunch,' added Raffaella. 'And we could meet the buffalo, perhaps.'

The girls had so many questions. Were buffalo big and scary? What flavour was the *gelato*? Would there be a playground?

'I am not sure about that,' Raffaella told them. 'It is a long time since I was there. But the gelato will be very good and they may let you pat the buffalo.'

The girls squealed at that: they wanted to pat farm animals and eat sweet treats. Could they come too please, they chorused.

'OK then.' With a sigh, Imogen relented. 'Tomorrow morning, yeah?'

'It's a plan,' I agreed, my brain already ticking over with thoughts. Would my cheese maker be there and if so, how would I recognise him? I was craving another win now, for myself as much as Grace. I wanted to prove I was good at this.

We finished our meal with wafer-thin almond biscuits and tiny cups of strong, sweet espresso. Then my sister trailed back to her sun lounger, lay down and draped a sarong over herself, immediately closing her eyes.

The girls and I helped clear up the dishes and tidy the kitchen. We had made a spectacular mess so it was a long job, and Imogen barely seemed to move in all that time.

'She needs her rest, I think,' said Raffaella, following my glance out of the window. 'Having young children is tiring.'

But the thing is she didn't need to rest, not usually. Imogen was like my mother, all fizzy energy and purpose. She never took an impromptu nap or lazed away an afternoon, not unless she was sick, and that hardly ever happened.

'You should rest too,' Raffaella urged. 'There must be more of those lounger chairs.'

'I can't find any,' I told her.

'Have you tried the small room at the far end of the house? That is where everything is stored – outdoor chairs, games for the children.'

I knew the room she meant. We had found it the first day when we were exploring and not been able to open the door.

'That room is locked,' I told her. 'I think it's full of stuff the owner doesn't want us to use.'

Raffaella insisted she would find the key then began searching along shelves and putting her hands into the jugs that lined them, refusing to give up, even though I tried to tell her it didn't matter and we would manage without whatever was hidden behind the locked door. At last she smiled, 'Yes, here it is.'

Unlocking the room revealed a treasure trove. Lots to please the girls: old-fashioned games and inflatables, as well as a ladder for when we wanted to swim off the rocks, a collection of outdoor chairs and a gas barbecue.

'All the things you need for your summer here,' said Raffaella, helping me drag the chairs out into the sunshine.

She stayed a while longer, watching me play energetic games with the girls, closing her eyes for a quiet doze as the afternoon wore on.

'Why is everyone asleep?' Farah whispered. 'It's daytime.'

'Wouldn't you and Darya like a nap too?' I asked, hopefully, because I was starting to puff.

My nieces shook their heads, claiming they were too old now to sleep during the day. What they wanted was for everyone to get up and join their fun.

'Grown-ups need lots of rests,' I told them. 'I'm going to have one right now actually.'

When you have a borrowed heart, it doesn't always act the way you think it will. In the mornings mine can feel like it is taking a while to get up to speed. And sometimes I need to stop whatever I am doing and give it a chance to find a resting rhythm.

My nieces have strong hearts – at least I hope so. They murmured with disappointment to see me flopping down on the lounger I had positioned next to their mother.

'You guys keep playing and I'll watch,' I told them.

Without me they quickly lost interest and started some game of their own invention amid the fallen bougainvillea flowers. Keeping an eye on them, I let my mind drift back to the search for Jamie's recipients. If this cheese maker did turn out to be one of us, wouldn't it be great to bring everyone together, here in this beautiful place, far away from the extra complication of Grace. The more I thought about the idea, the greater its appeal.

'Hey Imogen,' I woke my sister.

She squinted at me. 'Hmm?'

'Are you really OK with Tommy coming? And what about me asking Fiona?'

'Hell yeah, we need lots of people, let's have a party.'

'I thought you wanted to relax though.'

'Not for the whole summer, only right now.' She yawned

widely. 'And maybe for a few more days to be fair.'

'Imogen, is everything all right?' I wondered. 'It's not like you to want to sleep all the time.'

She rolled over onto her side and gave me a look. 'Show me a mother of young kids who isn't exhausted ...' she began, and right on cue the game my nieces were playing turned noisy. There was some squealing then Darya started crying and Farah proclaimed that it wasn't her fault.

'See what I mean?' said Imogen, throwing a sarong over her head as Darya's sobbing grew louder.

Raffaella was awake and out of her chair before I could get up and see to the girls. I don't know what she said, but the crying quietened surprisingly fast.

'That woman is great,' said Imogen. 'Do you think we can keep her?'

'We should definitely try,' I agreed.

My sister made a bit more effort after that. She climbed out of the sun lounger and made us all follow her down to the tiny beach, where we paddled in the waves foaming gently onto the pebbles and tried to convince ourselves the water was almost warm enough for proper swimming. Watching Imogen skipping and splashing, she seemed more herself again and I felt relieved. I didn't want my sister to ever be anything else.

Vivi

A text from Dan arrived the next morning while we were eating breakfast and getting ready for our outing to the mozzarella place. He said I should contact him as soon as possible as there was something he needed to tell me. Shoving my phone in my bag, I ignored it, even when it started ringing. I didn't want my old life invading this one, and surely there was nothing I needed to hear from him.

Eventually, after a lot of last toilet visits and a frantic gathering of all the items that were needed to accompany us, we piled into the car and drove down to the marina to pick up Raffaella. It was tricky finding her place and then she insisted on inviting us in for coffee and the girls were fascinated by the tiny house, which had been built into a wall of rock at the harbour's edge and was filled with all sorts of trinkets. So we were running late by the time we set off and I didn't look at my phone again until we were on the road, Imogen driving.

I had missed three calls from Dan and there was another text, insisting I was going to want to hear what he had to say. By now I was more intrigued: this had to be something interesting. But there was no mobile phone coverage so I couldn't call him anyway.

'Is someone trying to get hold of you?' asked Imogen, glancing at my screen then back at the twisting road. 'Is it mum and dad?'

'No, only unsuitable Dan.'

'Oh yeah, what does he want?'

'I don't know but he's being very insistent.'

In the back seat with the girls, Raffaella was dozing already. She was wearing a bright red dress today and had paired it with an orange scarf and tamed her hair.

'It might be a work thing,' I lowered my voice so as not to wake her. 'Something about the Vivi's Law campaign.'

'Are they still calling it that?'

'Apparently, yes.' I hadn't been able to stop myself checking the *Daily Post* website several times a day to see whose bylines were appearing and what they were writing about.

'You're not going to talk to him, are you?' Imogen was focused on the road. We were behind a truck that was too wide for the sharp bends and progressing frustratingly slowly. 'The man's a shit.'

I glanced at the back seat. Raffaella was definitely asleep and the girls absorbed in a game they were playing on their iPad.

'A complete shit,' I agreed. Still I was too curious to resist calling as soon as I had enough reception for my phone and a few moments alone.

We had taken the scenic route around a narrow coast road that was carved into the sides of the mountains. There were views across a glittering expanse of sea and the blues of distant land and sky, but there were also hairpin bends and less space than was needed for two cars to pass safely. Imogen didn't seem fazed. Her style of driving had come into its own here, and she hooted her horn like a local as she rounded every tight corner.

Eventually the road widened and turned towards the mountains. We passed fields of red poppies and picturesque old towns with crumbling ochre buildings and domed churches. The girls grew restless, waking Raffaella, who provided entertainment by teaching them an Italian children's song. Imogen and I joined in and the car was filled with the sound of our tuneless singing as it sped northwards.

*

Masseria Perretti was on the plains of Campania. Burly water buffalo grazed in fields and waded in man-made wallows, and there was a collection of scarred old buildings painted in pinks just like Villa Rosa, surrounded by neatly laid-out vegetable gardens and climbing with jasmine.

The girls wanted to eat *gelato* and explore but I was impatient to get on a tour and see if I could spot my cheese maker. All I knew was that he was English; not much to go on but Lynda had been breaking the rules to give me even that.

As we waited for a tour I was jittery, wondering how I would find a way to approach this guy, what I would say and how he might reply. There was a chance he wasn't here at all and this had been a wasted trip.

'English?' asked the tour guide, a small, dark woman in tight jeans and silver hoop earrings. 'I can take you in ten minutes, OK? There is a café to have a quick coffee or you could go to the leather store and see the beautiful handbags.'

'Handbags?' Imogen perked up immediately. 'Show me the way.'

My sister collects bags. It is her great extravagance. She has shelves of vintage ones and several with designer labels that Hamid has given her over the years, and she treats them like precious pieces of art.

'Ah, my happy place,' she sighed softly, as we found a room lined with a glass display case filled with leather bags in tawny shades, every shape and size, all of them gorgeous. 'I've lost you, haven't I?'

I had seen that expression before on Imogen's face – she was distracted by large totes with wide shoulder straps, drawstring pouches and mini satchels. Soon an assistant would be unlocking glass cases, so she could examine every pocket and clasp, touch the leather for softness; smell it too, probably. This was a process that was likely to take a while and would almost certainly end with a purchase.

The girls were clamouring for their *gelato* and Raffaella suggested she should take them, since she wanted to eat mozzarella, not watch it being made. That meant I returned on my own for the tour, but the guide didn't seem to mind.

She walked me past covered yards filled with dozing buffalo, talking slightly too fast in thickly accented English so I caught only about half of what she said. We stopped to pat one she claimed was friendly and touch its impressive curved horns. Then we left the smell of hot animals and drying dung behind and headed to the dairy. I had imagined we would be allowed inside but the guide explained this was impossible because of hygiene rules, so instead we could look through a large viewing window.

The room beyond the window was filled with large stainless steel vats. Four men inside were dressed identically in white Wellington boots, overalls and cap.

Again, the guide was talking much too quickly. She mentioned curds and whey, something about pH levels and stretching cheese, and I tried to follow while through the window all that the men seemed to be doing was hosing down equipment and the floor.

'I am sorry but they have finished making mozzarella for the day. This happens earlier in the morning,' the guide told me. 'A pity as it is very interesting to watch.'

I stared at the men, who were laughing together, sharing a joke. Was one of them my guy?

'If they have finished, could I meet one of the cheese makers?' I asked. 'Is there somebody who speaks good English perhaps?'

'This is not a part of the tour,' the guide said, firmly. 'It will not be possible.'

All those years on the *Daily Post* have taught me to never take no for an answer, so I tried a different tack. 'The thing is I'm a newspaper journalist and I've realised this could be a really interesting story.'

'You ought to have called in advance and let me know. I have a press pack with all the information and, of course, I could have arranged an interview and for you to see the cheese makers at work.' The tour guide sounded irritated.

'I'm in Italy on holiday, not for my job,' I told her. 'But I'm keen on writing about this place so it would help if there was someone I could talk to.'

She rolled her eyes, not bothering to hide her exasperation. 'I will see what I can do but there is only one cheese maker who speaks fluent English and he may not be available.'

'Thanks, I appreciate it.'

'I suppose you will want a tasting as well?'

I wondered if the milk they used was pasteurised. It didn't seem very likely and I'm not supposed to eat anything remotely risky.

The tour guide nodded resignedly. '*Va bene*. Wait there and I will see what I can do.'

She was gone for quite a while. While I was waiting, the white-clad men finished scrubbing out the dairy and one by one disappeared from view. I was beginning to think my chances of meeting a cheese maker were slim when the guide returned.

'Stefano will be with you in a moment. I am going back to the office now to find a press pack, OK?'

'Thanks so much.'

'No problem,' she said, in the tone of someone whose patience had been tested.

It was another ten minutes before Stefano appeared. He hadn't been among the men I had seen working in the dairy, although he was dressed the same way. Even in baggy white overalls and a cap he looked gorgeous. His skin was smooth caramel, his eyes and hair a true black and the angles of his face faultless.

'Hello. You are the journalist?' There was no trace of an Italian accent.

'That's right, I'm Vivi Palmer,' I said, slightly thrown by this vision.

'Stefano Perretti.' He took my outstretched hand and shook it firmly. 'How can I help you?'

I could hardly ask if he'd ever had an organ transplant so instead continued with my story, saying I wanted to interview him about the masseria. Stefano looked unimpressed, shaking his head as I spoke.

'How can you write a good article without seeing the mozzarella being made. That's the most important part, surely?' he said.

'Yes, it would have been preferable but I understand I'm too late so perhaps I can buy you a coffee and we'll sit down and talk about it instead,' I suggested.

'Are you are staying somewhere nearby?' he asked. 'Could you come back?'

'It's a bit of a drive away, further south.'

'But you could return?'

'Yes, I expect so,' I nodded my agreement. 'Even so, if you had time for a quick chat now that would be ...'

My sister was calling my name and I turned to see her approaching, large shopping bags in both her hands.

'Did you do the tour yet?' she called and, getting a proper look at Stefano, added, 'Oh hello ... who is this?'

'Stefano Perretti.' He held out his hand to her.

'He's the cheese maker I'm hoping to interview,' I explained.

'Right ... hi. I'm Vivi's sister Imogen.' She took his hand and smiled. 'How lovely to meet you.'

'We were about to head off to have a chat actually,' I told her. 'We'll be twenty minutes or so.'

'Aren't you going to join us for lunch?' asked Imogen. 'The girls and Raffaella are already at the restaurant.'

'No, I really need to do this interview ...'

'Eat with your family,' Stefano urged. 'Come back to the

masseria another day then I can spend more time with you and we will do things properly. Your article will be better if you see what we do here.'

I was impatient to know if he was one of Jamie's recipients and ready to do this now. 'I really think I …'

'You should definitely come back.' Imogen said, quickly. 'It would be crazy not to do things properly.'

'When would you like me to return then? Tomorrow?' I asked, not prepared to put it off any longer.

'You must come very early, OK?' said Stefano.

'Great that's all arranged then.' My sister smiled. 'Let's go and have some lunch, shall we? Stefano, would you like to join us? No? You're sure? Vivi will see you tomorrow then.'

I wondered if this really was my guy, if a part of him matched a part of me, and I found myself hoping so. Grace couldn't be disappointed in Stefano, surely?

'He's absolutely gorgeous,' breathed Imogen, as we headed towards the restaurant together. 'How is it even possible to look that good?'

'No idea,' I admitted. 'It seems unreal.'

'You think he's a part of your transplant family? He doesn't look like he's had a moment of illness in his life.'

'I know, but that doesn't necessarily mean anything.'

'It would be great if he was one of your donor twins, wouldn't it?' Imogen said, enthusiastically. 'Then you'd have to get to know him better.'

I laughed at that. 'Weren't you trying to matchmake me with Tommy the other day?'

'I'm open-minded,' said Imogen. 'So long as we keep you away from unsuitable Dan.'

Yes, Dan. I wondered if he was still trying to get hold of me. Quickly checking my phone, I saw there had been no more texts or missed calls. Hopefully after lunch there would be an opportunity to slip away from the others and see what he had wanted earlier.

'Dan and me are completely over,' I promised my sister.
'You've said that before.'
'This time I mean it.'
'I hope so.'

Raffaella was waiting at a table with the girls and had gone ahead and ordered. As we sat down, food was being ferried over: slices of dense bread and little dishes of butter, one dotted with herbs, another with flecks of sea salt.

Next, they brought us glossy balls of mozzarella along with a salad of basil-laced tomatoes and a plate of red peppers sautéed with anchovies and cubes of crisp oily bread.

'That looks good,' I said.

'Should you though?' worried Imogen. 'Be careful, the mozzarella might be on the banned list.'

'It's fine, stop worrying.'

'We don't want you getting sick.'

I was so incredibly over being careful, tired of missing out. What sort of a life was this if I had to be wary of cheese?

'Everyone breaks the rules now and then,' I told Imogen, reaching for the platter.

The mozzarella shredded into soft layers as I cut into it, milky brine oozing out. It tasted salty and pleasantly sour. Nothing terrible happened when I ate it and, although I could sense Imogen's disapproval, it didn't stop me taking another helping. There was a limit to how careful anyone could be.

Afterwards there was coffee and some sort of dessert involving buffalo yoghurt that I skipped but the girls seemed to adore.

'So how many handbags did you buy?' I asked my sister.

'Only two ... and one is for you.'

'Thanks, but you shouldn't have. I don't need a bag.'

'It's not about need,' argued Imogen. 'And anyway, yes you do and I enjoyed getting it for you.'

She gave me a little cross-body satchel. It was exactly the kind of thing I would have chosen for myself if I were the sort of person who ever bought things.

'Thanks, I do love it,' I said, watching as she started to transfer the clutter I carry: pen, notebook, lipstick, keys, sunglasses, phone and, of course, medications.

While she was distracted arranging every item in the ideal pocket and compartment, I took the opportunity to send Dan a quick message.

Sorry, been busy with family. Can I call you later?

His reply came back a little later.

No problem I've sorted it myself.

Sorted what?

Nothing for you to worry about.

The girls were hoping to see the buffalo and Raffaella wanted to buy mozzarella, so the afternoon had worn away by the time we started the drive back to Villa Rosa. Imogen had been drinking wine with lunch which meant I had to take a turn at driving.

My focus needed to be on the road, with its unexpected twists and motorbikes buzzing past. I couldn't afford to let thoughts of Dan distract me. All the same, as Imogen dozed or stared out of the window, and the girls chatted to Raffaella, my mind kept returning to him.

I tried calling when we got back to the house but Dan didn't pick up. After that I went straight through to his voicemail a couple of times and left messages telling him I was free to talk whenever he wanted to call me.

It was early evening by the time my phone did ping with a

message, and it was from Tommy rather than Dan. He was wondering if I might be able to FaceTime him.

I positioned my phone to show off the view, propping it against a pile of books, and called him straight away. It was good to see his face, looking back at me from England.

'I've got some good news,' he told me, smiling.

'Please tell me it's that you're coming to Italy soon.'

'Actually yes, I've managed to get the time off work and talked my ex-wife into letting the kids come with me, so I'm all set.'

'That's so great. I think you're going to love it here.'

I told him all about the house and gardens, the steep path that led directly down to the sea, about Raffaella and her great cooking, and the places we could take his children for *gelato*.

'Sounds great. For once I can't wait for school holidays to start,' he said.

Tommy had a second piece of news. Finally, we had received the official confirmation that we shared a donor.

'Fiona called me,' he explained. 'She got the letter this morning.'

We had been convinced of the link between us but to have it confirmed seemed important to Grace, and when Fiona took over negotiations with the Donor Records Department she had proceeded with quiet determination. Tommy and I supplied her with letters, and she got busy making phone calls. And now we had it in black and white: we were a family of sorts. There was no doubt about it.

'Good on Fiona,' I said. 'I knew she'd do it.'

'Yeah, she's a funny old thing, isn't she? Do you think she overwhelmed them with perfect manners and greetings cards?'

I laughed. 'Probably. I've been thinking about inviting her to come over to Italy too. What do you reckon?'

'I'm sure she'd love to be asked.'

I heard another phone ringing and saw Tommy glance away from his screen. 'That's my landline,' he said. 'I think it's Grace. I'd better get it.'

I made him promise to let me know the minute he booked some flights and then let him go. A few minutes later I was busy poking round in the fridge, trying to see if there was enough to put together for a decent supper, sure that Raffaella would have turned sausages and tomatoes into something delicious but not convinced I had the skill, when another message came from him.

Big news from Grace!

What? FaceTime me again.

I'm still on the phone to her. Stand by though.

I paced impatiently, wondering what was going on. It seemed ages before the next message.

This is going to take a while, sorry.

What's going on?

A second long, frustrating gap then at last:

Another of Jamie's recipients has turned up!

What? Who?

Hang on a minute.

By the time Tommy was free to FaceTime me again the sun was setting and I was desperate to hear what had happened.

'Well?' I said, impatiently. 'Tell me. What's the story?'

'Your old boyfriend, that editor guy Dan, he contacted Grace this afternoon and said the newspaper had heard from a liver transplant recipient who thinks Jamie might be her donor. Grace is pretty excited and wants to meet the girl. I was trying to persuade her to wait until one of us can go with her.'

'Who is this girl?'

'All Grace knows is that her name is Emerald.'

'Dan will have more details than that,' I said, confidently. 'If he's not sharing them it's because he thinks he'll get a story out of this.'

'Will you call him?'

'I'll give it a try.'

'Is this going to be difficult?' asked Tommy. 'Would you prefer me to talk to him?'

'No, it's OK.'

'Tell me what he says. I'm going to call Grace back now and let her know you're on the case.'

Dan was avoiding my calls. I knew his phone was always glued to his hand, so when there was no response, I was sure he had to be playing games. Sooner or later he would pick up. I made dinner in the meantime, a messy sauce of tomato and sausage with pasta shells and lots of grated cheese. Farah and Darya seemed to like it but then they were used to my sister's cooking.

'We need to get Raffaella back,' said Imogen, tasting it. 'I mean this is fine and everything, but she's so brilliant with the girls, isn't she? Do you think we could get her to move in?'

'I suspect not.'

'I'm going to ask her anyway,' said Imogen.

She was thrilled to hear that Tommy was definitely coming and began animatedly making plans: places we could visit, a go-cart track his son might like, a pizzeria a little way down the coast that had some great reviews online, a kayaking trip through the caves. As she was chatting away, I flicked a quick text to Dan:

Call me!

Keen to speak to me now are you?

Dan, just call me OK?

I'm in the pub, give me a sec.

I imagined him with the usual crowd, with their pints of beer and packets of crisps, and their voices growing louder as the night wore on. There was a part of me that missed all that, even if I was better off out of it.

When my phone rang, I went outside to answer. It was a clear and starry evening. The warm air smelt of jasmine and the tall white statue of Christ on the mountain was illuminated so it seemed to be hanging above us.

'Dan, hi,' I said.

'Ah Vivi Palmer, how's life for the rich and famous?' He sounded less than sober.

'Yeah, fine.'

'I suppose you want to know all about Emerald, lovely Emerald with the lovely liver.'

'Who is she? How did you guys find her?'

'Emerald found us, because she's a *Daily Post* reader. She saw a piece I put up the other day. Says she wasn't sure at first but the dates and details match up so I reckon she's one of your crew.'

'What's she like?' I sat down on a low bench beneath the bougainvillea-covered pergola.

'Pretty little thing ... I'm having a drink with her at the moment actually.'

'Whatever.' I wasn't sure if I believed him.

'I don't need your help any more,' he continued. 'The donor mum, Grace, got back to me the minute she heard about Emerald.'

'Leave Grace alone please, Dan. She doesn't want to be involved in any stories.'

'They can't wait to meet each other.'

'Dan ...'

I tried to argue but Dan was always going to do whatever made for the best headlines. If I didn't do something then he would be orchestrating a meeting between Grace and Emerald, with a reporter and photographer intruding, and probably someone shooting video too. A circus like that wouldn't be fair on either of them.

Saying a brusque goodbye, I had a moment of panic because I was too far away to be useful. Then, with relief, I remembered I had Tommy and Fiona to turn to.

The messages I sent found Tommy cooking dinner for his kids and Fiona at home in London. Our texts pinged back and forth, with me impressing on them both how determined Dan would be to turn this to the *Daily Post's* advantage. They agreed that Grace shouldn't have to deal with it alone but Tommy was too busy with work to help out. That only left Fiona, who was too well schooled in doing the right thing to refuse to be at Grace's side when she met Emerald, although it must have been the last thing she wanted.

Yes of course I'll be there. That makes sense. And don't worry, I can make sure the newspaper isn't involved.

Reading her reply, thinking of her sitting alone in her little flat and what a good woman she was, made me want to do something good for her too. Since Tommy was coming to Villa Rosa now, why didn't she too? The three of us could spend time together, in this beautiful place, and really get to know each other.

I sent another quick message asking, and there was a gap of time before her reply, a refusal, polite and wistful. Fiona told me it had been so long since she was abroad last, she wasn't even sure if her passport was up to date, or if her doctor would clear her to travel at this point.

Could you check on all that? We have a big house here and I know my sister would welcome you.

She had only ever been to Italy once before, a trip with her mother years ago when they were both well. She would love to visit again, but perhaps not right at the moment.

What a lovely idea though, Vivi. How kind of you to think of me.

My offer must have seemed too casual and impulsive to be genuinely meant. Even if she was tempted to come, women like Fiona have a certain way of doing things. It involves handwritten notes, at the very least a phone call, rather than a quick, careless message.

I went back inside, and found my sister in the kitchen drinking wine amidst the mess of the evening meal: crumbs of bread and crackers, knives sticking out of jars of Nutella and jam, tomato sauce-splattered plates and pans, lots of glasses with an inch of fruit juice left in them.

She wasn't a domestic goddess but she did know how to make people feel welcome. I explained about Fiona and before long she had her phone in her hand, was topping up her wine glass and asking for the number.

Filling the sink with sudsy hot water, I started on the dishes and listened to her side of the conversation.

'Hello, it's Imogen Palmer here. Vivi tells me she's asked you to come and stay. I do hope you will because I'm longing to meet you.'

She was silent for a moment and I pictured Fiona at the other end of the line, surprised, but hopefully delighted, that Imogen was following up with a proper invitation.

'Tommy is coming,' my sister was saying. 'Vivi will give you all the dates. It would be so lovely to have you both here together. I think that's what she is hoping for.'

Imogen was quiet again, then I heard her telling Fiona how much space we had at Villa Rosa, a garden so rambling you could almost get lost in it, plenty of peaceful places to escape and be alone in.

'We've found a local woman who comes and makes wonderful meals so you won't have to put up with too much of Vivi's cooking.' Imogen listened, then laughed. 'Yes, both terrible I'm afraid, neither of us has a clue, we're a culinary disaster zone. Do you cook? Oh, you do. Well, in that case we need you here ... we really do ... Yes, you certainly could help in the kitchen, that would be wonderful.'

My sister was persuasive; she could win over almost anyone. She finished the call having extracted a promise from Fiona that she would give it some serious thought, perhaps even look into flights.

And so it seemed there were going to be more people here soon, more dishes to wash, more chaos, more fun: two of my transplant twins were coming to Villa Rosa.

I finished the clean-up and joined my sister in a glass of wine to celebrate.

Vivi

It was easier going places alone. I woke early, ate quickly and was out the door with the minimum of fuss. The solo drive back to Masseria Perretti wasn't a lot of fun though. At least I was familiar with the route but it was a challenge negotiating the hairpins and the rough-walled tunnels blasted through rock.

I couldn't be late, as Stefano was waiting for me. He was planning to show me how mozzarella was made and I was going to tell him things he didn't know about himself. I would have been feeling nervously excited, even without the other motorists that kept overtaking me on perilous stretches of road.

The sun was only just beginning to warm the day when I pulled through the gates of the masseria. There were already a few cars parked, and even a tour bus today, and people were gathered in the café, some drinking coffee.

I went directly to the dairy and peered through the viewing window, hoping to spot Stefano. There he was in his white cap and overalls. I raised my hand to attract his attention.

This time they did allow me into the dairy. They dressed me in white overalls and boots, and Stefano made me scrub my hands and tuck my hair beneath some sort of hideous shower cap.

'Hygiene is very important,' he said, his tone businesslike. 'Please don't touch anything. You are here only to observe.'

It was hot in that room full of stainless steel vats and white-clad men; too hot to breathe almost.

'How do you stand working in here?' I asked Stefano.

He shrugged. 'I'm used to it. And we need the heat to make the cheese.'

Stefano began telling me about all the things that could affect the character of the mozzarella – the weather, the season, even the age of the animal. Most important of all was having the correct pH level for stretching and kneading the lumpy-looking curds in hot water and transforming them into smooth mozzarella.

He showed me how to shape the cheese by hand into differently-sized balls and plaits, and gave me some to taste, fresh and with a hint of sourness, soft and creamy.

'Mozzarella is the only cheese to be made this way,' said Stefano. 'And ours is the best of the best. Make sure you mention that in your article.'

I was keen to get out of that stifling room and strip off the unflattering overalls. Sweat was sheening my face and the white rubber boots they had given me were too big, so my feet slopped about in them, which made walking on the wet floors tricky. Stefano seemed to think I must be fascinated though. He was showing me a machine that produced perfectly shaped balls of cheese, popping them through small holes and into cooling brine. He was telling me that to make good mozzarella you had to be constantly on the move, looking and checking. That it was like the work of a sculptor and that cheese makers couldn't wear gloves because they would lose the sensitivity they needed to really feel the cheese, to know it intimately, to make it perfect.

'Amazing,' I said, because it was obvious he expected it. 'And is this your family's masseria? Is that why you became a cheese maker?'

'It belongs to my uncle. He trained me.'

'So you are Italian but you were brought up in England?'

'Yes.' Stefano didn't seem particularly interested in talking about himself.

'How long have you been here?' I persisted.

'A while now.'

'And how much time did it take to learn to make mozzarella?'

'I'm still learning.'

There was something about him that seemed cool and untouchable, a sort of stoniness to Stefano's good looks. I had a feeling he wasn't warming to me, which always makes me try even harder to win a person over.

'Would you show me round the rest of the masseria?' I was impatient now to get out of the unflattering overalls and the heat. 'I'd love to see the buffalo again.'

'Of course,' he agreed. 'The buffalo are where the cheese begins. There is still a lot I need to tell you for your article.'

Outside, the breeze felt fresh and welcoming. Stefano had made a joke that I might like to keep the shower cap as a souvenir of my visit, so he wasn't entirely lacking a sense of humour. And in the brighter morning light I could see traces of imperfection in his face, the finest lines around his eyes and beside his ears.

As we headed towards the covered yards to visit the buffalo, I wondered how I was going to tackle the real reason I was here.

'We're completely organic,' he was telling me. 'We've had none of the problems with mozzarella becoming contaminated. Our pasture is clean and our herd is treated well. We're an example of how things can be done, and hopefully others will follow us in the future.'

He led me to a pen where they kept the baby buffalo, which nuzzled into me and licked my hands like puppies. Overcome by how adorable they were, I wished Farah and Darya were with me. Stefano was still talking, telling me that they grew fond of the best buffalo and gave them names; all facts he was hoping I would include in my imaginary story. How could I stop that stream of words and ask him the questions I really wanted answered?

It wasn't until we were in the café and Stefano had ordered some mozzarella to be brought for me to taste that I found a way into the conversation.

'The milk it's made from isn't pasteurised is it?' I asked.

'No, of course not.'

'Strictly speaking, I'm not really meant to eat the cheese then. I'm a heart transplant patient you see, so am supposed to stick to a really safe diet like a pregnant woman. It's because of all the immune-suppressants I take.'

Stefano shrugged as if he couldn't be less interested. 'The dairy is perfectly clean and we use boiling hot water to make the mozzarella. I think you are safe to eat it.'

There were no questions about my transplant, no details about his own health, and I began to wonder if I had got it wrong and Lynda was only ever suggesting the masseria as an interesting place to visit.

'This mozzarella has spent a little longer in the brine so the taste is saltier,' Stefano explained. 'But it is important to eat it very fresh. Often when you get it at home in the supermarket it's been frozen and the texture is rubbery, the flavour bland ... terrible. Never buy cheese like that in London.'

'Is that where you're from originally, London?' I wondered, sensing an opportunity.

'I grew up there. But we used to come here every summer to stay with my uncle.'

'And you always wanted to be a cheese maker?'

'Not always,' he said.

'How did you end up doing it then?'

'This was the direction that life took me in,' he said, shortly.

I tried my tactic of leaving a moment's silence in the hope he would fill it with more details, but Stefano was going to be harder work than that.

'So, what happened?' I asked. 'What made you start training?'

'This is not for your article?'

'It can be off the record if you prefer.'

'When I was younger I had some health problems. A very severe form of an eye condition called keratoconus. I used it as an excuse not to try too hard at anything. I was lucky that my uncle had this place and offered to train me, to teach me this craft and give me a future.'

Finally, I was onto something. 'And your eyes? Did you have a corneal transplant?'

'That's right.' He nodded. 'Now with contact lenses my vision is good. I'm very lucky, as I said.'

'We've both had transplants then,' I said, trying to sound meaningful.

'Yes, we have that in common,' he agreed. 'A coincidence, although I think your surgery was much more difficult than mine.'

'Perhaps not such a coincidence ... and we may have more in common than you think.'

He frowned slightly 'What do you mean?'

Stefano listened to the news that I suspected we shared a donor, with an expression I couldn't read. Then he leaned back in his chair and said rather coldly, 'Is this why you've come? The article ... that was just a story, a lie?'

'No, I'd definitely like to write something,' I said, hastily.

'How did you find me?'

'A tip-off after a newspaper article I wrote, a phone call,' I said, another half-truth, but there was no way he would ever know that.

'I still don't understand why you would come all the way here.'

And so I explained. About the Vivi's Law campaign, about Grace, Fiona and Tommy, about Jamie, even about this woman, Emerald, that I hadn't met yet. It was a long explanation and he listened without a word, his silence unsettling.

'The plan is to bring us all together, everyone who was helped when Jamie died.'

'Why, though?' Stefano asked. 'What's the point in it?'

'To begin with it was purely for his mother Grace, because she wanted to meet everyone. Then I got interested too. If I'm right then we're all connected, aren't we?'

'We're strangers,' argued Stefano, his tone still chilly. 'I'm very sorry this woman lost her son but it has nothing to do with me. I was on the list for a transplant. If it hadn't been his corneas then it would have been someone else's.'

I was thrown by his attitude. 'Look, if you prefer not to have contact with Grace, that's fine. I haven't even mentioned you to her yet. But you may like a chance to meet the rest of us. Tommy is coming over to stay, possibly Fiona too.'

Stefano gave me a look, as if he was sizing me up and trying to decide if he trusted me.

'Why don't I give you my contact details, then you can think about it and decide?' I suggested.

'Sure, why don't you do that?' he agreed.

My old business card was useless now so I tore out a page from my notebook and wrote down my mobile number and email address.

'We're staying at a villa further south on the Basilicata coast. Maybe you could come for lunch on your day off?' I suggested.

Stefano glanced at my scrawled note then tucked it in his shirt pocket. 'If I decide to come then I'll be in touch.'

As he walked me back to my car he talked about how busy he was at the masseria, how there were things going on that demanded his attention and his days off were rare. My sense was that I wouldn't be seeing him again.

Getting into the car, I wound down a window to say goodbye then reversed out of the parking space. Stefano was holding up his hand in an awkward wave as I headed away.

Checking my rear-view mirror before I turned onto the road, I saw he was still there, watching.

Again, I had the feeling that I could have handled things better. As I drove and the plains of Campania gave way to the mountains of Basilicata, I replayed the meeting in my mind.

Stopping at a bar for coffee, I logged on to the free wi-fi and looked up his eye condition. Keratoconus: it sounded pretty serious. I imagined a younger version of Stefano, his vision blurring as his corneas thinned. Perhaps he had some of the symptoms the website listed, pain or sensitivity to light; obviously he must have worried about losing his sight. How had it been for him? I couldn't help feeling curious. There were so many questions I should have asked.

At Villa Rosa there had been a rainstorm. Clouds hung low over the mountains but the sun had broken through and Imogen was basking, her skin golden, her bikini tiny. There was a resinous smell of warm pine and the sweetness of jasmine, there was birdsong and the sound of my nieces playing happily, and there were all the many blues of sea and sky. Yes, it was a pity about my unfriendly cheese maker but at least I was here. And in England there was Emerald now and perhaps Grace might be content with that and I could stop searching and focus on enjoying the summer like my sister wanted.

Imogen stirred at the sound of my footsteps. 'Hey, you're back. I thought I heard the car. How did it go?'

'Not great,' I admitted.

'Doesn't he want to join your transplant family?'

'Apparently not.'

'Cheer up; I have better news. I heard back from your friend Fiona and she'd be delighted to accept my kind invitation to come and stay. She's going ahead and booking her flights so it's going to start feeling like a proper house party round here at last. We can get to know these people properly, do it together.'

Imogen seemed pleased, and so was I. With the weather hotter now I envisaged long, lazy days, swimming off the rocks beneath the house, lunches in the garden, maybe some adventures beyond it. There were no worries about us getting on; with Fiona and Tommy I couldn't imagine a problem. Stefano though: he was an entirely different proposition.

'I asked the cheese maker to lunch,' I told my sister. 'He didn't seem wildly excited but you never know, he may come.'

Imogen reached for her sun cream and began rubbing it into her tanned legs. 'What did you think of him? Tell me absolutely everything.'

And so I did, the way I pretty much always have, and my sister leaned back on her lounger, closed her eyes against the sun and heard me.

'You're going to hear from him again, I'm sure of it,' she said when I had finished. 'You just took him by surprise, that's all, and it's a lot to take in. He'll go away and think about it and won't be able to resist getting in touch. You'll see.'

I didn't share her confidence. Stefano hadn't been interested; he didn't feel connected. I could only assume that it must feel more intimate to have another person's heart deep inside your body than their corneas on the surface of your eyes.

Stefano

What Stefano loves most about making cheese is that there is a right way to do things and a right moment. Follow the rules and the result will be perfect, time after time; it is that precise. Walking back to the dairy, to make sure it has been cleaned thoroughly after the morning's work, he wishes all of life could be the same.

The stainless steel equipment has been scrubbed carefully. Stefano is sure the men he works with are reliable but makes the usual checks because his uncle has been clear how important it is. He was the one who trained Stefano, taking him on as an irresponsible boy, teaching him at his side and showing him how to do better. It is hot, hard work in the dairy and his uncle is glad to have stepped aside now, trusting Stefano to take over and continue his legacy.

Stefano finishes up, locks the door and goes to strip off his overalls, then takes a long shower before heading to the office. There is always work to do. Orders to process, winter feed to source for the buffalo, staff to manage. The masseria is a large operation and often Stefano works late into the evening to be sure every aspect of it is running smoothly.

He makes a habit of breaking for lunch with his uncle, no matter how busy he might be. It is the main meal of their day. They eat a plate of pasta, some fish or meat, a few vegetables, and a little cheese and fruit as they talk through anything that might be on Stefano's mind, problems with the business or his personal life.

Today he will speak about the girl who came, Vivi, and her belief they are connected. There will be several ways to handle the situation, but only one that is right, and Stefano wants to choose correctly.

His uncle is a good sounding board and Stefano has learned to be guided by his advice. This is a man who had the courage to do things differently, to rise above the corruption all around him and create a mozzarella to be proud of. They may only be glossy balls of cheese but they are perfect, time after time, and that is what matters.

He can often predict what his uncle will say about things, he knows him well enough now. But this girl arriving with her invented story then claiming that her heart matched his eyes, this is different; there is no way of guessing.

What Stefano loves about making cheese is the certainty. The buffalo milk may be different depending on the season, the timing may change, but get everything right and the result is consistently perfect. He sees no reason why the rest of life shouldn't be that way.

Vivi

Tommy arrived on a pristine July day. Everything about Villa Rosa seemed brighter and better – the pinks of the bougainvillea more intense, the sea so many shades of blue and drifts of delicious smells from the kitchen where Raffaella was cooking up something for lunch.

'Wow,' he said. 'I mean, just wow.'

'Isn't it perfect?' Imogen was smiling. She linked an arm through his and toured him around the gardens and down towards the sea before showing him the bedrooms she had picked out for him and his children. Ava and Liam were pale and serious-looking, older than my nieces, not an obvious pick for friends, and I found myself hoping they weren't going to be bored in this house with no wi-fi or television. But then, in the easy way kids do, they found things in common and before long were chasing lizards together along the grey stone walls and trying to climb a tree to pick lemons.

Lunch was served at the long table beneath the pergola, Raffaella bringing out a baked pasta dish studded with meatballs, and a salad of red peppers she had charred and blistered over the barbecue.

As we ate, Tommy updated me on the latest from home. Mostly he talked about Emerald: what a hit she had been with Grace, how they were planning to catch up again very soon, Fiona's impression, and his own from a couple of Skype chats. He said Emerald was charming and funny, smart, very pretty, really great; I was going to love her, apparently.

I tried to chase away the sense that an unwelcome guest

had joined my party. This was good news and hardly a reason for me to feel niggled.

'She's looking forward to meeting you,' said Tommy. 'I thought we could call her together at some point so I can introduce you. Maybe later on this afternoon?'

'Later on we're going swimming,' Imogen told him. 'There's a ladder you can help us carry down that fits onto the rocks. And then we're having drinks at one of the little bars down by the marina, then afterwards we'll come back here to picnic on leftovers and play cards.'

'Emerald will have to wait then,' agreed Tommy.

'I'm sure she won't mind,' I told him.

The sea was calm and inviting. Tommy jumped in first, swimming towards an opening in the rocks, cutting fiercely through the water, his stroke strong. His kids followed and I stayed behind with my sister, wrangling inflatables and coaxing Farah and Darya to jump in with us.

We didn't swim far, instead wallowing in the natural pool walled by rocks where it was shallow enough to be safe. With small silver fish jumping and a grotto to explore, it was ridiculously perfect.

'Did you get a look at Tommy?' Imogen asked me.

When he had stripped off down to his Speedos and put on swimming goggles there had been a few moments with his body on show before he plunged into the sea.

'Those arms ... like a work of art ... I hope it stays hot while he's here so he hardly ever wears clothes.'

I laughed, glancing at the girls on their lilos, too busy looking out for octopus and other scary creatures to be paying us any attention.

'He's very fit,' I told her.

'You don't say.'

'I'm confused. Aren't you supposed to be matchmaking me with the cheese guy now?'

'Changed my mind,' said Imogen. 'I'm back on Tommy again.'

'It doesn't matter anyway. Two transplant recipents getting together is a terrible idea.'

'Why?'

'We've got parts of the same person inside us, for a start.'

The water was starting to feel cold, numbing my fingers and toes, and I wanted to be back standing on the warm rocks in the sunshine with a towel wrapped round me. Kicking out, I swam away from her, steering Darya's lilo with one hand.

Imogen swam after me. 'You might be taking this whole transplant family thing too seriously. Tommy and you aren't actually related.'

I hauled myself up the ladder, reaching down to help Darya follow. 'He's my friend, that's all.'

'He's a good guy, and it's hard to find them out there.'

'I'm not looking for a good guy.'

'Don't be ridiculous, of course you are.'

My sister didn't get it and that was fine. This was no time to remind her that borrowed hearts don't last forever; I might not be around to see Farah and Darya grow up; we weren't going to get old together, she and I. That knowledge was always there, and even though I tried to keep it small and safe at the back of my mind, how could it not affect the way I lived the shorter life I was bound to have?

'Good guys aren't my style,' I said to Imogen.

Tommy was heading back now; he and his kids were racing, and I could tell he was slowing his front crawl so they would reach the ladder first. I saw the lean muscles ripple in his tattooed arms as he pulled himself out of the water and watched as he rubbed a beach towel over his wet body, knowing Imogen was doing the same.

*

Strictly speaking I don't drink much; I'm not really meant to. But it was cocktail hour in a seaside bar in Italy and everyone else seemed to be sipping on Aperol Spritz. For once I wanted what they were having.

Tommy ordered a sparkling mineral water and didn't touch any of the salty snacks the waiter brought out. He was always so disciplined. I don't think I'd ever seen him consume anything unhealthy.

'I'm only having one,' I told him, tasting the refreshing bright orange drink with its kick of alcohol. 'Maybe even just half.'

'Hey, I'm not judging you,' he said.

'I'm definitely having two,' declared Imogen, 'so please don't judge me either.'

We were sitting at a table beside the marina. The owner had a puppy, a little white Maltese that he seemed happy to let the children pat and play with. The sun was slowly sinking in the sky, there was Italian pop music playing and next to us a group of old men were gathered beneath a tree playing a card game.

'I feel like I'm in a movie,' said Tommy.

'What sort of movie would it be?' Imogen wondered. 'A romcom?'

'No, a heist drama, with car chases around that terrifying coast road and a lot of speedboats.'

'Oh, I love boats,' said Imogen. 'I think it's possible to hire them here and go on day trips round the coast. Should we do that?'

'I was thinking of taking Ava and Liam on a kayak tour through the grottos.' said Tommy. 'We like to stay active. It's good for the head as well as the body.'

'Kayaking is too energetic for me,' Imogen told him. 'Vivi will go with you though.'

'I might not be able to keep up.'

'Yes, you would,' Tommy assured me. 'The kids aren't

that fast either. Although don't tell them I said that.'

He was lovely as a father. Not overprotective, just attentive enough. He had encouraged Ava and Liam to go into the bar and order their own *gelato*, teaching them the Italian words for 'please' and 'thank you' and when Ava immediately dropped hers down her dress in a great sticky mess, he laughed, cleaned her up quite badly with a couple of serviettes and went back inside to get her another.

'What else would you like to do while you're here?' Imogen was asking him. 'Is there anywhere you particularly want to visit?'

'With the weather like this I'm happy to hang out at the villa, eat good food and get some exercise. Why go anywhere else when the place is so perfect?'

'I agree,' said Imogen. 'Let's just relax together.'

'I really appreciate us being included in your holiday like this,' Tommy told her. 'It's been tough for the kids with my illness and then the split with their mum. This is the nicest thing that's happened to all of us in quite a while.'

'It's nice for me too,' said Imogen.

I wasn't in any hurry to meet Emerald. Things seemed to be going perfectly well without me being involved. But then Liam started playing with his dad's phone and we realised the bar had free wi-fi so there seemed no good reason not to try to FaceTime her.

We propped up the phone against my empty Aperol glass and pulled our chairs closer together. When she didn't respond, Tommy was disappointed.

'That's a shame. But we're only an hour ahead of the UK here, right? Maybe she's still working.'

'Let's try again another evening,' I suggested. 'Shouldn't we be heading back to the villa now?'

Imogen wasn't about to be deprived of her second cocktail. And the service was so slow that by the time the drink arrived another twenty minutes had passed and Tommy was trying Emerald again.

This time her face filled the screen. Green eyes, wide smile, strawberry blonde hair and a soft Irish lilt. 'Hey Tom-Tom, are you in Italy?'

'Yeah, and I've got someone here for you to meet. This is Vivi.'

'Hi Emerald.' I waved at the phone. 'Nice to see you at last.'

'Oh my gosh, Vivi, amazing to see you too.' She waved back with both her hands. 'It's like I know you already because I've heard so much. Grace talks about you all the time. Isn't she a darling?'

'Have you been seeing a lot of her?'

'We've been spending a bit of time together. I've been trying to find ways to thank her. At the weekend I gave her a makeover. We should have FaceTimed then, she looked gorgeous.'

'It's great that you're hitting it off,' Tommy told her.

'It's so special isn't it? She's showed me loads of pictures of Jamie and we've found all these connections.'

'What sort of connections?' I asked.

'So like, I know this sounds weird but I started cycling after my transplant and eating some of the foods Jamie preferred, even listening to the same music. It's as if his cells inside me are remembering.'

'Which foods?' This was sounding very familiar. 'McDonald's by any chance?'

'No, Walkers salt and vinegar crisps.' She laughed. 'I know, amazing right. But I never touched them before. I always had a sweet tooth. And then there's this dream I started having, about an awful car accident.'

'You think it's Jamie's accident?'

'Maybe ... I don't know. It's really spooky though.'

We chatted for half an hour, Emerald talking about her

liver disease and the shock of being given five years to live when she was only twenty-one. She told me all about her transplant, her job as a hair and make-up artist, her family, her plant-based diet and even her cat. She was charming and funny like everyone had said. There was no reason not to like her.

'Talks a bit doesn't she,' said Imogen when the call finally ended and we were rounding up the kids so we could leave the bar and head home.

'She's really vivacious,' agreed Tommy.

Imogen gave me raised eyebrows but thankfully said nothing. The word my sister used to describe her later was 'ninny' which made me laugh, partly because it was so old-fashioned. It was late by then and Imogen had climbed into bed with me, so we could whisper beneath the covers like we always used to.

'On and on and on about herself … did the ninny ask you a single question? I don't think so,' she said.

'Lots of people are like that,' I argued. 'I get it all the time.'

'And the whole cell memory thing. Walkers salt and vinegar crisps. Seriously?'

'Grace will be loving it,' I told her. 'And actually, there are lots of stories around like that, people taking on the characteristics of their donors; it may really be a thing.'

'Shut up.' Imogen jabbed me in the ribs with her elbow. 'You hated her, I know you did.'

'I didn't hate her.'

'But …'

'I didn't love her either.'

'Do we really want her to join your transplant family?'

'We don't get to choose. She has Jamie's liver, she's a part of it. And if Grace likes her … and Tommy too.'

'You mean Tom-Tom.' Imogen made a choking sound.

'I know, I know.'

'This woman, Fiona, who's coming, she'd better not be a ninny too.'

'She isn't, you'll like her,' I promised.

Imogen snuggled into me, her breathing deepened and soon she was asleep. I listened to her soft snoring, as I lay awake hoping she really was going to like Fiona, that it hadn't been a mistake to invite her.

My transplant family. My sister always rolled her eyes a bit when she said those words. It was getting bigger now. There were more of us surrounding Grace and I hoped that was a good thing.

We hired kayaks the next morning, just Tommy, his kids and me, and with the Mediterranean glassily calm, we explored the rocky coastline. I feared being left behind, because I don't have much stamina, but Tommy hung back and we paddled side by side through a limestone grotto then out the other side to a hidden bay where the water was the same dazzling blue as his eyes.

I didn't want to go much further, in case I struggled on the return, but he was encouraging, climbing out of his kayak to help me through the shallows and taking us out towards the open sea. His kids were racing ahead of us, and I noticed how he didn't call them back or warn them to be careful.

'They'll be fine, they know what they're doing,' he said, then brought his kayak alongside mine and, holding onto each other's paddles, we drifted together in the sunshine, salty-skinned and warm, and it felt good to be alive.

Vivi

I wanted Villa Rosa to show its best face to everyone, so it was disappointing to wake to overcast skies and blustery breezes on the morning of Fiona's arrival. While Tommy drove to the railway station to pick her up, Imogen and I attempted to make a tomato tart for lunch. Mostly we made a mess, covering the kitchen in flour and managing to singe the tart despite trying to remember to check on it every few minutes and see if it was cooked.

'What if we scatter some herbs on the top to cover it up?' Imogen said, examining it. 'Should still taste OK, surely?'

'We're useless,' I told her.

'Yes we are,' my sister agreed, cheerfully. 'I'm going to call Raffaella and see if she'll come over and do dinner. It's short notice but you never know.'

'Fiona can cook,' I reminded her.

'We can't really have our guest slaving in the kitchen on the day she arrives … Maybe tomorrow though.'

As he drove through the gates, Tommy hooted his horn and we all rushed down to the car-parking area to meet them, me hoping my new friend was about to make a good impression.

Fiona looked lovely, of course, in a polka dot shirt, flared linen pants and very cool sunglasses. Stepping out of the car, she was surrounded by curious children and immediately folded into a welcoming hug by my sister. Tommy carried her suitcases up to the house while Imogen and I gave her the official Villa Rosa tour. Fiona was quieter than usual, only saying once or twice how lovely everything was. Standing on the rocks looking down at the sea I was surprised to see tears creeping out from beneath the lenses of her sunglasses and streaking her cheeks.

'Is everything OK?' I asked.

She took off her glasses and started dabbing at her eyes with a linen square she produced from her pocket.

'I'm a little overwhelmed,' she said, shakily. 'Being here, on top of everything you've already done for me, meeting your parents last month, seeing their garden ... it's ... well, I don't know how to thank you properly.'

Fiona had already sent her heartfelt thanks via several messages.

'Like I said, my mother loves taking gardeners around the place. It would have been a treat for her too.'

'She gave me so much of her time. And then your father met up with us and we had a glass of very nice champagne and talked about their charity work.' Fiona turned to my sister. 'And now to invite me here, when I'm a stranger to you, and to give me such a wonderful welcome ...'

'Of course you're welcome.' Imogen took her arm and began steering her back towards the steps. 'You've only just got here; we haven't even started to have fun yet; so many nice things are going to happen.'

'Thank you so much.'

'Let's go and have lunch now shall we? That might not be such a nice thing. Vivi cooked it.'

'Not fair, you can't blame me for the tart.'

'Totally can,' said Imogen. 'I never burn things usually.'

'That's because you never cook,' I pointed out.

'I'm sure lunch will be lovely,' Fiona said as we made the steep, heart-pounding walk up to the house, stopping several times so she could catch her breath.

Even she couldn't find anything nice to say about the tomato tart, which seemed to have shrivelled since we took it out of the oven. She gave it a sympathetic look, as if she felt sorry for it being left in our hands, and murmured, 'Oh dear.'

'I'm sorry,' said Imogen. 'I really wanted us to have a lovely first lunch together. But the food is terrible and the weather's crappy.'

'No, no, I think it's cheering up a little out there,' Fiona reassured her. 'And we can make something else to go with your little tart. Do you have eggs? A frittata is always nice.'

She opened the fridge and soon was wearing an apron and dicing an onion with a chef's skill. It is funny how people are in a kitchen. Raffaella seemed to slow down, chatting as she drifted round, appearing to make hardly any effort and yet somehow producing a delicious meal. Fiona was one of those cooks that cleans up as they go, careful and efficient, briskly productive.

We decided to risk eating outside and so Imogen and I set the table, picking armloads of wildflowers along the roadside to fill the jugs and vases, finding a vintage linen table cloth and green cut-glass tumblers. Fiona laid out the frittata, a salad of leaves from the garden, a salsa of ripe rock melon, some cheese and even our little tart. The sun was shining again and it all looked so lovely that we had to take photos.

Tommy had been for a long morning run and freshened up quickly in the outdoor shower. He came and sat down bare-chested with a towel wrapped round his waist and I avoided catching Imogen's eye, focusing on helping my nieces load their plates with food.

The children didn't stay at the table for long. They ate and went back to their games. But we adults lingered; Fiona fetched a bowl of peaches, Imogen drank wine. We chatted and laughed, and it felt like we were old friends, not people who had been brought together by tragedy and coincidence.

Imogen was sitting back in her chair, taking in the whole scene, glass in her hand, a smile lighting her face. 'Isn't this lovely?'

'It's what you wanted, isn't it?' I said.

'Yes, it is,' she agreed.

'Imogen has been desperate for a proper house party,' I explained to the others. 'So we're grateful you're here to help make it happen.'

'We're the grateful ones,' Tommy said. 'This place is a lot fancier than the caravan park me and the kids usually go to.'

'And I haven't any sort of holiday in so long,' admitted Fiona. 'I was worried about travelling, especially alone: it seemed too risky, with my health; I didn't want to get sick and end up in a strange hospital. But with us all here and in the same boat.' She stopped and cleared her throat. 'Actually, Vivi I feel I owe you an apology. As you know, I had my share of misgivings about you bringing us all together, I thought it was a mistake; but I was wrong. Such good things have happened. So thank you, I'm very glad.'

For the first time in quite a while, it felt like I had got something right. I grinned at Fiona. 'I'm very glad as well.'

Imogen raised the glass in her hand. 'Here's to you guys then, your transplant family.'

'Yours too.' Tommy told her, clinking his sparkling water to her wine. 'You get to be an honorary member.'

'Good, because I hate being left out.' Imogen took a long sip, topped up her glass with more Pinot Grigio and drank from it again.

Tommy was looking at her curiously, as if something had just struck him. 'It must have been tough for you growing up, having a sick little sister,' he remarked.

'Vivi was the one who had it tough. I just had to watch.'

'Watching is never easy though, is it?'

'She's doing well now; all of you are, thanks to that poor kid. So here's to him too.' Imogen raised her glass once again. 'He's what we're all really grateful for.'

Jamie, how could he ever be far from our thoughts, especially when we were together? All of us were silent for a few moments, gathered round that table strewn with the remains of our good lunch, listening to the laughter of the kids playing hide and seek in the garden, smelling jasmine, feeling alive and lucky, and all thanks to him.

The sun came and went that afternoon. Tommy disappeared for what he called a proper swim, Fiona explored the garden, Imogen retreated to her lounger, claiming to be keeping an eye on the kids. Meanwhile I headed off for my usual walk around the cliff path, past other holiday homes and down a long flight of steps to a pebbled beach, where I stopped for a rest and watched the waves breaking on the shore, then home again via a series of oleander-fringed lanes.

As I walked, trying to keep up a decent pace, it was Emerald I thought about – her spooky connections with Jamie, the dream she'd had, all her talk of cell memory. By the time I got back to Villa Rosa I seemed to have worked out what was worrying me. Everything about her was exactly what Grace wanted. I was suspicious of their quick and easy bond.

I had started this, the bringing together of strangers, so it was up to me to make sure it worked out OK. All afternoon a sense of disquiet kept nibbling away at me when everything ought to have been perfect.

Late in the day Raffaella arrived, summoned by my sister to prepare an elaborate dinner. Fiona grabbed an apron to help, insisting she was in heaven. Tommy was playing a noisy card game with the children, Imogen was painting her toes bright pink, the clouds had scattered and the sun was shining, and my thoughts kept going in circles, coming back to Emerald every time. Was I being unfair? It was entirely possible this woman was as lovely as everyone thought.

What I needed was to talk to someone else who had met her, a person who was clear-eyed about things like me, perhaps even a bit cynical. As much as I preferred not to contact Dan, there was no one else and I wanted to know what he had made of her.

I went wandering along the upper terraces and stood among the lemon trees, far enough away from the others not to be overheard. Calling his number, assuming he wasn't going to bother responding, I was surprised by his voice, that familiar south London accent, slightly high-pitched, his tone teasing.

'Vivi Palmer, the last person I expected to hear from.'

'Hey Dan.'

'Why are you calling?'

'Perhaps I just wanted to say hello.'

'I don't think so.'

'You're right,' I admitted. 'I need your advice.'

'My advice doesn't come for free. There's a price. Want to know what it is?'

No conversation with Dan was ever going to be uncomplicated. Stifling a sigh, I sat down on a low wall. 'Go on then, tell me.'

'I want an apology, Vivi. You walked out on me with no explanation.'

'I had my reasons,' I said, guardedly. For a moment there was near silence, only static at his end and the singing of cicadas at mine.

'You thought I was some sort of gold-digging bastard.' Dan sounded bitter.

That was exactly what I thought; there was no doubt in my mind. But when you make a habit of unsuitable men, picking them for their looks and charm, you can hardly complain when they act true to form. So actually, I blame myself. The mistake had been in thinking I could take things further. Dan was only ever meant to be a short-term thing and it was how I should have kept him, then there would have been no risk at all of disappointment.

'You disappeared out of my life, you didn't come back to

work, for God's sake. That's not fair. It's not even normal,' he pointed out.

And he was right, it wasn't normal. I had no argument for that.

'You had everything going for you – career, relationship – and you threw it all away.'

'OK ... sorry.' I breathed the word; it seemed the easiest thing to say.

'What is it you're after anyway?' he asked. 'Career advice, I assume? You don't walk out on the *Daily Post* without there being consequences. Your reputation is shot.'

'Actually, I wanted to talk about Emerald. I'm in Italy and haven't had a chance to meet her properly yet.'

'Holidaying in one of the family mansions, are we?'

'Don't be like that.'

'You want to know what I made of her?' guessed Dan.

'Basically, yes.'

'OK then,' he relented.

Dan always had good instincts. They had been honed over years of being a reporter and telling other people's stories, sensing when someone was embroidering the truth, weeding out the frauds, reaching for the real facts.

'She's a lot of fun,' he told me, 'really upbeat, probably quite ambitious – she seemed keen to do some work for the *Post* but wasn't too pushy about it.'

'So you think she's straight-up?'

'Yeah ... Why? What's bothering you?'

'She seems too good to be true,' I told him.

There was a soft chuckle. 'Ah, I taught you well.'

'Do you think she might be?'

'As I said, I liked her. I took her to the pub, had a few drinks, thought I might see her again perhaps.'

'Have you been in touch since?'

'Maybe I should give her a call. Is that what you're saying?'

I hesitated. 'I suppose if you fancied having a beer with her …'

'Always happy to have a couple of beers with a pretty girl,' he said, lightly. 'And I do appear to be single again, so why not.'

Dan was unsuitable, of course he was, but I remembered lots of good times together: the curry house suppers, nights cocooned in his flat, noisy evenings in the pub. I remembered his infectious grin, his easy laugh, and how he always made me feel just like any other girl, normal, ordinary. For the briefest moment I did feel sorry; it was impossible not to.

That night's dinner was the best yet at Villa Rosa. Our cooks must have got competitive in the kitchen, because they treated us to dish after dish. Soft shells of pasta drizzled in an oily slick of rendered broccoli and scattered with breadcrumbs and a crumble of crisp piquant peppers. White swordfish in a smooth sauce of roasted cherry tomatoes. Caciocavallo cheese melted onto toasted bruschetta. A puree of fava beans topped with wilted chicory. A plate of local wild mushrooms stewed and strewn with earthy roasted garlic. Raffaella sat down to share it with us while she and Fiona made plans. They were going to church together the next morning and then to some town in the mountains that was famous for its red aubergines. There was talk of a restaurant we really must have lunch at, of day trips and beaches, of more excellent dinners.

I realised this was enough – enough of a house party for my sister, as much happiness as anyone could expect, as much good luck. These people, all so different, with one thread to link us together, had come together in this beautiful place: a small group, sitting round a table, lit by soft lamps, looking forward to the days and nights we would be spending together; these were the people who mattered, and I didn't need any more.

When you stop wanting something, often that is when you get it. Glancing at my phone shortly before I went to bed, I found a message from Stefano. It said he had been doing a lot of thinking. Perhaps he was interested after all to meet the other people I had spoken about, the ones who shared his donor. If there was still an offer to come for lunch then he would to accept it. His day off was Tuesday. He hoped that would suit.

Sitting on the edge of my bed, head bent over my phone, I started to compose a message.

Sure, come for lunch on Tuesday. Bring cheese.

Imogen was excited at the news of Stefano's impending visit. With him and Tommy on the scene, she envisaged all sorts of possibilities for her matchmaking plans.

'I hate to be a disappointment but you're doomed to failure; I'm not interested,' I said.

'I don't believe it.' Imogen shook her head. 'I absolutely refuse to.'

The others were at church and we were walking round Triento, exploring its back streets, weaving through narrow lanes, climbing up and down steps with my nieces lagging behind in the hot sun and pleading for *gelato*. Imogen had been entertaining herself by weighing up the merits of the two men. Tommy was a little old for me and he had kids. Although he was lovely, the obsession with fitness could get annoying. Stefano seemed freer of complications but his extreme good looks bothered her. Men who were too handsome often didn't try making the effort to be anything else. That was what Imogen had found. What did I think?

I thought I had no business having either of them as a boyfriend. 'One of them has Jamie's kidneys, the other has part of his eyes and I have his heart,' I told her.

'Didn't we talk about this the other day and decide it makes no difference?'

'That's not how I remember it.'

'Yes, yes, I pointed out that you aren't actually related and Tommy is a good guy. I'm a stickler for details; don't try to argue.'

'Why are you so keen to pair me up with one of them, anyway?'

'What you need is someone like Hamid.' This was a familiar refrain. Ever since Imogen had met her reliable, hard-working husband she had wanted me to have the same. 'I think Tommy comes closest, although once I get to know Stefano I may change my mind. I'll let you know.'

My sister said those last words over her shoulder as I was falling behind now too. Climbing so many steps had left me slightly breathless and my heart felt heavy as if my blood had thickened and it was pumping more lazily than usual.

'Are you OK?' Imogen paused for me to catch up.

'Not really … Tommy says if I stick with the exercise I'll get fitter, but it doesn't seem to be happening so far.'

'Let's head back down to that bar in the piazza where we had coffee earlier,' Imogen suggested. 'We'll get the girls their *gelato*.'

We travelled back to the piazza more slowly, my nieces ahead of us now, the prize of a sweet treat in their sights, while Imogen was growing concerned, shooting me quick looks.

Reaching the bar, I was pleased to sit down, to rest my elbows on the table and put the weight of my head in my hands.

'Vivi?'

'Just give me a minute.'

'This seems more serious than a bit puffed. What do you need me to do?'

'I'd love some water,' I told her.

Once Imogen had gone inside to order, I leaned back and took stock. My breathing seemed normal, my heart had settled into a reassuring rhythm.

'Maybe you're pushing yourself too hard,' said Imogen on her return, sounding concerned. 'All these long walks you've been taking, you've overdone it.'

'No, Tommy is right, the exercise is good,' I insisted, not wanting to worry her.

We camped out at one of the bar's outdoor tables, the girls demolishing dishes of *gelato* covered in whipped cream and chocolate sprinkles, and Imogen making forays to the nearby shops, coming back to show me the treasures she had found. Linen tea towels, bright ceramic bowls, a scarf with giant appliqué flowers she was sure our mother would adore, a tray of cakes from the *pasticceria*. Meanwhile I sipped water in the shade.

When you have another person's heart inside your chest it is natural to worry about every flutter, each moment when your heart seems to skip a beat or hammer out too many, any sense of tightness or sharp pain. You don't shrug off those things, assuming there is nothing to be concerned about like other people might.

For a short time there on our walk I hadn't felt good at all. But I had drunk a couple of strong coffees and not enough water, this was a hot day and the streets were steep; all of that could be an explanation; this was not a crisis, there was no need to panic.

Still for the rest of the day I was watchful, constantly checking in with myself, taking a rest in the afternoon instead of going swimming with the others, feeling each heartbeat pumping blood around my body.

I remember how, right after my transplant, the feeling was euphoric, like I had been given a second chance and was going to last forever. Soon I learnt that while Jamie's heart was a gift, there were rules to live by to care for its muscle and valves. That Aperol Spritz I drank, the celebratory glasses of wine, all the creamy cheese I had been enjoying, the too-rich meals, the too-strong coffees – I was breaking the rules, taking risks and hoping to get away with it. This seemed like a sign that I needed to be more careful.

Watching Tommy's kids playing ping-pong, I made a promise to myself. From now on I would be sensible. Lots of fruit, low-fat everything, gentle exercise, no more alcohol. I was going to follow the rules and everything would be fine.

We had pulled the ping-pong table out beneath the pergola and there was a tournament in progress. Ava and Liam played with fierce concentration, Tommy challenged my sister, the little kids were put in charge of retrieving stray balls, even Fiona joined in for a few short minutes before sitting down, too breathless to continue.

Nothing had gone wrong with me, only a couple of minutes of not feeling a hundred per cent, and didn't that happen to everyone? My own heart may have been a failure, but Jamie's was going to be fine. That was what I kept telling myself.

Fiona

The body always wins. They warned Fiona that before she had her transplant. They said the lungs are large and when they don't belong to you the body is going to fight them.

On the hospital ward, recovering from surgery, she had put it out of her mind. All Fiona cared about was breathing in the sweet air, filling up with it. Then later there were so many things she could do again: walk briskly, dig a garden, climb stairs. It was like she had been reborn.

There were some good years before Fiona noticed the stairs felt steeper again and the earth was harder to turn with her spade, and she couldn't walk as far or as fast. None of this was unexpected. The doctors adjusted her medication, and she carried on, only with less breath than before.

She had frightened herself that first day at Villa Rosa when she got so puffed on the hilly climb back up from the sea. Even taking it slowly, each breath was an effort although she tried to hide it. Fiona isn't risking going down there again; refusing invitations to swim and staying closer to the house, pottering round the kitchen or exploring the garden.

Acute rejection. It sounds very bad but they say she could be this way for years and years and mustn't let it hold her back. So Fiona may have slowed, but she hasn't stopped. While she has enough breath left to walk and talk, she will continue taking tours of the Chelsea Physic Garden. She will do whatever she can.

At first Italy had seemed too much of an adventure and she almost didn't come. Now though, Fiona is glad she allowed herself to be persuaded. The sunshine, the food, the views, the drinking coffee in the piazza, the cooking and sharing of meals; it has all been so lovely.

Most of all Fiona is enjoying the company of new friends. She is useful here, and she likes being useful.

Next time she sees her doctors they will measure her lung capacity again. Fiona doesn't need them to tell her it is declining. She feels it every day, in all the things she does. There is no point in making a fuss about it.

Fiona doesn't run for buses any more. She takes the lift instead of the stairs. She never tackles hills. Gradually life is returning to the way it used to be. There is a fight going on, her body is battling against Jamie's lungs. And the body always wins.

Vivi

My sister was matchmaking; being very amusing, and I was happy to be amused. It took my mind off whatever was going on inside my body. Fluttering was what I called it, because I didn't like the word palpitations and besides they were only faint things: little moments of feeling as if my heart was racing, of a strangeness that almost might not be happening at all. I kept telling myself it was nothing.

Letting Imogen distract me, playing with her, had always taken the edge off my worry. When I was a kid before going in for medical procedures, and during that first crucial year of transplant recovery, my sister was always there, making me smile, providing the lightness. Although the games we played were different now, she was still doing it.

Imogen was hoping that Stefano's appearance at lunch would be the push Tommy needed to realise how much he liked me. While planning a menu and where we would sit, she worked up a romantic fantasy.

'Stefano will be paying you lots of attention and Tommy won't enjoy that,' she said, in full flight. 'Then it's only a matter of something happening to bring you together, a romantic moment. Maybe you'll stumble walking down the steps to the sea and he'll take your arm ...'

'Seriously Imogen, have you been reading too many romantic novels?' I was laughing. 'This is not how things work in real life.'

'How do first kisses happen then? Someone has to make the move, don't they?'

'I think people are usually drunk,' I told her.

'But all of you are too clean-living for that to work,' she complained.

'Anyway, it might turn out to be the other way round,' I said to my sister, playing along. 'Perhaps Stefano will come to lunch and decide I'm the love of his life.'

'You're right. I should engineer things so you get some time alone with him. I have to up-skill immediately.' Imogen pulled out her phone and began scanning and digesting information on websites, with lawyerly speed. 'There must be some good matchmaking tips around somewhere.'

'Anything?' I wondered.

'This one says I need to work out exactly what you're looking for. That's easy, anyone who isn't a shit like Dan.'

'Right, what else?'

'I'm advised to bow out for a while after you meet and let things follow their course.'

'Is that a strength of yours, bowing out?

'I may need to work on it,' conceded Imogen.

'I might need to work on my ability to stumble and clutch at someone's arm attractively.'

'Excellent; we have a plan.'

Lunch preparations took most of the morning, everyone together and busy. Fiona had offered to cook, and I helped her in the kitchen, confining myself to the simple tasks like chopping and stirring. My sister set the table and chose one of her own dresses for me to wear, because this was no time for a palette of boring black. Tommy went to the market for bags of white peaches that he was squeezing by hand to make some sort of alcohol-free cocktail. All we were waiting for now was Stefano, who had promised to arrive at midday.

He was late and we were at the table, in the seats Imogen had assigned us, by the time he appeared, apologetic, blaming last-minute work problems and bad traffic. Any first-meeting awkwardness was lost in a flurry of introductions. We stood up, hands were shaken, cheeks were kissed; then we all sat back down in the wrong places, Tommy and Stefano together at the far end of the table, which had not been my sister's plan at all. But she could hardly make us move again.

To my surprise the two men seemed to forge a connection at first. They were talking about football then moved on to cars, and it occurred to me that Tommy must have been missing male company.

Imogen looked deflated. The matchmaker's guide can't have covered this. We ate a tart of zucchini and gorgonzola with a sweet-sour caponata, half-listening to them chat, sipping sparkling peach drinks and finishing with a salad of juicy red tomatoes and the fresh mozzarella Stefano had brought.

'Is this what you guys do then? Take villa holidays together?' he asked.

'This is the first time,' Tommy told him. 'We haven't known each other all that long. But nice idea for it to become a tradition.'

'They think of themselves as a transplant family,' Imogen explained.

I expected him to have more questions, to ask about Jamie or Grace, but he seemed more interested in our holiday plans.

'You're staying here the whole time?' Stefano asked, disapprovingly. 'Don't you want to see some other places? What about driving over to Matera for a couple of days or exploring Puglia? Or you could head south through Calabria.'

'We're happy taking it easy,' said Tommy. 'Sightseeing with a bunch of tourists isn't my cup of tea.'

Stefano shrugged, as if food and sunshine weren't enough for a holiday and he was taking it personally that we weren't showing any interest in Italy's history, culture and architecture.

Seeing the two men side-by-side seemed to highlight all the differences between them, Stefano's smooth arrogance, Tommy's rougher edges, his honesty and warmth.

'Is there a point to all this?' Stefano was asking. 'Are you planning some sort of memorial to our donor? Is that why you've come together, or are you just hanging out?'

'A memorial is a good thought,' said Tommy. 'Perhaps we should check in with Grace, see how she feels.'

'What would we do though?' Fiona was interested in the details. 'Hold a church service perhaps. Although not everyone is religious.'

'I guess that's up to Grace. She might want us all to gather and give thanks.'

'It would be nice to do something more lasting. Perhaps we could plant a tree for Jamie, or donate a park bench in his name,' suggested Fiona.

Stefano was surprised to find we hadn't come up with any of this sooner. He thought we needed a solid plan, that the anniversary of Jamie's death might be a focal point, and one of us should be in charge of the organising.

'A first step is to put together all your ideas,' he said.

'There's Emerald too,' Fiona reminded us. 'She'll want to contribute, I'm sure.'

A long discussion followed that I failed to give my full attention to because I was distracted by that odd sensation in my chest, a few beats where my heart seemed to be skittering, before settling back to a comfortable rhythm. I waited and wondered, focusing on my breathing.

Once I was listening properly again, the conversation had moved forward. Now they were talking about Emerald and her sense that she was becoming more like Jamie.

'I've read about cell memory,' Stefano said, dismissively. 'There's no science to prove it. Why would having a liver transplant change your personality? It doesn't make sense to me.'

'Not everything makes sense,' said Tommy. 'There are mysteries in life, and maybe this is one of them.'

'She's imagining it; she wants to believe it,' argued Stefano. 'Have any of the rest of us changed?'

'Being ill changes you,' murmured Fiona. 'Obviously it does.'

'But no one else feels like they're taking on donor characteristics?' Stefano turned to me. 'Vivi, you're being very quiet about this.'

I thought back to that first meeting with Grace. It hadn't been a thing I had spoken about and I was reluctant to mention it now, but everyone was looking my way and waiting.

'There was this one odd moment ...' I began.

It came on suddenly, the feeling that my heart was skipping erratically. I gasped, partly from the shock, then I felt dizzy and put my head down on the table as quickly as possible, afraid I was going to pass out. Moments later it was over and I felt OK again.

'Vivi, what just happened?' My sister sounded scared.

'I'm not sure, I had a bit of a turn, like maybe an arrhythmia, just a tiny one.'

'Your heart ...' The colour had washed from her face.

Everyone was still looking towards me; all those concerned faces turned in my direction. Even the kids had picked up that something was wrong and quietened.

'It only lasted a few seconds, hopefully it's nothing serious.'

Imogen already had her phone in her hand. 'We need to get you checked out. There's a cardiologist about forty-five minutes away. I looked it up before I came away, just in case.'

'Let me make the call,' said Stefano. 'In case their English isn't great.'

My sister found the number and passed him the phone. We all listened as he conducted a terse conversation in Italian. I had the sense there was some sort of argument going on.

'They can't fit me in?' I guessed, as he finished.

'That's what they said at first but I convinced them they were wrong.' Stefano stood up, slinging his sweater round his shoulders. 'Let's go, shall we? The sooner we get there the better. Apparently you may need a few tests.'

That was the closest he and Tommy came to vying over me. Both men thought they would make the better escort. Neither would back down until finally my sister, growing impatient that time was being wasted, coolly started issuing instructions.

'Tommy, could you please stay and look after the kids. I'll go, and Stefano should come with us in case we need a translator. We'll call and let you know how we're going; but Fiona, if we're very late perhaps you might give the girls some supper. OK Vivi, let's get moving.'

Stefano insisted on driving, since he was more accustomed to these roads and sure to get us there quicker. He did drive fast, his sporty car eating up the kilometres, and Imogen, in the passenger seat, didn't tell him to slow down. She was silent, keeping all her worry contained, not wanting to bother me with it. That was how she was whenever anything went wrong: quiet and calm, because she was the strong sister, the healthy one.

'Is it much further?' she asked. 'Another ten minutes, do you think?'

'About that,' Stefano agreed, turning for a quick glance at me. 'You doing OK?'

'I'm fine,' I reassured them. 'It might have been just a blip.'

'Still, best to get you checked out, hey?'

'Definitely,' agreed Imogen.

They spoke some English at the clinic but Stefano stayed with us anyway, in case there were any misunderstandings. He was a calming presence, not fussing or worrying, only being there. He even sat in with me while I talked to the cardiologist, listening as I described the brief sensation I had felt, as though my heart was shorting out and then sputtered back to life again. The doctor said what I expected – it sounded like an arrhythmia, and given my medical history, a few tests were going to be necessary.

Over the years I have learnt to hand myself over to

medical professionals and let them get on with what they do; extract my blood, listen and look. Echocardiograms, scans and treadmill tests, biopsies; my heart has been through all of them before. I feel at home with the way a clinic smells, and under its strip lighting, I recognise the equipment they use and know what they are likely to say as they go about their work. This may have been Italy but none of it felt all that foreign to me.

In the end we didn't know much more than at the beginning. My heart muscle was strong, nothing was blocked, inflamed or failing, there were no obvious problems. So they prescribed more pills for me to swallow, gave me a monitor to take home and wear, then said goodbye for now.

I don't think Imogen felt particularly reassured; she would have liked a proper result, something definite. But the doctors were saying what I wanted to hear – don't worry, take your meds, carry on as normal. If my symptoms settled there was no need for me to hurry home and see the transplant team at Harefield.

'Perhaps you should go back anyway,' suggested my sister as we were driving back to Villa Rosa, 'just to be on the safe side. What if you have another arrhythmia?'

'Let's see how I go. I feel fine now.'

'You'll take it easy though, right?'

'They didn't actually tell her to take it easy,' Stefano interrupted. 'They said to carry on as normal.'

Imogen gave him a withering look but Stefano's eyes were on the road ahead so he may have missed it.

'If Vivi is going to stay in Italy then I'd like her to take it easy,' insisted my sister.

'Surely it's up to her what she does.'

'I really don't think this is anyone else's business,' said Imogen, tersely.

'My point exactly,' argued Stefano. 'It's Vivi's business, what she does, whether she takes it easy or not. Why does everyone think they get to take over and boss you round whenever you've got a health problem?'

'I'm her sister, I'm concerned about her.' Imogen's voice was steady enough although she must have been furious. 'Right now she needs to go carefully.'

'All I'm saying is she's not a child, she gets to make her own decisions.'

I spoke up from the back seat. 'I am actually here, you know. There's no need to fight about me.'

We were on the coast road now and he was taking it faster than either Imogen or I would have dared. For some reason it was the spark to flare my sister's temper.

'Could you slow down,' she hissed. 'There's no rush now.'

'Actually there is,' he responded, coolly. 'I need to drive home after this and in the morning be up early for work. So I'm in a hurry.'

Imogen didn't respond. She was probably too angry to speak. The rest of the trip was made in silence and when Stefano dropped us off at the gates of Villa Rosa it was me who thanked him for his help while Imogen slammed the car door and stormed back to the house.

'Thanks again,' I said.

'No problem, glad I was here to help. Look after yourself.'

'Of course.'

'Oh and Vivi ...' He gave me a smile. 'Taking it easy and being careful? That sounds boring to me.'

I smiled back. 'You're right, it really does.'

Imogen was bristling with all the ways Stefano was objectionable: arrogant, controlling, opinionated, insensitive, a terrible driver.

'At least you seem OK,' she said, pacing the length of the kitchen, her calm gone. 'You *will* be taking it easy though. And I'd better call Mum and Dad, let them know what's happening.'

'No, don't,' I pleaded. 'Let's not get them all anxious, not yet. I'm wearing the monitor in case I have any more episodes. If I have to go home, then I will. But for now, can't we carry on as normal, have a nice time and try not to think about it too much?'

The others were rustling up some supper. Both had been listening, obviously, but Fiona was too polite to interrupt and Tommy seemed worried. The moment I walked through the door he had been full of questions about what the cardiologist had said, wanting to know about the palpitations: were they normal, had I experienced them before, was it his fault for pushing me to exercise? Now as my sister and I fought, he stayed quiet.

'They're our parents, they need to know about this,' Imogen was arguing.

'Not unless it turns out to be something serious,' I argued. 'Isn't this my decision? Like Stefano said, I'm an adult.'

'Do *not* start quoting Stefano to me. Dan was bad enough, now this one ... ugh.'

What if I was attracted to men who were bad for me? Everything else in my life was supposed to be virtuous, so surely I was allowed one weakness. Unsuitable men wouldn't raise my blood pressure or my cholesterol. My heart might get broken but it wouldn't actually fail.

'I quite liked him actually,' I said, looking towards Tommy and Fiona. 'What did you guys think?'

Fiona only remarked that Stefano was young and very handsome so possibly that explained a lot, while Tommy was evasive.

'Here's hoping we won't be seeing much more of him,' said Imogen, pouring herself a glass of wine.

A short while later, when I found the message from Stefano on my phone, I didn't mention it to the others. He must have pulled over on his drive or stopped for coffee and sent it.

If life gets too quiet let me know. I might have some ideas to liven it up for you.

Vivi

I was at odds with my sister. She kept insisting I sit down, frowned whenever I wanted to go for a walk, and wouldn't let me take off my cardiac monitor for ten minutes to have a quick swim in case that was the very moment another attack of palpitations struck. Imogen said she was being the responsible one, that someone had to be; and I kept thinking how Stefano might have replied. This was my body after all, even if the heart had been a gift, and surely people should stop telling me what to do with it.

As lovely as Villa Rosa was, our days there weren't exactly exciting. In the mornings we went up to the village and the others had coffee, which I didn't drink now because I was being careful not to do anything that might spike my blood pressure and send my heart fluttering. There was usually some shopping after that but only for food, since we had exhausted the potential of the few other stores. And then back to the house, with me staking out a spot under the pergola to be sure my skin didn't burn.

Life seemed to be all about treading carefully. I still went down with the others to swim off the rocks at least once a day, but now I sat and watched rather than jumping in with them.

There was no more kayaking. Instead in the afternoons I helped Fiona, as she seemed to have decided it was a good idea to teach me to cook. We had progressed to simple sauces and even managed a risotto. She was a restful presence, chatting as we put a meal together with the minimum of fuss, and I was surprised how much I enjoyed the time spent together pottering round the kitchen.

My main activity though was messaging with Stefano. That was what kept me busiest and entertained. I was secretive about those messages, always with my phone close by and on silent, checking it constantly, with a burst of anticipation whenever it vibrated.

Sometimes he was irreverent and funny. Or he would tell me about his day and send photos: a sunset, a jacket he was thinking of buying, whatever he had eaten for dinner, normal stuff like that. The one thing Stefano never did was ask me how I was feeling.

Once or twice he referred to my sister as 'the fun police', which made me feel disloyal because everything Imogen did was in my best interests. Still, it felt good to be able to laugh. When you have electrodes stuck to your chest and a button you're meant to press if your heart starts beating erratically, life can start to feel too serious.

Stefano still thought that I needed to see more of Italy than the few kilometres around the coastline near Triento. He kept saying I was missing out and that he would like to show me some of his favourite places. There was a lot of chat about where we might go, and the place he kept coming back to was this amazing hotel his cousin managed where the rooms were caves carved into the limestone and you ate candlelit meals in an ancient church sculpted from rock. Stefano said if I visited this place then it would feel as if I was walking through history. 'Matera is incredible. You really have to see it.'

Getting caught up in his descriptions, I was content to imagine myself there. Then one afternoon when Fiona was lying down with a headache, and my sister and the kids were off feeding stray kittens they had found on the roadside, and Tommy was busy exercising, I looked up Matera, and the more I read, the more I wanted to go.

Why should this stay as a daydream? There were so many things I wasn't meant do, and no reason at all why this should be one of them. A couple of days away with a good-looking guy; where was the risk in that?

So then my messages turned into questions:

How long would we go for?

Could you get the time off work?

Would your cousin have any rooms free at short notice?

Who would do the driving?

Almost before I knew it we had a trip sorted. Stefano booked a couple of days leave, reserved us rooms for the night, and declared that he would drive us there.

Tell the fun police we'll be sure to take it easy!

He was right that Imogen was going to need some reassurance. But Matera had a hospital and Stefano spoke fluent Italian. I would be as safe there as anywhere. That was what I said on her return from feeding the kittens.

'I didn't go to all the trouble of getting a new heart so I could *not* live my life,' I reminded my sister, seeing the anxious frown on her face.

'Yeah, I know that,' she sighed.

'Fiona and Tommy will be here with you,' I continued. 'And I'll be back before you know it.'

'Do you promise to wear your heart monitor the entire time and go straight to the hospital at the first sign of any problem?'

'So long as you promise not to worry.'

'I've worried about you my whole life, I'm not likely to stop now.'

I hugged her then. Her hair was salt-caked ringlets from her morning swim, her skin smelt of sun cream and she pressed her head into my shoulder. 'I love you Vivi.'

'I love you more.'

It was what we used to say to each other as kids. The words weren't really necessary, we knew what we felt, but we liked the sound of them.

'You're not falling for this guy Stefano, are you?' She held me at arm's length, looking into my eyes. 'He's not a good idea.'

'Not even for a meaningless fling?'

'Is that what it is?'

'Probably.' Pulling free from her, I glanced at my phone in case there were any more messages. 'I mean, why not?'

'I do understand why you want to have a good time,' said Imogen. 'But don't make the mistake of thinking he's your guy. Because really he isn't.'

'I don't have a guy.'

'You do, I'm sure of it.'

Stefano must have risen at dawn, as when he arrived at Villa Rosa everyone was still in the process of waking and starting the day. I had packed a bag the night before, eaten some fruit for breakfast and was making coffee for the others when I heard a car horn hooting.

'That'll be him then,' said Tommy who was looking rumpled, still in shorts and the vest he had slept in. A rough diamond was how Fiona had once described him. I suppose it was the tattoo, and perhaps his northern accent too, that marked him out as different to her. Despite that, they seemed to get on.

I could tell that neither of them had warmed to Stefano. The news I was heading off to spend a night with him had been met with widened eyes and silence. Fiona had spoken first, politely hoping I would have a lovely time and the weather would be nice. Tommy said nothing but insisted on carrying my bag to the car and shook Stefano's hand, sternly telling him to look after me.

Stefano gave a low whistle as we reversed out of the gates and started up the hill. 'You escaped your guards; well done.'

'They're not that bad. All they want is for me to be safe.'

'No one is ever safe,' said Stefano, matter-of-factly, 'that's why it's so important to make the most of life.'

As I knew from my research online, his future was uncertain too. Corneas, like heart transplants, don't last forever. By the time he reached his forties Stefano might not be at the wheel of a car driving this coast road slightly too fast.

He whistled again. 'Wait till you set eyes on this place I'm taking you to Vivi, it's fantastic.'

The route started with more mountains, then a long road running between two reservoirs, and finally a motorway that was a chain of ugliness strung out over the countryside, lined with unfinished buildings. When Stefano told me it wasn't much further I couldn't imagine we were about to arrive somewhere lovely.

Then there was Matera, layers of stone stacked up a hillside, the spire of a cathedral reaching to a sky filled with darting swifts, and Stefano slowing down because these streets were narrow and not made with cars in mind.

Our hotel was in the oldest part of town. Stefano handed over the keys of his car and we headed up a flight of steps, through a little metal gate and down again into a courtyard made of sun-warmed stone. With a grapevine climbing over the arch of a doorway, a scattering of mismatched chairs and rustic wooden tables, and no one else around, this felt like some ancient dwelling and not a hotel at all.

Stefano's cousin wasn't there but one of the staff showed

us to our rooms. They really were caves, lit by candles and simply furnished.

Stefano looked pleased with himself. 'Do you love it?'

'Yes, I absolutely do.'

His room was three doors down from mine so, for all his breezy self-assurance, Stefano hadn't made any assumptions. He had plenty of other plans though: the rest of the day exploring the town, dinner in the hotel then a glass of Prosecco under the stars.

'People have been living here for thousands of years. I want you to experience it, feel the history, the timelessness.'

He warned me that we would be doing lots of walking through this town of steep streets and many steps, and said he wasn't planning on fussing over me every few minutes to make sure I was all right.

'So if you need to rest or you're feeling bad then tell me; otherwise I'll assume you're ready for anything.'

That was fine by me. We spent a carefree afternoon lost in the maze of narrow lanes, visiting the honeycomb of hollows in the rock where whole families once lived, and climbing to the highest points for the best views.

Stefano led the way to a bakery producing brown-crusted conical loaves where they let us taste slices drizzled with olive oil and oregano. To a restaurant that served folded ears of pasta covered in a creamy herby sauce for our lunch. Then up more steps to a church that seemed to rise out of the rock-face.

There was no resting. He wanted us to go across the ravine and view the town from the hillside opposite. Sit outside a bar listening to street musicians, look at ancient frescoes. Stefano was a restless companion, always on the move and expecting me to follow.

By the time I was back in my room, having a bath before dinner, I was tired enough to slip between the smooth white sheets of my bed and drift off to sleep. But that would have meant missing out. So I put on make-up, fixed my hair into a smooth ponytail, decided which black dress to wear and then, as a final touch, removed my heart monitor and tucked it out of sight at the bottom of my bag. It had no place in the night I was hoping for.

When I emerged from my cave room, Stefano was already out in the courtyard, sitting at a table with a view, sipping wine and snacking on pickled lupin beans and fat green olives.

'That was such a great afternoon, thank you,' I told him, taking a seat opposite.

'We're going to have just as good an evening.'

The two of us ate dinner beneath the vaulted ceiling of a vast deconsecrated church that had been chiselled from the limestone centuries ago. By the time we emerged it was late, but Stefano wanted to finish the night with a glass of Prosecco out in the courtyard.

'Just one glass then,' I agreed, because surely that couldn't hurt me.

It was dark and I could barely see Stefano's face once we sat down together, only the shape of him backed by a silvery hint of moonlight. The Prosecco was chilled and yeasty, and I sipped my one glass very slowly, savouring every mouthful.

'What's next for you, Vivi?' he asked. 'What will you do when the summer is over? Go back to London?'

'It's where feels most like home to me. I need to find some work and a place to live. I can't put it off forever.'

'Back to journalism then?'

'That's what I do.'

'And you love it?'

I remembered how Grace had asked the same question that night in Oxford, when she made me feel as if I wasn't living a life large enough to deserve the heart I had been given.

'It's fine,' I said. 'And career isn't everything, is it?'

'Maybe not, but it's important,' he argued.

'What about you then? Are you going to stay here in Italy making mozzarella?'

'Yes, of course, that's my passion now. There's nothing for me in England, just a lot of bad memories.'

'You don't miss home?'

'I don't think of it as home anymore. This is where I belong.'

Stefano started to talk, in a low and level voice, about all that had gone wrong when he thought he was losing his eyesight and none of the treatments were working.

'I wanted to escape, blot it all out ... I tried my hardest.'

'With alcohol?'

'With drugs; pot and pills mostly.'

Perhaps it was the depth of darkness that made honesty easier, or maybe he was always going to confide in me eventually. Stefano spoke of failing at everything, of leaving school with no future and not caring. About getting two new corneas that weren't thinning or bulging out of shape, but how it didn't seem to solve anything.

This out-of-control person he described seemed so unlike the man sitting opposite me. When I told him that, Stefano said it was down to his uncle.

'He set high standards and expected me to meet them. He didn't only train me to be a cheese maker.'

'He gave you another chance.'

'Yes, and the important thing now is to not waste it. No more missteps, no more losing my direction. My uncle has taught me whatever I do must be right otherwise there is no point in it.' He sounded so fierce and certain.

'Everything you do? That can't be easy.'

'Excellence isn't easy but it is worthwhile,' he said, with absolute certainty.

For a moment I stared at the dark shape of Stefano's face, trying to trace his features.

'What?' he asked the silence.

'You're a perfectionist,' I observed.

'You say it like a criticism; but what's wrong with striving for perfection?'

The darkness seemed to make my honesty easier too. 'I'm not perfect,' I told him, touching a hand to my chest. 'I have a scar right here, where they cut me open to take out my old heart. And the new one they gave me to replace it, the one that is skittering and fluttering now, I don't know what's going to happen to it.'

'You're scared?'

'Hell yes, who wouldn't be?'

Now it was Stefano that held the silence. I heard the steady sound of his breathing.

'The last thing I care about is being perfect,' I told him. 'I want to be ordinary, that's all.'

'My uncle would say that ordinary isn't something worth striving for.'

'Then I'm guessing your uncle has never closed his eyes at night thinking he might not open them again. Or been fearful of being a burden. Or worried about looking too far into the future.'

Stefano's breath was a sigh. 'I'm sorry, Vivi, that you feel like that. But how are you ever going to live if you're always scared about dying?'

'I live,' I said, defensively. 'Isn't that what I'm doing here right now?'

'If you've enjoyed yourself then I'm glad, but this was only a break and tomorrow you'll go back to real life, with your sister constantly telling you what you can't do. No wonder you're anxious.'

'Imogen is only trying to keep me safe.'

'And holding you back,' he insisted. 'I don't know how you stand it.'

Up till then our evening had been heading in one direction.

It had seemed set to end with us in bed together, and the anticipation had flavoured every moment of Matera for me, it was what I thought I wanted.

My mistake was in seeing this man as another Dan: fun, a bit irresponsible, a guy for good times and no expectations. But Stefano was the opposite of all that.

He was someone else who could make me feel small; and that was the last thing I needed.

I left my prosecco half drunk, left Stefano in the darkness finishing his own, made up some excuse about being exhausted after so much walking; and he let me go without any argument.

My cave room smelt of burning wax. Alone in the flickering candlelight I swallowed my scheduled dose of drugs, rubbed at my skin with a gauze swab and re-attached the electrodes of my cardiac monitor as tightly as I could. I lay down in bed, put the monitor on the nightstand, curled my body around a pillow, closed my eyes, felt my heart steady and slow, and trusted it to keep beating until morning.

Perhaps because so little natural light filtered in through the cave room's single small window, I slept later than I meant to. I found Stefano already at breakfast; his plate piled with cheeses and stuffed breads. If he was the least bit put out by the way the night before had ended, he showed no signs of it, outlining his plans for the day: a medieval ghost town I couldn't miss, a Benedictine monastery.

This trip had turned into a disappointment and it seemed pointless to keep it going.

'Actually, I'd prefer to head straight back this morning,' I told him.

'Back to the quiet life?'

'Yeah, I've had enough sightseeing I think, but thanks.'

We drove to Villa Rosa, with only a short stop for him to have coffee, talking about anything but each other. We were speeding down the long straight road between the reservoirs when I brought up the subject of Grace. I was hoping that now he might agree to meet the woman who helped change his life, but again I had read Stefano wrongly.

'Why would I do that?' he asked. 'Didn't I make it clear from the outset that I don't see any point?'

'But then you changed your mind, you came and met us,' I pointed out.

'Because I was curious, but you're all just people, like anyone else, there was no special connection.'

I was sorry, though not especially surprised. 'So you don't want the chance to thank Grace?'

'I talked to my uncle about it. He agreed I shouldn't feel obligated. She made the decision for her son to be a donor and I was the top of the list; that's all there is to it.'

Stefano's attitude clashed with mine. There wasn't a moment when I didn't feel I owed Grace a debt that I could never repay. I envied him in a way, being able to forge on so selfishly and single-mindedly. I liked him less for it too. And I wasn't quite as sorry about the way the night before had ended. Stefano was unsuitable, just in a different way than Dan had been.

My first glimpse of the house felt like a homecoming. Its terracotta roof standing over the wide band of sea, its pergola smothered in bougainvillea, the sound of the waves crashing on the rocks below, the smell of wood-smoke from garden bonfires and Tommy heading back from a run, surprised to see us arriving.

'We didn't expect you till much later.' Tommy's eyes locked onto mine. 'Everything OK?'

'Yes, it was all great,' I told him, stretching my legs as I climbed from the car. 'Cool hotel, beautiful place. We had fun.'

Tommy stood by and watched as I said goodbye to

Stefano. He lifted my bag from the boot of the car, closed it then tapped twice to signal it was OK for him to drive off.

Then he turned to me with a frown. 'There have been a few developments here since you left yesterday morning.'

My heart didn't sink, but it did a sort of flip-flop and for an instant I wondered if I should press the button on my monitor. 'What's happened?' I asked.

'Sorry Vivi, but I don't think you're going to like this.'

Tommy

This isn't the conversation he wants to have. The things he says to Vivi in his head are all entirely different. If he were a different man he might have spoken them aloud.

Telling her how he feels is such a risk. He has no confidence it will go well. Even so, he very nearly did it in those first few days at Villa Rosa when he knew for sure her boyfriend was off the scene and her sister seemed to be encouraging it.

Why had he held back then? It is why he has come after all, not to eat *gelato* or swim in the sea or sit on a beach. Tommy is here for her. And now he has missed his opportunity.

He wants to tell Vivi she is beautiful, to hold her for more than a moment, to be important in her life. Instead he has watched while another man drove away with her, a man who is all the things Tommy knows for sure he isn't.

Now she is back early and he assumes things haven't gone too well. The thought should be cheering except it is already too late; Tommy's chance has slipped away.

This isn't the conversation he planned to have with her. But he didn't know what to say before, how to put his feelings into words, the sorts of words she might want to hear.

He should have spoken to her, seized a moment as they were walking round the headland or swimming in the sea, while her sister was lazing on a lounger and Fiona was busy in the kitchen, when the kids were caught up in a game. Who knows how that might have gone, what she would have said?

Tommy thinks his feelings don't matter anymore, not at

this point. Things have changed; and that is exactly what he needs to explain to her.

This chance has gone. Still Tommy is holding onto a hope there may be another one. A small hope … an unspoken one.

Vivi

Everything had been taken out of my hands. While I was busy walking through history, other people were deciding on my future. In the shade of a carob tree, out of sight of Villa Rosa, Tommy explained it all, sounding so reasonable.

Imogen had got such a fright that day when I slumped on the table in the middle of lunch. She had been scaring herself with Google searches ever since. As soon as I was gone she was onto my parents, scaring them too.

Everyone had agreed that I needed to go home. My father's reach was long thanks to all his charity work, so if he wanted me to be seen by the transplant team at Harefield then it was the work of a moment for him to arrange it.

'But I'm not due for an assessment,' I told Tommy.

'An extra one, just to be safe and put everyone's mind at rest.'

'It's a waste of time. I haven't had any more palpitations.'

'We still don't know what caused the arrhythmia; that's what is worrying everyone.'

'Why don't they let me worry about myself?'

'It's a few more tests, that's all.'

'I had them all at the cardiologist's here,' I pointed out.

'Imogen ... and your parents ... they think it's a good idea to see your own team and possibly have a biopsy to check for signs of rejection.'

Perhaps I should have been more understanding. But I was tired of my life being shaped by other people's worry. And I was sick of the interference, being told what to drink and eat, what to do and when to rest. Stefano had been right about one thing: they might have been keeping me safe, but they were also holding me back. I told Tommy that and his face seemed to harden, until he interrupted.

'You're lucky to have people to worry about you. Look at Fiona. She doesn't have anyone at all.'

I had never heard that tone from him before – chilly, disapproving. 'You're on their side,' I said, accusingly.

'This isn't about sides. But yeah, I'd like to be sure you're getting the best care possible.'

'Do I have any choice in this at all?'

Tommy shook his head. 'They've booked you on a flight from Naples on the same day I'm leaving, so we can drive up together. And Fiona is going to stay here a while longer because Imogen didn't want to be on her own.'

I closed my eyes against the blue of the sky and the loveliness of the garden; made everything disappear. 'Imogen was the one who insisted I come here in the first place. Now she wants me to leave.'

'It's for a few days, that's all. Once you know you're in the clear you can come back and carry on with your holiday.'

'So my life is all arranged,' I said. 'Everyone is looking after me.'

'Seems that way,' agreed Tommy, putting his arm round my shoulder, giving it a reassuring squeeze.

I had two final days in Italy and wasn't going to tiptoe softly through them. With Tommy and his kids, I went kayaking again through the sea caves. I spent a morning at the lido letting the sun touch my skin and eating salty, cheesy pizza. I even took off my heart monitor and went for a swim. And Imogen didn't say a word, knowing she had said enough already.

The final afternoon I spent with Fiona, making our last supper together. We had bought soft spiced 'nduja sausage at the market, plump pods of fava beans and a punnet of salted ricotta. Together we made pappardelle and she let me knead the pasta dough until it was smooth then cut it into wide ribbons. For the second course there was a sweet-sour braise of chicken with lemon and rosemary. And Fiona showed me how to make a caponata of artichokes, celery and toasted pine nuts.

'Thanks to you, I'm not such a terrible cook any more,' I said, as I sautéed the celery golden.

Fiona smiled. 'You were never terrible; all you needed was a little practice. I suppose when you were a child you never helped your mother in the kitchen?'

'If I did then I can't remember.'

'There are lots of people like you who are daunted, thinking it's more complicated than it needs to be. It used to be my dream to do something to change that.'

'By teaching?' I asked, tipping the artichokes into the pan, along with the garlic oil, torn mint leaves and raisins.

'That's right.' Fiona nodded. 'My plan was to have a cookery school. Take people shopping for ingredients, bring them back to cook a meal, then sit down and enjoy it together with some delicious wine. I looked into it for a while, even found the perfect location.'

'And then you got sick,' I guessed.

'No, this was long before that. My brother discouraged me. He thought there was too much financial risk – I had to borrow money, you see – and perhaps he was right.'

Fiona was a good teacher, gentle and encouraging, and I couldn't help wondering aloud if this was something she could still do.

'It needn't cost that much. Maybe you could hold pop-up cooking classes in restaurants on the evenings they were closed,' I suggested. 'If you'd like then I could help you look into it.'

'Thank you Vivi, but it's too late for that now. It was just a dream, it wasn't meant to happen.'

We ate outdoors, as the light softened and faded. Everything was delicious, especially the chicken infused with sweetness and acidity; still none of us had much appetite. One by one, with the sky slowly darkening overhead, we made our excuses and went to bed early.

The morning we left was a stunner, hot and golden. Since I wasn't planning on coming back I took a last walk, saying goodbye to the place, went all through the gardens, down the steep path to the sea and back through the rooms of the pretty pink house. My summer was over and I needed to get on with my life now.

Kissing my nieces, saying goodbye to my sister and hugging Fiona, I climbed into Tommy's rental car and was driven away from Villa Rosa.

I'd had a long sleep the night before but even so drifted off again as we skirted the mountains and headed towards the motorway. I was woken by the sound of Tommy softly swearing because he had taken the wrong exit and now we were stuck in traffic trying to get back onto the proper road. That made us late to the airport and thankfully there was no time for a long, drawn-out goodbye. I grabbed my bags and ran, hoping to make the plane.

I slept again once I was in the air so it didn't feel long at all before England's patchwork fields were beneath us, hazed by cloud.

My parents were at Stansted to pick me up. They wanted to wrap their love around me like cotton wool and make me feel safer. So much love and I knew it made me lucky, and I should be grateful like Tommy said, but it felt suffocating anyway.

Sitting in the back seat of their Mercedes, I answered my mother's questions about exactly what had happened in Italy and how things felt right now.

'We'll put our faith in your doctors, like always,' she said, 'and pray it's nothing that can't be easily treated. We've cancelled all our commitments tomorrow so we can come to Harefield with you,'

'Mum, it's routine stuff, I won't need you.' I tried not to sound as impatient as I felt.

'We want to,' she insisted.

'I'm fine to go alone as usual.'

With them as my entourage everything was going be higher key and more serious. I would be Sir Lance and Lady Palmer's daughter, not just Vivi back for another check up.

'You'd really prefer us not to be there?' My mother sounded hurt.

My father is an astute businessman; he knows how far to push people, especially me. I saw him glancing at his rear-view mirror and the expression on my face.

'Leave it, Deb. We've got faith in her team, like you said, and Vivi's done all this before, she doesn't need a fuss.'

My mother didn't put up much fight once he got involved. She has learnt to trust his judgment when it comes to most things, but especially me.

'You'll remember not to eat any breakfast, won't you, in case they decide on a biopsy. And you'll call us as soon as you know anything at all,' she fretted.

'Yes, of course.'

'I'm sure it will all be OK,' she said.

My parents were doing their best to sound positive; still, I knew how anxious they were and the knowledge weighed me down. We were nearly home by then and I stared out of the car window at the shoppers in Upper Street, going about their lives and making their own decisions like normal, healthy people do. I was never going to be like those people. I wouldn't be ordinary; I wouldn't get old. That was just how it was and I had to accept it.

*

My coordinator Lynda and the rest of the transplant team at Harefield are like a bunch of old friends and it's good to catch up even if it does involve me having blood tests and a chest X-ray. They manage always to seem in such a great mood, keeping things light and making me laugh. How they do that all day and with every patient, I will never know, but I'm grateful for it.

This time everyone mentioned the Vivi's Law campaign, and it was nice knowing they were proud of me and I might have made a difference. Then there was a discussion about whether to do a biopsy, weighing up the risks with the benefit of it being the best way of making sure my body was still a happy home for my donor heart. In the end the transplant cardiologist decided, since it had been a while since the last one, they might as well go ahead. These were the people who had saved my life and I didn't argue with them. I never do.

Dressed in a hospital gown, I let them inject anaesthetic into my neck and dab me with bright pink disinfectant. The worst bit comes after they insert the cannula. At the end there's this long wire with clippers and it goes all the way to my heart and grabs little bits off. After a while a heart gets more reluctant to give and often complains by putting in extra beats or even skipping a few. This time I distracted myself by thinking about them all: Imogen and the girls in the sunshine at Villa Rosa, Fiona probably in the kitchen, Tommy home again and back at work, even Stefano busy making mozzarella. At least it was quick, fifteen or twenty minutes then the whole thing was over.

My final appointment of the day was at the clinic, re-assessing my medications with the transplant cardiologist. Afterwards I said goodbye to Lynda, who had come in with me. As she was walking away, at the far edge of my vision I noticed someone hovering and trying to attract my attention. The very last person I expected or wanted to see.

'Grace? What on earth are you doing here?'

She was flushed, apologising for being late and hoping everything was OK.

'How did you know where I'd be?' I asked her.

'Tommy told me. I thought it would be all right if I came along as a support person.'

'Did he tell you to?'

'No,' Grace admitted. 'I wanted to come though. You don't mind, do you?'

It felt wrong to have her there, in the hospital where her son's heart had been put into my body. It felt entirely wrong.

'What did the doctors have to say?' she wanted to know. 'Are you OK?'

'It'll be a couple of days before I get the results of the biopsy but nothing to worry about so far,' I reassured her.

'Thank God, I couldn't sleep last night . . . I was so worried about Jamie's heart.'

'It's still beating.' I told her.

'Can I listen? Would you mind?'

She had brought the stethoscope and for the second time I found myself in a public restroom with it pressed against my chest while Grace, eyes closed, listened intently.

'It's beating really strongly, just like last time.' She sounded relieved. 'It's good to hear it again, thank you.'

'You're welcome,' I told her, buttoning up my shirt, and wondering how many more times she would want this.

The hospital has a café where the food is tasty, and I was starving since I hadn't eaten all day. We headed there together, tiny me head-to-toe in black as usual, Grace statuesque in a bright summer dress: an odd-looking couple of friends.

Even though I couldn't mention Stefano, since he still hadn't changed his mind about meeting her, there was enough for us to catch up on over tea and toasted sandwiches.

Grace was open to the idea of some sort of memorial and we talked for a while about ideas – planting a tree, holding a service. She didn't seem to mind what happened, so long as we were all there together.

We ate our sandwiches and drank a second pot of tea. I needed to call my parents because they would be waiting but it was always hard to leave Grace. So we stayed and chatted a while longer. She told me about the part-time job she had taken in school administration and how nice it was to work in a place filled with young people. I talked about leaving the *Daily Post* and how I wasn't sure which direction to take but thought I would like to try life as a freelance writer.

'You should do it,' she encouraged me, 'take the risk, I'm sure you won't regret it.'

We were friends, sharing our thoughts with one another, like others at the tables around us. For a while we might even have forgotten what had brought us together in the first place; or at least it receded a little, it didn't seem like everything.

I started making noises about leaving. My bag was over my shoulder and I was on the point of standing up, when out of the blue Grace said, 'Someone wants to borrow money off me.'

'I'm sorry, what?'

'Quite a lot of money.'

'Who? One of us?'

She stared down at the table as if fascinated by the grain of the wood. 'I don't think I should say.'

'Grace, you've already given us so much. No one should be asking for more.' I was shocked.

'I've got some savings, Jamie's university fund,' she said, 'and I could borrow against my house if I needed to.'

'You haven't agreed to anything yet, have you?'

'I'd have helped Jamie if he needed it, I'd have done anything for him. This isn't so different.'

'None of us are Jamie though.'

'You're all that's left of him.'

'Grace, please will you tell me who it is.'

'I shouldn't have mentioned it at all,' she said.

Of course, I was sure it must be Emerald; I had never trusted her completely. I refused to believe it of the others. They were hardly wealthy – Tommy's business had gone under and Fiona was frugal – but surely neither of them would take advantage of Grace like that.

'How much money, exactly?' I wanted to know, but she refused to be drawn.

We caught a taxi together to the station and then a tube to the city, separating at Baker Street with promises to catch up again soon. Arguably if Grace wanted to give away her money, then it was none of my business. Except I had started this, I had brought us together to help her feel better and repay some of the debt I thought that I owed for having her save my life. If I failed to protect Grace now, what was the point of it?

Emerald was my number one suspect and Dan was on my radar again. We had talked about him having a beer with her and hopefully by now he had got round to it. I texted to ask what he was up to after work and got a fast reply.

Drinking! Why? Are you back in town?

Yep.

Don't suppose you want to come to the pub? Have a beer with your old colleagues?

Not really. Could we go somewhere else?

So long as you're paying and you take me somewhere fancy.

We went to Bar Américain in Soho for the art deco glamour, plus it is big and buzzy, and impersonal. This was the first time I had seen Dan since walking out on him and it felt awkward for the first daiquiri. But we had spent a lot of evenings sitting with a table of drinks between us, and it only took a couple to loosen him up.

I was sipping on something non-alcoholic that tasted of elderflower. I could tell he was already shrugging off his work self and turning into drinking Dan. His skin was flushed along the line of his cheekbones, he was laughing more and talking louder.

'So I suppose you want to hear about Emerald,' he said. 'Can't imagine I'd be getting free drinks from you if you didn't want something.'

He sounded bitter, but I shrugged it off.

'Did you get a chance to catch up with her again?'

'I may have.'

'And?'

'She's working with us on some stories around the Vivi's Law campaign. I reckon this change might actually happen. Think of it: hundreds, possibly thousands, more lives saved, thanks to the *Daily Post*. Emerald would be delighted to do anything she can to help. She can't do enough actually.'

'Do you think she might be trying to take advantage of the situation in some way?' I was convinced that it was her trying to borrow money from Grace. 'Is she on the make?'

'Isn't everyone?' Dan shrugged. 'Why don't you meet up with her yourself and make your own judgment?'

'There hasn't been a chance yet. Also, I trust your opinion.'

'Great, you do trust something about me, then.'

Dan's third daiquiri was almost finished. I didn't know how strong they were but they had gone down very fast.

'Let's eat,' I suggested. 'We must be able to find a good curry nearby.'

We walked round the corner to a cramped little place where we sat elbow-to-elbow at a counter and ate fierce Thai dishes, layered with spice and warmly comforting; ordering extra because Dan decided he was hungry.

'Aren't you going to ask me to take you back?' he asked, messily transferring a forkful of glass noodles from the clay pot they had been baked in to his open mouth.

I passed him a serviette. 'No.'

Come to my place,' he wheedled. 'Just one more night; you want to Vivi.'

If we kissed he would taste like garlic, ginger and spice. It was almost tempting. But I knew Stefano had been right about one thing. You can't keep on making the same mistakes, sometimes you have to try and get life right.

'Not tonight ... not ever, sorry,' I told Dan.

He tilted his head, looking at me through suddenly narrowed eyes. 'Seriously?'

I nodded.

'You had so much going for you,' he said, with conviction. 'Your career, us ... Vivi's Law could have been big for both of us. But you screwed it up, didn't you? The whole thing.'

'Maybe,' I said, although I didn't really think so any more.

I said goodbye to Dan outside the restaurant on Brewer Street. Walking away from him, looking for a taxi to hail, I thought how pleased my sister was going to be about this. I couldn't promise there would be no more unsuitable men, but I was definitely over this one.

Imogen

She wants another glass of wine but that would mean opening a bottle. There is one in the fridge but that would involve getting up to fetch it. Imogen isn't moving. She is on the lounger with her eyes closed while Fiona keeps her daughters occupied; she can hear them chattering away in the kitchen of Villa Rosa as they roll out pasta.

Imogen has been sitting out there since the message came that Vivi's test results were clear and everyone at home was celebrating. She has been having a little party of her own, a glass or two of wine.

One day Vivi will go for those tests and there won't be a celebration afterwards; all of them know that. Imogen wonders what it would be like without it always hanging over them.

Her entire life, or at least for as long as she can remember, her sister has come first and Imogen has never minded. How could she complain, when she was the one who went to school, played sports, partied, dated boys, while Vivi missed out?

What did Imogen do to deserve being the healthy sister? She thinks about it sometimes and usually concludes she doesn't deserve it at all.

This is a beautiful day, blue-skied and quite perfect; she almost wishes it wasn't. And that makes no sense; she ought to be happier. She should be making the most of it: swimming in the sea, walking on the beach, playing with her daughters, all the things Vivi can't do. Instead Imogen stays on the lounger, eyes closed against the bright day, while someone else teaches her girls to make lasagne.

The sun is shifting the shade and the afternoon is passing. There is a sauce simmering on the hob. Imogen has smelt it cooking all afternoon: beef, red wine, tomato, leafy basil. Soon they will be layering it with the sheets of pasta they have made, covering it with cheese and a blanket of béchamel and putting it in the oven. It is time for her to climb out of this lounger.

The kitchen is in chaos. There is tomato spattered up the wall, flour and offcuts of pasta scattered far and wide. Farah is trying to grate cheese. Darya is spooning up sauce and asking her to try it. Fiona is sitting down, looking a little bit shattered.

Imogen breathes and smiles. She tastes the spoonful of sauce that one daughter offers, helps the other with the grater and goes to the fridge where the wine is chilling. She opens another bottle. She wants one more glass.

Vivi

My father was opening champagne, a careful hand over the cork as he popped it, then four glasses poured without a drop spilt. We were celebrating the news that my biopsy results were in – no signs of rejection, nothing to worry about for now. The relief my parents were feeling was obvious and even Hamid seemed to sparkle as we toasted and sipped around my sister's messy kitchen table.

'You can go back to Italy now and carry on having a lovely summer,' my mother said, happily.

'Actually, I'm planning on staying in London.' I was busy searching the freezer for Imogen's supply of Waitrose mini sausage rolls. 'There are things I need to do here. Aren't you guys heading over there soon though?'

Hamid lost some of his sparkle as he explained that he wasn't sure if he would be able to get away as there was a high-stakes case reaching a critical stage. It wouldn't be the first time he had missed out on a holiday because his work was more important; it was one of the rare things he and my sister fought about.

'It's tricky for us too,' admitted my father, apologetically. 'We'll definitely be going, but there are a few issues: meetings I need to be present at, fundraisers we have committed to.'

'Imogen's not going to be impressed.' I told them, rattling the frozen pastries onto a baking sheet and shoving them in the oven. 'She won't like being there on her own with the girls.'

Relief at my tests coming back clear had washed away any last resentful feelings towards my sister. I could even see how maybe she had been right, and coming home to have a thorough check-up was the right thing. But I hadn't changed my mind about going back to Villa Rosa. A few more weeks of sunshine and pasta might be nice, but it was more important to start finding my own way again and work out who I was without my old job and my unsuitable boyfriend.

'There's plenty of time for that. No need to rush into anything,' said my mother, when I tried to talk about my plans.

As I carried on searching Imogen's kitchen for things to cook and eat, it occurred to me that in this family it was normal to drop everything for one sister and to be much too busy for the other. And I spared a thought for how Imogen must feel about that.

The next morning Fiona called me. I didn't recognise her number when it came up on my screen and her voice sounded different too, huskier and slightly breathless.

'Is everything OK,' I asked. 'Where are you?'

'I walked a little way,' she explained. 'I wanted to speak to you privately.'

Fiona was worried about Imogen. She couldn't put her finger on precisely what was wrong but both she and Raffaella thought it was more than the usual stresses of young kids and motherhood. The word she used was brittle, which seemed wrong because I knew Imogen was strong, she was made of steel and diamonds, and she didn't break easily.

'I'm so glad you've got a clean bill of health,' Fiona said. 'When do you think you'll be back?'

I repeated what I had told the others, this time with less certainty. That word – brittle – I didn't like the sound of it; particularly as I knew Fiona was a person who chose her words carefully

'Has something in particular happened?' I wanted to know.

'Not really, we've been doing the usual things, having a lovely time. I don't know Imogen very well, of course, perhaps she is often tense and tearful.'

'Tearful?' I was alarmed.

'Yes, ever since you left, tearful ... and drinking rather a lot ... even more.'

'I'll call her,' I promised.

'You won't mention that I said anything?' Fiona sounded anxious. 'I don't want her thinking I'm a busybody.'

On the phone a little later Imogen sounded the same as usual, upbeat about my test results, describing the things they had been doing and the meals they had eaten. As she spoke I could tell she was sipping something, probably wine, but Imogen often had a glass in her hand in the daytime, especially when she was on holiday.

Feeling uncertain, I put down the phone and started looking at flights just in case. Even if I did go back, there was no need to rush, surely? I wanted to meet Emerald and attempt to solve this mystery of who was trying to take Grace's money. And I needed a few more days in London, to put out feelers about freelance work and check out flats to rent.

I was online looking at rooms in shared accommodation, wondering if I should go east to Bethnal Green or Mile End, not really liking anything I was seeing and wishing I could bring myself to accept my parents' offer to buy me a place, when I started getting the messages: Grace, Stefano, even Emerald, all of them wanting to know if I'd had the results of my biopsy yet. Only Tommy failed to get in touch. While I was busy messaging everyone back with my good news, that struck me as unusual.

Ever since we had met, Tommy and I had been conducting a conversation, and whether it was via phone, Skype or face-to-face, it didn't seem to matter. But the last time there had been any contact was the day of my assessment and then it was only a quick reply to my text, a thumbs-up emoji. I had assumed he was busy with work and family but now as I sent him the same message as the others – biopsy all clear! – a worry began to niggle. Was Tommy upset with me?

I remembered us standing together under the carob tree at Villa Rosa, and how Tommy had been terse and made it clear he thought I wasn't grateful enough for all my family did. What if he had been put off me completely? It didn't seem likely but then it wasn't usual for him to hold me at arm's length like this. Something seemed wrong.

Calling his number, I left a message, apologising for being bratty and saying I missed him and hoped to talk soon. My phone stayed close for the rest of the day, but I didn't hear back. Alone in my sister's house, because Hamid was working late, the small worry grew. I started up a new thread of messages, asking if anyone else had been in touch with him. One by one they came back to me – Grace, Fiona, Stefano, even Emerald – and nobody had heard from Tommy.

Every time I tried him, the phone rang until I heard his familiar message - *Tommy here, I'm probably out for a run so try me again later* – and I wasn't sure what to do. I didn't have his ex-wife's details or the name of the business he worked for, or his kids' schools, or even his neighbours. There seemed no way to track him down. All afternoon and into the evening I kept thinking about him and wondering.

There was no food left in Imogen's house so in the morning I took myself out for scrambled eggs with buttery toast and sat in the café with my phone on the table, willing it to ring. Then I wandered down to Waitrose to buy some ready meals for Hamid and as I was busy stocking the freezer with them, felt the phone buzzing in my pocket.

Tommy's message was stark and short.

Am in hospital. Came off my bike. Will call in a bit.

As I read those words, it felt like my heart was sinking through my body and hitting the floor. Reaching for a chair, I sat down and rested my head on Imogen's kitchen table. Nothing bad could happen to Tommy. I needed him.

When he called, Tommy sounded terrible, not like himself, no warmth in his voice at all. 'Sorry, I was just with the doctor.'

'What's happened?' I was impatient to hear.

'I went out on a bike ride and got car-doored really badly. No broken bones, just cuts and bruises mostly.'

'Why are you still in hospital then?'

'I must have caught the door or the handlebars as I went down and I bashed myself pretty hard, unfortunately.'

'Your kidney,' I guessed, feeling my heart flutter and ignoring it. 'Please don't tell me you got injured.'

'It's my own fault. I wasn't wearing a shield, but I was heading to work and it's only round the corner so I never bothered.'

'Can they save your kidney?'

'I'm in the renal transplant unit at the Royal Liverpool. It's not looking good.'

'What are the doctors saying exactly?'

'Chances are the kidney will fail,' he said, bleakly.

'God, Tommy, I'm so sorry.' What I wanted most was to be with him. 'Shall I come up?'

'Bad idea, I'm not great company. If anything changes I'll let you know.'

He said goodbye and I sat in my sister's kitchen, dazed and indecisive. I wasn't even sure how to feel. But I felt like Tommy needed me. And I realised I needed him too.

The person I contacted was Fiona, and her reply steadied me. She agreed the best idea was to go to Liverpool and be there to support Tommy. In the meantime, she would reorganise her commitments so she could stay in Italy because she didn't like to leave my sister.

Now I had a plan and didn't waste more time. I threw a few things in a bag – a toothbrush, clean underwear – and caught a cab up to Euston Station so I could jump on the first available train. As it sped north, I wished I shared my parents' faith and could pray the way they always had whenever I got sick, but the only thing that was going to make me feel better would be setting eyes on Tommy. Hearing accents like his all around me as I walked through Lime Street station made me want to see him all the more.

Tommy didn't seem very pleased at the sight of me, turning his face away and demanding to know what I thought I was up to.

'I never said you should come here.' He looked pale, sounded sad and angry.

'I know, but I wanted to make sure you're OK.'

'Yeah well, I'm not.' His voice was a low monotone and he wasn't looking me in the face.

'This isn't fair,' I told him. 'You've done everything right, you're so healthy, it shouldn't be happening to you.'

He sighed, gave a shrug, stared down at the floor. 'If the worst comes to the worst I'll go back on dialysis. At least I've got that option.'

I could tell how much he was hating the thought of being hooked up to a machine several times a week, trapped for hours while it did the job his kidneys were meant to and cleaned up his blood. I imagined Tommy, with all that wild energy and drive, feeling like a caged animal. Still it was better than the alternative.

'You can lead a relatively normal life though?' I tried to sound encouraging. 'Could you get a dialysis machine to have at home?'

'Vivi, you should go now. I don't want to talk to anyone.'

'Can I come back later?'

'No.' His blue eyes met mine. 'Like I said on the phone, I'm not good company. Just go, please.'

I started to walk away, reluctantly pacing across a few metres of institutional linoleum. The further I got from Tommy, the worse I felt. I could have lost him if that accident had been worse, just like Grace lost Jamie. He might have been gone from the world without me seeing or speaking to him again. The thought made me cold.

I paused and right there, in the middle of the ward full of broken people, it came to me, the realisation that being careful didn't guarantee anything. In fact, sometimes it meant that you missed out on the one thing you really wanted.

Making up my mind, I turned and marched back to Tommy.

'Me again, sorry,' I said.

He stared at me helplessly. 'Vivi, you're the last person I want to see right now.'

That hurt. It was difficult to understand. 'Why?'

Tommy looked out of the window, his fingers drumming on his knee.

'I thought we were friends, really good friends.' I sat down beside him, putting my hand over his, stilling his fingers.

'Maybe I wanted more,' he replied, turning his open palm to mine.

'More than friends?' I asked, unsure if I had understood him.

'Yeah.' Tommy gave me a rueful half-smile. 'When that guy Stefano came and took you away to Matera for the night, I could have punched his lights out. Wasn't it obvious?'

'Nothing happened between me and him.'

'It doesn't matter now anyway.'

If that was how Tommy had been feeling, why hadn't he told me so?

I curled my hand around his. 'It does matter. You should have said.'

'I have nothing to offer a girl like you. I'm just a guy with fucked kidneys and a failed business. Why would you want to take me on?'

'Tommy, I ...'

'I had plans though. To get another business up and running, make something of myself again. It was starting to fall into place, then this happened.'

'Couldn't you still do all that?'

'No, I can't, it's over.'

Tommy kept saying that I didn't understand. Then bit by bit it came out. He needed premises and equipment, it would be a big investment, and with his track record the banks weren't going to lend him the cash.

'So you went to Grace?' I guessed. 'It was you who asked to borrow the money.'

I felt so bad about assuming it was Emerald, just because I hadn't especially warmed to her, but I never dreamed it would be Tommy.

He was surprised that I knew. 'She told you? You probably don't think I should have asked her, but how else was I going to have a future? Grace was my last resort, and she understood that. Helping me felt like helping Jamie; that's what she said.'

'She was going to give you the money she had saved for his university fund; she told me so.'

'I can't ask her to do that now, can I?'

'Because Jamie's kidney is failing?'

'It is failing and so am I ...'

There seemed no words. I sat beside Tommy, holding his hand, and all I wanted was to be closer. Sliding my chair over, I leaned in and touched his shoulder.

'Don't,' he said, but I hugged him gently anyway, my face buried into his shoulder, my arms stubbornly wrapped around him, and it felt like I fitted there, in the space made by the curve of his body. His skin smelt good. I didn't want to let go.

'Vivi, please don't. Like I said, I've got nothing to offer you now.'

'Tommy,' I responded, my voice slightly muffled. 'What if you're wrong about that?'

Hearts can only be gifted when they are no longer needed to support the life of their original owners. Kidneys are different. We are born with two; we can survive with one. What Tommy needed now was a living donor. He knew that, of course, because he had tried it the first time round and no one was a match or fitted the criteria. But his circle had widened; Tommy had us.

'None of you is going to be allowed to give me a kidney,' he said, not understanding.

'Yes, but we all have family and friends, that means a whole lot more people who may be willing.'

'I can't ask you to pester them.'

'You don't have to; we'll do it anyway. We're going to find you a kidney.'

Tommy squeezed my hand. 'Don't get your hopes up, Vivi.'

'We can do this,' I told him. 'I'm sure of it.'

When I was in Bar Américain with Dan he had irritated me by finding similarities between Emerald and I. His theory was that people like us, who had come close to dying from a chronic health condition, had a different sort of toughness. Maybe he was right, or perhaps I was my father's daughter, but in that moment, I was determined to make finding a new kidney for Tommy my absolute priority. I refused to accept the possibility of failure. This man deserved another chance. He was kind, he had kids that loved him … and now he had me. Whatever it took, I was going to help him.

'Tommy, you've got more to offer than anyone else I know,' I told him. 'Never think you don't.'

He kissed me then, there in the overheated hospital ward

beneath the bright strip lighting, he kissed me softly and slowly, and his lips on mine felt at once familiar and exciting.

'I've been desperate to do that … You've got no idea,' he said, holding onto me.

'Why didn't you then?'

'I wasn't sure you wanted it.'

'I always did … I was just too scared to admit it, even to myself.'

He kissed me and we might have been anywhere. The smell of antiseptic faded, I didn't hear the murmurings of other patients, wasn't aware of nurses or doctors. Only Tommy seemed to matter and the knowledge that we had been wasting so much of our precious time.

'I liked you from the very start,' he told me. 'That day when you turned up to interview me after the marathon and told me we shared a donor. In Italy I almost said something, but then you seemed interested in Stefano so …'

'I'm an idiot,' I said. 'So is Stefano actually.'

'I went for an extra long run that day after the pair of you drove away. Didn't make me feel any better though.'

'Nothing happened,' I reminded him.

'Good,' said Tommy, and kissed me again.

I hated leaving him when visiting hours were over. We held hands till the very last moment and I promised to come back the next day, whether he liked it or not.

I had managed to find a room in a hotel down by the river and spent a fidgety night alone, not sleeping properly, thinking about Tommy, alternately worrying and feeling ridiculously happy. His kidney was failing. We had kissed. It was a lot, all at once.

First thing in the morning I started trying to make a new kidney happen. A living donor would ideally be a blood and tissue match, in good physical and mental health and prepared to undergo surgery then several weeks of recovery. It was a big ask, but not one I was shy of.

I came up with a list: my family, old colleagues and school friends, anybody I could think of. Then I began messaging and calling. My parents said they would put the word out around their own network of contacts and I felt a surge of confidence. Somewhere out there was a kidney, a healthy, fully functioning one, and a person who was going to be convinced that Tommy deserved it.

When I called my sister, she picked up on the second ring, sounding worried. 'What's wrong?'

I gave her my good news first, and she squeaked on hearing about Tommy and I, telling me how pleased she was, her voice breaking on the words.

'Imogen, are you crying?'

'Maybe,' she admitted, 'but only because this is the best ever news. Finally, a nice guy; I'm so happy for you. And you really like him?'

'Yeah I do, really, but there is another thing ...' I hated having to tell her. 'And it's not great news. It looks like his kidney may be failing.'

For a couple of seconds there was a shocked silence. 'Vivi, that's terrible.' My sister seemed to be struggling to get the words out. 'Really terrible.'

I told her about the accident and Imogen listened quietly. I could hear the sound of her breathing

'It's going to be OK,' I told her. 'I've got a plan, and I need your help.'

Naturally, my sister promised to help, to tell her own friends and get tested to see if she was a candidate to be a donor herself, do anything at all that might make a difference.

'Mum and Dad said the same thing,' I told her. 'You guys are the best.'

'I'd do anything for you, Vivi. I guess that means I'll do anything for Tommy now too.'

Surgery would involve risks. Even if they were small ones I preferred someone other than my sister to take them. When I tried telling Imogen that, she refused to listen.

'I'm be coming home to be assessed. Anyway, it's not the same here now. Fiona is sweet, but the girls and I miss you.'

Visiting hours were my excuse to drop everything and go back to Tommy. With what felt like encouraging news to pass on, I walked through the doors of the Royal Liverpool Hospital in a far brighter mood than the day before. I was eager to set eyes on him, to hear his voice and wrap my arms around him. I wanted to reassure myself that he felt strong and healthy.

There was a WHSmith at the hospital so I stopped to pick up magazines, chocolate and fruit in case he was bored or hungry. As I was paying for them at the checkout I saw two faces I recognised among the drifts of people passing by, Tommy's children Ava and Liam. They were with a woman, small and dark like me, who must have been their mother.

I hesitated before following them up to the ward at a distance, not wanting to be noticed. The children started running when they saw Tommy and their mother called out a caution to be careful. I hung back and watched as, arms wide, Tommy caught and hugged them. Then he looked over at the worried-faced woman, smiled and said something, and she leaned in and dropped a quick kiss on his cheek.

Holding my bag of magazines and snacks, I held back. Tommy belonged to these people, they had years of history and had been through all of this before, the exact same hurt and worry. For now I was the outsider and it felt wrong for me to intrude. So I stayed just a few moments longer, looking on as Tommy comforted his kids, and I knew for sure I wanted to belong to him, to be together and try to make a new sort of family, even if it wasn't always going to be easy, even if it might mean hurt and worry.

In my *Daily Post* days Dan taught me a trick for dealing with stressful deadlines. His advice was to choose the most urgent item on a to-do list and focus entirely on it. Then at least you were in with a chance of achieving something.

It seemed the best course now. I was going to concentrate on helping Tommy find a kidney and try not to think about anything else. So I forgot about meeting up with Emerald; there was no urgency now anyway. And I didn't give a thought to finding the final piece of the puzzle, the person with Jamie's pancreas. That didn't seem to matter any more. There was only one recipient I cared about.

Leaving the hospital, I wandered for a while, lost in my thoughts. Ahead I saw a large modern building that I recognised as the Catholic cathedral. On a whim I went inside and sat at one of the pews. It was an airy space with light filtering in through the coloured stained glass windows. I remembered the prayers of my childhood and wondered if I should say one now? Closing my eyes, I said the words in my mind, 'Our Father, who art in heaven, hallowed be thy name.'

There was a sense of comfort in being there and I had no place else to go, so I stayed. No one bothered me and I didn't move. When the silence was broken, it was by a melody, a choir singing a psalm only for me, a clear treble voice soaring and sounding in my chest and swelling in my heart. I had listened to this music before in Westminster Abbey with Tommy and Grace, right at the beginning of all this. Hearing it again now, when so much had changed, seemed significant.

While the choir rehearsed, I let their music touch me and afterwards I asked one of them what I had been listening to.

'*Misere mei deus*,' he told me. 'It's about washing away sin and having a clean heart. We're giving a performance later in the week if you'd like to come to and hear it again.'

A clean heart, a heart full of love, a pure heart; we expect a lot of the organ that keeps us alive, of the 300 or so grams of muscle, chambers and valves that beats 100,000 times a day. I wasn't sure if my heart was pure and it certainly wasn't perfect, but I knew it was full of love, and more so than ever.

I was leaving the cathedral when my phone rang. Glancing at the screen I saw it was the one person I had put off contacting, because the conversation was bound to be a tough one.

'Grace, hi,' I said, answering.

'Emerald just called and said about Tommy. How is he?' she asked, anxiously. 'What's happening? Is Jamie's kidney going to be OK?'

For Grace this would feel like another tiny piece of her son was dying and it wasn't going to be easy.

'Jamie's kidney has kept Tommy going for seven years. Given him all that time of being fit and healthy. No matter what happens now, he'll always be grateful,' I told her, before sharing the details of what had happened.

'Another bike accident,' she said. 'Can you believe that? It's like a curse.'

'It's not going to be this time; there's something we can do.'

As soon as I explained about the plan to find a living donor for Tommy she demanded to be assessed.

'I have the same blood type as Jamie, and if his kidney was a good tissue match then mine will be too,' she said.

I wasn't sure if that was true. But I did know there were strict psychological tests to pass before you could be a living donor and it seemed unlikely that Grace would manage it.

'They might have issues with the mother of the original donor giving Tommy a kidney,' I warned her.

'I don't see why.'

'We weren't even supposed to be in touch with you in the first place.'

'But the fact is you are, and I'm sure Jamie would like this. If his kidney can't help Tommy any longer, then he'd want me to.'

'Grace, you are a truly amazing person.' I meant it.

'Tommy has kids, and they must need him, just like Jamie always needed me,' she said, simply.

I put her name at the top of my list as she had requested. Even though I foresaw all sorts of ethical issues, she deserved to have her wishes considered.

Vivi

The bad news was Tommy was back on dialysis. I kept clinging to the positive; there was no reason for him not to get a new kidney, if one became available.

I stayed in Liverpool for a few more days, messaging him now before turning up to make sure it was convenient and his family wasn't going to be there; for now they seemed to be more important. Still, we spent as much time as we could hanging out together, chatting or listening to music on his phone, and I did my best to keep him cheerful.

We didn't really talk about the future; Tommy seemed reluctant and I didn't want to push him. But we spoke about the past a lot. He told me about the man he had been before Jamie's kidney saved him: frustrated and angry, selfish, moody. I think he was afraid of turning into that person again, but I couldn't imagine it and kept telling him so.

I gave him my story, all about Sir Lance and Lady Deborah Palmer, how privileged I was, and how I struggled with that.

'So like, you're saying that you're really rich?' Tommy seemed to be finding it difficult to believe.

'Yes, or at least my parents are.'

'Shit.' He sounded devastated.

'It's their money, not mine. And they're busy giving it away.'

'Even so, what are they going to think of their daughter getting together with a broke, divorced cabinetmaker with stuffed kidneys? I don't even own a house. I've got nothing to offer.'

'My parents will love you. They'd love anyone who cared about me.'

Tommy's arm was round me and he squeezed me a little closer. 'They can't fault me there. If it only came down to caring about you, I'd score a hundred per cent. But it won't, Vivi. I'm too old, I've got a past and who knows what's in store for me in the future. I'm completely unsuitable.'

I laughed at that. 'Trust me, unsuitable is the one thing you're not.'

During the long hours I was alone in the hotel, I had been constructing a future for us in my head, looking at rental properties in Liverpool and thinking about what work I could do if I moved here. I put off discussing it with Tommy though. Until we heard whether he had a new kidney, I was wary of talking about any of it.

Soon he would be having his dialysis sessions at another hospital closer to his home on the other side of the river.

'Back in the old routine,' he said, wryly. 'The old way of life.'

It was time for me to head back to London, at least for a short while, as there were things I needed to do there. Meet Emerald, who was messaging me regularly now, sending inspirational quotes and aphorisms she must have harvested from the internet. And far more importantly, catch up with my sister, who had interrupted her summer and come home so she could be assessed as one of Tommy's potential kidney donors. Brittle … that was what Fiona had said about her. I needed to go back and see for myself if Imogen really did seem breakable.

It was difficult leaving him, as I had known it would be. I wanted to cling to him as we said goodbye, and I cried as my train headed south, because he had seemed smaller and more vulnerable, when usually his strength was the first thing you noticed about him.

Imogen was waiting for me, an open bottle of wine on the kitchen table although it was still mid-afternoon. 'I'm still in holiday mode,' she explained, seeing me glance towards it.

'You've leased Villa Rosa for a few more weeks, haven't you? If you're not a match for Tommy then you should go back there and carry on with your holiday properly.'

'We'll see.' She sipped her wine. 'I might want to stick around and support my sister and her new boyfriend.'

I smiled at the sound of the word; there was a warm feeling when I thought about Tommy as that. That night I made dinner for all of us, a very simple baked pasta dish that Fiona had shown me how to prepare. We sat around the kitchen table and I wished they were both there with us.

'You seem to have actually learnt to cook,' remarked Imogen, tasting it. 'Is there no end to all the ways you're going to surprise me?'

Once the girls were in bed and Hamid back at his desk catching up on work, my sister wanted to finish her wine in the little park that lies at the centre of the square she lives in. The gate is locked at dusk but Imogen has a foldaway step stool she bought purely so she could climb the railings and enjoy it after dark.

She likes sneaking in and breaking the rules, and softened by several glasses of wine, she was especially giggly that evening. We lounged about in the long grass, gazing up at what little you could see of the night sky dazzled by London's lights, and I told her all about me and Tommy.

'You must be so worried,' she said, lying flat on her back now, with her head in my lap, searching out stars.

'I'm trying not to be. I keep reminding myself that worrying won't get me anywhere. It's not easy though. I'm starting to see how it must have been for all of you.'

'Mum once planned your funeral; did you know that?' Imogen said, starkly. 'You were so sick and she wrote out exactly what she wanted – the venue, the music, the readings – knowing if she lost you she would be too distraught to think straight.'

'Poor Mum.'

'I thought you were going to die too,' said Imogen. 'More than once I picked out which teddies would go in your coffin with you.'

'Seriously?' I smoothed my sister's hair from her face. 'I had no idea.'

'I do it with the girls now. Would Farah prefer her baby doll or her plush puppy dog? Would Darya like to wear her pink princess dress.'

'But the girls are fine, they're not at risk.' Imogen had been tested so she knew before getting pregnant there was no chance of her passing on the gene mutation that had caused my heart problems.

'Not of cardiomyopathy, but of hundreds and thousands of other things; every day there are so many ways I could lose them.'

'And you worry about it?' I was stroking her head and looking into her face, my beautiful, funny sister.

'I try not to; it's pointless, like you said. But since having Farah and Darya, the worries are always there, bubbling under, and often they burst through and I get these thoughts in my head. Sometimes I . . .'

'What?'

'I worry I might hurt them myself on purpose.' Imogen half-whispered the words. 'I imagine doing it, almost like it's a film screening in my mind. I'm scared it might actually happen.'

'You never would,' I told her. 'I'm sure of that.'

'But when the thoughts come I can't get rid of them, it's like they're stuck there. And they make me so scared.'

'Imogen, you have to talk to someone about this,' I said, dismayed.

'I'm telling you. That's hard enough. I can't tell anyone else.'

'Does Hamid know? Or Mum and Dad?'

'I haven't said anything to them. I can't.'

My sister wasn't meant to be the fragile one; that had always been me. Reaching into my bag for the fleecy blanket I had brought in case the night air got chilly, I draped it over both of us.

'You've been going through all of this alone.'

'It always felt better when you were around, even if you didn't know.'

'But this is my fault, isn't it? Having me as a little sister and being so anxious for so long, always having to put on a brave face ...'

'It's my brain, Vivi; I don't think you can be blamed for the thoughts going through it.'

'Why then?'

Imogen shrugged. 'Perhaps it feels like I'm too lucky, I don't deserve my life, and it's bound to go wrong, like it seems to for you.'

My illness, it had caused so many problems, and they had rippled outwards, affecting everyone around me. I'm not sure I realised until then how much or how hard it must have been.

'Imogen ...'

There were people approaching. We heard men's voices and both of us quietened until they had passed, not wanting to be noticed. We were the same as little kids, sneaking off where we weren't supposed to, being careful because we knew getting caught would spoil the fun. Imogen was always trying to find new rules to break; and she was my big sister so I went along with her.

'Imogen, you should have said something,' I told her, when the men had passed.

'Your problems always seemed so much worse than mine.'

I repeated what Stefano had once tried to tell me. 'Being afraid all the time: it's no way to live.'

'So long as the girls never guess ... so long as I don't ruin their childhood.'

We stayed together in the dark, beneath the blanket, Imogen sitting up to finish her wine, me lying down and putting my head in her lap. It took a while for me to persuade her to see a therapist. She had a lawyer's arsenal of arguments for why it wouldn't work, and I wasn't used to standing up to her. Still, I couldn't back down. Her problem was serious and it scared me. I had been given a new heart; she had been left to struggle on without so much as a bandage.

By the time we climbed back over the railings, Imogen had agreed to get some proper help. We walked towards the house arm in arm, smelling the night-scented stock and jasmine from people's window boxes as we passed by.

'Love you,' she said, before opening her front door.

'Love you more,' I promised her.

Grace

Grace's body is already covered in scars. Some are old like the neat line of her Caesarean or the collection of cuts and burns from clumsy moments in the kitchen. There are newer scars engraved on her wrists, scars she tries to conceal even from herself because she hates to remember how close she came.

Now Grace is preparing to be scarred again. It will be quite a wound, a slash across her abdomen, and she expects it to look ugly. Everyone keeps telling her how courageous she is, but this isn't really about courage. Grace is only finishing what Jamie started.

For a long time she asked herself if she should have fought harder for her boy. The doctors said there was no hope, but doctors can be wrong. And later she read those stories about people who woke up from their comas, and was tormented by the thought she had given up too soon. It kept on worrying away at her, for years and years.

Now Grace is not going to give up on Tommy. This kidney is hers to give and the decision is easy, not one made in grief and panic. She feels better about it than she ever did about donating Jamie's heart, his undamaged kidney, his liver and pancreas, his corneas. It is clear-cut, uncomplicated.

Not that she is looking forward to being in hospital; the smell of them takes her right back. Weeks of recovery, pain, and time off work, there are plenty of reasons not to do this. Grace has listed them in her head and discounted them all. Tommy needs a kidney and she has one to spare; it doesn't seem such a sacrifice.

It is much too late to fight for Jamie; but that doesn't mean she should stop fighting at all. Grace is ready for another scar.

Vivi

It was such slow going. Tommy had been assigned a donor coordinator, a breezy, no-nonsense woman who was guiding us through the process. She kept stressing that giving him a kidney was going to involve a lot of tests for someone. Blood and urine, heart and kidneys, all got a work-over. And then there was a meeting with a therapist to assess mental health. And after that another check to be sure there was no pressure to donate, no payment or coercion. It went on and on.

In all my life I had never been so impatient. If it had been possible to speed things up by buying a kidney for Tommy then I would have done it, and paid with my parent's money too. It was all taking too much time.

When the ideal match turned out to be Grace, she was nonchalant about it; hadn't she known that would be the case? But Tommy and I both had concerns.

'Could I even accept her kidney? Would it be morally right?' he asked me, one evening via Skype.

I was sitting on my bed in Imogen's spare room and could tell he was in his living room because a corner of his trophy cabinet was visible in the background.

'You were prepared to accept her money before,' I pointed out.

'That's different: it was a loan and I was sure I'd be able to pay her back at some point.'

'She really wants to do this for you.'

Grace had said that several times, on the phone and again in Oxford as I drank more cups of tea in her living room, surrounded by photographs of Jamie. She told me this was a good choice, and it felt right or she wouldn't have offered.

'If Grace is willing to go through this then we should let her,' I told him. 'Anyway, I don't think you'll stop her. She's determined.'

Tommy yawned and I felt worry flare. Was he tired? Had he been overdoing it? I knew he was exercising again, trying to build himself up slowly, and that concerned me. I wasn't used to being the person who worried. It had always been something that others did for me. Now I could feel my heart beat faster as my mind filled with anxiety.

'Are you OK? Do you need to rest?' I asked him.

'In a bit, not yet.' Tommy said. 'I meant to tell you, I've broken the news about us to the kids.'

'How did they take it?'

'Ava claimed she knew already, Liam went quiet. I think he must have been hoping that my ex-wife and me would get back together. But they're OK. They'll get used to the idea.

'You should tell her too, before one of them does. Better coming from you.'

Tommy nodded. 'Yeah, I know that.'

'And you need to meet my parents soon. There's a lot for us to deal with, isn't there?'

'At least we're dealing with it all together.'

The urge to hug him was overwhelming but all I could do was reach out and touch his face on the screen. 'I'll be coming up to see you soon, maybe on one of your dialysis days, just so it won't be so boring.'

'That would be nice.'

'You're only a couple of hours away, you know. I can come up any time you need me.'

'I know that.' Tommy touched his own screen, reaching for my face. 'I wish you were here now.'

'So do I.'

Ending the call, seeing him disappear, I lay back on the bed and stared up at the ceiling. The worries crowded in.

What if Tommy's transplant wasn't a success? What if therapy wasn't the answer for Imogen? What if bad things happened to everyone I knew? I wasn't used to this. My heart pounded.

I don't know what Grace said when they were grilling her at all those one-on-one meetings. Later she told me her greatest fear had been that she would start crying and she was proud of managing not to. She must have put on a brave face to convince them she was steady enough to be a living donor; she must have been determined.

The day we were given the news she had been approved, I was literally giddy. Imogen opened champagne and danced around the kitchen, while I sat there feeling thrilled for Tommy, but terrified for him too.

My mind kept returning to those weeks we spent together in Italy. I hoped there were more times like that ahead for all of us: Tommy and his kids, Imogen with hers, definitely Fiona, maybe even Emerald and Stefano too, my new extended family, my transplant twins. It was the view I looked towards in the far future, way out in the distance beyond the hospital beds and the surgeons. It was one thing that kept me going.

The other was Grace. In the days leading up to giving Tommy her kidney we drew closer. It felt like we needed each other.

Everyone kept saying that surgery for a living donor was more complicated than it was for a recipient. They kept making sure she knew the risks. I didn't want her feeling anxious on her own in Oxford, so we asked her to come to stay with us in London.

Grace turned out to be Imogen's ideal houseguest, falling in with her crazy schemes, and the days were filled with treasure hunts for the girls and shopping trips for nightwear covered in love hearts for her to wear in hospital.

The Sunday before the day scheduled for surgery we were in St James's Park feeding lettuce to the swans because someone had told Imogen they loved it. Grace couldn't seem to get enough of being with the girls. She was watching Darya approaching the large white birds, smiling at the expression on her face.

'She's nervous but she's doing it anyway,' she said, approvingly.

We were meant to be walking around the lake, because Grace had been told to step up her exercise, but she couldn't tear herself away from my nieces. So instead we were sitting on a bench, watching the swan flap its wings, and Darya, alarmed by it, darting behind her sister.

Grace smiled again. 'Do you think you and Tommy will ever have kids?' she wondered.

'What?'

'It's so lovely that you're together.'

'Thanks to you,' I reminded her. 'If you hadn't asked me to find Jamie's recipients then Tommy and me would never even have met.'

'Thanks to Jamie then.' Grace turned away from the swan-feeding scene and looked into my face. 'Vivi, if you did have a baby, would I be an honorary grandmother?'

I was startled by the tears welling up in my eyes, and so was Grace.

'Now I've upset you.' She rummaged in her bag for a tissue. 'What did I say wrong?'

'Nothing at all,' I promised her, once I could speak without my voice wobbling. 'If we were going to have kids then you would definitely be their honorary grandmother, but Grace, we can't do that. It wouldn't be fair of us.'

'Why not?' She passed me a packet of tissues.

'My heart, his kidneys, we both have hereditary conditions and I'd be scared of passing them on to a baby. Besides, neither of us has the promise of a long life. So even if things do work out for us, children will never be an option. We can't take the risk.'

'That makes no sense at all,' Grace said bluntly. 'Jamie was perfect and he died. Would I have never gone ahead and had a baby in case something bad happened? Of course not.'

'That's different,' I said.

'I don't see why. Wouldn't you rather be alive, even with your health problems? Wouldn't you rather that Tommy was too? Anyway, who knows what medical science will be able to do for people like you in the future.'

'It's still too much of a risk,' I insisted. 'I decided years ago that it would be better not to try to take it.'

'Don't you want a baby?' she wanted to know.

'There would tests to take before we even tried and a pregnancy would be complicated,' I told her. 'Dangerous for me even.'

'But do you want a child?'

'Yes,' I admitted. 'Of course I do.'

She smiled. 'You'd make such a lovely mother, Vivi. You care about people and you're full of love. In the end that's all that matters.'

I lost it completely then. Grace had to hold me until I stopped crying. It has never been imaginable, a baby of my own. Holding my nieces when they were newborns, I gave my love to them. And now there would be Tommy's kids and I hoped they might accept some love from me too, once we had grown used to one another. But a baby of my own … It didn't seem possible and I had never dared to dream about it.

'There's one thing I can tell you for sure,' Grace finished. 'You've got a courageous heart, Vivi, but then I think you always have had.'

Sitting on a bench in the middle of the busy park, I unbuttoned my shirt, just enough to expose a little skin and the very start of my scar, then I took Grace's hand and placed it flat against me so she could feel that courageous heart beating.

'Thank you,' I said. It was one word and could never be enough; still it was everything.

Friends rallied round for Tommy, the old and the new ones. Implanting the kidney would be a routine surgery – unexciting was the word the renal surgeon used – but that didn't cheer me up. I was full of fear for Grace too, convinced it wasn't possible for everything to go right.

In Liverpool on the day it was set to happen, it felt like they were all there with us in a way, everyone with a tiny piece of Jamie, sharing their strength. Reading the messages aloud to Tommy, I was a little calmer than I had been. There was one from Fiona, sending her love, another from Emerald filled with positive thoughts, even a line or two from Stefano. We had people on our side; we were full of love and like Grace said, in the end it is all that matters. There was no stopping this now.

'In a day or so I'll be feeling good again,' Tommy kept repeating, determined to be nothing but hopeful. 'It's Grace who'll need us. They say it's pretty awful once the morphine wears off.'

'Will they remove Jamie's kidney before they put Grace's one into you?' I wondered.

'I don't think so. His kidney is embedded now, a part of me, even if it isn't working any more.'

'So we'll still have some of the same DNA inside us then.' The thought was comforting, not weird at all. Anything that held us closer together made me happy. 'You'll carry on being a part of our transplant family?'

'Always,' Tommy promised. 'I can't imagine life without it.'

How it begins again …

This is a funeral but no one is wearing black; they have been asked not to. My mother is bright in a floral dress, Imogen looks elegant in dusky pink, Hamid and my father have chosen pale jackets and lively ties. This is a funeral and it is beautiful.

The church is more crowded than I imagined it would be and full of faces I don't recognise, but some of them are familiar. Grace is next to me, holding my hand, not crying but very solemn. Soon she will be giving a eulogy and while she won't tell me exactly what she is going to say I am certain she will talk about Jamie, and the gift of extra life he gave, and how the decision she made on that day haunts her, but still she is glad to have made it. Grace has said all those things already while trying to comfort me; now she will say them again.

There was always going to be heartbreak, but even when you know it is coming its arrival feels unexpected. I am trying to hold myself together by focusing on all the beauty, the stained glass windows, the choir singing, the colourful clothing of the congregation, and the flowers, of course, so many of them strewn over the willow coffin. Most came from the place that Fiona loved most, the Chelsea Physic Garden, picked by the other volunteers who are filling the pews and raising their voices in her favourite hymn, 'I Vow to Thee, My Country'.

This was Fiona's church and she worshipped here every week, so the priest knew her and his words are heartfelt. He speaks about how bravely she faced the knowledge her lungs were failing, becoming gradually more and more breathless, finding it difficult to do the things we take for granted and only able to visit her beloved gardens if someone took her there and she could sit very quietly in a favourite corner.

Fiona had hidden her decline until it became too rapid and she couldn't any longer. Over a few short months, every time I visited, she seemed worse. When you can't breathe properly, you can't do anything, life stills and grows small. That is how it was for Fiona.

She never stopped thanking me for the holiday in Italy and telling me how much she had adored it: cooking with Raffaella, people-watching in the piazza, pottering round the gardens of Villa Rosa and most of all the friendship and feeling she was useful. Back when we were still hoping that there might by a chance of a second lung transplant, we talked about going back there.

The last time we saw each other, I was the one hiding something. It seemed insensitive to force my happiness on her when she had so little left. But Grace was with me and she wasn't keeping secrets. Putting a hand on my belly, gently smoothing down my loose top to show the swollen rise of it, she beamed and said, 'I'm going to be a grandmother.'

And actually, Grace was right; it was good to have some joy in the room with us that day. Fiona lit up at the news. Very tentatively, she reached out to touch my tummy too and then she smiled.

Now Grace stands up to give her eulogy and Tommy passes me his clean handkerchief because he knows I'm going to need it. Grace's voice is shaky as she starts, but it steadies and she says the things I expected, and more. She talks mostly about hope and how for a long time hers was gone, but thanks to Jamie so many other people's lives have been filled with it. She shares memories of Fiona and speaks about grief. I listen to every word, my eyes fixed on her face, one hand resting on my belly, feeling its rise and fall, and the occasional tiny movements like butterflies fluttering.

There is no hiding the fact I am pregnant now: my belly is proud with it. I am draped in a dress covered in a print of bright flowers, looking like a whole meadow full of them, according to Tommy. He is proud too. This baby is one more thing we could only hope would happen. Still, there are risks, although as Grace keeps reminding me, risks are everywhere even when you can't see them, so it is better we know what we are facing and take them with purpose.

Her words don't stop me worrying. Worry is a feature of my life now, like the rented Georgian townhouse in Liverpool with its high ceilings and sash windows, and the morning sickness that is only just easing, and the queen-sized bed I share with Tommy, and the freelance writing career I am trying to get off the ground. Imogen says worry is normal, no mother can ever be free of it entirely, that I will get used to it eventually and find it is worth it.

Now it is time for the prayer that Fiona chose, a special one for gardeners. 'May we grow with our flowers in gentleness,' the congregation repeats. 'May our lives be filled with beauty and love; may we live peacefully through the seasons given to us and return to the earth at the end.' Not trusting my voice, I close my eyes and listen, wishing Fiona were here so she could see and hear how many people cared about her.

Next my sister gives a reading. Today there is no sign of the playful Imogen. Her therapist has told her she must stop that, find some quiet and allow herself to feel sadness and fear. Like everything, my sister does therapy well. Her voice breaks in the middle of the poem and it takes several breaths before she can speak again.

A single chorister starts to sing '*Ave Maria*' and the others join with him, their voices building. My mother turns and looks at me, giving an encouraging half-smile. She hates to see me upset so I manage to smile in return. Finally I have accepted a little more help from her and my father. There was no choice in the end, because as they pointed out, I was free to live without things myself, but I couldn't deprive their grandchild.

This little baby is going to have a wealth of people to love it and Grace will be one of them. She has already given us the teddy bear Jamie used to sleep with, so tattered and patched in places I think it might have been sharing her own bed through some of the hardest nights. Now it lives on a shelf in our nursery waiting for a new child to arrive. Girl or boy, we don't know yet, but all of us think Jamie sounds like a good name either way.

I hope I am strong enough for this baby. I hope I can do this. Tommy will be there, and my new stepchildren have promised their help too, but my body has to manage this first bit, carry our baby, bring it into the world, and I am praying it won't let us down.

Tommy moves his hand, spreading it next to mine across my belly, and from his smile I know he feels what I do, a fluttering and quivering, our baby's kicks.

It is scary what lies ahead for this child and us. Feeling my heart thump in my chest, I can't pretend it isn't. But there is no life without being scared; and it is exciting and wonderful too.

My heart is less than one per cent of my body; it is only a tiny piece of me. All I can do is trust it will keep beating, that its valves will open and close, pumping blood round my body. All I can do is hope and live, like everyone ... like other ordinary people.

Thank you . . .

When I started on this novel I knew very little about any of the things I was planning to write about. There has been a lot of learning and I am grateful for the help of loads of people.

A big thankyou goes to the transplant recipients who kindly shared their personal stories. Heidi Harty-Eugster, Anna Maharaj and Troy Stapleton, your courage astounds me.

I may have made mistakes but thank you to all the professionals who did their best to make sure I didn't: Raffat Shameem, Ian Dittmer, Janice Langlands, Tricia Casey, Helen Gibbs and Rebecca Oliver.

For marathon running details, thanks to Mary Lambie; for reminding me about life in a newsroom, thanks to Miryana Alexander, and for letting me pat buffalo and taste their excellent mozzarella, thanks to Richard and Helen Dorresteyn of Clevedon Buffalo Co.

As always, a huge thanks to my agent Caroline Sheldon and everyone at Orion, Hachette New Zealand and Hachette Australia, but in particular to my editor Victoria Oundjian for her kindness and patience.

Thanks to Carne for overcoming his loathing of caves in Matera.

Thank you to the booksellers and librarians who will put this novel (hopefully) in people's hands.

Most of all thanks to Stacy Gregg and Sarah-Kate Lynch, because friendship is everything and everyone needs friends like them.

ALSO BY NICKY PELLEGRINO

For sale: historic building in the picturesque town of Montenello, southern Italy. Asking price: 1 Euro

Cloudless skies, sun-soaked countryside, delicious food . . . In the drowsy heat of an Italian summer, four strangers arrive in a beautiful town nestled in the mountains of Basilicata, dreaming of a new adventure. An innovative scheme by the town's Mayor has given them the chance to buy a crumbling historic building for a single Euro – on the condition that they renovate their home within three years, and help to bring new life to the close-knit local community.

Elise is desperate to get on the property ladder. Edward wants to escape a life he feels suffocated by. Mimi is determined to start afresh after her divorce. And there's one new arrival whose true motives are yet to be revealed . . .

For each of them, Montenello offers a different promise of happiness. But can they turn their dream of Italy into reality?

The best adventures are waiting for you to follow your heart . . .

Kat is an adventurer, a food writer who travels the world visiting far-flung places and eating unusual things. Now she is about to embark on her biggest adventure yet – a relationship.

She has fallen in love with an Italian man and is moving to live with him in Venice where she will help him run his small guesthouse, Hotel Gondola. Kat has lined up a book deal and will write about the first year of her new adventure, the food she eats, the recipes she collects, the people she meets, the man she doesn't really know all that well but is going to make a life with.

But as Kat ought to know by now, the thing about adventures is that they never go exactly the way you expect them to . . .

'Nicky Pellegrino goes from strength to strength and A Year at Hotel Gondola shows her skill in full flight . . . If you enjoy intelligent clear-eyed writing – and great recipes – this is the book for you'
NZ Herald

'Warm, engaging and truly delicious'
Rosanna Ley, author of *The Little Theatre by the Sea*

Two women, one house – one at the beginning of her life, one nearing the end. Alice is in London, working in the kitchen of a top restaurant and determined to live life fast and to the full. Babetta is living in a lonely house in southern Italy and trying to hang on to the quiet life she has made for herself.

When the two women meet one summer life changes for both of them. This is a novel about what we run from, and the places that make us stop and consider. Drenched in sunshine, it's about friendship and growing up, food and love.

'A slice of pure sunshine'
Good Housekeeping

'An amazing book . . . it's a wonderful and enchanting read . . . one of those books you want to read and reread. It's endearing, entertaining and inspiring.'
Novelicious.com

'The author delivers not only on every sensory front – combining her love and knowledge of food with her passion for the Italian coast – but also with her energetic writing, layering every character with shades of darkness and believable charisma.'
The Australian Women's Weekly

Help us make the next generation of readers

We – both author and publisher – hope you enjoyed this book. We believe that you can become a reader at any time in your life, but we'd love your help to give the next generation a head start.

Did you know that 9 per cent of children don't have a book of their own in their home, rising to 13 per cent in disadvantaged families*? We'd like to try to change that by asking you to consider the role you could play in helping to build readers of the future.

We'd love you to think of sharing, borrowing, reading, buying or talking about a book with a child in your life and spreading the love of reading. We want to make sure the next generation continue to have access to books, wherever they come from.

And if you would like to consider donating to charities that help fund literacy projects, find out more at **www.literacytrust.org.uk** and **www.booktrust.org.uk**.

THANK YOU

*As reported by the National Literacy Trust

Credits

Nicky Pellegrino and Orion Fiction would like to thank everyone at Orion who worked on the publication of *Tiny Pieces of Us* in the UK.

Editorial
Victoria Oundjian
Clare Hey
Olivia Barber

Copy editor
Laura Gerrard

Proofreader
John Garth

Audio
Paul Stark
Amber Bates

Contracts
Anne Goddard
Paul Bulos
Jake Alderson

Design
Rabab Adams
Joanna Ridley
Nick May
Helen Ewing

Editorial Management
Charlie Panayiotou
Jane Hughes
Alice Davis

Finance
Jasdip Nandra
Afeera Ahmed
Elizabeth Beaumont
Sue Baker

Marketing
Brittany Sankey

Production
Ruth Sharvell

Publicity
Kate Moreton

Sales
Laura Fletcher
Jen Wilson
Esther Waters
Victoria Laws
Rachael Hum
Ellie Kyrke-Smith
Frances Doyle
Georgina Cutler

Operations
Jo Jacobs
Sharon Willis
Lisa Pryde
Lucy Brem